D0234287

A few moments later she felt without seeing when Varo came to stand directly at her shoulder. He was greeted warmly by everyone, but it was Ava he had come for.

"I hope you realize, Ava, as I am the captain of the winning team, you owe me a dance. Several, in fact," he said, with his captivating smile.

"Of course, Varo."

She turned to him, her eyes ablaze in her face, brilliant as jewels. Inside she might feel pale with shock, but outside she was all color—the golden mane of her hair, dazzling eyes, softly blushed cheeks, lovely deep pink mouth. She was determined now to play her part, her only wish to get through the night with grace.

For all he hadn't been completely honest with her, Juan-Varo de Montalvo would never leave her memory—even when he disappeared to the other side of the world.

ARGENTINIAN
IN THE OUTBACK

BY
MARGARET WAY

MILLS
BOON

First published in Great Britain 2012
by Mills & Boon, an imprint of Harlequin (UK) Limited,
Eton House, 18-24 Paradise Road, Richmond, Surrey TW9 1SR

© Margaret Way, Pty., Ltd 2012

ISBN: 978 0 263 89455 4
ebook ISBN: 978 1 408 97130 7

23-0812

Harlequin (UK) policy is to use papers that are natural, renewable and recyclable products and made from wood grown in sustainable forests. The logging and manufacturing processes conform to the legal environmental regulations of the country of origin.

Printed and bound in Spain
by Blackprint CPI, Barcelona

Margaret Way, a definite Leo, was born and raised in the subtropical river city of Brisbane, capital of Queensland, Australia, the Sunshine State. A conservatorium-trained pianist, teacher, accompanist and vocal coach, she found that her musical career came to an unexpected end when she took up writing—initially as a fun thing to do. She currently lives in a harborside apartment at beautiful Raby Bay, a thirty-minute drive from the state capital. She loves dining *alfresco* on her plant-filled balcony overlooking a translucent green marina filled with all manner of pleasure craft—from motor cruisers costing millions of dollars and big, graceful yachts with carved masts standing tall against the cloudless blue sky, to little bay runabouts. No one and nothing is in a mad rush, and she finds the laid-back village atmosphere very conducive to her writing. With well over one hundred books to her credit, she still believes her best is yet to come.

CHAPTER ONE

THE French doors of her bedroom were open to the cooling breeze, so Ava was able to witness the exact moment the station Jeep bearing their Argentine guest swept through the tall wrought-iron gates that guarded the main compound. The tyres of the vehicle threw up sprays of loose gravel, the noise scattering the brilliantly coloured parrots and lorikeets that were feeding on the beautiful Orange Flame Grevilleas and the prolific White Plumed species with their masses of creamy white perfumed flowers nearby.

As she watched from the shelter of a filmy curtain the Jeep made a broad half-circle around the playing fountain before coming to a halt at the foot of the short flight of stone steps that led to Kooraki's homestead.

Juan-Varo de Montalvo had arrived.

She didn't know why, but she felt *excited*. What else but excitement was causing that flutter in her throat? It had been a long time since she had felt like that. But why had these emotions come bubbling up out of nowhere? They weren't exactly what one could call appropriate. She had nothing to get excited about. Nothing at all.

Abruptly sobered, she turned back into the room to check her appearance in the pierglass mirror. She had dressed simply: a cream silk shirt tucked into cigarette-slim beige trousers. Around her waist she had slung a wide tan leather belt that showed off her narrow waist. She had debated what to do with her hair in the heat, but at the last moment had left it long and loose, waving over her shoulders. Her blonde hair was one of her best features.

Cast adrift in the middle of her beautifully furnished bedroom, she found herself making a helpless little gesture indicative of she didn't know what. She had greeted countless visitors to Kooraki over the years. Why go into a spin now? Three successive inward breaths calmed her. She had read the helpful hint somewhere and, in need of it, formed the habit. It *did* work. Time to go downstairs now and greet their honoured guest.

Out in the hallway, lined on both sides with gilt-framed paintings, she walked so quietly towards the head of the staircase she might have been striving to steal a march on their guest. Ava could hear resonant male voices, one a little deeper, darker than the other, with a slight but fascinating accent. So they were already inside the house. She wasn't sure why she did it but, like a child, she took a quick peek—seeing while remaining unseen—over the elegant wrought-iron lace of the balustrade down into the Great Hall.

It was then she saw the man who was to turn her whole life upside down. A moment she was destined never to forget. He was in animated conversation with her brother, Dev, both of them standing directly beneath the central chandelier with all its glittering, singing crystal drops. Their body language was proof they liked and respected each other, if one accepted the theory that the distance one maintained between oneself and another said a great deal about their relationship. To Ava's mind these two were *simpatico*.

Both young men were stunningly handsome. Some inches over six feet, both were wide through the shoulders, lean-hipped, with hard-muscled thighs and long, long legs. As might be expected of top-class polo players, both possessed superb physiques. The blond young man was her brother, James Devereaux Langdon, Master of Kooraki following the death of their grandfather Gregory Langdon, cattle king and national icon; the other was his foil, his Argentine friend and wedding guest. Juan-Varo de Montalvo had flown in a scant fifteen or so minutes before, on a charter flight from Longreach, the nearest domestic terminal to the Langdon desert stronghold—a vast cattle station bordered to the west and north-west by the mighty Simpson, the world's third-largest desert.

In colouring, the two were polarised. Dev's thick hair was a gleaming blond, like her own. Both of them had the Langdon family's aquamarine eyes. De Montalvo's hair was as black and glossy as a crow's wing. He had the traditional Hispanic's lustrous dark eyes, and his skin was tanned to a polished deep bronze. He was very much a man of a different land and culture. It showed in his manner, his voice, his gesticulations—the constant movement of his hands and shoulders, even the flick of his head. Just looking down at him caused a stunning surge of heat in her chest that dived low down into her body, pretty much like swallowing a mouthful of neat whisky.

There was far too much excitement in her reaction, even if it was strictly involuntary. She was a woman who had to defend her inner fortress which she had privately named Emotional Limbo. Why not? She was a woman in the throes of acrimonious divorce proceedings with her husband Luke Selwyn who had turned nasty, even threatening.

She had long reached the conclusion that Luke was a born narcissist, with the narcissist's exaggerated sense of his own importance. This unfortunate characteristic had been fostered from birth by his doting mother, who loved him above all else. Monica Selwyn, however, had pulled away from her daughter-in-law. Ava was the woman who had taken her son from her. The pretence that she had been liked had been at times more than Ava could bear.

When she'd told Luke long months ago she was leaving him and filing for divorce he had flown into a terrible rage. She would have feared him, only she had tremendous back-up and support from just being a Langdon. Luke was no match for her brother. Why, then, had she married him? She had thought she loved him, however imperfectly. Ava knew she couldn't go on with her life without asking herself fundamental questions.

In retrospect she realised she had been Luke's trophy bride—a Langdon with all that entailed. Her leaving him, and in doing so rejecting him, had caused Luke and his establishment family tremendous loss of face. That was the truth of the matter. *Loss of face.* She hadn't broken Luke's heart, just trampled his colossal pride. But wasn't that a potentially dangerous thing for any woman to do to a vain man?

Luke would mend. She was prepared to bet her fortune on that. Whereas she now had a sad picture of herself as a psychologically damaged woman.

Maybe everyone was damaged—only it came down to a question of degree? Some would say one couldn't *be* damaged unless one allowed it, furthermore *believed* it. Unfortunately she had. She felt she was a coward in some ways: afraid of so many things. Afraid to trust. Afraid to stand her ground. Afraid to reach out. Almost afraid to move on. That hurt. For all her lauded beauty, at her core was painfully low self-esteem. Her skin was too thin. She knew it. Pain could reach her too easily.

Ava had lived most of her life feeling utterly powerless: the *granddaughter*, not the all-important *grandson* of a national icon. In her world it was *sons* who were greatly to be prized. But surely that was history? Women through the ages had been expected to make as good a marriage as possible, to honour and obey her husband and bear him children. In some privileged cases for the continuation of the family dynasty.

She didn't give a darn about dynasty. Yet she had found enough courage—perhaps courage was the wrong word and *defiance* was much better—to fly in the face of her authoritarian grandfather's wishes. He had despised Luke and warned her off him. So had Dev, who'd only had her happiness and wellbeing at heart. She had ignored both of them—to her cost—she had got it badly wrong. Proof of her poor judgement.

It would take her some time before she was able to pick herself up and walk back into mainstream life. She had so many doubts about herself and her strength. Many, many women would understand that. It was a common pattern among besieged women trying so hard to do the right thing, with their efforts totally disregarded or held in contempt by their partners. She sometimes wondered if genuine equality between the sexes would ever happen. Women were still receiving horrific treatment at the hands of men all over the world. Unbearable to think that might remain the status quo.

To be truthful—and she believed she was—she had to own up to the fact she had never been passionate about Luke, or indeed any man. Certainly not the way Amelia was passionate about Dev. That *was* love—once in a lifetime love. In Ava's eyes, one had to be incredibly blessed to find it. Ava was an heiress, but she knew better than anyone that although money could buy just about anything it couldn't buy *love*. Her marriage, she acknowledged with a sense of shame, had been an escape route from her dysfunctional family—most particularly her late grandfather.

Her grandfather's death, however, had brought about swift changes. All for the better. Dev now headed up

Langdon Enterprises, of which Kooraki, one of the nation's leading cattle stations and beef producers, was but an arm; their estranged parents were back together—something that filled her and Dev with joy; and Sarina Norton, Kooraki's housekeeper for many years and her grandfather's not-so-secret mistress, had taken herself off to enjoy *la dolce vita* in Italy, the country of her birth.

And last but not least Sarina's daughter—the long-suffering Amelia—was putting the seal on her life-long unbreakable bond with Dev by getting married to him. Ava had long thought of Dev and Amelia as twin stars, circling a celestial field, never far apart. Now at last they were coming together, after delaying the wedding for some months as a mark of respect for Gregory Langdon's passing.

She now had the honour and privilege of being Amelia's chief bridesmaid—one of three. Together the lives of Dev and Amelia had gained their ultimate purpose. They would have children—beautiful children. Mel was strong. Ava had always been stunned by Mel's strength. Beside Mel she was very conscious of her own frailty. Despite the fact that all her own hopes had vanished like a morning mist she couldn't be happier for them. Dev was gaining a beautiful, clever wife who would be a great asset to the family business enterprises, her parents were gaining a daughter-in-law, and she was gaining the sister she had longed for.

Triumphs all round for the Langdon family. The past had to make way for a bright future. There had to be a meaning, a purpose, a *truth* to life. So far it seemed to Ava she had struggled through her existence. How she longed to take wing! She had suffered through the bad times—surely things could only get better?

From her vantage point it was plain to see their visitor projected the somewhat to be feared "dominant male" aura. Man controlled the world. Man was the rightful inheritor of the earth. In a lucid flash of insight she realised she didn't much like men. Her grandfather had been a terrifying man. But at the end of the day what did all that power and money matter? Both were false idols. Strangely, the dominant-male image didn't bother her in her adored brother. Dev had *heart*. But it put her on her guard against men like Juan-Varo de Montalvo. He looked every inch of his six-three— the quintessential macho male. It surrounded him like a force field. Such men were dangerous to emotionally fragile women wishing to lead a quiet life. In her case, she came with baggage too heavy to handle.

De Montalvo, she had learned from Dev, was the only son and heir of one of the richest land-owners in Argentina— Vicente de Montalvo. His mother was the American heiress Caroline Bradfield, who had eloped with Vicente at the age of eighteen against her parents' violently expressed disapproval. Not that Vicente had been all that much older— twenty-three.

The story had made quite a splash at the time. They must have been passionately in love and remained so, Ava thought with approval and a touch of envy. They were still together. And Dev had told her the bitter family feuding was mercifully long over.

Why wouldn't it be? Who would reject a grandson like Juan-Varo de Montalvo, who made an instant formidable impact. He had the kind of features romance novelists invariably labelled "chiselled". That provoked a faint smile— but, really, what other word could one use? He was wearing a casual outfit, much like Dev. Jeans, blue-and-white open-necked cotton shirt, sleeves rolled up, high polished boots. Yet he still managed to look…the word *patrician* sprang to mind. That high-mettled demeanour was inbred—a certain arrogance handed down through generations of a *hidalgo* family.

Dev had told her the Varo side of the family had its own coat of arms, and de Montalvo's bearing *was* very much that of the prideful Old World aristocrat. His stance was quite different from Dev's New World elegant-but-relaxed posture, Dev's self-assured nonchalance. Only as de Montalvo began moving around the Great Hall with striking suppleness a picture abruptly flashed into her mind. It was of a jaguar on the prowl. Didn't jaguars roam the Argentinian *pampas*? She wasn't exactly sure, but she would check it out. The man was dazzlingly exotic. He spoke perfect English. Why *wouldn't* he speak perfect English? He had an American mother. He would be a highly educated man, a cultured world-traveller.

High time now for her to go downstairs to greet him. She put a welcoming smile on her face. Dev would be expecting it.

The wedding was in a fortnight's time. The bride-to-be, Amelia, was still in Sydney, where she was finishing off work for her merchant bank. Dev was planning on flying there to collect her and their parents and some other Devereaux guests. That meant Ava would be playing hostess to Juan-Varo de Montalvo for a short time.

The season was shaping up to be absolutely brilliant for the great day: the sky was so glorious a blue she often had the fancy she was being drawn up into its density. Despite that, they were all praying the Channel Country wouldn't be hit by one of its spectacular electrical storms that blew up out of nowhere and yet for the most part brought not a drop of rain. For once rain wasn't needed after Queensland's Great Flood—a natural disaster that had had a silver lining. After long, long punishing years of drought, the Outback was now in splendid, near unprecedented condition.

Kooraki was a place of extraordinary wild beauty, with every waterhole, creek, billabong and lagoon brimming with life-giving water that brought an influx of waterbirds in their tens of thousands. So the station was in prime condition—the perfect site for the marriage between her brother and her dear friend Amelia.

Guests were coming from all over the country, and Juan-Varo de Montalvo was, in fact, the first overseas visitor to arrive. In his honour Dev had arranged a polo match and a post-polo party for the coming weekend. Invitations had gone out, generating huge interest. Most Outback communities, with their love of horses, were polo-mad. De Montalvo would captain one team, Dev the other. The two men had forged their friendship on the polo field. Dev had even visited the de Montalvo *estancia*—a huge ranch that ran Black Angus cattle, located not all that far from the town of Córdoba. So here were two polo-playing cattlemen who had every reason to relate to each other.

How Juan-Varo de Montalvo would relate to *her* was an entirely different matter. As she moved, her heart picked up a beat a second. Sometimes the purely physical got the better of the mind. She consoled herself with that thought.

Both men looked up as Ava began her descent of the curving staircase, one slender hand trailing over the gleaming mahogany banister. Ava, herself, had the oddest sensation she was walking on air. Her blood was racing. She felt in no way comfortable, let alone possessed of her usual poise. How could feelings run so far ahead of the rational mind?

"Ah, here's Ava," Dev announced with brotherly pride.

Dev's eyes were on his sister and not on Juan-Varo de Montalvo, whose dark regard was also fixed on the very fair young woman who was making her way so gracefully to them. He had known in advance she was beautiful. Dev had boasted many times that he had a beautiful sister. But the reality far exceeded his expectations. He was used to beautiful women. He was a man who loved women, having grown up surrounded by them—doting grandmothers, aunts, female cousins. He adored his mother. He had three beautiful sisters—one older, very happily married with a small son, his godchild, and two younger, with legions of admirers—but something about this young woman sent a jolt of electricity shafting through his body.

He could see beneath the grace, the serene air and the poise that she was oddly *vulnerable*. The vulnerability seemed inexplicable in a woman who looked like an angel and had grown up as she had, with every material advantage. Dev had told him about her failed marriage. Maybe she saw it as a humiliation? A fall from grace? Maybe she was guilty of heedlessly breaking a heart—or worse, inflicting deliberate pain? He had been brought up to frown on divorce. He had lived with two people—his mother and father—who had made a wonderful life together and lived side by side in great harmony.

She had to tilt her head to look up at him. There was a curiously *sad* look in her jewel-like eyes, the same dazzling aquamarine as her brother's. She had flawless skin, with the luminescence of a pearl. Few women could claim a face so incandescent.

It was in all probability a symptom of jet lag, but he felt a distinct low-pitched hum in his ears. Her smile, lovely and effortlessly alluring, seemed to conceal secrets. He had a certainty it was she who had ended her marriage. A cruel thing for an angel to do. One would expect such coldness only of a young and imperious goddess, who would only be loved for as long as it suited her.

Ava released a caught breath. "Welcome to Kooraki, Señor de Montalvo," she said with a welcome return of her practised poise. Heat was coming off the Argentine's aura. It was enveloping her. "It's a pleasure to have you here." It was necessary to go through the social graces even when she was *en garde* and taking great pains not to show it.

"Varo, please," he returned, taking her outstretched hand. His grip was gentle enough not to crush her slender fingers, but firm enough not to let her escape. "It's a great pleasure to be here. I thought it impossible you could be as beautiful as Dev has often described, but now I find you are even more so."

She felt the wave of colour rise to her cheeks but quickly recovered, giving him a slightly ironic look, as though judging and rejecting the sincerity of his words. "Please—you mustn't pander to my vanity," she returned lightly. She couldn't remember the last time a man had caused her to flush. She didn't like the enigmatic half-smile playing around his handsome mouth either. The expression in his dark eyes with their fringe of coal-black lashes was fathoms deep. She was angry with herself for even noticing.

"I had no such thought," he responded suavely, somehow establishing his male authority.

"Then, thank you."

There was strength behind his light grip on her. As a conductor for transmitting energy, his touch put her into such a charged state it caused an unprecedented flare of sexual hostility. It was as though he was taking something from her that she didn't want to give.

The warning voice in her head struck up again. *You have to protect yourself from this man, Ava. He could burn down all your defences.*

That she already knew.

"I find myself fascinated with Kooraki," de Montalvo was saying, including Dev in his flashing white smile. "It is much like one's own private kingdom. The Outback setting is quite extraordinary."

"From colonial times every man of ambition and means came to regard his homestead as the equivalent of the Englishman's country manor," Dev told him. "Most of the historic homesteads were built on memories of home— which was in the main the British Isles."

"Whereas our style of architecture was naturally influenced by Spain."

Dev turned his head to his sister. "As I told you, Estancia de Villaflores, Varo's home, is a superb example."

"We have much to be proud of, don't we?" de Montalvo said, with some gravitas.

"Much to be grateful for."

"Indeed we do." Brother and sister spoke as one.

Ava was finding de Montalvo's sonorous voice, with its deep dark register, making her feel weak at the knees. She was susceptible to voices. Voice and physical aura were undeniably sensual. Here was a man's man, who at the same time was very much a *woman's* man.

He was dangerous, all right.

Get ensnared at your peril.

They exchanged a few more pleasant remarks before Dev said, "I'm sure you'd like to be shown your room, Varo. That was a very long trip, getting here. Ava will show you upstairs. I hope you like what we've prepared for you. After lunch we'll take the Jeep for a quick tour of the outbuildings and a look at some of the herd. An overview, if you like. We have roughly half a million acres, so we'll be staying fairly close in for today."

"I'm looking forward to it," de Montalvo returned, with a sincere enthusiasm that made brother and sister feel flattered.

"Your luggage is already in your room, Varo," Ava told him, aware she was struggling with the man's magnetism. "One of the staff will have brought it up by now, taking the back entrance." Although de Montalvo had travelled a very long way indeed, he showed no signs whatever of fatigue or the usual jet lag. In fact he exuded a blazing energy.

"So no one is wasting time?" De Montalvo took a small step nearer Ava. An inch or two above average height, Ava felt strangely doll-like. "Please lead on, Ava," he invited. "I am all attention."

That made Dev laugh. "I have a few things to attend to, Varo," he called as his sister and his guest moved towards the grand staircase. "I'll see you at lunch."

"Hasta luego!" De Montalvo waved an elegant hand.

Ava had imagined that as she ascended the staircase she would marshal her defences. Now, only moments later, those defences were imploding around her. She had the sense that her life had speeded up, entered the fast lane. She had met many high-powered people in her life—none more so than her grandfather, who hadn't possessed a shining aura. Neither did Montalvo. It was dark-sided, too complex. It wasn't any comfort to realise she had been shocked out of her safe haven. Worse yet to think she might be shorn of protection.

How could any man do that in a split second? The impact had been as swift and precise as a bolt of lightning. Maybe it was because she wasn't used to exotic men? Nor the way he looked at her—as if he issued an outright challenge to her womanhood. Man, that great force of nature, totally irresistible if he so chose.

The thought angered her. Perhaps it was borne of her sexual timidity? Luke had early on in their marriage formed the habit of calling her frigid. She now had an acute fear that if she weren't very careful she might rise to de Montalvo's lure. He was no Luke. He was an entirely different species. Yet in some bizarre way he seemed familiar to her. Only he was a stranger—a stranger well aware of his own power.

As he walked beside her, with his tantalising lithe grace, glowing sparks might have been shooting off his powerful lean body. Certainly *something* was making her feel hot beneath her light clothing. She who had been told countless times she always appeared as cool as a lily. That wasn't the case now. She felt almost *wild*, when she'd had no intention let alone any experience of being any such thing. To her extreme consternation her entire body had become a mass of leaping responses. If those responses broke the surface it would be the ultimate humiliation.

His guest suite was in the right wing. It had been made ready by the household staff. Up until their grandfather's death the post of housekeeper had been held by Sarina Norton, Amelia's mother. Sarina had been most handsomely rewarded by Gregory Langdon for "services rendered". No one wanted to go there…

The door lay open. Varo waved a gallant arm, indicating she should enter first. Ava had the unsettling feeling she had to hold on to something. Maybe the back of a chair? The magnetic pull he had on her was so strong. How on earth was she going to cope when Dev flew off to Sydney? She was astonished at how challenging she found the prospect. What woman reared to a life of privilege couldn't handle entertaining a guest? She was a woman who had not only been married but was in the process of divorce—she being the one who had initiated the action. Didn't that qualify her as a woman of the world?

Or perhaps one could interpret it as the action of a woman who didn't hesitate to inflict pain and injury? Perhaps de Montalvo had already decided against her? His family of Spanish origin was probably Roman Catholic, but divorce couldn't be as big a no-no now as it had been in the time of Katherine of Aragon, Henry VIII's deposed, albeit lawfully wedded, wife. Not that taking Katherine's place had done Anne Boleyn much good.

Ava put the tension that was coiling tighter and tighter inside her down to an attack of nerves. It was all so unreal.

The guest room that had been chosen for de Montalvo was a grand room—and not only in terms of space and the high scrolled ceilings that were a feature of Kooraki's homestead. The headboard of the king-sized bed, the bed skirt and the big cushions were in a metallic grey silk, with pristine white bed-coverings and pillows. Above the bed hung a large gold-framed landscape by a renowned English-Australian colonial artist. Mahogany chests to each side of the bed held lamps covered in a parchment silk the same colour as the walls. A nineteenth century English secretary, cabinet and comfortable chair held pride of place in one corner of the room. The rest of the space was taken up by a gilded Louis XVI-style sofa covered in black velvet with a matching ottoman. All in all, a great place to stay, with the added plus of a deep walk-in wardrobe and an *en suite* bathroom.

He said something in Spanish that seemed to make sense to her even though she didn't know the language. Quite obviously he was pleased. She did have passable French. She was better with Italian, and she even had some Japanese— although, she acknowledged ruefully, keeping up with languages made it necessary to speak them every day. She even knew a little Greek from a fairly long stint in Athens the year after leaving university.

De Montalvo turned back from surveying the landscaped garden. "I'll be most happy and comfortable here, Ava," he assured her. "I'm sure this will be a trip never to be forgotten."

She almost burst out that she felt the same. Of course she did not. She meant to keep her feelings to herself. "I'll leave you in peace, then, Varo," she said. "Come downstairs whenever you like. Lunch will be served at one. Dev will be back by then."

"Gracias," he said.

Those brilliant dark eyes were looking at her again. Looking *at* her. *Through* her. She turned slowly for the door, saying over a graceful shoulder, *"Nuestra casa es su casa."*

His laugh was low in his throat. "You make a fine attempt. Your accent is good. I hope to teach you many more Spanish phrases before I leave."

Ava dared to face him. "Excellent," she said, her tone a cool parry.

CHAPTER TWO

THEY set out after breakfast the next day, the horses picking their way through knee-high grasses with little indigo-blue wildflowers swimming across the waving green expanses. Dev had flown to Sydney at first light, leaving them alone except for the household staff. She would have de Montalvo's company for a full day and a night and several hours of the following day before Dev, Amelia and co were due to fly back. So, all in all, around thirty hours for her to struggle against de Montalvo's powerful sexual aura.

For someone of her age, marital status and background Ava was beginning to feel as though she had been wandering through life with her eyes closed. Now they were open and almost frighteningly perceptive. Everyone had the experience of meeting someone in life who raised the hackles or had an abrasive effect. Their Argentine visitor exerted a force of quite another order. He had *roped* her, in cattleman's terms—or she had that illusion.

Dinner the previous evening had gone off very well. In fact it had been a beautiful little welcoming party. They'd eaten in the informal dining room, which was far more suitable and intimate than the grand formal dining room only used for special occasions. She'd had the table set with fine china, sterling silver flatware, and exquisite Bohemian crystal glasses taken from one the of numerous cabinets holding such treasures. From the garden she had picked a spray of exquisite yellow orchids, their blooms no bigger than paper daisies, and arranged them to take central pride of place. Two tall Georgian silver candlesticks had thrown a flattering light, finding their reflection in the crystal glasses.

The menu she'd chosen had been simple but delicious: white asparagus in hollandaise, a fish course, the superb barramundi instead of the usual beef, accompanied by the fine wines Dev had had brought up from the handsomely stocked cellar. Dessert had been a light and lovely passion-fruit trifle. She hadn't gone for overkill.

Both Dev and his guest were great *raconteurs*, very well travelled, very well read, and shared similar interests. Even dreams. She hadn't sat back like a wallflower either. Contrary to her fluttery feelings as she had been dressing—she had gone to a surprising amount of trouble—she had found it remarkably easy to keep her end up, becoming more fluent by the moment. Her own stories had flowed, with Dev's encouragement.

At best Luke had wanted her to sit quietly and look beautiful—his sole requirements of her outside the bedroom. He had never wanted her to shine. De Montalvo, stunning man that he was, with all his eloquent little foreign gestures, had sat back studying her with that sexy half-smile hovering around his handsome mouth. Admiring—or mocking in the manner of a man who was seeing exactly what he had expected to see? A blonde young woman in a long silk-jersey dress the exact colour of her eyes, aquamarine earrings swinging from her ears, glittering in the candlelight.

She was already a little afraid of de Montalvo's half-smile. Yet by the end of the evening she had felt they spoke the same language. It couldn't have been a stranger sensation.

Above them a flight of the budgerigar endemic to Outback Australia zoomed overhead, leaving an impressive trail of emerald and sulphur yellow like a V-shaped bolt of silk. De Montalvo studied the indigenous little birds with great interest. "Amazing how they make that formation," he said, tipping his head back to follow the squadron's approach into the trees on the far side of the chain of billabongs. "It's like an aeronautical display. I know Australia has long been known as the Land of the Parrot. Already I see why. Those beautiful parrots in the gardens—the smaller ones—are lorikeets, flashing colour. And the noisy ones with the pearly-grey backs and the rose-pink heads and underparts—what are they?"

"Galahs." Ava smiled. "It's the aboriginal name for the bird. It's also a name for a silly, dim-witted person. You'll hear it a lot around the stockyards, especially in relation to the jackeroos. Some, although they're very keen, aren't cut out for the life. They're given a trial period, and then, if they can't find a place in the cattle world, they go back home to find alternative work. Even so they regard the experience as the adventure of a lifetime."

"I understand that," he said, straightening his head. "Who wouldn't enjoy such freedom? Such vast open spaces virtually uninhabited by man? Our *gauchos* want only that life. It's a hard life, but the compensations are immense. Kooraki is a world away from my home in Argentina," he mused, studying Ava as though the sight of her gave him great pleasure. "There is that same flatness of the landscape. Quechua Indians named our flatness *pampa*—much like your vast plains. But at home we do not know such extreme isolation at this. There are roads fanning out everywhere from the *estancia*, and the grounds surrounding the house— designed many decades ago and established by one of our finest landscape designers—are more like a huge botanical

garden. Here it is pure *wilderness*. Beautiful in the sense of
not ever having been conquered by man. The colours are
indescribable. Fiery red earth, all those desert ochres mixed
in beneath dazzling blue skies. Tell me, is the silvery blue
shimmer the mirage that is dancing before our eyes?"

"It is," Ava confirmed. "The mirage brought many an
early explorer to his grave. To go in search of an inland
sea of prehistory and find only great parallel waves of red
sand! It was tragic. They even took little boats like dinghies
along."

"So your Kooraki has a certain mysticism to it not only
associated with its antiquity?"

"We think so." There was pride in her voice. "It's the old-
est continent on earth after all." Ava shifted her long heavy
blonde plait off her nape. It was damp from the heat and the
exertion of a fantastically liberating gallop with a splendid
horseman who had let her win—if only just. "You do know
we don't call our cattle stations *ranches*, like Americans?
We've kept with the British *station*. Our stations are the
biggest in the world. Anna Creek in the Northern Territory
spreads over six million acres."

"So we're talking thirty thousand square kilometres
plus?" he calculated swiftly.

"Thirty-four thousand, if we're going to be precise.
Alexandria Station, also in the Territory, is slightly smaller.
Victoria Downs Station used to be *huge*."

He smiled at the comparatives. "The biggest ranches in
the U.S. are around the three thousand square kilometres
mark, so you're talking ten times that size. Argentine *estan-
cias* are nowhere in that league either. Although earlier in
the year a million-acre *estancia* in north-west Argentina was
on sale, with enormous potential for agriculture—even eco-
power possibilities. Argentina—our beautiful cosmopoli-
tan capital Buenos Aires—was built on *beef*, as Australia's

fortunes were built on the sheep's back—isn't that so?" He cast her a long glance.

"I can't argue with that. Langdon Enterprises own both cattle and sheep stations. Two of our sheep stations produce the finest quality merino wool, mainly for the Japanese market. Did Dev tell you that?"

"I believe he did. Dev now has a great many responsibilities following your grandfather's death?"

"He has indeed," she agreed gravely, "but he's up to it. He was born to it."

It was her turn to study the finely chiselled profile de Montalvo presented to her. He wasn't wearing the Outback's ubiquitous akubra, but the startlingly sexy headgear of the Argentine *gaucho*: black, flat-topped, with a broad stiff brim that cast his elegant features into shadow. To be so aware of him sexually was one heck of a thing, but she strove to maintain a serene dignity, at the same time avoiding too many of those brilliant, assessing glances.

"Your father was not in the mould of a cattleman?" he asked gently.

Ava looked away over the shimmering terrain that had miraculously turned into an oasis in the Land of the Spinifex. The wake of the Queensland Great Flood had swept right across the Channel Country and into the very Red Centre of the continent.

"That jumped a generation to Dev. He was groomed from boyhood for the top. There was always great pressure on him, but he could handle it. Handle my grandfather as well. The rest of us weren't so fortunate. My father is much happier now that he has handed over the reins. My grandfather, Gregory Langdon, was a man who could terrify people. He was very hard on all of us. Dad never did go along with or indeed fit into the crown-prince thing, but he was a very dutiful son and pleasing his father was desperately important to him."

"And you?"

Ava tilted her chin an inch or so. "How can I say this? I'm chiefly remembered for defying my grandfather to marry my husband. Neither my grandfather nor Dev approved of him. It soon appeared they were right. You probably know I'm separated from my husband, in the process of getting a divorce?"

Varo turned his handsome head sideways to look at her. Even in the great flood of light her pearly skin was flawless. "I'm sorry." Was he? He only knew he definitely didn't want her to be married.

"Don't be," she responded, more curtly than she'd intended. He would probably think her callous in the extreme.

He glimpsed the flash of anger in her remarkable eyes. Obviously she longed to be free of this husband she surely once had loved. What had gone so badly wrong?

"I too tried very hard to please my grandfather," she offered in a more restrained tone. "I never did succeed—but then my grandfather had the ingrained idea that women are of inferior status."

"Surely not!" He thought how his mother and sisters would react to that idea.

"I'm afraid so. He often said so—and he *meant* it. Women have no real business sense, much less the ability to be effective in the so-called 'real' world. Read for that a *man's* world—although a cattle kingdom *is* a man's world it's so tough. Women are best served by devoting their time to making a good marriage—which translates into landing a good catch. Certainly a good deal of time, effort and money went into me."

"This has led to bitterness?" He had read much about the ruthless autocratic patriarch Gregory Langdon.

Ava judged the sincerity of his question. She was aware he was watching her closely. "Do I seem bitter to you?" She turned her sparkling gaze on him.

"Bitter, no. Unhappy, yes."

"Ah…a clarification?" she mocked.

"You deny it?" He made one of his little gestures. "Your husband is not putting up a fight to keep you?" Such a woman came along once in a lifetime, he thought. For good or bad.

Ava didn't answer. They had turned onto a well-trodden track that led along miles of billabongs, creeks and water-holes that had now become deep lagoons surrounded on all sides by wide sandy beaches. The blaze of sunlight worked magic on the waters, turning them into jewel colours. Some glittered a dark emerald, others an amazing sapphire-blue, taking colour from the cloudless sky, and a few glinted pure silver through the framework of the trees.

"One tends to become unhappy when dealing with a divorce," Ava answered after a while. "My marriage is over. I will not return to it, no matter what. Dev at least has found great happiness." She shifted the conversation from her. "He and Amelia are twin souls. You'll like Amelia. She's very beautiful and very clever. She holds down quite a high-flying job at one of our leading merchant banks. She'll be a great asset to Langdon Enterprises. Mercifully my grand-father didn't pass on his mindset to Dev."

"Dev is a man of today. He will be familiar with very successful women. But what do *you* plan to do with your-self after your divorce comes through?"

She could have cried out with frustration. Instead she spoke with disconcerting coolness. "You are really inter-ested?"

"Of course." His tone easily surpassed hers for hauteur.

She knew she had to answer on the spot. Their eyes were

locked. Neither one of them seemed willing to break contact. They could have been on some collision course. "Well, I don't know as yet, Varo," she said. "I might be unequal to the huge task Dev has taken on, but I want to contribute in any way I can."

"Then of course you will." A pause. "You will marry again."

It wasn't a question but a statement. "That's a given, is it? You see it as my only possible course?" she challenged.

He reached out a long arm and gently touched her delicate shoulder, leaving a searing sense of heat. It was as though his hand had touched her bare skin.

"Permit me to say you are very much on the defensive, Ava. You know perfectly well I do not." The sonorous voice had hardened slightly. "Dev will surely offer you a place on the board of your family company?"

"If I want a place, yes," she acknowledged.

He gave her another long, dark probing look. "So you are not really the businesswoman?"

She shook her head. "I have to admit it, no. But I have a sizeable chunk of equity in Langdon Enterprises. Eventually I will take my place."

"You should. There would be something terribly wrong if you didn't. You want children?"

She answered that question with one of her own. "Do you?"

He gave her his fascinating, enigmatic half-smile. "Marriage first, then children. The correct sequence."

"Used to be," she pointed out with more than a touch of irony. "Times have changed, Varo."

"Not in *my* family," he said, with emphasis. "I do what is expected of me, but I make my own choices."

"You have a certain woman in mind?"

It would be remarkable if he didn't. She had the certainty

this dynamic man had a dozen dazzling women vying for his attention.

"Not at the moment, no," he told her with nonchalance. "I enjoy the company of women. I would never be without women in my life."

"But no one as yet to arouse passion?" She was amazed she had even asked the question, and aware she was moving into dangerous territory.

Her enquiring look appeared to him both innocent and seductive at one and the same time. Did she know it? This wasn't your usual *femme fatale*. There was something about her that made a man want to protect her. Possibly that was a big mistake. One her husband had made?

"I don't think I said that," he countered after a moment. "Who knows? I may have already succumbed to *your* undoubted charms, Ava."

She raised a white hand to wave a winged insect away—or perhaps to dismiss his remark as utterly frivolous. "It would do you no good, Varo. I'm still a married woman. And I suspect you might be something of a legend back in Argentina."

"Perdón—perdonare!" he exclaimed. "Surely you mean as a *polo player*?" He pinned her gaze.

Both of them knew she had meant as a *lover*. "I'm looking forward to seeing you in action at the weekend." She declined to answer, feeling hot colour in her cheeks. "It should be a thrilling match. We're all polo-mad out here."

"As at home. Polo is the most exciting game in the world."

"And possibly the most dangerous," she tacked on. "Dev has taken a few spectacular spills in his time."

He answered with an elegant shrug of one shoulder. "As have I. That is part of it. You are an accomplished rider," he commented, his eyes on her slender body, sitting so straight but easy in the saddle. Such slenderness lent her a deceptive fragility, contradicted by the firmness with which she handled her spirited bright chestnut mare.

"I should be." Ava's smile became strained as memories flooded in. "My grandfather threw me up on a horse when I was just a little kid—around four. I remember my mother was beside herself with fright. She thought I would be hurt. He took no notice of her. Mercifully I took to riding like a duck to water. A saving grace in the eyes of my grandfather. As a woman, all that was expected of me was to look good and produce more heirs for the continuation of the Devereaux-Langdon dynasty. At least I was judged capable of expanding the numbers, if not the fortune. A man does that. I expect in his own way so does Dev. Every man wants a son to succeed him, and a daughter to love and cherish, to make him proud. I suppose you know my grandfather left me a fortune? I don't have to spend one day working if I choose not to."

"Why work at anything when one can spend a lifetime having a good time?" he asked on a satirical note.

"Something like that. Only I *need* to contribute."

"I'm sure you shall. You need time to re-set your course in life. All things are possible if one has a firm belief in oneself. Belief in oneself sets us free."

"It's easier to dream about being free than to accomplish it," she said, watching two blue cranes, the Australian brolgas, getting set to land on the sandy banks of one of the lagoons.

"You thought perhaps marriage would set you free?" he shot back.

"I'm wondering if you want my life story, Varo?" Her eyes sparkled brightly, as if tears weren't all that far away.

"Not if you're in no hurry to tell me," he returned gently, then broke off, his head set in a listening position. "You hear that?"

They reined in their horses. "Yes." Her ears too were registering the sound of pounding hooves.

Her mare began to skip and dance beneath her. In the way of horses, the mare was scenting some kind of danger. De Montalvo quietened his big bay gelding with a few words in Spanish which the gelding appeared to understand, because it ceased its skittering. Both riders were now holding still, their eyes trained on the open savannah that fanned out for miles behind them.

In the next moment they had their answer. Runaway horse and hapless rider, partially obscured by the desert oaks dotted here and there, suddenly burst into full view.

De Montalvo broke the fraught silence. "He's in trouble," he said tersely.

"It's a workhorse." Ava recognised that fact immediately, although she couldn't identify the rider. He was crouched well down over his horse's back, clinging desperately to the flowing black mane. Feet were out of the stirrups; the reins were flailing about uselessly. "It's most likely one of our jackeroos," she told him with anxiety.

"And he's heading right for that belt of trees," De Montalvo's expression was grim. "If he can't pull up he's finished. *Terminado!*" He pulled the big bay's head around as he spoke.

The area that lay dead ahead of the station hand's mad gallop was heavily wooded, dense with clumps of ironwood, flowering whitewoods and coolabahs that stood like sentinels guarding the billabong Ava knew was behind them. The petrified rider was in deep trouble, but hanging on for dear life. He would either be flung off in a tumble of broken bones or stay on the horse's back, only to steer at speed into thick overhanging branches. This surely meant a broken neck.

"Stay here," de Montalvo commanded.

It was an order, but oddly she didn't feel jarred by it. There was too much urgency in the situation.

She sat the mare obediently while de Montalvo urged the powerful bay gelding into a gallop. Nothing Zephyr liked better than to gallop, Ava thought with a sense of relief. Nothing Zephr liked better than to catch and then overtake another horse. That was the thoroughbred in him.

The unfortunate man had long since lost his hat. Now Ava recognised the red hair. It was that Bluey lad—a jackeroo. She couldn't remember his surname. But it was painfully clear he was no horseman. One could only wonder what had spooked his horse. A sand goanna, quite harmless but capable of giving a nervous horse a fright? Goannas liked to pick their mark too, racing alongside horse and rider as though making an attempt to climb the horse's sleek sides. A few cracks of the whip would have settled the matter, frightening the reptile off. But now the young jackeroo was heading full pelt for disaster.

Ava held up a hand to shield her eyes from the blazing sun. Little stick figures thrown up by the mirage had joined the chase, their legs running through the heated air. She felt incredibly apprehensive. Señor de Montalvo was their guest. He was a magnificent rider, but what he was attempting held potential danger for him if he persisted with the wild chase. If he were injured… If he were injured… She found herself praying without moving her dry lips.

Varo had been obliged to come at the other horse from an oblique angle. She watched in some awe as he began to close in on the tearaway station horse that most likely had started life as a wild brumby. Even in a panic the workhorse couldn't match the gelding for speed. Now the two were racing neck and neck. The finish line could only be the wall of trees—which could prove to be as deadly as a concrete jungle.

Ava's breath caught in her throat. She saw Varo lean sideways out of his saddle, one hand gripping his reins and the pommel, the other lunging out and down for the runaway's reins. A contest quickly developed. Ava felt terribly shaken, not knowing what to expect. She found herself gripping her own horse's sides and crying out, "Whoa, boy, whoa!" even though she was far from the action. She could see Varo's powerful gelding abruptly change its long stride. He reined back extremely hard while the gelding's gleaming muscles bunched beneath its rider. Both horses were acting now in a very similar fashion. Only a splendid horseman had taken charge of them, bringing them under tight control.

The mad flight had slowed to a leg-jarring stop. Red dust flew in a circling cloud, earth mixed up with pulped grasses and wildflowers. "Thank God!" Ava breathed. She felt bad enough. Bluey was probably dying of fright. What of Varo? What an introduction to their world!

The headlong flight was over. She had a feeling Bluey wasn't going to hold on to his job. She was sure she had heard of another occasion when Bluey had acted less than sensibly. At least he was all right. That was the important thing. There had been a few tragic stories on Kooraki. None more memorable than the death in a stampede of Mike Norton, Sarina Norton's husband but not, as it was later revealed, Amelia's actual father. Sarina Norton was one beautiful but malevolent woman, loyal to no one outside herself.

Ava headed off towards the two riders who had sought the shade to dismount. Her mare's flying hooves disturbed a group of kangaroos dozing under one of the big river gums. They began to bound along with her.

It was an odd couple she found. Bluey, hardly more than a madcap boy, was shivering and shaking, white as a sheet beneath the orange mantling of freckles on his face. Varo showed no sign whatsoever of the recent drama, except for a slick of sweat across his high cheekbones and the tousling of his thick coal-black hair. Even now she had to blink at the powerful magnetism of his aura.

He came forward as she dismounted, holding the mare's reins. They exchanged a measured, silent look. "All's well that ends well, as the saying goes." He used his expressive voice to droll effect. Far from being angry in any way, he was remarkably cool, as though stopping runaway horses and riders was a lesson he had learned long ago.

Ava was not cool. He was their guest. "What in blue blazes was *that* exhibition all about?" she demanded of the hapless jackeroo. She watched in evident amazement as the jackeroo attempted a grin.

"I reckon I oughta stick to motorbikes."

"I've seen you before, haven't I?" Ava asked with a frown.

"Yes, miss." The jackeroo sketched a wobbly bow. "I'm Bluey. This gentleman here did a great job of saving me life. I'd have broken a leg, for sure."

"You'd have broken a great deal more than that," Varo pointed out, this time making no attempt to hide the note of reproof.

"It was a mongrel goanna." Bluey made a wild gesture with his skinny arms. "About six feet long."

"Nonsense!" Ava shook her head. "It was probably a sand goanna, half that size. You must have alarmed it."

"Well, it rushed me anyway," Bluey mumbled, implying anyone would have reacted the same way. "Sprang up from under a tree. I thought it was a damned log, beggin' your pardon."

"Some log!" It was all Ava could do not to tell Bluey off. "You could have frightened it off with a few flicks of the whip."

"Couldn't think fast enough," Bluey confessed, looking incredibly hot and dirty.

The expression on Juan-Varo de Montalvo's handsome face conveyed what he thought of the jackeroo's explanation. "You're all right to mount your horse again?" he addressed the boy with clipped authority in his voice.

"Poor old Elvis." Bluey shook his copper head. "The black mane, yah know? I thought his heart would burst."

"The black mane?" Varo's expression lightened. He even laughed. "I see."

Ava was finding it difficult to keep her eyes off him. He looked immensely strong and capable, unfazed by near disaster. His polished skin glowed. The lock of hair that had fallen forward onto his tanned forehead gave him a very dashing, rakish look. He wore his hair fairly long, so it curled above the collar of his shirt. She tried not to think how incredibly sexy he was. She needed no such distraction.

As they paused in the shade small birds that had been hidden in the safety of the tall grasses burst into the air, rising only a few feet before the predatory hawks made their lightning dives. Panicked birds were caught up, others managed to plummet back into the thick grass. This was part of nature. As a girl Ava had always called out to the small birds, in an effort to save them from the marauding hawks, but it had been an exercise in futility.

"What were you doing on your own anyway, Bluey? You should have been with the men."

Bluey tensed. "Headin' for the Six Mile," he said evasively. "You're not gunna tell the boss, are you?" he asked, as though they shared a fearful secret.

Varo glanced at Ava, who was clearly upset, her eyes sparkling. He decided to intervene. "Get back on your horse. I assume the red hair justifies the nickname! We'll ride with you to the house. You'll need something for those skinned hands."

"A wash up wouldn't hurt either," Ava managed after a moment. "Think you'll be more alert next time a goanna makes a run for your horse?"

"I'll practise a lot with me whip," Bluey promised, some colour coming back into his blanched cheeks. "I hope I didn't spoil your day?"

"Spoil our day?" Ava's voice rose. "It would have been horrible if anything had happened, Bluey. Thank God Varo was with me. I doubt *I* could have caught you, let alone have the strength to bring the horses under control."

"Sorry, miss," Bluey responded, though he didn't look all that troubled. "I could never learn to ride like *you*." Bluey looked to the man who had saved him from certain injury or worse.

"You can say that again!" Ava responded with sarcasm.

"Thanks a lot, mate." Bluey leaked earnest admiration from every pore.

Varo made a dismissive gesture. "M-a-t-e!" He drew the word out on his tongue.

"Well, that's *one* version of it." Ava had to smile. Did the man have any idea what a fascinating instrument his voice was? "Well, come on, Bluey," she said, giving the jackeroo a sharp look. "Get back up on your horse."

Bluey shook himself to attention. "Dunno who got the bigger fright—me or Elvis." He produced a daft grin.

As they rode back to the homestead Ava couldn't help wondering if Bluey would ever make it as a station hand. His derring-do could prove a danger to others. From fright and alarm he had gone now to questioning his hero about life on the Argentine pampas, confiding that everyone— "I mean everyone!"—would be turning up to see him play polo at the weekend. "You got one helluva lot of strength inside you," Bluey told the South American visitor with great admiration.

"Just as well. It was a titanic struggle," Ava said, resisting the impulse to call Bluey the derogatory *galah*. "Common sense goes a long way. If I find you've used up eight lives…?" She paused significantly.

"Please don't tell the boss, miss," Bluey begged. "One more sin and he'll kick me out."

"And there goes your big adventure." Ava shrugged, thinking admonition might well fall on deaf ears. "It could be later than you think, Bluey. Now, let's get you cleaned up."

CHAPTER THREE

WHEN they arrived back at the homestead, Varo sent the jackeroo off to the first-aid room.

"Let me have a word with this young man." He inclined his head towards Ava.

"You think you can talk some sense into him?" she asked sceptically. "I remember now—he once put Amelia in danger with one of his ill-conceived stunts."

"I think I can make him see sense," he answered with quiet authority. "He knows there's a strong possibility he will be sent home if Dev hears about this."

"Maybe we should tell Dev?" she suggested with utter seriousness. "In rescuing Bluey you put yourself at considerable risk."

"One doesn't think of that at such a time." He dismissed the risk factor, looking deeply into her eyes.

"All right," she consented, trying not to appear flustered. "I'll see to lunch. This afternoon I thought I might show you the hill country. It's not all low-rise on Kooraki. The hills reach a fair height. A good climb, anyway—and there's so much to see. Aboriginal rock paintings. And there really *was* an inland sea—but we're talking pre-history. There are drawings of crocodiles on the rock walls. X-ray depictions of fish. We even have a waterfall of sorts at the moment. It plunges downhill into the rock pool beneath it. Not even a trickle in the Dry, of course."

She knew the rock pool would be a great place for a dip. The waters were fairly deep, and crystal-clear, but Juan-Varo de Montalvo made her feel far too aware of herself as a woman to risk donning a bathing suit.

"We will ride there?" he asked, already filled with fascination for the fabled Outback.

She shook her blonde head. "We'll take the Jeep. I'll even let you drive." She gave him a quick smile which he thought as alluring as any water nymph. "There's no wrong side of the road."

"Gracias, Señora," His black eyes glittered as he acknowledged her marital status.

It was quite a job to keep her expression composed. Infatuation was the last thing she had seen coming.

From the passenger window Ava eyed the Wetlands, home to thousands upon thousands of waterbirds. The vast expanse of water had joined up with the lignum swamps to the extent one didn't know where the lignum swamps ended and the Wetlands started up.

"In times of drought this great expanse of water will dry up," she told Varo, who drove like he did everything else. With absolute skill and confidence. "The parched surface becomes crisscrossed by cracks and the footprints of the wildlife—kangaroos, emus, camels, wild pigs, snakes, or any human walking across the dry ochre sand."

"Camels I *have* to see," he said, giving her a quick sidelong smile.

"You will," she promised. "The Afghan traders brought them in the early days. 1840, to be precise. They thrived here. We even export them to Arab countries. They're part of the landscape now, but they can be very destructive. Not as much as hoofed animals, however. Their feet are adapted for deserts. They have soft pads, but they eat everything in sight, depleting the food supply for our indigenous species. They're very dangerous too, when the male goes on heat."

"The *male?*" One black eyebrow shot up.

"Bizarre, but true. At the last count there were over a million feral camels scattered over the desert areas of the Territory, Western Australian, South Australia and Queensland's desert fringe. The introduced water buffalo of the Territory do tremendous damage to the environment and the ecosystem. Even our dingoes were introduced."

"But I thought they were native Australian animals?" He glanced back at her. She had taken her beautiful hair out of its plait. Now it was sliding over her shoulders and down her back in shining, deep sensuous waves. She had changed for lunch, as had he. Now she was wearing a blue T-shirt with a silver designer logo on the front. The clingy fabric drew his eyes to the delicate shape of her high breasts.

"They've been here for thousands of years," she was saying, snapping him back to attention, "but they came from South East Asia originally, where they must have been domestic dogs. Over the four or five thousand years they've been here, they've established themselves in the wilds. They're our number-one predator. They can attack, even kill—especially if the victim is small, like a child."

"One doesn't like to think of that," he said gravely. "What about sheep? Mature cattle would be able to fend them off, surely?" He was frowning slightly.

"Not the calves. The alpha male is especially dangerous. So is the alpha female. They hunt in packs. We don't have the Great Wall of China, but we do have the longest man-made fence in the world."

He was quick to reply. "I have heard of the famous Dingo Fence."

"We'll take you to see Kooraki's section of it before you go home," she offered.

Even thinking of his departure gave her a distinct wrench. That only added to her sense of unreality. Who could expect to be so susceptible in such a very short time? She had to be aware her sense of trepidation was spiced with undeniable excitement. She only hoped he wasn't witness to it.

"The Dingo Fence is close to six thousand kilometres long," she carried on, her tone rather clipped. "It was shortened from well over eight thousand kilometres in 1980 because of the high repair costs. Six feet of wire mesh with steel and timber posts. It's a never-ending job maintaining it, but it protects over twenty-six million hectares of sheep and cattle grazing country. You're in trouble big-time if you forget to shut a gate."

"Who would know out here?" He waved a hand at the empty miles that ran for as far as the eye could see.

"You'd be surprised. Everyone keeps an eye out. Everyone knows if there are tourists or strangers in the area. Cattle-and-sheep men would never be guilty of such an offence."

He could see the jagged shape of the hills off to the northwest, their broken peaks and domes silhouetted against the cobalt-blue sky. The furnace-red of the earth made a wonderful contrast to the cloudless blue sky and the amazingly green trees and vegetation. The most beautiful tree he had seen along their route Ava had told him was the Outback's iconic Ghost Gum. It was easy to understand why. The tall upright tree with pendulous dark green leaves had a smooth, near blindingly white trunk and branches that made it glow in the sunlight. Even the distant hills were changing colour from brown to an orange that deepened into the red of the earth.

"You can stop here," Ava said as they arrived near the foot of a tumbling white waterfall.

Once out of the Jeep they could hear the loud murmur of the waters and their splash into the circular pool. A surprising amount of water was falling into it.

Varo moved closer, looking down into the depths. The silvered mirror-like surface threw back his own reflection. That too of the beautiful blonde Ava, who stood at his shoulder like an ethereal vision.

"It's so hot. A swim would be most welcome." He turned to her, the movement of his wide shoulders causing a flutter of air to cross the pool and form ripples.

"Bathing suits optional?" The coolness of her voice was intended not to give her inner turmoil away.

"You don't think it the duty of a good hostess to—"

"Varo, I know you're teasing," she protested, looking up into his brilliant mocking eyes.

"Even if you're really tempted?" He seemed to be towering over her. "The water is crystal-clear." He bent to dip a hand into it. "And so refreshingly cool."

"Varo, I'm getting a little nervous around you," Ava murmured.

He straightened. "You are *very* safe with me."

"I know that," she said hurriedly. "You also know what I mean. If you want a swim we have many lagoons. Dev, Amelia and I spend countless hours swimming in our favourite lagoon, the Half-Moon. The most gorgeous water lilies on the station grow there—the sacred blue lotus. They decorate the perimeter, along with all the water reeds. The lagoon is very deep in the middle. One day you can swim there. Maybe have a picnic."

"With you?" He fixed his dark eyes on her.

"Maybe," she said, half turning away.

"Maravillosa!" He had an instant vision of her, naked

as a water nymph, her long golden hair cascading over her shoulders, her beautiful skin with the lustre of a pearl.

Ava, for her part, was glad of her gift for composure— even if it was being giving an almighty workout. She pointed upwards, a pulse beating in her throat. "There's a big cave up there that goes so far back into the hills I used to be terrified I would get lost if I ventured too far. See, Varo?" She glanced at him, only to find him looking at her. "It's the one partially camouflaged by those feathery sprays of acacia. You'll have to duck your head at the entrance, but the interior at the central point is over two metres high."

"The roof has never caved in on anyone?" he asked, beginning to stare upwards.

Ava gave a little shudder. "Never. But I didn't dare to venture into the cave's recesses like Dev. Even Mel was scared. We have a famous mystery novel called *Picnic at Hanging Rock,* written by Joan Lindsay. It was made into a film way back in the 1970s. It tells the story of the disappearance of several schoolgirls and their teacher during a picnic at Hanging Rock on St Valentine's Day. The book is in our library at home. I've read and re-read it. It's a haunting tale. The missing party was never found."

"You think you will disappear as well?" he asked in teasing fashion.

"Wait until you're inside the cave," she replied, her composure regained.

"You think I'll get cold feet?"

"Laugh all you like." She gave him a sparkling look that was like a brief taunt. "I've known visitors to our great desert monuments, the aboriginal sacred sites Uluru and Kata Tjuta, come away stunned by the atmosphere. Why, some find the Valley of the Winds at Kata Tjuta very scary—especially when the winds are blowing. It's another world."

"One I intend to visit." He put out his elegant tanned hand. "Let me help you."

His wonderfully expressive voice sounded so tender her heart shook. She had no recourse but to put her hand in his, feeling his long fingers close around hers. She had known from the start nothing was going to be *normal* with this man. The suppressed excitement, the assault on her senses was way out of her experience. She had not dreamed of anything like this.

Together they climbed. A rock wallaby, startled by the approach of two figures, bounded back down the steep slope, making short work of reaching the bottom. Once when Ava's foothold slipped Vero gathered her close, wrapping one arm around her. She gave an involuntary little cry. She knew it wasn't fright. It was something far more dangerous that had her catching her breath.

At that height the rumbling of the waterfall was much louder. Big splashes fell over them—not enough to soak on such a hot day, but having a wonderful effect. Ava found herself taking droplets of cold water into her dry mouth. She wondered if this was how Amelia felt with Dev. There was a palpable ache inside her. It was sexual.

Gradually the footholds became narrower, but she turned her feet sideways just as she had done as a child. Varo might have been an experienced rock climber for all the trouble *he* was having. For all she knew he might have made an attempt on Mount Everest at one time. His own majestic Andes were close by his *estancia*, with a splendour rivalling the Himalayas.

In a final burst they reached the top, both of them turning to stare down at the infinite plains that spread out to the horizon. Not a single cloud broke up the dazzling peacock-blue of the sky.

"This is magic!" Varo exclaimed. "Superb!"

He still kept an arm around her. Maybe he had forgotten?

"And there's much more to see." She broke contact, restless and madly energetic. She might have caught fire from him. "Keep your head down until I tell you to lift it," she warned, preparing to enter the cave first.

In their shared childhood she, Dev and Amelia had always brought torches so they could explore inside. On a fairly recent climb she and Dev had left a lantern behind. When lit, it threw a very satisfactory light over the interior.

Varo reached out to pull away the curtain of vines that wreathed the neck of the cave.

"It's dark inside," she said over her shoulder. "Don't forget to keep your head down."

He nodded. He had no need to be told. In actual fact he had kept right behind her, to catch her should she slip on all the loose pebbles as fine as gravel.

Then the plunge into the tunnel!

It wasn't as dark as he'd expected. Although no ray of blazing sunshine pierced the cave, it still managed to cast a luminescence. He was able to judge the moment to stand erect. He saw her kneeling on the ground near one wall of the great tunnel, then there was suddenly light. Golden light that lit the cave and danced over the sandstone walls.

Varo stood mesmerised, his eyes tracking the images of the primitive art gallery. Even Ava, who had been inside the cave many times, stood rapt. More than anything she wanted their guest to be stirred and fascinated by what he saw. Varo moved closer to inspect one smooth, clean wall of the great cavern. It was dominated by a highly stylised drawing of a great serpent—a python—executed in chalky white with dark bands encircling the body and a black neck and head. The powerful reptile wound its sinuous body around two sides of the cave, its head high on the rock ceiling.

Evidently the great serpent was an important, even sacred creature from the aboriginal Dreamtime. Human figures with white circled eyes were represented only in stick-like form. The female forms with pendulous breasts. There were animals—kangaroos, emus—trees, and flocks of birds radiating over the walls, but what was most incredible, just as Ava had told him, was an outstanding drawing of a *crocodile*. It was surrounded by what could only be tropical palms. Fish too were represented, and what appeared to be turtles. Human handprints acted like a giant frame.

He turned back to Ava, who was watching his expression and trying to gauge his reaction. "This has to be a significant site!" he exclaimed. "Quite extraordinary."

"It is," she confirmed, "but very few people get to see it. It's not a sacred site, but it has to be protected. That's *our* job."

"Then I'm honoured. Thank you for bringing me here." He resumed his tour of the gallery, taking his time. As he walked he talked about the Inca civilisation of Peru, and the culture that had been shattered by the cruel and bloody Spanish Conquest. "Ancient temples and tombs were pillaged by the Conquisadors. Gold and silver booty to enrich the coffers of the Spanish Crown. In return Catholicism was forced on them."

"Your family is Catholic?"

He shrugged without answering.

"I've often wanted to visit South America," she said. "Especially since Dev came home filled with the marvels of your world. You were the one who took him to Machu Picchu?"

"Ah, yes—the secret cloud-shrouded ceremonial city of ancient Peru. That vast empire included the north-west of Argentina. Machu Picchu is one of the must-see places one should visit before one dies, Ava. Anyway, when you come to Argentina it will be my privilege to show you all we can offer." He turned suddenly, bending his dark head so he could whisper softly in her ear. "I'll even teach you how to dance the tango."

"Of which you are a master?" She felt the flush rise to her face.

"Of course."

It was so quiet inside the cave it was almost as though they were in some ancient cathedral, cut off from the rest of the world.

Varo was looking at the tunnel that led off the main cavern and went as far as anyone knew back deep into the eroded hills. It appeared as if he were debating whether it was wise to explore it.

"*No,* Varo!" she found herself exclaiming. "No one has ever mapped any of the passageways. No one even knows if there are exits. You're not Indiana Jones."

He turned back. The brilliant dark glance that swept over her was amused. "Maybe not. But I have been in some very scary places—including the South Pole. You're frightened I might want to explore in there?"

"I'm frightened I might lose you," she said.

"That won't ever happen."

It was said so gently, yet Ava thought she would remember his expression for as long as she lived. "We *must* go," she implored. "Back into the sunlight."

"We've only just arrived. You realise this would probably lead to a whole cave system?"

"The hill country is honeycombed with them," she admitted. "But even Dev backed off after he had gone a good distance. In some places there's only crawling space. I have to tell you I'm a bit claustrophobic." She wrapped her arms around herself as though she were cold.

He remained quite still, not making any move towards

her. "There's no reason to be frightened, Ava," he assured her, his voice pitched low.

"I'm not frightened. I'm more *worried*."

He gave her a slight and dangerous smile. "That you'll find yourself lost?" Now he made a move towards her, extending his hand to lift her face to him. "You fight the attraction?"

It was so strangely quiet she could hear her blood whooshing through her veins. "What attraction?" Unnerved, she tried to deny the obvious.

"*Our* attraction," he said. "You think it inevitable I might want to kiss you?"

"Don't, Varo," she whispered, shaking her head. This man could mesmerise her.

"One moment in time," he coaxed. "It occurs to me you are suffering in some way."

"I've had years of it." She hadn't intended to say it, but she had.

"Then you need a new start."

Just like that.

The note in his voice sent her head spinning. She felt herself sway towards him even before he gathered her into his arms in a way no man had gathered her to him before. She couldn't move away. She didn't want to move away. Why she was allowing this she didn't want to understand. She should feel daunted. Their instant connection was near incomprehensible. Yet every last little thing about him was proving an intoxicant. Even the cool air inside the cave was aromatic with the scents of the wild bush.

"I love that mouth of yours," he muttered, his handsome head poised over hers. "A man might only dream of kissing it." He touched her lower lip with the pad of one finger, effectively opening up her mouth to him.

That ignited such a response inside her she feared her

heart might stop. She was desperate for this, but all the while she felt deeply perturbed. From here on she was in his power. Yet she didn't push away, or ask him to stop. She knew he would if she did. Only right at that moment she knew this was what she wanted. She *had* to have it before she let go.

He was kissing her, tasting her, cupping her face with strong but exquisitely gentle hands. He kissed her not once but over and over, each time more fully, more deeply. A thousand brilliant stars were bursting behind her closed eyelids. Her hands had come up to clutch at his shirt, bunching it, her long nails maybe even hurting him if they pierced the fine cotton. This was longing, *desire*, on a grand scale, and the sensation was worth anything. She was far, far more vulnerable than she could ever have imagined. A near stranger had taken her captive when her husband had never succeeded in even pushing her to a climax.

He didn't stop. Perhaps he couldn't. If so, neither could she. She was utterly bewitched. He would have already identified that. He understood the power of the flesh would be too great. Ava felt as though her bones were dissolving, her flesh melting, yet the delta of her body felt oddly *heavy*. One of his hands was hard at her arched back. The other swept over her breast. Her nipples were standing erect with the height of arousal that was in her. His every action, so masterful, demolished all coherent thought. She felt in another moment they would sink onto their knees before falling back on the sand. Neither of them stopping. Neither of them prepared to try.

You've got to fight out of this delirium.

Her inner voice was crying out to her, desperate for her to listen. This could turn out to be a bitter, very traumatic mistake.

Make yourself care. No matter what you feel, this could come back to haunt you.

Her eyes flew open, coming slowly into focus, though she still felt bound to him.

For an instant Varo felt profoundly disorientated. Then he realised it was her soft moan that had forced him back to reality, back to control. He hadn't been able to get enough of her. The pressure on him had been unrelenting. Never in his life had he wanted a woman more. Locked in his arms, she'd seemed to him to be the very image of man's one great desire. But it was all so very complicated. This beautiful woman was still married—however unhappily. She was the much loved sister of his friend. He was a guest on Kooraki.

He told himself all this as he fought down the tumult inside him. Without thinking he raised a hand to brush her tumbling cascade of golden hair away from her face and over her shoulders. "There's no point in denying attraction, Ava," he said quietly. "Your life is complicated at the moment, but I can't think kissing you was a mistake."

"A woman is to be enjoyed?" she asked, brittle-voiced. Her tone was far sharper and more cynical than she'd intended.

There was a hush before he answered. "Do not demean the moment, Ava. Come, let's go back into the light."

She caught his arm as he started to turn away. "Forgive me, Varo. I didn't mean that the way it came out. I'd given up feeling—" She broke off.

"Did you love your husband at all?" He stared down into her eyes.

"If you had asked me back then I would have claimed I did."

"But he loved you? He continues to love you?"

The air around them seemed to be trembling. "Leave it there, Varo," she advised. "You know nothing about it."

His dark, handsome features tautened. "I know you want an escape."

"What else should I do?" she burst out with too much emotion. "Come on, tell me. Stay in a loveless marriage?"

"On *your* side," he pointed out.

"So judgemental?" Now there was an immeasurable distance between them. She might have known. "With your strict moral code I'm shocked you resorted to kissing me. Me—a married woman!"

He shrugged a wide shoulder. "Maybe I've been possessed, enchanted, bewitched…whatever. Temptation clings to you like a diaphanous veil. You're a very beautiful woman, Ava. Surely there have been other men in your life?"

"Irrelevant!" she said, with a downward chop of her hand. "Let's think of this as a summer storm. Over as quickly as it began."

Except it wasn't over. They both knew that.

CHAPTER FOUR

Ava spent a sleepless night. Never for a moment could she get Juan-Varo de Montalvo out of her mind. He might have been sleeping alongside her, so palpable was his aura. The power he had over her had arisen on its own. She hadn't invited it. Her conscience was clear on that point. Neither had she planned it.

It was some comfort to realise he too had surrendered to the massive force that had reached out for them and held them fast. The electrical charge that flowed between them was mutual. What had happened—and really were stolen kisses so illicit?—had caught him up too. He had not persisted when he heard her involuntary little moans. He had swiftly drawn back, only to brush back the wild mane of hair that had tumbled all around her face, with golden skeins clinging to the skin of his face and his neck.

But, *oh!* She had never known a kiss could make one's heart rise like a lark. It had been so unbelievable to take wing. She thought she would always be able to recall that weightless feeling, the shooting stars behind her eyes. Why hadn't Luke kissed her like that?

He didn't know how. He simply wasn't capable.

Yet she had been faithful to him. She wasn't the sort of woman who indulged in meaningless flings. Until now. If one could call rapturous kisses infidelity. For the first time all thoughts of Luke blurred. It was the past. Luke would move on.

Or so she believed.

Dev flew in around noon, with his bride-to-be Amelia and their parents, Erik and Elizabeth, for so long estranged, now back together again, and looking happy and wonderfully fit after a trip to beautiful Tasmania. There were three other passengers, all Devereaux relatives, including her cousin Karen.

Karen's parents were supremely self-assured people, partners in a blue chip law firm, and Karen too was a very confident, good-looking young woman, but remarkably exacting—almost driven, to Ava's mind. Two years older than Ava, she had always adopted a patronising attitude towards her younger Langdon cousin. There was plenty of money in the family. Like her, Karen had no need to work, but Karen was in fact a successful interior designer of the minimalist style. Whenever she stayed at Kooraki she had a habit of mooching around the handsomely decorated rooms—so many collectors in the family—as though she'd like to clear the lot out and start again.

Surely that would be like obliterating the past? In any case Kooraki was the Langdon stronghold. She remembered her grandfather referring to Karen as "that very unpleasant girl."

Thank God for Amelia, Ava thought as she hugged her. Amelia was a kindred spirit—the sister she'd never had and now would.

Karen locked on to Juan-Varo de Montalvo the instant her startled dark eyes fell on him. If expressions were anything to go on their Argentine guest had come as an enormous surprise. Indeed, her mouth fell half open as if in shock. Ava even thought she heard a gasp.

How fantastic was this!

They were all assembled in the Great Hall, with Dev making introductions.

Varo had no difficulty in recognising what qualities his friend Dev saw in his bride-to-be. Not only was Amelia beautiful in the Italianate fashion—large, lustrous dark eyes, lovely olive skin and wonderful thick dark hair—her manner would always draw people to her. As far as he was concerned she suited Dev perfectly. The Devereaux relatives, however, were quite different from the warm and friendly Langdons. They acted as though they owned the earth, their manner, to Varo's mind, almost ridiculously regal. Same with the daughter, Karen.

She was much too thin for her height, but graceful, with a long elegant neck, good bones, long almond-shaped brown eyes, and glossy dark hair cut in a bob with a deep fringe to draw attention to her unusual eyes. She was dressed from head to toe in black. Skin-tight black jeans, black T-shirt with a white logo, black high-heeled boots. She stood staring at him with such intensity she might have been testing to see if he were real.

All three Devereauxes, he thought, were surprisingly *arrogant*. He had to use that word—but on the basis of what? Having money and a position in society appeared to be an end in itself. Dev, his beautiful Amelia and of course Ava displayed no such characteristic, and they were the ones with the *real* money and a fantastic ancestral home.

Ava had the job of escorting her relatives upstairs. Her mother and father headed off to their old suite of rooms. Natalie Devereaux nodded her approval of the guest room with its adjoining *en suite* bathroom. Mercifully it would do. Karen stalked ahead to her room, just down the hallway, turning on Ava the minute they were inside the door.

"Why on earth didn't you tell me that man was going to be here?" she demanded, her brown gaze snapping so sharply it could drill holes.

Ava took her time to answer. "That man?" she queried gently.

"De Montalvo," Karen said with a frown. "Oh, for God's sake, Ava, don't play silly games. He's *gorgeous*!"

"Much too *masculine* for gorgeous, don't you think?"

Karen ignored her cousin as though her opinions were of little importance. "I've never seen such a stunning-looking man. And that voice! God, it nearly melted my bones. He is no doubt rich?" She shot Ava another piercing look. "Any Argentine of that class means rich."

"Varo's *parents* are rich," Ava offered mildly. She didn't add that Varo's mother was an American heiress.

"How long has he been here?" Karen continued her interrogation in an accusatory voice.

"Why do you ask?" Ava took a moment to push a beautifully scented pale apricot rose further into its copper bowl. Pal Joey, she recognised.

"Well, you will have been *alone* here, wouldn't you? With Dev in Sydney?" Karen opened her narrow eyes wide.

Ava's smile was amused. "I promise you, Karen, we didn't indulge in wild sex."

"As though you could!" said Karen, and threw her a pitying look. "You still have that virginal look, Ava. You must know that. How's the divorce going, by the way?"

Ava allowed herself a sigh. Karen never had been a sympathetic person. In fact Karen had given her rather a bad time of it when they were both at boarding school. It was Amelia who had always come to her rescue—like a protective big sister.

"Luke has been...*difficult*," she confessed. She didn't

mention the threatening letters and e-mails. "He believes it's my clear duty to go back to him."

"Well, he's a lovely man!" Karen said, on a wave of disapproval.

That hurt. Was Karen deliberately trying to hurt her? "What would you know about it?" Ava countered. "All he ever did was butter you up." The more over the top the compliment, the more Karen had swallowed it.

"He never *did*!" Karen protested, clearly outraged.

"The compliments were so thick you could eat them," Ava said. It suddenly struck her that Karen would have made a far more suitable bride for Luke than ever she had. "Maybe it's better if we don't talk about Luke."

"Especially as he's not here to defend himself," Karen huffed. "No, let's talk about Juan-Varo de Montalvo." Karen took a seat on the antique chest at the end of the four-poster bed. "He's not married? If he were his wife would have been invited."

"Of course. No, he's not married—but I would think he has legions of adoring admirers."

"South American women *are* very beautiful," Karen said, nibbling hard on her lower lip. "Where have you got him?" She fastened her eyes on her cousin.

"Got him?" Ava was rather enjoying acting dumb.

Karen shook her head so vigorously her thick fringe lifted off her smooth forehead. "Okay, you're having a little joke. Which one of the guest rooms is his?"

"You plan to drop in on him?" Ava lifted a delicate brow.

Karen leaned back on her hands. "No need. Are you sure *you* know what you're doing, cousin?"

"Meaning?" Ava's tone took on a surprising briskness.

"Maybe you should take care?" Karen cautioned. "Luke wouldn't like to hear you were alone in Kooraki with the sexiest man on earth."

"Is this a way of threatening me?" Ava held herself very still. "You plan to tell him?" Her years of tolerating Karen appeared abruptly over.

Karen must have grasped that fact—if not in its entirety. "Don't get me wrong, Ava. I've tried to keep a cousinly eye on you all our lives. I'm a real softie that way."

"What a pity I never realised that," Ava said, making a decision to leave before Karen upset her further. That was her style. "I'll leave you to unpack. Lunch at one."

Karen rose languidly to her feet, her legs as long and thin as a crane's. "When is he leaving?" she called.

Ava turned about. "Whenever he wants. He's most welcome to stay. He's our guest, Karen. He's come a long way."

Karen wasn't finished with her questions. "But after the wedding?" She moved abruptly towards Ava. "After Dev leaves on his honeymoon?"

"Dev won't be going on his own," Ava reminded her, not holding back on the sarcasm.

Karen scowled. "Does she *know* how lucky she is to get him—what with that mother of hers?"

Her cousin was on dangerous ground. "I'm astonished you haven't got the message, Karen," Ava said. "Dev is madly in love with Amelia. He's loved her since childhood. If I were you I wouldn't bring up the subject of Sarina Norton. In a very short time Amelia will be mistress of Kooraki."

"Never liked Amelia," Karen muttered.

"I well remember. She always did get the better of you. So heed my warning. Amelia and her mother are off limits."

Karen, a confident horsewoman, threw up her hands as though to quieten a fractious horse. "Yo, cousin!" she cried. "Yo! We're *family*. Surely we can have a private chat?"

"Certainly. Only you must remember Amelia is family too. I'm absolutely delighted to have her as a sister."

Karen quickly mustered some common sense. "She'll make a beautiful bride," she admitted, trying not to show her long-standing jealousy of the luscious Amelia. "I can see that. I'd let you see my own outfit, only it's going to be a big surprise. I had thought Amelia would ask me to be one of her bridesmaids. I mean we *did* go to school together."

Sometimes the clever Karen could be remarkably obtuse. "Be glad you were invited," Ava said, waggling her fingers. "See you soon."

"Can't wait for the polo match!" Karen called, a lift in her voice. "I have another outfit planned."

"Bet it cost plenty." Karen hardly wore the same outfit twice.

"Around a thousand bucks," she answered casually.

Ava closed the door after her. So Karen was going to spend her time trying to capture Varo's attention? At least she was a free agent, and she could be charming when she chose to be.

There was no reason to think Varo wouldn't respond. What she and Varo had shared had been a kind of enchantment—a surrender to an overpowering sexual desire. There were different words for it. Love was a long, long way from that.

The days flew, with everyone in high good spirits. Karen seemed to be laughing from dawn to dusk, changing several times a day, and all the while skipping around with Dev and Varo, as enthusiastic as a teenager, accompanying them on all their tours of the station. Or as many times as Dev allowed, being well aware where his cousin's interests lay.

"She's got it bad!" Amelia breathed softly in Ava's ear as Karen hurried out through the front door to join the men.

"She told me she thinks Varo is as magnificent as a black panther." Amelia paused a moment. "Actually, he *is*." She pulled a comical face. "A paragon of masculinity!"

They both laughed.

"It seems to me that if his eye is anywhere it's on *you*, Ava," Amelia continued shrewdly.

"Varo enjoys women," Ava said, glad her long hair was partially obscuring her expression. "Anyway I can't look at anyone—even someone who puts Karen in mind of a black panther—until my divorce is final."

"I wouldn't be *too* scrupulous," Amelia advised. "Luke doesn't deserve it."

"I know. He wants me back."

"Of course he does!" Amelia exclaimed, no admirer of Ava's weak, excessively vain husband. "You're a prize. He's stupid enough to think once he has you back again he can continue to control you."

"That's not going to happen." Ava sounded very firm. "It's just taking a while for it to sink in."

"He contacted me, you know," Amelia confessed after a considered moment.

"What? Just recently?" Ava struggled not to show her anger.

"Before we came away. He's a desperate man. We spotted him at a reception. He says he loves you. He adores you. If this divorce goes through it will destroy him."

"What did you say?"

"Exactly what you'd expect. I told him it was over. Dev and I think he was one lousy husband. Not worthy of you. It's his colossal pride that's hurt, Ava."

"No one knows that better than I," Ava murmured, checking a pang of regret for what might have been. "Let's go for a swim," she suggested.

"Good idea!" Amelia swiftly agreed. She stood up, glowing with health and energy. A woman on the eve of marrying her one true love. "Half-Moon?"

Karen usually spent time in the homestead's swimming pool, doing endless laps up and down. No matter how thin she was Karen thought she could be thinner. It was impossible to change her mindset.

"Half-Moon it is."

In the heat they took one of the station vehicles to the lagoon, where the silvery-blue heatwaves were throwing up their fascinating illusions. They might have been lost in the mirage.

Amelia parked at the top of the slope leading down to their favourite lagoon. She was wearing a black nylon-Spandex one-piece that fitted her beautiful body with its hourglass curves like a glove. Ava had chosen one of the four bikinis she kept in her closet. Spandex top and bottom, its colours were a mix of ocean hues—cobalt, emerald and aquamarine.

They raced across the sand, leaving their things in a heap and moving to the water's edge. As always the perimeter was decorated with exquisite blue lotus lilies.

Amelia turned with a smile. "All right, let's get it over!" she challenged.

Both knew the water would offer a shock of cold in the golden heat of the day. With a cheer Amelia waded into the shallows that quickly fell away to the deep, but Ava, always fleet of foot, beat her into a dive. It sent up glittering arcs of spray that fell back into the lagoon. Ava was actually the better swimmer of the two, but built for speed not stamina.

After their invigorating swim they padded back up onto the pale ochre sand, patting themselves dry before spreading out their towels. They had moved back so all their faces and bodies received of the sunshine was a dappled light through the overhang of trees. Amelia, with her olive skin, tanned easily, but she wasn't after a tan for her wedding day. And Ava had always had to protect her "lily-white" skin. As Amelia's chief bridesmaid she wanted to look her best.

As they lay there, eyes closed, they discussed all aspects of the big day. Dev and Amelia were to honeymoon in some of the great cities of the world—London, Paris, Rome—before jetting off to the U.S.A. New York first, then San Francisco, before returning home. Two months in all. It wasn't either one's first time in any of those cities, but this time they would be together as man and wife.

"It will be so *exciting*!" Amelia breathed, suddenly pulling herself up to lean on one elbow and looking back over her shoulder. "Looks like we're having visitors."

Her beautiful face was vivid with delight. Amelia and Dev were every inch and for all time passionate about each other.

Ava sat up very quickly her heart giving a rhythmic jolt as she turned her head in the same direction.

"Look—it's Dev and Varo." Amelia sprang, laughing, to her feet. She looked gloriously happy. "Karen too." A dryness entered her tone.

Ava, however, was pierced by embarrassment. Always comfortable in a swimsuit—she was very slender without being bone-thin like Karen—she suddenly felt a strange panic that Varo's eyes would be on her. She didn't want that. She wanted to keep calm. She knew she was being foolish, but there it was. She could hardly reach for the sarong she had draped around her hips. That would be too obvious a cover-up. Instead she waved a hand as Amelia moved to greet the new arrivals.

She stood up, paused a moment, then headed back into the water as if wanting to cool off on this steamy hot day. Maybe they would be gone before she emerged? She knew she was acting like an overly shy and modest schoolgirl, but she felt incredibly self-aware around Varo. She was actually shivering a little in reaction. She had so little experience of the powerfully sexual. Luke had never been a turn-on, she fully realised.

When she came up, blinking the lagoon water out of her eyes and off her lashes, she saw with a kind of dismay the party of riders were stripping off, obviously intent on cooling off in the crystal-clear water.

"Oh, my God!" Her breath whistled between her teeth. They were coming in.

Dev and Varo had stripped to dark-coloured swimming briefs. Karen had exposed her ultra-thin body in a postbox-red one-piece with a halter neck. She stood at the water's edge, squealing at the cold as she put a toe in. She didn't even bend to splash her face. No preliminaries to accustom herself to the cold water. Both men charged past her like young gods, diving in unison into the water. Amelia was still at the water's edge, perhaps saying a few coaxing words to Karen, who now had her long arms criss-crossed over her body. Ava began to wonder if her cousin would come in at all.

There was a flat rock platform on the other side of the lagoon. It overhung the emerald-green waters by two or three feet. As children they had often used it as a diving board. She, Dev and Amelia had often sat there to sunbake and be alone. Now she struck out for the platform, proposing to sit there for a short time while the others took their refreshing dip. Dev always had pressing things to do. She would wait it out.

Amelia had joined Dev now, continuing the little rituals of childhood, diving under the water and chasing after each other like a pair of dolphins. Karen had evidently decided the water was too cold for her liking. She had retreated to the shade of the trees, keeping a keen eye on them all. Especially Varo.

He was a born athlete. Ava *knew* he was going to swim over to her. She knew for sure.

He did, his teeth flashing white in his handsome dark face, his skin pearled with drops of water.

"So, I always suspected you were half-mermaid," he mocked. "All you need is a circlet of sparkling crystals and emeralds around your blonde head. You need nothing else. Not even the covering of a swimsuit, however brief." With one lithe movement he hauled himself onto the platform. A trained gymnast couldn't have done it better. "You took one look at me and swam away," he accused her. "You should have been swimming *towards* me, don't you think?"

Now his lustrous dark eyes settled on her, touching every part of her body: Her long wet hair, drying out in the warm air, over one shoulder and down her back, her face, her throat, her breasts, taut midriff, slender legs. All was exposed to his eyes.

"Ava," he said, very gently.

She managed a soft reply. "Yes?"

"Nothing. I'm just saying your name."

She loved the way he said it. Unlike anyone else. There was that tension again. The high, humming *thrum* of sexual energy. He had a superb body, evenly tanned, no betraying untanned skin below his waist above the line of his black swimming trunks. The sun had hit everywhere. He was bronze all over. Totally unselfconscious. Unlike her.

"It is very clear to me, Ava, that you are avoiding me." There was a glinting sardonic look in the depths of his dark eyes.

He shocked her by leaning over to brush her bare shoulder with his mouth, licking up the few remaining sparkling droplets and taking them into his mouth.

"Varo!" She tried to move, her little cry blending with the call of a bird.

"You fear someone is watching?" he asked. "Dev and his beautiful Amelia are totally engrossed in each other, as it should be. It is only your cousin who has the binoculars trained on us."

"Surely not?"

"A joke," he teased. "Though I am quite sure if she had a pair handy we would be in her sights." His voice took on an amused note. "She is very jealous of you, is she not?"

Ava turned her head all the way to him, her expression one of actual disbelief. "Of course she isn't."

His look seemed to say he knew more about her than she would ever know herself. "I think she *is*. Why are you so nervous of me? It's perfectly natural for a man and a woman to sit and talk like this."

"I talk a lot easier when I'm wearing clothes," she confessed on a wry note.

He kept looking at her. "I want to touch you." His voice was low, so emotive he might have been exulting in his own desires. "I want to make love to you. I want to press kisses all over your body. I want to kiss you where you have never been kissed before." His hand moved so that his fingers closed over hers.

She felt a sharp, knife-like thrust deep in her womb, leaving a dull ache. "Why are we going with this, Varo?" she whispered, even with no one to hear.

"Isn't it obvious to you?" His fingers tightened. Very firm. He wasn't going to let her get away. "You have enchanted me."

She could barely answer. "I have made it clear I'm still married."

"You will soon have your freedom. That's what you want, isn't it?" He didn't tell her that her cousin, Karen, had sought to convince him Ava could have been the inspiration for *La Belle Dame sans Merci*. The memory of her words flooded back without prompt.

"Ava might look like vanilla ice cream, but I assure you she has another side," Karen had told him. "We call it the Langdon syndrome. They're tough people, the Langdons. Her husband, Luke, is a lovely man. He idolises her. Puts her on a pedestal. Such a terrible shame, but Ava didn't care to inhabit the role of wife. At least not for long."

Ava now turned to him, her eyes huge. "I shouldn't stay here."

"No," he murmured, his eyes lingering on her. "Your beautiful skin might get burned."

"I haven't *your* olive skin," she said defensively.

He lifted a hand to stroke the side of her neck. "Yours is as lustrous as a pearl. *'Full beautiful'* you are, Ava." He began to quote softly, dark and honey-tongued, "*'Her hair was long, her foot was light, and her eyes were wild.'*"

In truth he was the one doing the seducing, Ava thought. "I love Keats," she said on a surprised note. "Fancy your knowing that poem."

He shrugged. "A famous English poet, a famous poem. *La Belle Dame sans Merci*."

"And I brought it to mind?" Was that how he saw her? Cool to cold? A little cruel?

He didn't answer. He fell back into the water and held up his arms. "Come here to me."

Little thrills of excitement were travelling the length of her spine. Yet she hesitated, aware Karen could see them. She was a cautious person, not at all adventurous, but it seemed her whole life was changing.

"Come," he repeated.

Her breath shook, but there nothing else she could do but allow herself to fall blindly into his outstretched arms.

They went under together. Down…down…into shimmering crystal depths shot through with rays from the sun. Varo held her body locked to his, as though she would never get away. His mouth pressed down with great ardour over hers. Surely this only happened in dreams? It was simply… *magic*.

But he was in need of more…a man held in captivity by an enchanting woman.

His hand had a life of its own. It plunged into her tiny bikini top, taking the weight of her delicate breast, the pleasure boundless. They were locked together so long Ava thought they might drown. She couldn't seem to care. Somehow this was not real. The moment was timeless. Locked together in the cool silvery-green depths yet burning with passion. This was a secret place of great beauty, the waters like silk against the skin. Best of all, they were far, far away from prying eyes.

They were moving to another stage. It was like a dreaming. They were weighted under water but not conscious of it. Only Varo, his strong arm locked around her, broke the idyll. They shot to the surface, faces turned up to the sky, both gasping for air. Dev and Amelia were lazily stroking their way back to them. Karen was standing right at the shoreline, one arm waving frantically, as though signalling to Ava and Varo to get out.

Ava knew she was in for a good talking-to. Karen hadn't been jealous of her before now. Her cousin had always acted like someone of elevated status—far superior to the younger Ava. She realised Karen had spent a lot of time trying to put her down, deflating any tendency towards a burgeoning self-confidence. Karen would be full of admonitions and she might even talk to Luke. Get in touch with him. Ava wouldn't put it past her. Karen was on Luke's side. She had no loyalty to Ava. She had to remember that. Karen could cause trouble.

Karen waited her moment until they were back at the homestead.

The men, Dev and Varo, refreshed, had returned to the Six Mile, where a thousand head of cattle were being yarded in advance of the road trains that were scheduled to arrive the following day.

Ava had taken a quick shower, washing the lagoon water out of her hair before changing into fresh clothes. She and Amelia planned on continuing their discussions with Nula Morris, the new housekeeper. Nula was a part aboriginal woman married to one of their best stockmen. Amelia's mother, the by now notorious Sarina Norton, had trained Nula as well as the rest of the domestic staff. She had done an extremely good job of it. No one could deny that.

Food and drink had to be planned for the coming polo weekend, and for the buffet at the party on Saturday night. For those who stayed on until Sunday, either camping out or finding a place in the station dorms, there would be a lavish Sunday brunch. All in all, the first big test for Nula—although she would have lots of help. The wedding reception, of course, would be fully catered.

Inevitably, Karen showed up at her door, charging past her. She spun to drill Ava with an accusatory look. Small wonder Amelia had long since christened Karen "The Snoop."

"You're spending a lot of time with Varo," she burst out, not beating about the bush.

Ava didn't hotly deny the allegation. Instead she said, very quietly, "Forgive me, but is that any of your business?" She was determined to hold on to her composure.

"Of course it is," her cousin hissed. "I've been looking out for you since we were kids. I never thought you capable of wayward impulses, Ava, but it seems you are. I believe I have the right as your cousin to point out that you've got your feet planted on the slippery slope." She stared at Ava intently, the pupils of her dark eyes black and huge.

"Which slope would that be?"

"Don't evade the issue, Ava."

"What? My wayward tendencies? You never stop, do you?" Ava sighed. "You have to show me you're far wiser, far more sophisticated than I. For years you were the superior schoolgirl. Now you're the experienced woman of the world. So far *you're* the one who has been chasing after our guest, Karen. We've all noticed."

Karen's face turned red. "Maybe a little," she confessed, trying to make light of it. "But *fun* is all it is," she maintained vigorously. "A bit of a release from my tight work schedule in the city. In any case, I'm a free agent. I have no commitment to anyone. Unlike *you*."

"And you can't help feeling a bit jealous?"

"Yo!" Karen did her extraordinary reining-in gesture. "Don't be so ridiculous! It has never occurred to me to be jealous of you, Ava. *Protective* is the word. We're cousins. Family. Right now you must be feeling very vulnerable. Don't think I can't see how easy it would be for you to fall for someone like Varo. Those dark eyes…the way he looks at a woman like she's the most desirable woman in the world. The smile. The charisma. It's all South American macho stuff. That's the way they are. Let me tell you, Varo is used to making conquests."

"I'm sure of it," Ava returned. "I can't think why you're working yourself up to such a state. Varo hasn't stolen my heart."

"Then *what*?" Karen demanded to know. "I'm a remarkably good judge and I'd say he has."

"I don't know if you're a good judge or not, but you're

remarkably interfering," Ava said. "You are my cousin, but you're also a guest here. I really don't need any lectures."

"Why take it like that?" Karen issued a protest. "Amelia has always carried on scandalously, so *she* won't advise you."

Ava's eyes sparkled dangerously. "I'd take that back, if I were you."

"Okay, okay—but Amelia is not you. Surely you recognise that? She's a very sensual woman. You're the Snow Maiden."

"I haven't been a maiden for years now, Karen. And I've told you before not to discuss or criticise Amelia or her mother. I consider Amelia my champion in all things. Not you."

"Well, then, make a fatal mistake!" Karen exclaimed, angry and affronted.

"Another one, you mean? You've shown far more loyalty to my husband than you've ever done to me."

"Why shouldn't I turn to Luke? He's my friend. He's a good man, Ava, and you've deliberately cast him aside. So much for your marriage vows. Luke loves you. Only now you've got all that money you want to be free."

Ava started walking to the door. "Maybe it's best if you leave now, Karen. You'd make a terrible marriage guidance counsellor. No one on the outside can see inside a marriage. If Luke considers himself unhappy, he made *me* unhappy for most of our married life. Like you, he took pleasure in putting me down, eroding my self-confidence."

Karen shook her glossy head. "I never remember him doing that. I strenuously deny it in my case. You're too thin-skinned, Ava. You take offence too easily. I didn't mean to upset you, but certain things have to be said. You know nothing about Juan-Varo de Montalvo beyond the fact he's Argentine, stunningly handsome, of good family and a splendid polo player. You're very beautiful, in your quiet way. It's nothing to him to start up a flirtation, even an affair. Ask him about the young woman he's left behind."

Ava couldn't ignore the stab of apprehension. "You know about such a woman?"

"I don't *know*," Karen replied in her familiar arrogant tone, "but I suspect it from a few things he's let drop. Think about it, Ava. He's nearly thirty years of age. His family will be expecting him to choose a bride soon. He wants a family. It's *time*. I wonder you haven't thought of all this. He's simply playing you for all it's worth."

"It's a wonder you haven't kept notes," Ava said, maintaining her cool. "Strange, I didn't think Varo had had the time, with you fussing over him, but thank you for your concern. If that's what it *is*. I would appreciate it if you kept all your insights to yourself for the rest of your stay. We Langdons want nothing to spoil this happy time. I could be mistaken—if so I'm sorry—but I think you're out to upset me."

Karen stalked to the door, her dark head held high. "I've simply told you what you need to know," she said sanctimoniously.

"You'll stay in touch with Luke?" Ava asked.

"Are you suggesting I don't?" Karen threw up her chin aggressively. "I'm not taking sides in this. I care for you both."

Ava ignored that spurious claim. "I'm sure he knows you're here. You both think you're in the perfect position to keep tabs on me."

"I'll forget you said that, Ava."

Ava took little heed of the tone of deep hurt.

"Better if you *remember* it," she replied.

CHAPTER FIVE

THE polo day was as brilliant as promised.

There was a great stir of excitement from the crowd as the Red Team, captained by James Devereaux Langdon, and the Blue Team, captained by the visiting Argentine Juan-Varo de Montalvo, cantered onto the field to wave upon wave of applause. Horses were part of Outback life, so it was no surprise polo was a great attraction, drawing crowds over long distances even by Outback standards. Polo was the fastest game in the world, and it had the seductive element of danger.

"Oh, isn't this *exciting*?" Moira O'Farrell, a very pretty redhead and a polo regular, threw back her head, rejoicing in the fact.

Four men to a team, all of them were tall, with great physiques and good-looking to boot, but all female eyes were on the Argentine. He was so *exotic*, so *out there*. Dev Langdon was taken, after all. No use looking to him. All these guys were seriously sexy. All at this point of time bachelors. That was of profound interest and concern. The polo "groupies" were among the most involved spectators. Would it be so amazing if one of them caught the eye of the devastatingly handsome Argentine? Not difficult to see oneself as mistress of some fabulously romantic *estancia* on the *pampas*.

Not to mention the high life in Buenos Aires, home of the dead-sexy tango.

In the main it had fallen to Ava to organise the weekend's events. Never one to sing her own praises—Ava was modest about her abilities—she actually had exceptional organisational skills. As her mother Elizabeth told her, with loving pride, "Far better than mine, my darling!"

Multi-coloured bunting decorated the grounds, aflutter in the light cooling breeze. Prominent amid the fluttering little flags was the Argentine, pale blue and white—Argentina was the polo capital of the world, a Mecca for top players—and the red, white and blue of Australia, a polo-playing nation. The polo field itself was a good three hundred yards in length and more than half that distance in width. Today, after concentrated maintenance, it was a near unprecedented velvety green. The going had to be just right for the game. Too hard would jar the legs of the polo ponies. Too soft would slow down the action.

Several of the players on the polo circuit had travelled overland with their string of ponies—though *ponies* was a traditional term. The polo ponies of today were full-sized horses, either thoroughbreds or thoroughbred crosses, their legs protected by polo wraps from below the knee to the fetlock. Long manes were roached, tails braided. Nothing could be allowed to snag the rider's mallet. The taller the horse, the longer the mallet. Both Dev and Varo were six-footers-plus.

Amelia was wearing a polka-dotted navy and white shirt, with chinos in bright red accentuating her long legs. There was no doubting which team Amelia was barracking for. Ava had found herself choosing a pale blue silk shirt to go with her white lightweight cotton jeans. No coincidence that her outfit bore the colours of the flag of Argentina. Karen wore dazzling white. Karen was always given to block colours. All black, all white, or all neutral beige. Once she had claimed she was channelling Coco Chanel. With some success, Ava had often thought. The tall, super-thin Karen always looked elegant. Today for the afternoon match she wore a collarless white shirt tucked into very narrow-legged white jeans with high heeled wedges on her feet. As a concession she had quite dashingly tied a blue silk scarf patterned in sun-yellow around her throat.

Behind her designer sunglasses Karen's dark eyes gleamed. She thought she was on to something. It wouldn't take her long to find the answers. She sat with the family—Erik and Elizabeth Langdon, Ava and Amelia the bride-to-be, and her own parents, who were giving the distinct impression they weren't all that keen on sport in general, and were apprehensive of such a dangerous sport as polo. For all they knew a charging player could lose control of his pony and plough into the area where they were sitting.

"You've done a great job, kiddo." Amelia complimented her friend and chief bridesmaid with real enthusiasm.

"I'm happy with it." Ava was watching Varo riding the bay gelding Caesar for the first chukka. The horse's hide had been lovingly burnished until it gleamed in the sunlight. Rider and polo pony looked magnificent. Out of the corner of her eye she saw Karen wave to Varo, as if he was her champion in a medieval joust. Ava transferred her gaze to her adored brother, who lifted a hand to them, then laughed as Amelia jumped to her feet waving a red bandana. Both young women laughed back in response. It was going to be a great day.

Ava had had the tall collapsible goalposts freshly painted in the colours of the two teams. Even the big white marquees that had been set up for food and drink had been decorated with the teams' colours. Adjacent picket fences had received a fresh coat of white paint.

The periods of play had already been decided. Six chukkas, each the traditional seven minutes long. Dev and Varo would only be playing two ponies, both well-trained Kooraki throughbred crosses. They had the right temperament, and proven speed, stamina and manoeuverability skills. Dev was used to all four ponies, and Varo had taken a hour or two to familiarise himself with his mounts' abilities.

Two members of Dev's team had brought along half a dozen good polo ponies between them, the idea being they could switch a tired pony for a fresh one between chukkas. Ava knew all the players. She had seen them play many times before, so she knew they were highly competitive. Dev's team, all from Outback properties, weren't going to let the Argentine's team win.

They were aiming high.

The best player on a team was usually the number three—the tactical leader and the most powerful hitter. Dev and Varo both wore a large white number three on the back of their coloured shirts, worn over the traditional fitted white breeches and glossy black riding boots. All players wore helmets with a chin strap. This was a dangerous game, with powerful young men wielding hardwood mallets.

"That's one sexy outfit!" Moira was really on a roll. She made the excited comment to the amusement of those around her.

It was a very friendly crowd, with lots of exchanges between spectators. Not that Moira wasn't spot on. Polo always attracted women who just happened to fancy the players more than the game.

It soon became evident that the number three players—the captains, the high-handicap players, hard-hitting, hard-riding, with an impressive armoury of strokes—were the best on the field. Neither was giving any quarter. In fact it was obvious to all the game's fans that the arrival of the dashing Argentine was proving a great stimulus to players and spectators alike.

It was a hard-played, hard-drawn contest, but in the end only one team could win. During the third chukka Tom McKinnon, number one on Dev's team, took a fall while covering the opposition number four. Tom swiftly and gamely remounted, but the Blue Team had gained the advantage. It was Varo who hit a magnificent winning goal that near stupefied the crowd so quickly and unexpectedly had it happened.

The Blue Team won, with good-natured cheers soaring to the cobalt-blue heavens.

It had been a wonderful match. The best for a very long time.

"Let's face it. The Argentine lifted the game. The captains were matched, but the others weren't in the same class."

It was Ava who was to present the cup to the captain of the winning team. Up close to Varo, she was perilously conscious of his sizzling energy, the sheer force of his sexual attraction that blazed like a brand. Indeed, to the crowd she looked like a beautiful and delicate porcelain figurine before him.

"Congratulations, Varo," she said sweetly, though the nerves in her body were leaping wildly. "That was a very exciting match."

"Gracias, señora," he said, silken suave, but with that mocking glint in his eyes. "I thoroughly enjoyed it." Bending his dark head, his hair as high-sheened as a bird's wing, he kissed one of her cheeks, and then the other,

breathing into her ear, "You look as cool as a camellia, *mi hermosa*."

She knew her cheeks pinkened but she moved back smilingly to present him with the silver cup. It was no everyday sort of thing, and one he would be happy to take back to Argentina.

Fresh waves of applause broke out. The crowd had melted for the Argentine. He had such animal magnetism—like some wonderful exotic big cat. Everyone was basking in his physical exhilaration.

Dev joined them now, his hair as golden as Varo's was raven-black. He threw an arm around his friend's shoulder. "My team will make a comeback," he joked. "That was a great game, Varo. You inspired us all."

Not to be left out, Amelia made a move up to them. Dev caught her around the waist, his aquamarine eyes sparkling with health and vigour. Brother and sister side by side could have been twins, which had been remarked on since childhood.

"Let's get ourselves a cold drink," Dev said, and started to move off to a marquee.

Karen bit her lip hard. She wasn't going to be denied her moment. She followed them and caught Varo's arm firmly, causing him to swing about. "May I add my congratulations, Varo?" She brushed his cheek with her hand. "That was a splendid match," she told him with warm enthusiasm, tugging at her blue and yellow silk scarf with its Argentine flag colours.

Varo responded gallantly. "Thank you so much, Karen. I enjoyed it too."

"I'm sure every woman in the crowd was urging you on," Karen said archly. "I know Ava was." She transferred a pointed gaze to her cousin.

"Well, *partly*," Ava responded lightly. "I wanted Dev's

team to win at the same time. But as we all know there can only be one winner."

"And winner takes all!" Karen's tone was decidedly provocative.

"Why did we ever invite that woman?" Amelia asked Ava later.

"Beats me," Ava responded. "We're from different galaxies. But she's family. It doesn't always mean families are nice."

"She always was a pain in the neck," said Mel, giving Ava a hug. "Don't let her bug you. Obviously she's trying to. Jealous, I'd say."

Ava gave a little grimace. "You're the second person who's told me recently Karen is jealous of me."

"So are you convinced?" Mel asked with a quirked brow.

"Getting there," Ava admitted with a laugh.

"I bet it was Varo who made the comment," Mel said very softly in Ava's ear.

"In a word, *yes*." Ava blushed.

Mel's lustrous dark eyes were fixed on her friend's face. "Both of you are playing it ultra cool, but it's not hard to see the attraction. It pulses around you. I'm sure you're aware Karen is keeping you under observation? To report to Luke, I wonder?"

Ava felt a hot prickling sensation all over her body. "There's nothing to report," she said huskily.

"You deserve to be happy, Ava," Mel said with the greatest affection. "Don't turn your back on your chances."

And so they came to the night of the party.

Ava knew she had far more in the way of formal eveningwear than most women. God knew she had attended any number of grand and boring balls, parties, fundraisers and other functions. She counted herself most fortunate in lots of ways. Not all. Luke had once sent her back upstairs to change one of her gowns because he had considered it not stunning enough. In actual fact it had been a designer outfit, purchased when she and her mother had been in Paris, the City of Light. It just went to prove Luke knew nothing about style and *haute couture*.

For tonight's party she chose the same full-length gown. Her mother had insisted on buying it for her because of its masterly cut and glorious colour. She knew Mel had a beautiful gold full-length gown, with bare shoulders and a richly embroidered top. Karen would be channelling Chanel again. Probably slinky black. Karen was forever quoting the infamous Wallis Simpson remark, "A woman can't be too rich or too thin." The other women guests would have brought something to dazzle. Every woman loved to dress up, and there weren't all that many occasions. When one arose they made the most of it.

Ava debated whether to pull her hair back or leave it loose. Men loved long hair. In her experience they considered it an unparallelled look for a woman. In the end she decided to go with movement. She did a little teasing to her thick gleaming locks, and even she thought the end result was very glamorous. It was party-time, after all. The satin gown in a lovely shade of purple hugged every curve, every line of her body. The bodice, ruched from below the bust, was held up by a shoestring halter with a long scarf-like pleat falling down the centre of the gown. Right now Ava felt as attractive as she could get.

For her twenty-first birthday her parents had given her a white-gold sapphire and diamond necklace, with matching sapphire and diamond drop earrings.

She realised what was happening. She was making herself as beautiful as possible for *one* man. Even thinking it brought out a rosy blush. Juan-Varo de Montalvo had had an enormous impact on her from the moment her eyes fell on him. Now she knew all about his powerful charm.

Turning about, she addressed her glowing reflection. "You've changed, Ava. You're almost a dual personality."

Cool, calm Ava and the woman who turned to flame in a near stranger's arms. A man, moreover, from another land.

For all she had lived life as a married woman, she had never felt remotely like this. She had never been in this intensely emotional state or felt such feverish excitement. And she was taking a huge gamble. One she might never win.

"It isn't like you at all," she told herself. "But it's magic!"

And how was it going to end? There were always consequences to actions.

On one side euphoria. On the other a certain trepidation which she sought to subdue but couldn't. She really knew very little about Varo. She could be playing with fire and she had always thought of herself as governed by cool logic. Falling madly in love was madness in its way. And she had a past. Some men didn't like a woman to have a past. Not to marry, anyway. Was it conceivable Varo could be regarding her in some way other than she believed? There was passion on both sides. Neither could deny that. But she would die of shame if he was only thinking of her in terms of a wild affair. How did she really know if he didn't have someone waiting for him at home? Now, *that* was logical. A man like Varo—a man of strong passions—surely would have a special woman tucked away. Karen had hinted at it. But Karen was not to be trusted. Karen only wanted to hurt her.

Momentarily her heart sank. Then she made the effort to throw off any negative feelings. She was like a woman who had been buried alive. Now she was going to enjoy herself. Enjoy life. She had been unhappy for such a long time. That had to change. She had to work at making her life change.

She wanted to be a stronger woman than she had ever been. It seemed to her this man who had come into her life, Juan-Varo de Montalvo, was helping her be just that. Her anxieties dissolved.

A few minutes later, looking supremely beautiful and composed, she made her way down the rear staircase to the kitchen, greeting Nula and her helpers with a warm smile. "Everything going okay?"

"All under control!" Nula assured her.

"Great!"

"You look absolutely beautiful!"

Nula spoke for all of them, charmed and delighted. Miss Ava, such a lovely, friendly person, had never been treated the way she should have been. The Old Man, Gregory Langdon, had been a genuine tyrant. Everyone on the station, family and employees alike, had taken a good deal of punishment from him. Miss Ava's husband—from the viewpoint of the staff, at least—wasn't half good enough for her. Good riddance, they all thought, now they knew Miss Ava was well into the process of divorcing him. She deserved and hopefully would find a far better man.

The party had already started. Music was playing through the house. All the exterior lights, and the lighting around the pool, the pool house and the landscaped gardens, were turned on, transforming the whole area into a fairyland. Couples were dancing in the Great Hall and out on the rear terrace. She had a good view of Dev, with his beautiful Amelia clasped in his arms. Her heart shook with love and gratitude. Everything at long last had turned out so splendidly for them. These were two individuals who had been made for each other. Wasn't that a source of wonder? Everything was so much better with Mel around. She found herself rejoicing that in one week's time Mel would become her sister-in-law—the sister she'd never had.

The instant she spotted the fabulous Argentine momentarily alone Moira O'Farrell broke away from her group, crossing the room swiftly to speak to him while she had the chance. Ava's cousin, the pretentious Karen Devereaux—so terribly hard-edged, wearing a very stylish black jersey dress—had actually unbent sufficiently to tell her Juan-Varo de Montalvo had picked *her*, Moira, out of the crowd.

"It's your wonderful red hair, darling," Karen had pointed out in a voice that hid insincerity. She really disliked red hair.

So he *had* noticed her! Moira had the sensation she was awakening to a dream. The Argentine was *gorgeous*, and Karen had let drop that he came from a fabulously wealthy family. Not only that, he was unattached. She didn't know if she believed that was true or not. How could such a man be unattached?

Well used to the ways of women, especially women dead set on chasing him, Varo was soon alerted to the redhead's intentions. She was very pretty, her small neat head a mass of silky curls, and she was wearing a lovely spring-green dress, but all he could think of was Ava and when she was going to appear.

The intensity of the feelings he had for his friend's sister was threatening to overwhelm him. He was always gentle with women, and tender too, he supposed, but he had never experienced such a potentially dangerous passion. He wanted her. Very, very badly. He had not been prepared for her. He wasn't one to fool around, treating women with a callous hand.

He had no idea where these feelings were going. Ava

was still married. He could not stay in Australia, despite the country's great appeal to him, the people, the way of life. He had to go home. He was his father's heir. He and his father had great plans. He might be able to grow to love Australia, especially the vast Outback, but a woman like Ava would be extremely unhappy away from her homeland. That was if her feelings even came remotely close to his own.

At the moment it was a dilemma. All of it. He cared too terribly much.

The redhead raced up to him, her face full of animation and, it had to be said, invitation. "Please, Varo, I'd love to dance—wouldn't you?"

She was so sweet, so openly flirtatious, he couldn't help but smile back at her. Very gallantly he took her arm, leading her out onto the terrace where everyone was in a rather *loving* dance mode.

"Fabulous party, Ava," one of the male guests said as she passed him. "You look glorious!"

Ava didn't reply, but she smiled and blew him a kiss. Invitations to join different groups were called to her as she made her way from the Great Hall into the living room, wondering all the while if Varo was out on the terrace. He was so tall, so much a stand-out figure, she would have spotted him easily had he been inside the house.

Easier still to spot him on the terrace. He was dancing with Moira O'Farrell. Moira's pretty face was uplifted to him, her expression one of almost delirious excitement.

Ava found herself standing perfectly still, her heart rocked by an unfamiliar pang of jealousy laced with an irrational sense of betrayal. Surely Varo could dance with whomever he pleased? He couldn't help being so devastatingly attractive to women. He appeared to be staring down into Moira's melting blue eyes. There was very little space between their bodies, although in height they were mismatched. Varo's raven head was bent to hear what Moira was saying. Ava saw him smile—that beautiful white flash that lit up his polished bronze complexion. He would draw any woman and compel her to follow him.

Unnerved, inhaling quickly, breasts steeply rising, Ava turned back into the living room. She was caught by a sudden fear that Varo might be toying with her. Then she reminded herself she had always suffered from a lack of confidence.

About time you took trust as a maxim.

Some time later, someone suddenly and very precipitately bumped into her.

"Oh, for heaven's sake. I'm sorry, Ava." It was Moira O'Farrell doing the apologising.

From looking radiant, Moira now looked hectically flushed and, yes, distressed. What on earth had happened to cause such a change?

"That's okay, Moira," Ava said companionably. "You look like you're leaving?" She was half joking, half serious. She put out a steadying hand. Moira was a guest.

"No, no. I'm having a marvellous time," Moira's protest had a touch of mild hysteria. "Look, I shouldn't say this, but that bitch of a cousin of yours, Karen Devereaux—" Moira broke off as though she'd suddenly realised to whom she was speaking.

"Whatever has she said to upset you?" Ava asked, staring into Moira's face. She took Moira's slender arm, moving them away to a relatively quiet corner.

"It was unforgivable, really." Always chirpy, Moira now looked both downcast and angry.

"Sure you're not being over-sensitive?" Ava questioned.

"She's nothing like you!" Moira shook her head so vigorously her curls bounced. "I always thought she was a bit on the vicious side."

"*Tell* me, Moira," Ava insisted.

Moira's face contorted into a grimace. "She tried to make a fool of me. You'd better ask her."

"I'm asking *you*, Moira. I prefer to speak to you." Ava spoke firmly.

"All right!" Moira made her decision. "She told me Varo had picked me out of the crowd. Her very words. *Picked me out of the crowd.* The implication was he fancied me. Like a fool I believed her. Men *do* fancy me, as I expect you know. But obviously she was having a good laugh at my expense. I practically forced Varo to dance with me. Don't get me wrong. He's a great guy—a perfect gentleman, lovely manners, and a *super* dancer. Stupid me, pressing myself against him... I could die. But it seems he has a girl back home. Of course he would, wouldn't he? A drop-dead gorgeous guy like that. Oh, God, I feel such a fool." A sound like a hot rush of self-loathing escaped her.

"Why would you?" Ava tried hard to sound understanding. Indeed she *was*. But her own fearful thoughts were spinning out of control.

"Oh, Ava, I was so *obvious*," Moira wailed. "I was flirting with him for all I was worth."

Ava gathered herself. Her voice, miraculously, sounded nice and normal. "Nothing much wrong with that, Moira. If you look around, everyone is playing the flirting game. It's a party. Cheer up." There seemed little else she could say.

Varo has someone back home. He's admitted it. Moira wouldn't lie.

"I've never told you this before," said Moira, "but that smug cousin of yours is very jealous of you. I've wanted to tell you for a long time now. You're so lovely too." Moira's

eyes were suddenly brimming with tears. "Just you be careful of her."

Ava lent forward and spontaneously kissed Moira's
flushed cheek. "Come on, Moira. So Varo has a love interest at home? You can easily find one right here. Blink the
tears away and go enjoy yourself. That's an order."

Moira lifted her head with smiling gratitude. "Thanks,
Ava. You're an angel."

They parted company with Moira looking brighter. Ava,
however, had to take her usual three calming breaths. She
tried hard to hold on to some steadying memory. Surely
her mother had once said, "You're always good in a crisis,
Ava."

She had to cling to that.

Varo, promised to someone else, had got in over his head.
So had she. It had all happened so fast. The effects had been
mesmerising.

Ava moved to join Dev and Amelia's group. "You look
ravishing, Ava!" Dev's tone spoke volumes of pride, while
Amelia's expression showed her shared pleasure. "I have
two beautiful women in my life."

Dev hugged Amelia to him. Plainly the two of them were
enjoying themselves immensely. What she had to do now
was not spoil things.

Plant a smile on your face.

A few moments later she felt without seeing that Varo
had come to stand directly at her shoulder. He was greeted
warmly by everyone, but it was Ava he had come for.

"I hope you realise, Ava, that as the captain of the winning team I am owed a dance by you. Several, in fact," he
said, with his captivating smile.

She knew their guests were waiting for her response.
And Mel, sharp as a tack, was watching her rather closely.

"Of course, Varo." She turned to him, her eyes ablaze in her face, brilliant as jewels.

Inside she might feel pale with shock, but outside she was all colour—the golden mane of hair, dazzling eyes, softly blushed cheeks, lovely deep pink mouth. She was determined now to play her part, her only wish to get through the night with grace. For all he hadn't been completely honest with her, Juan-Varo de Montalvo would never leave her memory, even when he disappeared to the other side of the world.

Varo took charge, as was his way. He clasped her hand in his, entwining his long fingers with hers, then led her away. Shaken, sobered, incredibly Ava felt *desire* course through her. Where had all this sensuality come from? These wildly extravagant reactions that touched every sensitive spot in her being and body? She had never experienced those feelings before. They had been drawn out of her by this man who had stolen her heart. There was just no fighting it. The connection was too strong.

Oh, God, she thought prayerfully. *Oh, God!* Her head was telling her what to do. Her body was ignoring the dictates of her mind. She had imagined him making love to her. Not a day had gone by when she hadn't fantasised about it. She felt possessed by him. Drawn like a moth to the flame. The huge problem was she couldn't seem to turn away from the flame, though she knew it could devour her.

"Wait," he murmured, steering her to the far corner of the loggia, just as she had known he would. In the light-dappled shadows he slowly turned her into his arms, his brilliant gaze questing. "What is troubling you, Ava?"

The sound of his name on her lips was like the softest swish of air. Yet pressure was expanding in her. *Be brave. Tell him.*

"Nothing." To her surprise her voice sounded normal. Or normal enough.

"Do you think I don't know you by now?"

The honeyed tenderness was almost her undoing. "But you don't *know* me, Varo. I don't know *you*."

He gave a soft laugh. "That is not quite correct." He took her into his arms as though the sole purpose for their coming to the far end of the terrace was to find a relatively quiet area to dance. "This is not the ideal moment to sort it out," he said humorously. "Too many people. Too many glowing lights. I cannot embrace you, or kiss your lovely mouth. I can only tell you I want you desperately." His full attention was focused on her. "You look incredibly beautiful." His arms tightened around her, guiding her in slow, sensual, graceful movements. *"Exquisito."*

What should she do? Their bodies were touching. She *couldn't* break away. Her muscles seemed to be locked. All she could do was stare into his dynamic dark face, wondering how she could live her life without him. It was quite frightening that she should think this way. But passion *was* frightening in its way.

He was wearing a white dinner jacket that served to emphasise his darkly tanned olive skin. It had to have been tailored for him because it fitted his wide shoulders like a glove. "Are you trying to woo me, Varo?" she asked, gripped by her undeniably erotic reaction. But this man *was* erotic. She had grasped that from the moment she had first laid eyes on him.

He was sensitive to her as well, because he had picked up on her mood. "Ava," he sighed over her head. "Ava. You want me to *win* you? Is that it?"

She placed a staying hand on his chest, feeling his heart beating strongly beneath the pristine white dress shirt. "You can't do that, of course," she said with a flare of spirit. "You have to return home soon."

"What *should* I do?" he countered swiftly, as though daring her. "Not for us coffee and conversation. Tell me, please, Ava."

It was a demand couched in exquisite gentleness. She struggled to find an answer but she was encased within his arms, her own heart beating as fast as a wild bird confined to a cage. "Is this all part of the adventure, Varo?"

The tenderness had alchemised to anger. Abruptly he pulled back, his handsome features tautening. "An adventure? What adventure?" A vertical line formed between his black brows. "I should stop your mouth with my own. Only I want to hear about these feelings that are plaguing you. You think me insincere? A social playboy?" He looked passionately affronted at the very idea. "I've fallen in love with you, Ava. Love is a force. The most powerful force on earth. I didn't expect any of this. I was not prepared. But we made an instant connection. You cannot deny it. Except, of course, as you say I don't really *know* you. However, you've allowed me to believe you are seriously affected as well. Or are you a witch?"

"I am *not* a witch," she said with adamance.

It was clear to her she had challenged his pride. He didn't like it. The deep dark emotions that were growing between them were as threatening as any storm. How long could they continue this fraught sensual dance before people began to notice?

Her face was turned up to his. She drew closer. "What about the woman you've left behind?" she accused. "The girlfriend? You told me your attentions were not engaged. Was that a lie?" Abruptly she recognised the fact she was madly jealous of the unknown young woman who no doubt would be stunningly beautiful. There would be strong approval from both families as well. That was the way it was done.

"Woman?" he rasped, as though she were completely stupid. "My God, is *that* it?"

"Of course that's *it*." Her supple body had gone rigid. The careless arrogance of his tone!

He wasn't going to let her go. He retained one of her hands as he stepped down a few steps into the garden and beyond to the radiant moonlight. He went first, compelling her to follow him into the scented darkness.

"Varo, what are you doing?" Her voice shook in alarm. "Where are we going?"

"Do not worry," he said. "Everything will be fine." He kept to the softly lit pathway, mindful of her evening shoes and her lovely long skirt.

She could smell gardenias. All kinds of beautiful blossoming flowers, native and exotic, and the scent of freshly clipped grass. "Varo!" she repeated breathlessly. If she had learned anything about herself it was that she couldn't resist him.

As they moved off the path into the deep shadows of the trees he caught her around the waist. "Who have you been speaking to?" he demanded. "Don't tell me. Sweet little Moira?"

She made no attempt to deny it. The brief conversation she had had with Moira had made her suffer. "You told her you had a special someone waiting for you at home." It was plain accusation.

"Maybe I was simply trying to get a message across?" he countered, his arm tightening around her as he drew her body, arched away from him, in close. "I'm not married. Who else to protect me but the woman I left behind?"

"Whose name is...?" The sad joke was on her!

"There *is* no one, Ava," he said very gently. Although

she knew he wouldn't forgive her if she continued to doubt him. "Just part of my ploy so pretty little Moira wouldn't waste her time," he explained. "If you raise your head a little I can kiss your cheek. You have such beautiful skin. A perfect camellia comes into my mind. Sadly I can't kiss your mouth as I want, because you can't return to the house *sin carmín*. Your hawk-eyed cousin Karen would be so upset."

Why hadn't she figured it all out for herself? The idea of Varo confiding in Moira had affected her so badly she had made a quantum leap. "It was Karen who played a trick on Moira," she confided abruptly. Her whole body was under siege at his touch. "She told Moira you had picked her out of the crowd."

He tilted her head back so he could run his mouth down her cheek, over her delicate jawbone to the column of her throat. "I would say your cousin is a woman full of tricks." His mouth was warm against her skin. "*Peligrosa.* Teacherous. Poor Moira was deliberately led astray. But one wonders why…?"

"Karen wants to see what will happen, Varo."

"Destino," he said, his hand sliding down over her breast with unparalleled sensuality.

She shuddered, on the brink of surrender. "We have to go back inside." It was imperative for her to take action before the pressure became too great.

"Soon. I need this badly." He sounded as if he was in pain.

Ava bit her lip hard, so a moan wouldn't escape her. The spell was at work again, holding them captive.

"Varo!" She forced her eyes open, her hand closing over his at her breast.

"I know… I know…" A sigh was on his lips. He lifted his head, his deep voice slightly slurred.

"I can't be sure," she told him in agitation, "but I think

there's someone moving beneath the trees." The trees were strung with countless tiny twinkling white lights, but there were dark spots.

Varo turned his head, his eyes trying to pierce the dappled dark. "A female puma, perhaps?" he mocked. "Why not acknowledge her?" There was more than a hint of derision in his tone. His resonant, fascinatingly accented voice lifted, carrying on the breeze. "We're over here, Karen," he called. "Feel free to join us. Ava is showing me the most wonderful night-blooming *cereus.*"

He was quick witted—and he obviously knew the plant, native to Mexico. Because the cactus with its enormous breathtakingly beautiful creamy cups brimming with golden stamens was twined around a tree not a few feet away from them.

Silence.

"Perhaps I was mistaken?" Ava whispered, her whole body aquiver.

"Give it a minute." His voice was low in her ear. "Ah, the stalker shows herself!"

The ultra-thin figure of Karen, well camouflaged in her black gown, now appeared on the path, all but stomping towards them. "Oh, there you are!" she cried out in an artlessly playful voice that would have fooled no one. "I needed a break from all the noise. I expect you did too."

"What *is* this woman's problem?" Varo, still with his head bent, was murmuring in Ava's ear.

"I think she hates me." Karen was acting more like the enemy than her family.

"She will have to get to you through *me.*" All of a sudden Varo sounded very cold and hard.

"I don't remember any night-blooming *cereus,*" Karen was remarking caustically, looking dubiously around her.

"Ah, but Ava is far more knowledgeable." Varo spoke

with charming mockery. "You are standing midway between it and us."

"Oh, the cactus, you mean?" Karen's tone reduced the stunning beauty of the night-blooming *cereus* to that of a paper daisy.

"Breathtaking," Varo exclaimed, turning his raven head to Ava. "But I think it's high time for us to return to the party, don't you, Ava? *Muchas gracias* for showing me such beauty. Such a mystery why it only blooms at night."

CHAPTER SIX

THERE were not enough days in the following week. They flew by on the wings of mounting excitement. Nothing like a wedding to bring the thrill of joy. Although the great day had been organised down to the last little detail, there still remained things to do.

Amelia had been dropping weight with all the excitement; consequently her beautiful bridal gown needed adjustments.

Amelia's mother, Sarina, had been invited purely as a gesture, everyone knowing full well that Sarina was too busy living the good life in Tuscany.

Ava's husband, Luke Selwyn, had not been invited at all. He and Ava were divorcing, after all, and the split was far from amicable. Luke Selwyn made no bones about wanting Ava back, although he had told Ava many times he wasn't happy with her. There had always been something she wasn't getting quite right. But he *wanted* her. No mistaking that. And she *was* the Langdon heiress.

The homestead, with its twelve bedrooms extended from the original ten, all fitted with an *en suite* bathroom, was full up. So too was the accommodation at the men's quarters, the dormitories, and all the various bungalows—including the one-teacher schoolhouse—that sat like satellites around the main compound.

People streamed through the house, carrying all sorts of boxes for all purposes. A huge consignment of glorious flowers had been flown in from Sydney, along with a renowned floral designer and his team. Top musicians had arrived. Food and drink and a team of caterers were to be flown in first thing Saturday morning.

The ceremony, in the lovely tranquillity of the garden, was to take place at four p.m., after the heat of the day had abated. Vows would be exchanged beneath an eighteenth-century gazebo with carved stone pillars and a delicate white cupola. Great urns nearby had been filled with white cymbidium orchids that had been flown in from Thailand. No expense had been spared. This was a once-in-a-lifetime event—a marriage that was destined to endure.

Dev's best man and his two grooms had arrived in the best man's private Cessna. Amelia's other bridesmaids arrived on Friday. A rehearsal was to take place in the late afternoon.

The reception was to be held in the Great Hall, a large multi-purpose building separate from the house. A celebration barbecue had been organised for Kooraki's staff. It was scheduled to begin at the same time as the main reception. This was a splendid occasion, affecting everyone on the station.

Amelia had bypassed the traditional structured duchesse satin style for a much lighter look perfect for a hot early summer's afternoon. The bride and her three bridesmaids were to wear the same exquisitely hand embroidered chiffon over full-length silk slips. Amelia had chosen for her bridesmaids the soft colours of one of her favourite flowers, the hydrangea. Amelia's own gown, ivory-white, was lightly embroidered with tiny pearls and sparkling beads to within some six or seven inches from the hem, where the embroidery burst into large silver leaves that gleamed like a work of art.

Ava was to wear not the blue of the hydrangea but another colour that suited her beautifully: an exquisite mauve. The other bridesmaids, Lisa and Ashleigh, would be wearing hydrangea-blue and pink. Slender arms were to be left bare. Instead of a veil Amelia would be wearing a floral diadem to encircle her dark head. So too would her bridesmaids. All would wear their long hair loose and flowing. Each bridesmaid's heart-shaped posy would feature one of the flowers in the bride's white bouquet, whether rose, peony, butterfly orchid, hydrangea or lily.

It had been a close collaboration, with input from each bridesmaid as to colours and styles. It was a great good fortune all were tall and slim with long flowing hair. Amelia did not want a *grand* wedding, as such. She wanted a lovely summer's day fantasy. A romantic wedding above all.

Amelia's room was crowded with her bridesmaids, the dresser and hairdresser and Elizabeth, Dev and Ava's mother. Even Karen had found her way in, standing near the open French doors, studying them all with a strange expression—never pleasure or excitement—on her tight-skinned face. She had chosen to wear a black and white outfit, extremely smart, but Ava thought it would have been nicer had she worn a colour.

The instant before Ava stepped into the corridor after the others Karen caught her arm. "Surely you're thinking of someone outside yourself today?" she asked in a steely voice.

Ava turned around, resolving to keep her temper. "Please don't upset me, Karen. It would be entirely the wrong day. What *is* your problem with me, anyway? You've always had one."

"I've had a purpose," said Karen, "to look out for you. And I place a lot of importance on marriage vows." She lowered her voice as Amelia looked back over her shoulder to check on them.

"Wait until *you* get there, Karen," Ava said. "How old are you now?"

Karen's expression became slightly pinched. "I've had any number of offers, Ava. I'm taking my time. I don't intend to make a mistake, like you. And you *are* making a mistake. Luke loves you. He wants you back. Hard to understand why, when you've treated him so badly."

The unfairness of it all!

Ava shook her cousin's hand off just as Amelia moved back to them, a slight frown on her beautiful face.

"Tell me you're not trying to upset Ava?" She stepped right up to Karen, so Karen had to fall back a step or two.

Just like in their schooldays, Ava thought. Mel stepping in to protect her.

"Mel, everything's okay," she said, ever the peacemaker.

But Mel, of Italian descent, had a volcanic temper when aroused.

"Let's say I was trying to talk sense to Ava." Karen adopted a self-righteous pose. "I happen to care about her. She *is* my cousin. I care about Luke too. He's suffering."

"Suffering?" Mel exploded. "Are you serious? Luke Selwyn is your classic narcissist. And a womaniser. As if you didn't know. If you like him so much, Karen, he'll be available in the not so distant future. Look him up. Offer comfort. But, for now, keep out of Ava's affairs. She is *not* your concern. And another thing! How dare you cause upset on *my* wedding day?" Mel's delicate nostrils flared. "Honestly, Karen, you're so stupid you don't even know you're stupid. Here's a word of warning from the bride: *behave.*"

Karen visibly deflated. Amelia had always had that effect on her—that was why she hated her. She gave a strangled laugh. "I can assure you, Amelia, I'll do the best I can."

"Be sure you do," said Amelia with a sharp nod.

"You look wonderful, by the way."

"Thank you so much, Karen," Mel said ironically. "Come along, Ava. This is one bride who isn't going to be late for her wedding."

At four o'clock, in a haze of emotion, the wedding ceremony took place. Bride and groom exchanged vows beneath the shelter of the white wrought-iron lace of a cupola decorated with white flowers and satin ribbons. Amelia stood in her exquisite bridal gown, sewn all over with sparkling crystals, staring up into her beloved Dev's eyes.

It was an ageless ritual but incredibly moving. Ava, ethereal in her mauve bridesmaid's gown, bowed her blonde diadem-encircled head in prayer, the inevitable tears rising to her eyes.

God bless and protect you all the days of your lives. God grant you beautiful children to love and raise to the highest possible level of happiness, confidence and morality.

Dev and Amelia were strong people. They had endured years of conflict—as had she. Only she had been the one who had been openly frightened of her grandfather but desperately anxious to win his approval. Her father had had the same experience, but those days were gone. Life had become more complicated, but in a way very much simpler. They were all working towards the same goal: personal fulfilment within a secure family environment. Dev had his adored wife. She had a sister. Their parents, reunited, had their eyes set on the future. And, needless to say—grandchildren to love and very likely spoil.

The ceremony over, the newly married couple yielded

completely to the bridal kiss. Emotion spread across the garden area. Women guests happily dabbed tears from their eyes, irresistibly reminded of *their* wedding day.

"The happiest day!" Elizabeth Langdon, looking lovely in a short blue silk shift with a matching lace jacket and a filmy blue picture hat whispered to her daughter, "Your perfect day is yet to come, my darling."

Hope that had glimmered, brightened, strengthened by Ava's wildly blossoming emotions, turned as insubstantial as gauze.

In the reception hall white-linen-draped buffet tables were laden with a succulent gastronomic feast: hams, turkeys, chicken dishes—hot and cold—roast duck and lamb, all manner of scrumptious seafood, whole Tasmanian salmons—cold and smoked—reef fish, lobsters, prawns, sea scallops, mussels and oysters, salads galore…

Good-looking young waiters were almost pirouetting, pouring champagne, white wine, red, and the popular rosé. There was also a well-stocked bar for anything stronger, and gallons of icy cold fruit juices and soft drinks.

There was a separate table groaning under the weight of desserts: apricot, peach, banana, mango, berries, citrus cakes and tarts, coconut cakes, and the all-time favourite chocolate desserts. No one would go away feeling hungry. This was a *serious* banquet the like of which was seldom seen.

From the upstairs gallery in the homestead Amelia, now mistress of Kooraki, threw her exquisite grandiflora bouquet: white roses, luxurious white peonies with the faintest flush of pink, gardenia *"magnifica,"* a perfect velvety white, a single large head of white hydrangea and a small cluster of butterfly orchids. She threw it directly towards her chief bridesmaid. Such was her accuracy, Ava had no option but to catch it.

Karen, who was behind Ava, leaned forward to whisper, "I seem to remember you've *already* been given in wedlock."

Nothing, it seemed, could stop Karen. It was a wonder she didn't shout it from the top of her lungs. She wasn't a woman of great subtlety. Even so, Ava found it hard not to remember that fact too. She had ignored all good advice. For once she had made her own decision. Well, it had cost her.

But her grandfather had left her financially set for life. Probably he had never trusted her to determine her own future. Even now she had fallen madly in love with a man who would soon return to his own country, his own life. She had thrown herself wide open to him. They couldn't go backwards. They could only go forward. Varo was only seeing what he wanted to see. Varo wanted her. She knew that. Fate had put her in his path. But Varo had other people to think of. His family in Argentina. They would have important concerns and plans for their only son. In her wildest dreams she didn't think they would accept a divorced woman. Their son could have *anyone*! Any beautiful young woman in their circle. Not a woman from another place. One who couldn't even speak Spanish.

Had Varo's American mother been fluent in Spanish when she'd run off with her Argentine husband? In all likelihood she hadn't been, but neither of them had cared.

By seven o'clock the newlyweds had left to fly to Sydney. The following morning they would board a fight to Singapore, staying at Raffles for a few days before heading off for London, their first European port of all.

This was the signal for the party to step up a gear. No

one wanted the wonderful day to end. It was all so exciting, with everyone so friendly. The older guests retired to the house for long in-depth conversations; the under forties were dead set on having a good time.

There was a great deal of laughter, flirting and, it had to be said, drinking. And dancing to a great band that became more and more high-powered as the night went on was on everyone's agenda. The band members were enjoying themselves every bit as much as the guests. They'd been well fed, and they hadn't gone short on liquid refreshments. No one was counting.

Varo pushed his chair back towards the shelter of a lush golden cane in a splendid blue and white Chinese jardinière. He had been enjoying more than his fair share of female attention, and now he was thankful to be on his own for the moment—free to watch Ava make her way down the staircase with her signature flowing grace, a romantic fantasy in her lovely softest mauve dress. She had removed the silver diadem she had worn around her head for the ceremony. It had suited her perfectly, enhancing the ethereal look. He had loved the idea of the diadem for a headdress. It had been set here and there along its length with tiny real roses nestled into little sprays of sparkling crystals.

Dev had given each bridesmaid a necklace to match her gown. Varo imagined they would treasure it: hand-made pendants featuring large diamond-set gemstones hanging from delicate white gold chains. Ava's gemstone was an amethyst, Lisa's a pink sapphire, Ashleigh's a blue topaz. They had all looked beautiful, with their long flowing hair and filmy summer dresses. He had danced several times with both Lisa and Ashleigh. Now he was waiting for Ava, who was proving as elusive as a woodland nymph.

As he looked towards the staircase he felt a sudden chill

that had him turning in his chair. It couldn't be. But it was. Cousin Karen had appeared again.

"Hi, there!"

She pulled up a chair close to him, crossing her long legs. She was looking very elegant in her black and white gown, but he found himself feeling astonishingly hostile to her. This rarely happened to him—especially with a woman. But there it was!

"Well, that went off extremely well, didn't it?" Karen had prepared a big smile, and was speaking in an enthusiastic kind of voice that didn't fool him one bit. "Slightly odd, Amelia throwing her bouquet to Ava," she slid in, her dark eyes hooded.

"You expected Amelia to throw it to *you*?" he asked suavely.

"No, no!" she protested laughingly. "Lord knows *I'm* in no hurry to marry. I simply meant Ava is already married. Divorce may be streamlined here in Australia—one year and one day of separation. Why the extra day?" she trilled. "But it has to *be* that before an application can be filed in the court. A hearing date can take a couple of months. You may not know this, but that separation date hasn't yet been reached."

"Why are you telling me this?" Varo asked, successfully staring her down. He really wanted to get away from this woman as he would want to get away from a snake.

She made a sound like a strangled giggle. "Go figure! I thought you and Ava were on the verge of having an affair?"

He recognised malevolence when he encountered it. "You think this, do you? Or do you fear it? And would it be *your* business either way?" His voice he kept low, but his black eyes took on a brilliant diamond-like glitter.

Karen could see he was angry. He really was a magnificent man. "Well, I've made it my business because I care about Ava, Varo," she insisted—not for the first time. "And Luke. As I've told you, he worships her."

"Apparently she missed that," he said, with heavy irony.

"Oh, no!" Karen shook her shiny dark bob that was groomed to racehorse perfection. "It was apparent to everyone who knew them or met them. Luke adores her. She's his perfect princess."

"So it's all Ava's fault? Is that it?"

Karen sighed, holding up one of her manicured hands to avoid his penetrating eyes. "Fault? No, I never said fault. But Ava is a fragile creature. She always has been."

"Perhaps she needs a *real* man and not your Luke?" Varo suggested smoothly. He rose to his impressive six-three, a stunningly handsome man, and stared down at Ava's poisonous cousin. "Would it clarify anything in your mind if I said you cannot hide your jealousy of Ava? I suspect it has always been there. She's so beautiful, and I have noted she takes into account *everyone's* feelings. I would say before her own."

Karen appeared genuinely shocked by his action. She too rose to her feet, colour flagging her high cheekbones. "It's much too soon for you to make an assessment, Varo. I'm only trying to prevent a huge mistake."

"And you would be desolate if your little plan came awry?" he challenged. "I think this is all a deliberate attempt at sabotage, Ms Devereaux. Now, if you will excuse me, I plan to dance with Ava."

Karen shook her head sadly. "My conscience is clear. I've done my level best."

"I would say you have. Only it's your motivation that is being questioned. Rest assured, Ms Devereaux, we can handle this ourselves."

Karen blushed and turned away, a white-hot fury moving through her. She would get even with Ava if it was the last thing she did. She was already going along that road, blind to anything else. She didn't really know or understand *why*, but she had always wanted to rob her cousin in some way. She especially wanted to rob her of any chance she might have with the arrogant, supremely macho Argentine. To think she had half fancied him too! He had certainly got her adrenaline going for a while. Now she hated him. Few men intimidated her. Juan-Varo de Montalvo did.

Varo drained a vodka before he went in search of the elusive Ava, who had disappeared. Eventually he found her out on the terrace, dancing with one of the polo-players, a long-time family friend and, as he correctly guessed, a long-time admirer of Ava.

He tapped the polo-player's shoulder, his name having sprung to mind. "May I cut in, Jeff?" he asked lightly. "Ava has promised me my quota of dances."

Jeff didn't look the least put out. "You're saying I've had mine?" He laughed, lingeringly releasing Ava. "Indeed, I have."

"Muchas gracias!" Varo smiled at the other man, who smiled back. Varo then took Ava very smoothly into his arms, their feet immediately fitting the soft, slow romantic beat. "You see me. You disappear again," he chided gently.

She tilted her face to him, caught up in the same physical exhilaration, the sense of *belonging*. "I saw Karen pull up a chair beside you. I didn't like to interrupt."

He gave an exaggerated groan. "Please *do* if there is ever a next time."

His arresting face was all high cheekbones, striking planes and angles in the shadowy golden light. "What was she saying this time?" she asked.

His voice dropped to a low, confiding whisper. "You don't want to know." He gathered her in close, feeling his hunger for her tighten into the now familiar near-painful knots of tension. He only had so much strength to resist such magical allure.

"Possibly what Karen should do is train to become a private investigator," Ava said thoughtfully.

"I promise you she'd be good at it." He laughed.

"So what *did* she say?" Ava persisted, very glad her cousin was going home the following day.

"Same old thing." Varo shrugged. "Your husband wants you back." He hesitated a moment, then said, "Could you tell me how long it is since you've been separated from him?"

They seemed to be dancing alone. Other couples had drifted away. "Ah, now, I'm ninety-nine point nine percent sure Karen told you."

His tone was taut. "I don't listen to Karen. I listen to *you*."

"Why talk about it on a day like today?" She sighed, swaying like a feather in his arms.

"Why refuse when it is something that is important to me?" he countered, steering her into the light so he could capture her exact expression.

Ava realised his intention. "Luke and I are two months short of mandatory separation time, Varo," she said. "Which is exactly as Karen must have told you: one year and one day. The day after my solicitor will file my application in the court. Luke no longer has a hold on me, Varo. My marriage is over."

"You think the court will look favourably on your application for divorce?" They had stopped dancing, but he was holding her in place.

"Why not?" she fired, her beautiful eyes ablaze. "My solicitor—he's a top man—has assured me it will."

"Your husband may throw difficulties in your way," Varo said. She felt so soft, so silken, so fluid in his arms she might have been naked beneath her exquisite sheer dress. "Perhaps you will be told to provide more information?"

The music had stopped. Now it started up again. Of all things, the famous Bolero. It was being played by the band with a compulsive up beat and a strong tango rhythm. Instinctively their interlocked bodies reacted. Along the length of the terrace other couples devoted themselves to their own form of the tango, while trying to keep within the spirit of the dance. Certainly the embrace was high on their list, with strong body connections, heads and faces touching.

"I know I have to be careful," Ava said, her voice unsteady. "I think we both know Karen will be reporting to Luke the minute she gets back home. If she hasn't done so already. I have come to the sad conclusion there's nothing my cousin wouldn't do to hurt me."

His body was finding it impossible not to move into the dance he knew so intimately. What woman could he desire more than Ava? When he was with her he felt somehow complete.

"When does she leave?" he asked rather curtly beneath his breath.

"Midday tomorrow."

He held her in a formal open embrace, gauging her knowledge of the dance. She followed him in total communication, arching her upper body away in the "ballroom" style of tango she would have been taught. She would know the famous dance had originated in Buenos Aires, but she didn't as yet know the striking difference between the Argentine tango and the positions and steps she had learned.

Only he would show her...

Ava felt rapt, carried along by sensation and responding perfectly to his signals. "You're such a beautiful dancer, Varo," she breathed, in a trance of pleasure.

"So are you. But your style is a little…formal. Let me show you." He moved her in close. Her breasts were against his chest, but there was a space between their hips. "Relax now. Relax totally," he said hypnotically. "Follow where I lead. Argentine tango continually changes. It is very improvisational. Emotion is extremely important. We have that, do we not?"

She felt desperately moved by his words. Did he *mean* them? Or was he giving way to infatuation? She was still so unsure of herself. Karen's planned intervention hadn't helped. They were dancing around the perimeter of the broad spacious terrace. The rhythm in his body, the musicality, seemed sublime. She had never known anything approaching it. It lifted her own dance skills, which she had been told many times were exceptional. But not like *this*. This was a communion of bodies…of souls…

No one cut across them. Everyone was now sticking to their own "lane", casting frequent glances at Varo and Ava and what they were doing. It might have been a master class, with a group of advanced students following the master's lead.

After a while—though Ava was scarcely aware of it, so caught up was she in the dance—the other couples cleared the terrace until it resembled a stage. The tango was the most passionate, the most exciting dance of them all. And here it was being so beautifully, so thrillingly performed on this wondrous day of days.

The wave upon wave of applause was sincere. Couples surrounded them, clapping and chanting, *"Bravo!"*

"That was the best example of the tango I've ever seen," exclaimed a flushed-faced Moira O'Farrell—no mean dancer herself. "I had no idea you were such a terrific dancer, Ava. So *sexy!*"

"This is the day to kick over the traces," her partner supplied.

In fact Ava had surprised them all—almost transfigured from the lovely, serene Ava they knew. She had packed so much *passion* into the famous dance it had been startling to those who knew her. Of course the Argentine was a past master. And the right partner was of tremendous importance. But neither had in any way been consciously showing off. It had passed way beyond that. It had appeared more like one glorious, even blatant, seduction.

The party broke up about three o'clock. The band had ceased playing an hour before that. Time to catch a few hours' sleep before the lavish brunch that was being served from eight o'clock onwards.

All the older guests had long since turned in. Finally the last stragglers went in search of their accommodation. Ava felt it her duty to remain at the party until the very end. Her mother and father had gone off on the crest of a wave, some time before one a.m., declaring themselves thrilled everything had gone so well.

"You don't see a lot of Karen, do you, darling?" her mother had asked, after kissing her goodnight.

"Not really." Ava had kept her smile.

"Good. I never liked that girl. She's rather unpleasant. For once I agree with your late grandfather. He never liked her either. You've got your own life, darling. She has hers. Hate to say it, but I don't trust her." Elizabeth's fine eyes had met those of her daughter's. "Be on your guard," she'd warned.

Ava went around the ground floor turning off all the main lights but leaving on a few lamps. There was no one around now. Oddly enough she didn't feel in the least tired.

She felt wired. It was a kind of refined torture—wanting someone desperately, having to keep oneself apart.

Varo had raised the point of the period of separation. Her application was a few months off being filed. She had an enemy in the house. In her cousin. Luke, for whatever reason, did seem intent on getting her back. Control was natural to men. Maybe even the *best* of men. She could pay a heavy price for allowing herself to have become so involved with Varo.

God, it's worth it!

She took the rear staircase to the upper floor, moving cautiously so as not to make any noise. Now, why did she do that? Was she deliberately playing with fire? Was she out of control? She could see Varo had not gone to bed, although they had said their formal goodnights thirty minutes ago. His bedroom was still illuminated. A shaft of light was raying under the door. She stood in the corridor, staring down the length of it. Wall sconces remained on, shedding a soft light.

All was silence. All was utterly still. The house slept.

She moved on soundless feet towards Varo's door, as if it was some forbidden rite. Her long chiffon skirt softly swished around her ankles. Her heart was beating in a frantic, unnatural way. She tossed her long hair over her shoulder, although golden strands clung to her heated cheeks.

What are you doing?

Her inner voice spoke up so sharply she backed away from the door, feeling a surge of panic.

You're not divorced from Luke yet.

Even so, she stood glued to the spot.

If I'm punished, I deserve it.

Astonishingly, as if he had a super sixth sense, Varo's door came open and his strong arm drew her swiftly inside as if she were a puppet on a string. Tingles started up all over her body...exquisite...probing. She began to flush from head to toe, as though molten liquid was being poured into her. She felt radiant, intoxicated, fearful.

"Varo, what are you doing?" Even her voice sounded afraid.

"Waiting for you. What else?" His dark eyes glittered as they rested on her. Her long blonde hair floated sinuously around her lovely camellia-skinned face, framing it. He could clearly see the pulse beating in the hollow at the base of her neck. That excited him. Her sparkling eyes were huge. Such emotion, such appeal was in them, it only served to inflame his passion.

"Dear Lord," she whispered. "This is *madness*!"

Madness. The word seemed to echo around the room, bouncing gently off the walls.

"Far better than doing nothing," he returned tautly, drawing her into his warm, close embrace. "Let me tell you about my mother and father when they were young. They surrendered to madness too—only they called it *love.*"

Words of protest kept coming and going inside her head, but she didn't utter a one. She knew full well she was doing something dangerous. She knew she should be careful. But she wasn't a thinking woman in his arms. She lifted her face to him like a flower to the sun in the sky for its blessing. Tenderly he began to trace the contours of her mouth with a padded finger.

The sensation that poured into her made her shudder. She took his finger into her mouth, her tongue caressing it.

"Don't be afraid," he said.

"Varo, I am. Technically I'm still married." Her voice was strained, full of intensity.

His answer was a mix of hard authority and deep emotion. "It's not you and Luke any more. It's you and me."

"But *how*? You will go away soon. You could forget all

about me. You might say you'll call me, e-mail me—God knows I'd spend my time checking—but once you get home things will be different. Family affairs will keep you very busy. You said you and your father had big plans." She knew she might be left with nothing but a broken heart.

Except he said, very simply, "We wait a while."

Was she to agree to that? Why could she not find her voice? Of course she *had* to wait. Even without Luke's throwing up difficulties, and if her application was successful, the decree nisi would only become final one month and one day from the date of the divorce order. She still didn't know how soon her application would come before the court. What she did know was that she and Varo had reached the point of no return. She had confirmed that by hovering outside his door. He with his finely tuned sensibilities had known she would come to him. He had been waiting as though it were her decision.

Wasn't that your objective? her inner voice questioned sharply.

Yearning rose in her body as his mouth came down across her hair, her forehead, her nose, her cheek. She tipped her head back so he could kiss her throat, before he came back to settle on her receptive open mouth. No feigning of emotion with Varo. No pretence. No mechanical movements. No sense of a deep inner loneliness, lying beneath a man unfulfilled. Varo had lit up every last little part of her with passion. Pure passion. How often did one meet a man with whom one was in perfect accord?

She stood quietly while he removed her beautiful glimmering dress with extreme care, leaving her body covered by the mauve silk slip. Her light, slender limbs had turned heavy, as if she wanted to lie down. He must have known, because he lifted her high in his arms before placing her very gently on the turned-back bed.

"I would not harm you for the world, Ava," he murmured. His lustrous eyes burned. "I only want to love you a little. Give you pleasure. I will wait for you. For the right time. Have no fear. You have only to tell me to stop if you fear I go too far. I want making love to you to be so *natural*." His eyes on her were very brilliant, very tender.

Her whole body was drowning in sensation. She closed her eyes, feeling the heat of her sex but knowing this time was not to be their ultimate encounter. There were demands to be met. "Everything is natural with you," she whispered, as he kissed her inner wrist with its white translucence and faint tracery of blue veins.

"As it should be," he said softly, bending his head to kiss her gently, so gently, cupping her face with his hands.

All he knew was his desire, but he had made a vow not to seduce her into giving herself. The depth of feeling he had for her, the tenderness, the sense of protectiveness, was as potent as it was astounding. He broke contact with her mouth, controlling the fever. His eyes followed his hands. He drew them, imperceptibly trembling, down over the length of her, the indentation of her narrow waist, her hips, her thighs, her long slender legs. He didn't realise it but he was murmuring in Spanish.

"You are a revelation to me."

Such beauty!

He was inhaling the fragrance that rose from her body, his sex hardening, but that was something he could not control. Lovemaking without penetration could be an enormous stress on a man's body, but the lovemaking still retained many elements of rapture.

Convulsively Ava moved, so he could lie more comfortably beside her on the bed. These were Varo's hands on her, kissing, stroking through the silk of the light bra and wisteria-coloured silk slip that covered her. Oddly, it seemed incredibly erotic. At some point she felt the cool breeze hit her naked breasts. Her senses were flooded with the warmth and the clean male scent of him. Lovemaking with Varo was an extraordinary bewitching ritual. She could hear little whimpering sounds. They were issuing from her own lips. All there was was her desire for him; his desire for her. She kept her eyes tightly closed, lost in a world of exquisite sensation.

At one point she found herself gripping his strong naked back in an effusion of heat and light, desperate to give him as much pleasure as he was giving her. He had thrown off his shirt long ago. They were both turning and twisting, bodies interlocking, totally absorbed the one in the other, their bodies imploring, wanting consummation. Varo wanted to know the whole of her, her glorious white flesh. She was allowing it. He was finding it near impossible to hold off the brilliant, overpowering rush of blind sex. Her beautiful body had already dissolved beneath his hands. He knew, like him, she could barely withstand the flood of sensation.

His steely resolve was under threat. She was his. Those inciting little exhalations! They were like a torch held against his skin.

With a deep groan, his handsome face near tortured, he began to breathe deeply, mustering control. Then he very gently began to ease her bra and her silk slip back onto her delicate white shoulders, kissing one and then the other.

"Ava, I have to stop," he muttered.

She opened her jewelled eyes to him. "I know." She put up a caressing hand to stroke his handsome chiselled face, moving her hand to clasp his nape, damp from his rising temperature. Their lovemaking, however curtailed, had been agony and ecstasy both. A rapture too extravagant to describe. She had to marvel, and then bless Varo's capacity for control. She had been lost, adrift in a sea of sensation.

He fell back on the bed beside her, staring up at the orante plaster rose in the ceiling. "I knew it would be you," he murmured, almost to himself. "I knew it in that very first moment."

"As did I." Ava's response came from the depths of her heart.

That was the great mystery of it all. Destiny at work. Only the heart, once given, could never be recalled.

Ava knew beyond all question that she had given hers.

CHAPTER SEVEN

THE first thing Luke Selwyn did when he got up that morning, after yet another anger-racked night, was check his e-mail. He was hoping for some communication from Karen. Karen was a good sort—a loyal pal. He should have married someone like Karen, only she was totally lacking in sex appeal. *That* his poor Ava had in abundance. The joke was she didn't know it.

He was absolutely furious—his parents were too—that they hadn't been invited to Langdon's wedding to *that woman's* daughter. He would always think of Amelia as that. The irony of it all. She was now mistress of Kooraki, wife to the man in control of the Langdon fortunes. Amelia—who had looked at him with blazing contempt.

Bitch!

Karen hated her too. There were five messages from her in his in-box. Only *one* was he interested in. He opened that message first, read the contents—his wife was having a great time, was she?—then opened the attachment, wondering what it would contain.

What he saw made him sit down joltingly hard at his desk. How dared she? *How dared she?* A peculiar fury was racing through him. He had always had the upper hand with Ava, physically and psychologically. She had never rebelled, never protested—except at anything a bit adventurous he had wanted in the bedroom. Such a prude!

Her first and only deliberate act of rebellion had been in defying that tyrannical old bastard of a grandfather to marry *him*. Her second major rebellion had been in leaving him. Her betrayal would have left him desolated—only he knew he could force her back, and when he did he'd make her pay. No one was going to ditch him. Not even the heir-ess Ava Langdon-Selwyn. Her shocking lack of allegiance would cost her. He couldn't wait.

He clenched his fists in his lap, biting down involuntarily on his tongue. He tasted blood in his mouth. The attachment showed three shots of his wife dancing with some South American gigolo. As flamboyantly handsome as any mati-nee idol and a polo-player of all things. He couldn't believe their body language. *His* Ava! She looked like a member of some professional dance troupe, strutting her stuff. The final shot had him swearing aloud. The dance was a tango. Anyone would know that. And there was his precious frigid Ava, holding a pose that should never be. This was his *wife*, dammit! The fact that Ava could act in this abandoned way made him dizzy with rage. She wasn't going to be allowed to make a fool of him. No way!

The insufferably arrogant Langdon was away on his honeymoon with his equally arrogant wife. He hoped they had a miserable time of it. Terrible weather. Food poison-ing. Lost luggage. Anything to spoil their dream time. He hated his brother-in-law with a passion. Now he hated his own wife. But he still wanted her. Oh, yes, he wanted her. He enjoyed their life together. He enjoyed controlling her. Only she had hurt him. So it was only fitting he would hurt her. The gigolo wouldn't present a problem, even if he did manage to stay on a while after Ava's parents returned home. He could easily find out when the Langdons were back in town. Arranging a charter flight to Kooraki would be easy enough.

Perhaps he ought to adopt the grieving-husband role? Enlist the gigolo's sympathies if he were still there? He was the husband, after all. It might not be far off but the application for divorce had not been filed. There was time for reconciliation. Ava knew her duty. Her duty was to him. The gigolo would see that. It wasn't as though he was after commitment. His life was in Argentina. Ava would never go there. The very thought of being away from her family would alarm her. A real cream puff was Ava.

Nevertheless, the shock of what he had seen had him still sitting in his chair a good twenty minutes later, staring all the while at a silver-framed photograph of his beautiful wife. It had pride of place on his desk. He still had her photograph on his desk at the office too. He knew Ava so well he took cold comfort in the fact she was extremely cautious by nature. No way would she have sex with a stranger. God, no! Ava had dozens of ardent admirers, who would give anything to spend a stolen hour with her. But Ava had never been unfaithful, was totally loyal. He trusted her completely. He'd had other women, of course. But that was different. Men were different. Men had different needs.

Her parents stayed on for a few days, at peace with one another and clearly enjoying themselves. They had taken a great liking to Varo, drawing closer to him every day. Clearly he was an exceptional young man who loved his family, his extended family, his country.

"Varo has a wonderful blend of sense and sensibility," Elizabeth remarked to her daughter. "It has such power to attract."

Elizabeth and Erik had derived great enjoyment from Varo's sense of humour, and his fascinating tales of Argentina and his family life there. He had invited them to stay at Estancia de Villaflores whenever they visited South America, which he hoped would be soon. The invitation had been issued with such genuine warmth both felt they might indeed take him up on it. Varo had assured them most charmingly that the *estancia* had as many guest rooms as Kooraki. His parents loved entertaining.

On the morning Ava's parents were to return home, Elizabeth sought a few private words with her daughter.

"You're in love with him, aren't you?" Elizabeth asked calmly and without preamble. She was half reclining on the chaise in Ava's bedroom, looking across at her daughter, who was sitting very quietly on the carved chest at the end of her bed.

Ava took a deep breath. She'd known this was coming. Her eyes met those of her mother. "I thought I was being *friendly*," she said, with a wry smile.

Elizabeth couldn't help laughing. "My darling, I'm a woman. I'm your mother. I understand perfectly why you're in love with him. What woman wouldn't be? He has *everything*." Elizabeth made an expansive little gesture. "He's everything Luke isn't."

Ava looked out at the gently swaying palms. "Of course he is. Do you think he loves me?"

Elizabeth smiled. "I may not have personally experienced the legendary *coup de foudre*, but I would say you two have. Your father agrees. He's very happy about it. The more the two of you attempt to play down your feelings, the more intense they appear. Have you slept with him?"

Ava felt her hot blush. *"Mum!"*

"Sorry, darling," Elizabeth apologised. "Only, you have

the radiance of a woman who is not only in love but is loved. What is Varo saying about the future?" she questioned with a slight frown. "He has deep ties to his family. He loves his own country."

Ava sighed. "I know that, Mum. All he says is, 'We wait a while.'"

"Implying?"

"I don't ask." Ava's shrug was a shade helpless. "I can't believe what is happening to me, Mum. I need a little time for the miracle to sink in. I never thought I could ever feel like this. I even thought I had a cool heart, if not cold. No, don't scoff. Luke was forever driving that point home. Maybe I can't believe it could ever work out for Varo and me. I can't even believe the divorce will proceed without incident. Luke is storing up trouble. He's like that. He'll throw anything he can in the way of holding up proceedings."

"So who's to talk?" Elizabeth asked derisively. "We're a thousand miles from anywhere. Luke knows nothing. Although I realise that dreadful girl Karen has always been his informant. Are you sure she's not keen on him herself?"

Ava shook her head. "Luke doesn't find Karen attractive. In fact he's said many an unkind thing about her. Her figure, in particular. How thin she is. He uses her, that's all."

"She could tell him about your famous dance…" Elizabeth said reflectively.

"Heard about it, did you?" Ava asked. Her parents had gone to bed before then.

"Certainly did." Elizabeth laughed. "You've always been a lovely dancer, but from all accounts you excelled yourself."

Ava's eyes were glitter-bright. "You know perfectly well how a wonderful partner can raise your performance. The tango is in Varo's blood."

"I bet!" Elizabeth laughed again. "The two of you must promise a repeat performance some time." Reluctantly she rose. "The wedding was simply marvellous. And it was lovely to hear from Dev and Amelia and know they're so blissfully happy." And now it seemed to Elizabeth her beloved daughter might have found the man of her dreams. "When is Varo going home?" she asked as they walked to the door. "He's come a long way. He will want to see lots more. The Red Centre was mentioned. Uluru and Kata Tjuta. He's so enjoying himself."

"I'm not pressing him for an answer," Ava said. "Rather the reverse."

She didn't say such thoughts and accompanying fears were never far from her mind. What would Varo's inevitable return to Argentina do to their relationship, for one? That was the burning question. She had to accept conflicts would arise. Could she give up her homeland for Varo? Could she leave the people she loved? She couldn't see that far into the future. Really, it all came down to Varo. If Varo loved her, all would be well.

Elizabeth put her arm around her daughter, hugging her close. "I want you to be happy, Ava. I pray for you to be happy. You're a lovely woman—inside and out. A wonderful loving daughter. Don't let Luke Selwyn intimidate you. I know it was the case in the past, his manipulation, though you never said anything. Dev and Amelia will be back home by the separation date—the year and the day. You have me and your father. We will be with you. Staying with a loveless marriage would be like being in a prison. The divorce *will* go through, my darling. You've a top lawyer. You're going to come out of this."

"One day, Mum," Ava said, her lovely smile a touch on the melancholy side.

* * *

She had to go in search of Varo. They had seen her parents off, and had a leisurely lunch over which they'd discussed where they would go on the station that afternoon.

It was a strange time for Ava, a euphoric time. She had the feeling the whole universe had changed. Simultaneously she wouldn't be shocked if it reverted to what it had been. Love affairs always started out with high hopes. She had even had hopes for herself and Luke, but never euphoria. Euphoria was like riding an ocean wave.

She thought she might take Varo out to see Malyah Man. The extraordinary rock formation was semi-sacred to the aboriginals on the station. It was a truly amazing spectacle, some eight feet tall, and resembled an aboriginal head atop a fiery limestone column rather like a Henry Moore sculpture or the Easter Island figures. Malyah Man stood alone in the remoteness, quite a distance beyond where they had so far gone.

She had been in awe of the rock all her life. There was something daunting about it, but it was certainly a sight worth seeing. Like all the rock formations on the station it changed colour from dawn to dusk. At midday it was a furnace-red that quickly lost intensity and became a reddish brown. By the end of the day it glowed a deep purple. She had seen Malyah Man in all his colours. What he was doing out there on his own in the wilderness no one knew.

She finally found Varo in a storeroom, crouching before a cupboard.

"Come on in." He made a wide sweep of his hand.

He looked wonderful to her eyes. Blazingly alive, exuding energy. What would she do if he disappeared out of her life? The pain would be excruciating.

Everything in life has its price.

She understood that. There might be a crushing price for her behaviour, although she and Varo had not slept together as her mother might have supposed. In any case, they had both become very aware of the proximity of her parents. It was agonising not to be together, but what option did they have? The high emotion of the wedding day had taken them by storm, sweeping aside their defences. Neither had set out with the intention of deliberately seducing the other. Fate had to take responsibility for that.

And here they were again.

Quite, quite *alone*.

She moved into the well stocked room, wondering what he was doing. "Can I help?"

"I'm after a powerful torch," he explained, turning his dark head to her. "The most powerful you've got."

"They're in the drawer over there." She pointed to the opposite wall of cabinets. "There are any number of powerful torches in use around the house. We have had floods and loss of power situations. The station store supplies the workforce."

"Presente!" Varo gave a cry of satisfaction, withdrawing a handheld torch. Ava could see the flashlight comprised an LED, not an incandescent bulb. This was the most powerful version of torch they had, with a solid waterproof assembly.

It suddenly struck her what he wanted the torch for. "You want to explore the hidden cave?" Her voice rose in sharp alarm.

"Ava, Ava… I will be very careful, you understand?" He put the torch down and came to her, taking her face between his hands.

"But it could be dangerous, Varo," she protested. "Dev hasn't gone all that far."

"Well, I intend to go a little further," he said, bending his head to kiss her not once but several times—tantalising little kisses promising much more. "It's in the nature of things, *mi querida*."

"Well, please leave *me* out!" Ava wrapped her arms tightly around him, revelling in his wonderful physicality. "As I told you, I'm more than a bit claustrophobic."

"But you *must* come with me," Varo insisted. "My concern for you will control my actions. I've done risky things. I've taken chances. I am a man, after all, and I will tell you I am considered a fine mountaineer. In my university days I led a team up one of the unexplored peaks of the Andes near the Chilean border. It was an unbelievable experience. I have made the ascent of active volcano Volcán Villarrica several times over the years. Thrilling, and not what *you* would consider safe. Climbers have fallen into lava pools and crevasses."

"Ugh!" Ava shuddered. "All in a day's climb?"

"Australia is different. You do not have our Andes, which as you know connect with the mighty Rocky Mountains."

"No, but we do have our Great Dividing Range," she reminded him with a smile. "I think it's the third longest in the world. I know it bears no comparison with the mighty Andes or the Rockies, but I still say exploring our cave system might be a tad dangerous even for you."

He traced the shallow dent in her chin with his fingertip. "I swear to you, Ava, I won't do anything foolish. Why would I? I will have you waiting for me."

The critical voice inside her started up again. *It could be dangerous.*

The problem was Juan-Varo de Montalvo wasn't your everyday man. A man of action, it would be nigh on impossible to stop him.

As a safety measure they had packed hard hats. Outside the cave the sun was at its zenith, blindingly hot and bright. Inside the cave the temperature had chilled. Varo donned

his hard hat, shining the powerful torch around the cave.
The great crocodile seemed to be slithering across the roof.
The stick figures had picked up their dance.

It was quite spooky, Ava thought, shining her own torch.
God knew how many tonnes of rock were over their heads.
She couldn't help thinking of Joan Lindsay's famous story,
Picnic at Hanging Rock. The hill country was ancient, its
peaks eroded over millions of years. The thought of losing
Varo, the man she knew she loved and her guest, sent waves
of terror through her. Her heart was even bumping against
her cotton shirt.

Varo looked down at her with brilliant eyes. "Give me
your blessing."

She opened her mouth to say something, but no sound
came out.

"Do not worry. I'll be fine. One kiss before I begin."

"You're crazy," she whispered.

"About you."

They kissed open-mouthed. His tongue traced the lovely
shape of her lips. He stroked her cheek reassuringly and then
moved away to the neck of the tunnel, bending low to make
his entrance. She already knew there was a long narrow
passageway, leading to a chamber where a tall man could
stand up with his head clearing the roof by about a foot.
Dev had told her that. She also knew cave systems could
go on for miles. And that highly experienced cave explor-
ers could and did get lost. But this was a man used to high
adventure. Clearly their cave system intrigued him.

She sat down on the sand, her back against a smooth un-
painted section of the wall. It took her several moments to
realise she was holding her breath. Around her was absolute
silence. She couldn't hear Varo at all. Knowing so much
about the aboriginal people and their legends, their sacred

places and their taboo places, she began to wonder if the all-powerful spirits thought of them as trespassers. She knew if the cave turned pitch-black she would scream her head off. Maybe she and Varo would never leave here, like the party of schoolgirls who had simply vanished from the face of the earth.

Get a grip, Ava, said the voice in her head. *Too much imagination.* No harm had come to Dev, although he'd admitted he hadn't been too keen on exploring all that far. For one thing their grandfather would have been furious if he'd ever found out Dev had made the attempt. Quite simply, Dev had been the most important person in the world to their grandfather. Even then the planned heir, over their father.

Varo wasn't feeling Ava's apprehension. Body and mind were set on establishing what lay ahead. He had spent a great deal of time exploring rocky caves and slopes. Here it didn't seem especially dangerous, although the air smelled strange—as though it had been trapped in the cave system for millions of years. And the entry tunnel was easily negotiated, even if it seemed to go on too long. He realised he was on a descending slope, going deeper into the bedrock. Twelve minutes by his watch and he was able to clamber out into a large cave, with tumbled boulders like devil's marbles acting as giant stepping stones to the cave floor. This was Dev's cave.

He trained his powerful torch on the roof of the cavern. No rock paintings here. The roof looked quite smooth, as did the walls. The action of water over the millennium? Who knew? There had been an inland sea at the centre of this great continent in prehistoric times. Surely proof was in that rock drawing of the great crocodile, the fish and the sea creatures? He was a bit disappointed, however. He wanted excitement, achievement.

The atmosphere had turned several degrees colder. He pointed the torch downwards. The sand beneath his feet appeared speckled with gold.

"Fantastico!" he breathed aloud. He knew Dev had felt he had to call a halt on his exploration at this point. *He* intended to go further, but without putting himself at risk. He was acutely mindful of Ava's anxieties. This entire area that the family called the Hill Country—the aboriginals would have another name for it, like all indigenous people—he knew to be honeycombed with caves.

He trained his torch on the next narrow opening. It would be a tight squeeze for a man his size...

Ava thought of going in after him then rejected the idea. She hated confined spaces. She didn't even like travelling in an elevator on her own. Even the best had problems. She had to trust Varo's judgement just as she had trusted Dev's.

But it was close on forty minutes now. How long should she wait? She wondered how much trusting she could fit inside her chest. Men and their adventuring, always tilting at death. Women spent more time considering the dangers and the consequences. Women were much more careful. Women wouldn't start wars.

She completely ignored the fact that she had given the tough game of polo a go. Her grandfather had protested on the grounds that it was not a fitting game for a female. Not because she might injure her precious limbs. Oh, no! She hadn't complied. She'd been rather good at polo, although naturally down some levels from the top notch. She loved horses and they loved her. She didn't think there was a horse she couldn't ride.

A bird—a hawk—swooped, and then flew into the neck

of the cave. She let out a strangled screech that matched the predatory bird's, but in the next moment it had flown out again. She jumped to her feet because she was so agitated.

Sounds came first. Then the beam of the powerful flashlight.

Thank God! Varo was coming back. Her emotions were bobbing up and down like a cork in a vat.

He all but swam out of the cave. Clear of the tunnel wall, his arms shot out sideways, as if he were taking wing.

"Varo!" Her cry was both relieved and anxious.

He was swiftly on his feet. He didn't even stop to catch breath. If a man's face could be called radiant, then it was his. "You have to come back with me," he said, yanking off his hard hat and thrusting a hand through his tousled jet-black waves. "It's *fantastico*!" He caught at her hand, the skin of his face as cold as if he'd been out in a snowstorm. "I've never seen anything like it before."

"Like what?" Despite herself she felt caught up in his excitement.

"I won't tell you. You must see. I should tell you first there's a narrow passageway that turned out to be a bit of a squeeze for me, but you'll slide through it."

"Am I free to refuse?" she asked, with humour and a trace of real fear.

"Of course. But there's no danger. I don't know about further into the cave system. There could be real danger there. One would need the proper equipment. But so far so good, as they say." He reached down to pick up her hard hat. "Here—put it on. You will be safe with me, my love. Bring your torch. You can't say no, Ava. You will be missing something."

He sounded and looked as exhilarated as she imagined Howard Carter might have looked and sounded when he opened up Tutankhamen's tomb ninety years before.

Ava took the hard hat from him, settling it on her head. With Varo beside her she could conquer her fears one by one.

"Lead the way," she invited.

In the "squeeze" passageway she felt a split second of over-whelming claustrophobia. She wanted to scream, but she didn't have enough air in her labouring lungs. What did the air smell of anyway? Bizarrely, she thought of shingle at low tide. Salt, sand, a whiff of fish and sea creatures. How crazy was that?

Just as she was about to fall flat on her stomach and stay there a minute or two, the passageway opened up.

Varo was through, reaching back for her. He pulled her out with as little effort as he might expend on a child. They were standing on a huge slab of limestone roughly ten feet square—one of many flat slabs descending to the cavern floor. To Ava's astonished eyes the huge area looked like a theatre, held up by fabulous twisting pillars The sight was so fantastic, so surreal, it almost hurt her to look. Yet she felt quite secure.

She pushed her shoulders back. Her breathing eased. Varo's strong arm was locked around her. She felt there was no space between them. She had fallen so madly in love the other versions of herself had faded into the past. This was the start of a whole new Ava.

"*Vaya!* Well?" He unfastened his headgear, then hers, dropping the hard hats on the huge slab.

His vitality was like an electric field. It sent charges siz-zling through her. "Oh, my God!" she murmured, her awe mixed with reverence. "This is utterly fantasmagorical—if there is such a word."

Stalagmites, stalactites—she wasn't sure which was which—marvellous curtain-like draperies, giant toadstools apparently formed from ochre mud, others the shape of the water-lily pads that grew in such profusion over Kooraki's billabongs and lagoons, all filled the grand space. In one area there was an organ like structure she thought might thunder if it was ever played.

The smell of the sea inside the cavern was even stronger, yet there wasn't a visible drop of water about them. No shallow pools. Certainly no underground river. They were, however, over the Great Artesian Basin. The cave was as dry as ancient bones.

"These are natural heritage objects, are they not?" Varo asked, turning his lustrous eyes on her.

She nodded in wonderment. She was finding it hard to process all she was seeing. They were holding two powerful torches, but the brightness inside the chamber was hard to explain. She looked up. The sun might have been shining through a hole in the roof of the cavern, except of course it wasn't.

"Protected by law," she confirmed. "One can't break even the tiniest piece off. Which are the stalagmites? I should know."

"The ones growing vertically from the cavern floor," he replied. "The stalactites are the curtains. See how they touch each other, forming the draperies? This wonderful scene was formed by dripping or flowing water perhaps a million years ago. Your famed inland sea?" he suggested.

"It could well be," Ava said. Her whole being was aglow. "To think it has all been here for probably thousands of years. I should think the early aboriginal tribes would have known about these caves. And the rock paintings."

"The ones that did know would have died out."

"But they always passed on their legends. And what about all the sparkles on the floor of Dev's cave?"

A smile swept his dynamic face. "Fool's gold?"

She lifted her face to the mighty organ, with shifting prisms of light bouncing off its cylindrical pipes. "Do you think we should be here?" she asked softly. "This could be a sacred site for all I know."

"Frightened, are you?" There was a pronounced tease in his voice.

"Not with you. We're together." She had never said such a thing before. Never felt like this before. "Have you ever heard the legend of Lasseter's Reef, Varo?" she asked, prompted by the mystery glitter. Opal matrix had been found on the station. But no gold-bearing quartz veins. *As yet!*

His face relaxed into his devastatingly attractive smile. "I am sorry, but no," he said gently. He was gaining enormous pleasure from her reactions, and the fact she had conquered her claustrophobia. That was brave.

"Then I'll tell you the greatest mystery of our gold fields."

"I'm listening, but let's go down." He kept an arm around her, guiding her as they descended the staircase of toppled slabs. Memory was stirring. Something he had read some-where, some time. That riveting word *treasure!*

"Debate continues to this day." Ava was staring around her in a wondering way. What would Dev and Amelia make of this? She couldn't wait to tell them. "Gold was the back-bone of the nation then. There were huge gold strikes all over."

"I've heard."

"Prospectors came from all over the world." She crouched over the extraordinary "lily pads", awestruck. They might have been cast in stone over a living plant. "Harold Lasseter was a young prospector who became hopelessly lost when he was prospecting for rubies in the MacDonnell Ranges."

"That's the Red Centre?" Varo asked. He was looking

forward to seeing the great desert monuments. Ava *had* to be with him.

Ava nodded. "It was long ago—around the late 1890s. My family, the Langdons and the Devereauxes, were here, pioneering the cattle industry. Anyway, Lasseter claimed when he was found, starving and dying of thirst, he had stumbled across a fabulous reef of gold and taken samples. An Afghan camel driver actually saved his life. Three years later, restored to health, he went back with a surveyor. They claimed to have re-found the reef, taking bearings with their watches."

"Only to find when they got back to civilisation their watches were incorrect?" Varo guessed.

"You've heard this story," she said wryly.

Varo only shrugged.

"Other expeditions followed, but it was all too dangerous. Forbidding territory, and the tribes were well equipped to defend their land. Spearing of the invading white man was common, which meant the Government of the day wasn't keen on sending expeditions into the desert to be killed or die of starvation and thirst."

"Okay—you tell me this so we can go and find it?" he asked, amused.

"Many people believe the reef is out there." She was speaking now in a hushed whisper.

They began to pick their way with the utmost care across the floor of the cavern, avoiding all the extraordinary formations. The bone-dry sand crunched beneath their feet.

"This is out of this world!" Ava exclaimed, enraptured by such a spectacle.

"The best news is we are quite alone," Varo said "*Finally*. I do like your parents. I enjoyed their company. But I longed for us to be together." He put out a hand, bringing her to her feet. He tugged gently on the silk scarf that tied back her hair, releasing it in a flood of gold.

"You want to make love?" she asked, on a long, voluptuous sigh.

"Need you ask?"

The expression of tenderness in his eyes almost brought her to tears. "This could be a sacred place, Varo."

"What we feel is sacred, is it not?" he asked, very gravely. "You fall in love with me. I with you."

She expected her inner voice to step in. Only it didn't. There was nothing to explain this. Nothing to gainsay it either.

All was quiet. The fantastic formations might have been ancient statues, quietly watching on. This was a dream, not a nightmare.

"Come here to me."

Varo took her torch from her, set it down beside his so the combined lights spread their illumination all through the cavern. There were no dark shadows, only wondrous natural sculptures. Could any woman resist an invitation like this?

Ava buried her face against his chest. "You *made* me love you."

"Is that the start of a song?" he mocked gently.

She lifted her head, her heart in her eyes. "Neither of us planned this, Varo. I wasn't ready for it. It's all happened so very, very quickly."

"Can one call *destino* a bad thing?" His deep dark voice crooned gently against the shell of her ear.

"Destiny?" That was the way she saw it. "I'm in love with you, Varo," she admitted freely. "I'm in love with a man from another land."

Emotion made his voice rough. "I will never leave you, *mi querida*. You will never leave me."

"How can that be—?" She started to speak, but his mouth covered hers so passionately her heart contracted. She was consumed.

"You understand it will take a little time?" Slowly, almost dazedly, he lifted his head.

"I *will* be a divorced woman, Varo." She felt compelled to point that out. "Your parents, your sisters, your family might not approve of a divorced woman in your life."

"My family will have their say of course," he admitted without hesitation. "All families do—especially one as close as mine. But *I* make the decisions. Besides, you are an angel."

"No, I'm not!" Her jewel-like eyes blazed. She didn't want Varo to put her on a pedestal.

"Not you're not!" he agreed gently in his throat. "You're a woman. All woman. *My* woman."

His dark, dark gaze was ardent, diamond-bright. In one smooth motion he had her blue and white striped cotton shirt free of her jeans, easing it off her shoulders.

Was it her over-active imagination or was the cavern lit in a golden glow?

"You're feverish!" His mouth was gliding all over her satin smooth exposed skin. Shirt and flimsy stretch lace bra had since fallen to the sand.

"On fire," she whispered back.

Very tenderly he lowered her to the sand. It didn't feel crunchy at all. It felt more like a velvet quilt. He couldn't leave her after this. He *couldn't*. This was not only a ravishing physical experience. It was spiritual.

Varo bent his head to kiss the tears away from her eyes. "We pick our path, my beautiful Ava. Nothing feels wrong to you, does it?" he asked with marked tenderness.

"How could anything be wrong when we are together."

Ava knew now she would put up the fight of her life to hold on to her love.

Varo.

She had been too malleable too much of the time. Too afraid to reach out. She wasn't there yet. But she would be. That was her vow.

CHAPTER EIGHT

HE HAD little difficulty chartering a flight to Kooraki Station from the domestic terminal at Longreach. It cost him, but Luke had never felt so determined on something in his entire life. He wanted Ava back. He was going to get her back. And, by God, he would make her suffer when he did. Not physically—never physically. He was after all a gentleman. But he had special psychological powers over his wife.

She had as good as accepted she hadn't been a good wife to him. In his world, the *real* world, the *man* reigned. He had quickly learned how to control Ava's spirit. She was too gentle by far, too tender, too sensitive. She had always been frightened of conflict. That old bastard Gregory Langdon with his Midas touch must be answering for a lot, he thought with intense satisfaction. Ava had been terrified of her grandfather. And she hadn't been the only one. Most people had. Except for Amelia's beautiful conniving mother, who had been left a considerable fortune by her long-time lover. Great to know she was an outcast now, shunned by all.

There was no one about when he landed. He waited on the tarmac until the pilot turned the nose of the Cessna about. Then until he was taxiing down the runway to take off. He hated flying in light aircraft. As far as he was concerned light aircraft had a bad reputation.

Two sulphur-yellow helicopters were grounded to the right of the giant silver hangar emblazoned on its roof with the station's name. He strolled over to a station Jeep, saw with relief the keys were in the ignition. Why not? Who was there to steal the vehicle? The Langdons ruled this Outback kingdom. James Devereaux Langdon, his revered brother-in-law, wore authority like a cloak. Quickly he pitched his suitcase in the back, then climbed into the driver's seat. No way was he going to walk up to the homestead. It was a hell of a distance, and he had always hated the dry inland heat. The Jeep was a gift.

He had a plan in place. The Argentine was still there— a favoured guest. Elizabeth and Erik Langdon were back in Sydney. Karen always had kept him well informed. Pity she wasn't more attractive. Well, she *was* in her way, and extremely smart, but her fine-boned featured face was a bit too much on the hard side. Actually, Karen Devereaux was a genuine bitch. No friend to Ava, but she had come in handy over the years when he needed information.

His idea was not to confront his wife in anger. Dear me, no! He had to get this de Montalvo guy on his side. Perhaps Ava hadn't done anything wrong. Perhaps the Argentine hadn't done anything wrong either. To split them, thus bringing any budding relationship to a halt, he intended pouring his husbandly woes into Montalvo's ear. By and large *he* was the innocent party. He, the long-suffering husband. Ava had led him an excruciating emotional dance. Ha-ha—not the tango. He had accepted all the punishment she had meted out. The thing was he loved her. He adored her. He saw no life, no future without her.

He had few peers when it came to winning people around. He was, he knew, an unsung genius. He had a top job. No one was about to steal his wife away from him. Certainly not a South American gigolo.

The housekeeper was at the front door to greet him. No, *greet* wasn't the right word, he quickly saw. From the expression on her dark-skinned face she was tossing up whether to slam the door on him or reluctantly admit him. She ought to be dismissed.

Her liquid black eyes bored into his. "Ms Ava is not at home," she announced, clearly challenging him to dispute it.

For a moment he felt like giving her a good shove out of his way. Rude bitch! He had encountered her before. "That's all right," he returned very mildly, as though he had plenty of time. "Where is she? It's Mrs...isn't it?" He couldn't for the life of him think of her name.

She didn't supply it. For God's sake, didn't she know how a housekeeper was supposed to behave?

"I'm hoping to stay for a few days," he said, preparing to sweep past this formidable woman. "My wife and I need to talk. Perhaps you could show me my room? When are you expecting my wife back?" he asked, playing up the *wife* for all he was worth. They had been estranged for more than nine months now and time was running out. This surprise visit was very serious.

The woman gave a twirl of her hand. "I have no idea. Miss Ava is not on Kooraki at this time. She is showing a guest around Alice Springs and our most famous desert monuments."

He forced an untroubled smile. "That's nice. The Langdons are extremely hospitable people. I'm in no hurry. I have a week off to expedite a couple of outstanding matters. I'd like to see my room now, if it's no trouble? It was a long trip getting here. Lunch would be nice—in, say, an hour?"

With hidden amusement he watched the housekeeper inhale hard through her wide nostrils. But what could she do? Throw him out? He *was* Ava's husband, after all. He was being perfectly respectful. He had deliberately used the word *expedite*. To all intents and purposes he was here to agree to a divorce, throwing no objections into the pot. It was all politics. He spent much of his time pretending this and that.

Ava and Varo flew back into Kooraki late afternoon the following day. Nula Morris hadn't wasted a moment leaving a message for Ava at the hotel where they'd been staying—in separate rooms—so they were prepared for a confrontation of some sort. Luke Selwyn would never have dared to set foot on the station with the Master of Kooraki at home, but Dev and Amelia were currently in Rome.

To Varo it was quite simple. He was here to keep Ava from all harm. He wasn't concerned about Ava's husband. From what he had gleaned from Dev and Amelia, and around the station, Luke Selwyn was held in poor regard. He had been judged by one and all as an unsuitable husband for Ava. They had all known Ava had been desperate to escape an unhappy home life. But her hopes of happiness had sadly unravelled along the way.

Nevertheless Varo had not been prepared to meet such an outwardly pleasant and good-looking man. He resembled an English actor whose name eluded him—the one with the floppy fair hair and earnest blue eyes. It was obvious Luke Selwyn was still deeply emotionally involved with his beautiful wife. Indeed, when he had come downstairs to greet them his blue eyes had momentarily shone with tears. He appeared to be taking Ava's wish for a divorce with stoicism, and a considerable degree of pain that he sought to hide—or was going all out to create that impression. There was no sign whatsoever of fuming jealousy, hostility, let alone paranoid rage. Not that Ava had spoken out against her husband. He thought Ava was prepared to shoulder her own share of blame.

Only it couldn't be easy to throw one's husband aside, jettison a marriage. Selwyn would have to be some sort of ogre figure. He certainly didn't present himself as one. And he had risked coming out here, where he clearly wasn't wanted. But then things happened in a marriage. For better or worse.

Ava flatly refused to sit down opposite her husband for dinner. "We're finished, Luke," she told him firmly. "Why are you here?" She raised her elegant brows. She knew Luke was well into role-playing and she disapproved strongly.

"I hope it's not an inconvenience for me to come here, Ava. I wanted to say—I just wanted to clear up a few points."

He thought he looked the very picture of embarrassment to the Argentine standing at Ava's shoulder. De Montalvo was very tall and devilishly handsome, but not in any matinee idol way. He looked damned formidable. He had been hoping for a bit of a playboy. No such luck! The man had real charisma. And obviously, going on everything about him—his manner, his speech, his air of confident authority—he came from a privileged background. That was the big surprise.

Karen had spoken about de Montalvo as though his main attraction was phenomenal sex appeal. Indeed, she thought de Montalvo so sexy she could hardly contain herself. He could see the sex appeal, all right. But *daunting* was a better word. De Montalvo was no one's fool either. It would be an enormous coup to turn this man off Ava. But it was *possible*. Anyway, wouldn't a guy like that, who had it all, have a girlfriend back home? Hell, a string of girlfriends. He *was* a hot-blooded Latin, after all.

In the end Ava relented. He had been counting on that.

They were all adults, civilised people, weren't they? Dinner actually went smoothly, considering just the three of them sat down and there were so many subterranean currents. Nula was an excellent cook. He had to give her that. He was very particular about his food. And drink, of course. Kooraki maintained an excellent cellar.

For starters they were served quietly and unobtrusively with crab and mango salad and wafer-thin fresh coconut slices, followed by duck breast on a bed of hot steaming wild rice. An exquisite *millefeuille* with passionfruit curd was wheeled in for dessert. No complaints there.

Ava could put a decent meal together at a pinch, but she wasn't in the same class as her mother. But she was *so* beautiful, with her tender, angelic face. He felt like reaching out and slapping it. Not able to do that—he could just imagine how de Montalvo would react—he continued drawing the Argentine out about life in his own country as though he were really interested. They had already discussed Uluru and the Olgas, for God's sake. Been there, done that.

Of course the two of them had slept together. There was no doubt whatsoever in his mind. Ava had an astonishing *glow* about her. A luminescence that lit up her blonde beauty. Unfaithful bitch! How he didn't leap to his feet and savage them both with furious accusations he didn't know. Or perhaps he did. The upshot might have been de Montalvo knocking him flat. Instinct told him the Argentine would be quite the wrong man to cross. And he looked so damned athletic—physically superior at every level.

But did he want Ava? That was the burning question. Or did he have an affair in every part of the world he wandered into? It was hard to gauge the Argentine's thoughts. The coal-black eyes were brilliant but quite unfathomable. Surely it couldn't be an act, de Montalvo's displaying interest in what he had to say? Then again, he had been told more than once he was an excellent conversationalist. De Montalvo had even asked him if he had ever played polo. He had answered regretfully that he had never had the time. What he'd actually meant was, had he ever considered playing the game of polo he would have needed his head read. Life and limb were much too precious.

Now all he had to do was keep his cool, act brain-dead in relation to their trip together and his wife's scandalous behaviour, and get de Montalvo alone. He wasn't sure if he should play his trump card. It was a horrendous lie, and it could prove dangerous, but he suspected he might have to use it. He had to change the Argentine's opinion of Ava, who was still *his* wife. That called for drastic measures.

All's fair in love and war, old son!

Fortune smiled on him. He had to control a mad desire to fall to his knees and give thanks. By an incredible stroke of luck one of the Langdon circle—a near neighbour Siobhan O'Hare, the one who had lusted after Langdon but lost out to Amelia—took a trip over to Kooraki to visit. No doubt to find out if the honeymooners were surviving the honeymoon, he thought waspishly. Obviously hope sprang eternal. If ever the marriage broke down, the ever-faithful Siobhan would be waiting in the wings. God knew how she thought she could ever replace the glorious, voluptuous Amelia. But most women had inferior reasoning powers.

Juan-Varo de Montalvo, *hidalgo* that he was, was on hand to say hello to Ava's visitor—who, let's face it, looked at de Montalvo with a suspicion she couldn't hide in her eyes. Why was the glamorous Argentine still on Kooraki? Shouldn't he have already gone on his way?

He knew exactly the thoughts that were ticking over in little Siobhan's head. Ava was still married. To *him*. Luke Selwyn. Blue-chip lawyer. What was *he* doing on Kooraki, for that matter? Initially she had looked as though she had stumbled into a war zone, but with his natural charm of manner he had made it clear there was no animosity between him and Ava. She was permitted the sneaking feeling he was secretly devastated, but hiding it like a man.

To celebrate this wonderfully timely intervention he suggested to the Argentine they take a run around the station in the Jeep that was parked out at the front.

"Might be my last time here," he said, with a pained air of regret. "Ava said at dinner she intended taking you out to see Malyah Man?" He had found the weird sandstone monument bloody terrifying, but he had to get de Montalvo somewhere out there, where they wouldn't be interrupted. Malyah Man was ready to hand. "I could show you," he said, giving the other man a friendly smile.

Varo stared down at Selwyn, wondering what was going on beneath the convivial exterior. The man could be a sociopath for all he knew. He knew a sociopath's destructive qualities were not easily recognised. They could be charming when required. He had heard Ava's husband was a very self-centred man. Whatever Selwyn was, he knew he could handle him.

"You have a camera?" Luke asked, rubbing his chin.

"Sure."

"You might like to take photos," he suggested. "It's an incredible structure—rather like those Easter Island statues. The girls can enjoy morning tea and a chat without us around. We'll be back in little over an hour. It really is an exceptional sight."

When de Montalvo went off in search of Ava he stood in the Great Hall, rocking in his boots. He had gained valuable time with his wife's lover. He had to make the most of it. He would really like old Malyah Man to topple and fall in a great crush on the Argentine. He wouldn't mind that at all. But he knew it wasn't going to happen.

Ava wasn't at all happy Varo had agreed to go for a trip around the station with Luke. But what could she do? If she said she didn't want him to go with Luke, it might appear to him as if she had something to hide. Her way to prevent Luke from giving his side of the story.

She hesitated, her mind racing. Luke was up to no good. She knew him too well. He would be out to squeeze the last little drop of sympathy he could out of Varo. That was the role he had chosen to play. The wronged husband. Helpless to keep a wife who no longer wanted him or needed him. She came from a rich family, but now she had no sense of dependency on anyone—much less her husband. Her grandfather, thinking she would never be able to stand on her own two feet, had made her totally independent for life.

Ava's nerves were jangling. She couldn't help feeling a creeping apprehension. If Luke couldn't have her, Luke would be out to destroy her. Or her one big chance at happiness.

"Well?" Varo questioned humorously, as she hesitated.

"I had intended showing you Malyah Man myself." She tried not to show any trace of her inner agitation.

Varo shrugged. "Then Selwyn and I will go some place else. There—that's decided."

Siobhan's clear voice piped up from the seating area behind them. She could feel Ava's tension. And why wouldn't she be tense? It was obvious to her there was something between Ava and the dashing Argentine. Luke Selwyn must be feeling it too—not that she had ever liked him. But one *could* feel pity. "Oh, Malyah Man is marvellous, Varo. You must see it before you go home," she enthused.

Ava took a breath. "Well, I suppose if Luke wants to show you, then go by all means."

"Not if you're upset about it?" Varo took no heed of the overly curious neighbour. It was all he could do not to draw Ava into his arms, hold her tight against his chest.

Ava raised a smile. The last thing she should appear was anxious. Or, even worse, *guilty*. "Of course not. Don't be long."

"Just over an hour, Selwyn said."

"Lunch at one," she reminded him, turning to her uninvited guest, whose ears and eyes were agog. "You're staying, of course, Siobhan?"

Siobhan pinkened up. "Love to," she gushed. She couldn't wait to tell her mother all about this. The Argentine was so sexy she felt a throb in her own blood.

Poor old Luke!

Blazing sunlight flooded the plains. On the far side of them the jagged outline of the ancient Hill Country stood fierily against a cobalt sky. Never until the day he died would Varo forget the sublime experiences he and Ava had shared.

He had seen many extraordinary and extreme sights so far in his life, taken many adventurous journeys. He and two friends had once loaded their backpacks and climbed to the top of a spurting volcano, where they'd had to don masks and protective gear. With the same companions he had gone extreme white-water rafting in turbulent waters. He had visited Antarctica—amazing beyond belief—and the Galapagos Islands with their wonderful evolutionary marvel the giant Galapagos Turtle and magnificent marine iguanas—the only sea-going lizards in the world.

He had followed the Argentine revolutionary Che Guevara's journey on his own motorcycle, half believing in the Curse of Che. It was well documented that the Bolivian politicians and generals who had shared responsibility for his death had later met with violent accidental deaths themselves. He had visited all the wonders North and South America could offer. He had seen the great awe-inspiring desert monuments of Central Australia.

But he had never before made passionate love to a woman while lying on the velvety sand of an ancient cavern with fantastic pre-historic formations gazing down at them. It was an experience that had great meaning for him, because he knew the passion he felt for Ava was true.

Luke Selwyn's voice jolted him out of his lingering euphoria. "Almost there," he announced, with a sidelong grin. "He looks a cantankerous old bugger, Malyah Man. I know Ava was always frightened of him. But then Ava has phobias." He paused for a moment, gnawing his lip. "I love her, you know."

"Love her or want to hold on to her?" Varo asked bluntly, glancing across at Ava's husband.

"Of course I want to hold on to her," Luke freely admitted, almost banging his fist on the wheel. "What man wouldn't? She's so beautiful."

"She is. But she has many other qualities to be greatly admired," Varo clipped off.

"Of course, of course," Luke agreed at once. "She's the loveliest person in many ways. But it broke my heart that she didn't want children. I know what was at the bottom of it, of course," he said with deep regret. "For all the fact she was a Langdon, she had a miserable childhood. She was terrified of her grandfather. He was an immensely powerful, tyrannical man."

Varo felt his heart flip over in his chest. Ava didn't want children? Could Selwyn, who appeared genuinely brokenhearted, possibly lie about something like that?

He suddenly remembered how his eldest sister, Sophia,

had sworn she would never go through the experience of childbirth again after Alvaro, his nephew, had been born after a prolonged and difficult labour. Sophia, however, had changed her mind. She had brought adorable little Isabella into the world, with none of the trauma associated with Alvaro's birth. Maybe his beautiful Ava felt threatened by the pain of childbirth? Men couldn't totally understand. He had friends who had been overwhelmed by their wives' first pregnancy. Over-protective, over-anxious—living the pregnancy. He felt he might be like that too. One's wife would be the most important woman in the world.

"Are you okay?" Luke was asking with concern. "You've gone quiet on me."

"Have I? I was thinking about my sister, actually," he said, choosing his words. "You were telling me Ava doesn't want children?"

Luke took a deep breath before continuing—a man trying to calm himself. "I was. It blew me away. There was never a hint of it before we were married. I naturally assumed Ava would want children as much as I do. My parents were longing for a grandchild. But Ava's attitude firmed with every passing day. I wanted her to have counselling about it, but she flatly refused. Please don't think I didn't try to calm her, Varo. I believe she really fears childbirth. Some women do. It got to the point where I was getting a bit paranoid myself. And then we discovered she *was* pregnant. My God!" he said quietly. "I was the *enemy* from that moment. Something must have gone wrong with her contraception method. It happens. I have to confess when she told me I couldn't help but be *thrilled*. The longed-for child! I promised Ava I would do anything—everything—to support her, that we would get her safely through pregnancy together—" He broke off, overcome by emotion.

The towering figure of Malyah Man loomed ahead, but

Varo was seeing it through a blinding haze. He had to grit his teeth. Even his breathing was constricted. Out of the clear blue he was abruptly unsure of anything. He might just as well have stepped off a cliff. Ava was in his blood-stream. He had come to think of her as part of his destiny. But what did he *really* know of her? Indeed, what did she know of *him*? The two of them had been swept away by the force of their feelings. It was a classic case of the heart ruling the head, the fatal *coup de foudre*. Still, a big part of him was highly suspicious of Selwyn, the self-styled wronged husband.

"Let's park the Jeep first," Selwyn suggested, like a man trying to buy time. "I can't go on for the moment. I get too damned upset. Ava was the centre of my world. A child would have made us complete. I was *absolutely* certain Ava would come around. I really felt that her peculiar fears would pass. A kind of phobia, I suppose. Not all women long to have a child. Many elect to go childless these days. Some don't even want a man as soon as they become financially independent. Sorry if I'm drawing you into this, Varo," he said, with an apologetic half-smile. "But it's good to be able to talk to someone. You know—like strangers on a train. I can't talk to my parents. I wouldn't dream of talking to our friends—"

"But surely you have Karen Devereaux's ear?" Varo broke in, feeling the heat of anger but fighting it down. He wanted to grab hold of Sewlyn, drag him out of the vehicle, beat the truth out of him. Yet his question was asked suavely, with a touch of sarcasm.

Selwyn responded at once, as though anxious to clear that point up. "As though I'd talk to Karen about Ava!" he exclaimed, lifting one hand off the wheel and throwing it up for emphasis. "Poor old Karen has been competing with my wife all her life. She is horrendously jealous of Ava. She has every reason to be. No, I couldn't confide in Karen," he said ruefully, shaking his head, "although she likes to keep in touch. She rings me from time to time. Karen doesn't trust many people, but she trusts me."

Varo kept silent. His nerves were drawing tighter every second. He could see Selwyn wanted to tell him more. He wasn't at all sure how he would react. He would never have thought for a moment Ava might not want children. He had assumed she was a woman who loved children as he did. Now he was no longer sure of anything. He would bide his time, hear Selwyn out.

Like the vast desert monuments Uluru and Kata Tjuta, rising as they did out of the featureless plains, so too did Malyah Man. The striking sandstone pillar was set in the middle of nowhere, surrounded by grassy flats that were thickly sewn with some pink flowering succulent he later learned was *parakeelya*—an aboriginal word. The stock liked to feed on it.

"Fantastic, isn't it?" Selwyn commented, as they stepped out of the Jeep. "Ava never would come here alone."

"So you said." Varo walked to the foot of the ancient formation—probably the only remaining relic of some pre-historic plateau. He tried to keep his mind focused on the natural formation. It reminded him strongly of tribal sculpture. African or Toltec-Mayan. There was a great dignity to the extraordinary "human" head. Certainly it wasn't a welcoming figure. It was a *guardian* figure. He was sure of it.

Selwyn was somewhere behind him, obviously keeping his distance.

Varo turned around. "It seems you suffer your own apprehension?" he said with a vague taunt.

"Well, he *is* a scary-looking guy." Selwyn tried a laugh that didn't quite come off. But to prove himself he moved over to where Varo was standing. "I hope I haven't upset you?" he asked, studying the Argentine's handsome profile. It was set in stern lines.

"In what way?" Varo glanced sideways, stared the other man down.

"A man would have to be blind not to notice you're attracted to my wife," Luke offered, holding up his hands in peace.

"I would think any man that laid eyes on her would be attracted," Varo returned. He rested a reverent hand against the sandstone folds of Malyah Man's "cloak".

Luke sighed. "I just wanted you to get things right," he said. "There's so much I could tell you."

"Go right ahead," Varo invited, covering the deep stabs of anger.

Luke lowered his voice, as though talking to himself. "I have to get this off my chest, Varo. It's been killing me. You have no idea how lost and wretched I feel. I'm a man who believes in marriage. I believed in *my* marriage. I love Ava with everything I am. Body, heart and soul."

"Apparently you weren't able to convey your deep feelings to her?" Varo said, shooting his companion a derisive look.

"You don't understand." Luke rubbed fiercely at the nape of his neck. Something had stung him, dammit! "The pregnancy ended in catastrophe." His voice dropped to a hoarse whisper. "Ava—my beautiful Ava, who looks like an angel—aborted our child."

This time Varo couldn't control himself. He lashed out on instinct, grabbing hold of Selwyn by his smarting neck. "You're lying," he rasped.

He looked so daunting Luke Selwyn moaned aloud. "Please…" Luke struggled to get free, but the Argentine held him fast. He was inches taller, fitter, stronger, and his black eyes were glittering with rage. "You don't *want* to believe it. I understand. I *have* to tell you. I refused to believe it too. Only it's too true. Ava aborted our child. She confided in Karen. At least Karen was always there for her. Her family don't know. I *know* it sounds appalling. It *is* appalling. I realise now I shouldn't have told you. This is something I should have kept to myself. Forgive me, but I thought you deserved to know. I'm sorry."

Varo didn't loosen his grip. On the contrary, he strengthened it, knowing he was spinning out of control. Selwyn was lying. It couldn't possibly be true. Ava had aborted a child? Unthinkable. He *loved* her. He knew now he had never fallen in love before. How could he not be shaken to his very core?

"Varo?" Luke Selwyn's voice quaked. He had taken a risk and now it looked as if his desperate ploy had backfired. His heart started to thump. He had never felt so exposed. For all he knew the Argentine was going to kill him.

Out of nowhere a hot, gusting wind suddenly blew up. It was so fierce Luke felt a kind of desperation to find shelter. Not so the Argentine, who seemed to be part of it all. Was a desert storm about to roll over them? The Outback was such a dangerous, unpredictable place.

Even as he wondered, de Montalvo thrust him away as if he was beneath contempt.

How dared he?

Luke fell heavily, wondering if something terribly untoward was on its way. His wife's lover, of all people, intended to beat the living daylights out of him. And in the middle of a dust storm. They might have been in the Sahara. He could taste red dust in his mouth, clogging it, preventing speech. He looked up, as if impelled. It was a mistake. At that precise moment a fist-sized rock broke away from the towering sandstone formation, sending him into a cowering position. The rock appeared to hang for a split second in mid-air, before it fell with a clunk on his head—although he was covering it, and his ears.

Hell and damnation!

He felt the throb. There was probably a horrible amount of blood.

For a second even Varo was transfixed. The wind that had gusted up so violently in the next minute had fallen away. It was a perfectly clear day. Not a cloud in the densely blue sky. He looked to Selwyn, huddled on the ground. "Are you okay?" He wasn't going to offer comfort, but he had to check on the man.

"I'm not right at all!" Selwyn yelled, spluttering and muttering invectives. "The blasted rock hit me." He staggered to his feet, holding a hand to the side of his head.

"I assure you, *I* didn't throw it," Varo said, turning to stare up at the regal desert monument. "Maybe Malyah Man didn't like what you were saying?" he said, with a hard, cutting laugh.

"Don't be ridiculous!" Luke examined his right hand. It was streaked with blood. He would have thought the blood would be more copious…

"Better get it cleaned up," Varo suggested with no trace of sympathy. "I'll drive."

"It's *hurting*, I tell you." Selwyn was now holding his head with two hands. He kept moaning, a continuing stream of colourful expletives flowing from his lips.

"Could have been worse," said Varo, giving Malyah Man a parting salute. He had seen many strange things at different times, but nothing the likes of that.

Selwyn was already sprinting away to the Jeep, obviously fearing a barrage of rocks.

I can't—won't—believe what he has told me.

Yet how could he ask her? If it were the truth she would be mortally wounded, exposed. A lie and she would be furious with him for even giving it a moment's credence. Either way, he was compelled to find out.

But what if it is true? It will change everything.

He couldn't begin to go there. There were life-changing moments along the way.

Selwyn was still moaning as they made their way into Kooraki's homestead. Ava, on trigger alert pretty well the whole time they had been away, was on hand to meet them in the Great Hall.

She wore a smile that faded the moment they entered the front door. "What on earth has happened?" She looked from Varo to her husband. She hardly recognised him. Luke stared back glassy eyed, his fair hair standing up in tufts, streaks of red dust all over his face.

"I'll tell you what happened." He drew a harsh, rasping breath. "Montalvo here seems to find it a joke. A big rock fell off that pillar. Size of a meteor, it was. It hit me on the side of the head. It could have *killed* me." Real tears glinted in his eyes.

Varo didn't mean to, but he laughed. "Actually, I really and truly believe it was Malyah Man who pitched it at you," he said, with no trace of humour. Indeed his temper was rising.

"You're saying a piece of sandstone fell off the monument? Is that it?" Ava asked, feeling sorry for the usually impeccable Luke. He looked such a mess he might have gone through a turbulent experience.

"Not *fell* off," Luke gritted. "The bastard aimed it right at me," he said, setting about putting his hair to rights. "Don't look so surprised, darling. You were always frightened of the thing."

"In *awe* of, Luke," Ava corrected, seeing Varo visibly tauten at the "darling". "I didn't think Malyah Man was *threat-*

ening. Well, not to me. But I wouldn't have offended him for the world." Ava's eyes met Varo's. "You okay?" she asked.

Something more had happened out there. She could tell. There was something *different* about Varo. She couldn't place it. But it was in the quality of his brilliant black gaze. It was as if he was looking at her with fresh eyes. Luke would do anything to sully her good name. The possibility he had attempted to do so was real. She didn't have an inkling what he might have said.

"I keep on the right side of the Ancients too," Varo said.

Ava was having trouble even thinking about Luke and his cracked head. Up until the time they had left, Luke had been playing the good guy. That alone made her stomach contract with nerves. Luke simply *wasn't* a good guy. He was a man who liked to get square. A man who would always seek revenge for the slightest hurt or word out of place. What had he said to Varo that made him look at her differently? What was there *to* say, for God's sake? She had always been gentle, respectful, restrained. She had never looked sideways at another man, even when she'd known plenty of men looked at her.

Finally she threw out an impatient hand. "Let's get you cleaned up, Luke, shall we? Is it painful?" God knew, Luke was no super-hero. He had always made a terrible patient, even with a head cold. "Do you think it might need a few stitches?"

"Of course it doesn't," Varo broke in, sounding incredulous. "It was more in the nature of a shot across the bows. Let's hope it worked."

Ava's eyes swept Varo. She dearly wanted to know exactly what Varo had meant by that, but she couldn't ask him there and then. It would have to wait for later. Or maybe she would never find out?

Luke was complaining wanly that he needed "peace and quiet". He could have his peace and quiet. He could stay the night, but she had organised the first leg of his trip back to Sydney for the following day. Station supplies were being flown in mid-morning. Luke could fly out with the freight plane. He could take care of himself after that. She still didn't know why he had come. They had discussed nothing. No doubt he was biding his time.

Luke was. He moved off in the direction of the first-aid room, comforted by the fact his ploy was actually working. He'd got the bandwagon rolling. All he had to do was sit back and watch proceedings. Innocent or guilty, it was a well-documented fact mud stuck. He could see how upset the Argentine was, even if he was doing a great job of keeping his feelings under wraps. Particular lies had a huge advantage. How could Ava ever prove her innocence? She could protest, sure. But would de Montalvo believe her? Would *anyone* believe her? He knew he had Karen on side. Karen would back him. Uphold his lie. You had to understand Karen's powerful jealousy of her cousin. *He* did. It had worked for him in the past. Lies could and did ruin affairs of the heart.

Luke felt no pang of guilt. Ava was his wife. She would take her punishment and then they could get on with life. The Argentine was a man who would want children. Probably a dozen or more. De Montalvo's perceptions of his angelic Ava had already shifted. He had almost heard the crash as Ava had fallen off her pedestal.

Serve her right!

He also blamed her for that whack on the head. People liked to pretend there were no such things as spirits and guardian figures. They should visit the Outback. He would swear he'd heard old Malyah Man make a deep throaty sound like *yahggh* as the rock began to fall. Weren't the old Kadaitcha Men supposed to have hissed that over their dying victims?

* * *

There was no opportunity for Ava to speak to Varo. Lunch was served, and Luke had recovered sufficiently to leave his sickbed. She could see he wasn't altogether happy with salad Niçoise and seared Tasmanian salmon escalopes. No starters. There was, however, a lemon tart to save the day.

Siobhan gave him lots of sympathy, thinking someone had to. The Argentine had a hard impatience etched on his stunning face. Ava was trying to hide some upset. "It's a wonder you weren't concussed," she said in a show of solidarity. Her tone was sugary at times, even cloying.

Luke frowned. "Perhaps I *am*." His injury was still hurting. He would need another couple of painkillers. He had to ready himself for a little talk with his wife. In his head he was tweaking it. All a man had to do was stick to his guns.

"One never knows," Siobhan pondered, looking towards her silent hostess. "When I was little I toppled head-first off a trampoline. Everyone thought I was fine but I had a concussion."

Luke didn't respond. He was always bored with problems outside his own.

Ava had to stop herself from sighing aloud. Siobhan was overdoing the sympathy. Was it deliberate? She could see Varo stir restlessly. The sooner Siobhan was on her way the better. She had flown over in her father's helicopter. Siobhan was Outback born and bred. A woman of the land. She would make a grazier cattleman an excellent wife. Of course she had been in love with Dev for years. Still was. Ava had been reminded of that constantly, with Siobhan's questions about the honeymooners. Ava hoped Siobhan would get over Dev soon. There had only ever been one woman for Dev. That woman was his wife.

CHAPTER NINE

VARO offered to drive Siobhan to Kooraki's airstrip, which seemed to cheer her immensely. She blushed.

Ava, however, spoilt the twosome by saying she would come too. After Siobhan had flown off home she would suggest to Varo they go for a drive. Maybe back to Malyah Man, as he appeared to be active. She was desperate to know what the barely perceptible change in his manner was all about. But it was there. The familiar easy charm hadn't been as much in evidence over lunch, although he had responded to all of Siobhan's thirty or so questions. One might have thought Varo came from an unknown part of the planet about which Siobhan knew nothing...

"All right, then. Goodbye." Siobhan smiled up into Varo's handsome face. "I expect you will be going home soon, Varo?"

"No, no—not *soon*," he responded, drawing out the *soon*, knowing Siobhan was storing up all she had seen and heard for relaying her family.

His response cut the goodbyes short.

Siobhan climbed into her Bell helicopter and in no time at all ascended into the wild blue yonder.

Ava looked at Varo, asking rather hesitantly, "Would you like to go for a drive?"

"As you wish," he answered smoothly.

It wasn't the answer she wanted. "Is something wrong?"

"Why would you think that?" he parried.

She gave a short laugh. "I've seen you in different moods, Varo. Sometimes I allow myself to believe I know what you're thinking."

"So what am I thinking now?"

A sudden uncharacteristic anger took hold of her. Her eyes flashed like jewels. "It's Luke, isn't it? What did he say to you?"

"What could he say?" Varo shrugged, not knowing which way to go with this. He would be so glad to be rid of Selwyn. He was even glad Siobhan O'Hare had flown off home.

"He sees you as a rival," Ava said hotly. They were, she realised with a shock, on the verge of their first argument. "Please don't answer my questions with a question, Varo. He said something to upset you. That seems clear to me. He may not have exhibited that side of him, but Luke is an extremely possessive man." Even the words in her mouth tasted bitter. "You didn't get into a fight, did you?"

Varo's voice was amused and disgusted. "Believe me, Malyah Man struck your husband the blow. I didn't have to do a thing."

"So you're not going to tell me?" Ava said. Her whole body felt as if it was going into a dejected slump.

He couldn't help touching her cheek. Her skin was as soft as a flower petal. He could smell the scent of her skin. Wound up as he was, he still wanted to take her in his arms, hold her body in an arc of intense pleasure tautly against him. Instead he said, "Let me get you out of the sun. We can't afford to bake your beautiful skin."

Ava didn't say anything until they were almost at the Jeep. "I don't want to go back to the house, Varo," she said in a strained voice. "Not with Luke there." This time her voice registered her disdain.

"So we go for a drive." Varo held the passenger door, waiting for her to get in before he closed it.

He took his time walking around to the driver's side. Luke Selwyn's disclosures had shocked him to the core. He couldn't deny that. At the same time he couldn't accept them either. His beautiful Ava not wanting children. Let alone cruelly terminating a pregnancy. He couldn't imagine the overriding guilt a woman might feel. But the Ava he knew seemed utterly guilt-free. One part of him wanted to tell Ava what Selwyn had said; the other part urged him to remain silent. Selwyn could be an utter scoundrel, a pathological liar. His reasoning would be if *he* couldn't have Ava no one else would. He couldn't bear to see Ava upset, the lovely colour gone from her face. But he actually feared he would do more harm than good confiding in her.

"So, where to?" he asked, putting the vehicle into gear.

She touched her slender fingers to her forehead. "Blue Lagoon," she said jaggedly. "We can sit on the bank beneath the trees. I know you're finding it hard to talk to me, Varo. And I know there's a reason. Luke told you something about me that has you terribly disappointed in me. In all fairness, don't you think you should tell me so I can defend myself?" she appealed to him.

Varo turned a grave face to her. She had a point. "I could be doing entirely the wrong thing, Ava," he said after a moment's consideration, "but I need to ask you. Have you ever been pregnant?"

Ava felt her heart jump in her breast. There was a long and awful ringing silence. Luke had told Varo she had fallen pregnant at some time? She literally couldn't speak she was trying so hard to control her outrage. "Excuse me—would I have kept that from you?" she demanded, fully communicating her anger.

"I don't really know, Ava," he answered quietly. And he

didn't. He wasn't by nature a judgemental man. And this was the woman he loved. "It is, after all, your business. I can understand if you had a miscarriage you might not like to talk about it. The memory could be too painful."

Ava was torn between bursting into tears and ordering him to stop the vehicle so she could jump out. "You hit Luke, didn't you?" she accused him. "Not that Luke wouldn't have had it coming."

"Would a jaguar swat a fly?" Varo returned bluntly. "I certainly wanted to—but, no, the rock fell away from the sandstone pillar. I watched it. For a split second it was stationary in mid-air, and then it dropped with a satisfactory crunch on your husband's head."

"My husband?" That hurt. Ava stared straight head. "He's *my husband* now?"

"He *is* your husband," Varo pointed out quietly.

"And you're my lover?" she asked with surprising fierceness. The writing was already on the wall. She was going to lose Varo. One way or another Luke had seen to that.

"I'm very seriously involved, Ava. We both know that." He turned off the main track, driving too fast towards the chain of lagoons. But what was in their way? These were the vast empty plains. Varo sensed she wanted to get out of the Jeep. He was finding it desperately confining himself.

"Involved? Is that the precise word?" Ava was losing the battle to keep her voice steady. "Not in love with? No? You prefer *involved*?"

"You haven't answered my question." The expression on Varo's striking face was unreadable. "I can understand if you kept it from me. You weren't sure how I would deal with it. How I would react."

"How you would react?" Ava exclaimed, her lovely face suddenly flushed with blood. She closed her eyes tight, shaking her head from side to side.

Varo believes Luke, that miserable, beastly liar. Don't men always stick together?

Luke was out to harm her in the most horrible way. He *knew* she had fallen in love with Varo. How could she hide it? Even she knew there was a special glow about her. Now she had to suffer for her perceived betrayal. She could picture the two of them talking out in the desert. Luke playing the tortured husband to the hilt. Varo feeling horrified and let down because she had kept such an event from him. She could see the residual anger still in Varo's brilliant eyes. If he hadn't actually made a physical attack on Luke he had erupted, not far off it.

"Stop the Jeep, Varo," she said furiously, and then made a huge attempt to lower her voice. "I want to get out. It seems you don't know me at all."

Varo ignored the order. He threw out a strong restraining arm across her breasts. "Sit still," he said tautly. "We're almost there."

Even the birds seemed to be singing melancholy songs. Ava stalked away from Varo down to the water's edge. This beautiful lagoon had always calmed her. Here she and Varo had sunk beneath its glittering emerald surface to steal heavenly kisses out of sight. She looked for a long time at the glorious flotilla of water lilies that steeped the lagoon in so much beauty. Nut grass and little wildflowers of flashing colours wove a sweet-scented tapestry, cloaking one area of the pale ochre sands. She had always thought this particular lagoon cast a primeval spell, but today it couldn't calm the tumult of her mind.

What else did Luke say while he was at it? She had been unfaithful? Not once but several times? Of course he had forgiven her. He could even have gone the whole hog and suggested he might not have been the father of the child? The child that never was.

She wouldn't put anything past Luke.

"Ava!" Varo called to her.

She turned back to where he was standing, in the shade of a line of feathery acacias. Such a wonderfully charismatic man. She loved him with all her heart. It was a hot, sultry, breezeless day. Shade would be welcome. Earlier in the day she had heard a series of muted thunderclaps that just as suddenly stopped. It was possible they would have a short, sharp afternoon shower. It might even be accompanied by a burst of hail. There were a few big, tumbled clouds appearing on the horizon in a peacock-blue sky.

"Let's sit down," Varo said, not knowing how to proceed exactly if Ava wouldn't confide in him. "I'm sorry if I've upset you."

Ava sighed deeply, thinking the wonderful harmony that had existed between them was as good as wrecked. She gave a raised right hand gesture, almost signifying defeat, and then sank onto the warm dry sand, drawing her legs up and clasping her arms around her jeans-clad knees.

Varo put out his hand, turning her head to him. His long fingers had a life of their own. They caressed the satin smoothness of her cheek and jawline. "Talk to me," he urged quietly.

Ava jerked her head away more forcefully that she'd intended. Her long blonde hair broke out of its clasp, spilling down her back and over one shoulder. "About what?" she asked bleakly.

"The truth. That's all I ask," he replied gravely.

Her eyes were gleaming with unshed tears. Luke had pushed all her buttons. He knew how she would react. Wind her up and let her go. "Which implies you believe I haven't been entirely honest with you?" she countered angrily. "For that matter, have *you* been entirely honest with *me*, Varo?" She was going out on the attack she was so overwrought. "Have I learned *everything* I need to know about you? You're nearly thirty years of age. You're not only a striking-looking man—a man who would compel the eyes of women—you're a man of strong passions, sexual vigour, high intellect. It's inconceivable you haven't had many affairs these past years, which you naturally don't want to expose. It's even possible you could have fathered a child and not known anything about it. It has happened countless times before today."

Varo too felt anger spurt into his veins. Anger Luke Selwyn's disclosures had caused to erupt. Now this! "Don't insult my good name, Ava," he said curtly. "I won't allow it—even from you. If a young woman had fallen pregnant to me she would have known to come to me. I would never desert such a woman, the mother of my child. However, no such woman exists. I've had my affairs. Of course I have. But I had come to believe I had never truly been in love."

"Past tense?" she said bitterly.

"It's not *me* I wish to talk about, Ava," he said, trapping her hand and holding it fast. "I have been entirely honest with you. I am, I hope, a man of honour. I was brought up to be. You are changing the subject."

"The subject being that I was pregnant to Luke?" she said hotly. "I lost my baby and I neglected to tell you about it? What is it you want me to say?"

"I've told you. I only want the truth."

"And you get to ask the questions?" The bitter note rang in her voice. She loved him so much and he didn't trust her.

"When did this happen?" he asked, feeling her anguish, desperate to understand.

At that point Ava totally lost it. She raged out of control. Her right hand—the hand nearest him—came up with the full intention of slapping his dark, handsome and arrogant face. Only he caught her wrist, bringing her arm down to her side.

"Let go of me." She couldn't endure his touching her. She began to struggle wildly, only he continued to hold her captive.

"Do not be frightened. I would never hurt you." Still, there was a little flame in his lustrous eyes. "I should never have asked you this."

"No, you *shouldn't*!" She managed to get in a sharp little punch to his chest.

The thought of losing him filled her with dread. But it was inevitable, wasn't it? She was doomed to losing the only man she could ever love. She didn't know what was happening to her because all of a sudden she was fighting him, her face flushed, her movements frantic. Anger and hopeless desire were mixed up inside her. Her every movement held an erotic charge. Not only to her. But to him. Their desire for each other was like a powerful drug that raced unchecked through the bloodstream.

Of course with his man's strength he triumphed. She was soon lying flat on her back, her body pinned to the sand. It felt much coarser than the velvety sand of the cave. Varo loomed over her, holding her down as easily as if she were a child.

He was breathing heavily, biding his time until the wild tumult of passion that was inside him miraculously cooled. This was Ava, and he was treating her with hard male dominance. The tiny top button of her pink cotton shirt had come undone. As she struggled so did the next. Now her lacy bra was exposed, and the shadowed cleft between her white breasts. His head was swimming. Her body was exquisite. He needed it so badly he almost felt like pleading for it.

"Are you going to let me up?" Her clear voice challenged him. This was a new side of Ava.

"The moment your anger passes," he announced very tensely. "A woman has never attempted to slap my face before."

"Even when you badly needed it?"

A violent hunger was washing through her. She wanted him to take her. Drive into her. Leave his brand. No way could she deny it. She was simply playing sex games. Desire was never far from them—even now, when there was so unexpectedly furious anger. The fury was actually inciting them. And it wouldn't go away. It was pumping strongly through both of them. She thought she couldn't stand it, but her body's response was just the opposite.

Still holding her arms, Varo sought her beautifully shaped sensuous mouth. He kissed her deeply, passionately, until she stopped struggling and was quiet while his hands moved over her. She should have been shamed by her surrender. Instead her senses were so exquisitely sharpened she abandoned herself to this feverish sexual onslaught. He was immensely desirable to her. Her arms came around him. Locked.

I'll never let you go.

The reasoning part of Varo was stunned by his intense hold on her delicate woman's body. Only she was egging him on, glorying in his tight embrace, even if they both remained grimly silent. There were no tender words of love. Tenderness had no place here. The hunger was boundless; the opportunity to make the other suffer as they suffered…

They were naked, their limbs tangled, bodies forming, re-forming, responding to their own rhythms that nevertheless matched perfectly. Her long blonde hair was wildly mussed. Together they were caught in a tempestuous love dance with a total lack of inhibition, willing slaves to the senses. But what kept Ava from screaming out how much she loved him? What kept Varo from responding with great ardour how much he loved her? Both were stubbornly holding on to the raw hurt and confusion Luke Selwyn had sparked.

They were one body. He brushed hard against the swollen bud of her clitoris, augmenting the pleasure. Then he was buried so deep inside her she gave an involuntary cry that swiftly softened into satiated little gasps. At such a crucial point, when nothing else existed outside of the pounding waves of pleasure and excitement, she could do nothing other than cry out his name.

Varo was unable to control his own massive response, his thrusting deep, his possession of this woman total. He felt as if his whole being was going out of him into her.

Above their heads the sun filtered down through the trees. And still neither of them spoke.

When Ava was finally able to get to her feet she had to lean against him for support. "At least I know you want me," she said, her voice low-pitched and trembling with emotion.

She was astounded at the wild abandon with which she had responded to Varo's lovemaking. It couldn't have been wrong because it had felt so right.

"As you want me," he rejoined. "Forgive me if I was a little too rough."

She gave him a soft look. "I was as caught up as you, Varo. Just give me a minute and we'll go. I have the feeling we could get a heavy shower of rain. Maybe even hail."

"Let's hope so," he said tautly. He kept one arm around her waist, absorbing her body heat. "I for one need cooling down."

We were so happy!

Ava drew back her hair, fastening it once more with the gold clasp. Finally she looked up, regarded him with the glitter of tears in her eyes. "It's all so sad."

The greatest part of him wanted to tell her he loved her,

adored her. She was his woman. He would never let her go. His fears were too dominant at that moment. Difficult to accept Ava might fear having children. But that could be handled with lots of tender loving care and support. And the rest? He couldn't bring himself to reveal anything more Selwyn had said. In fact he believed in his heart it was a lie.

"You ought to talk to me, Ava," he said, pinning her sparkling gaze. "Not now. But later." Varo was striving for a detached calmness he did not feel. His desire for her would never abate. Nevertheless he said, "Both of us need a little time to cool down and reflect."

Ava turned away sharply. Her body was still throbbing. Her nipples, her breasts, her sex. She would simmer for hours. It was a new Ava Varo had set loose. A new woman he had called forth. She had lost too much time dissociating herself from her painful past. Her defeats were many. Her triumphs were to come. Nothing was going to stop her having it out with Luke. She would even holler at him if she had to. She—ever so peaceful, confrontation-hating Ava. She felt shame for how biddable she had been. A great deal of it had to do with her childhood. She was a woman now.

They both got splashed with rain and light hail as they ran from the Jeep to the short flight of front steps. Ava paused, shaking the quickly melting hail from her hair. The strong smell of ozone was in the air. Both of them had remained quiet on the journey back from the lagoon. Both knew much had to be said.

Luke watched them return. He stood at the French doors of his guestroom—not as large or as handsomely furnished at the spacious room he and Ava had always occupied, he thought with fierce resentment. He would get square. He would go back and have more of a rest before he showered, dressed and went down to dinner. He was actually looking forward to it. Knowing Ava as he did, she would have reacted to any accusations de Montalvo might have made with her usual pained silence. Ava was all politeness. She couldn't assert herself for love or money.

He didn't have to do a damned thing. All he had to do was bide his time. The Argentine wouldn't waste a moment getting himself organised to leave Kooraki and the beautiful Ava behind. Before the separation time was up he was convinced he would have his wife back. With more revenge to come. Ava had let him down very badly. How could she avoid punishment? Subtle, of course. He had learned exactly how to manipulate her. Not that he hadn't had *his* affairs, but there was no question his wife could have one and get away with it. Punishment had to fit the crime.

Some time later, when Ava burst in on him, he looked up with genuine astonishment. "You could knock," he said, displaying his annoyance.

At the sight of him lounging on the bed Ava's fury increased. "You were *not* invited to this house, Luke," she said. "You are *not* a guest. We are separated. I am filing for a divorce. All this is known to you, yet you came here. Now I know why. To cause me as much pain as you possibly could."

"Don't imagine you don't deserve it," he said in his coldest voice, rising slowly from the bed. He would never forgive her for what she had done, but he now felt a driving sexual hunger. Ava had never really given herself to him. He knew that. He knew he had never truly aroused her. Something inexplicable to him. He had no such trouble with other women. She looked fantastically beautiful, as though she had suddenly stepped down from her white marble pedestal to become *woman*.

"I never deserved *you*," she said, her remarkable eyes

flashing. "I've arranged for you to fly out with the freight plane tomorrow, Luke, so you might as well do your packing tonight. The plane arrives at midday. It doesn't take long for the station supplies to be unloaded. Be ready."

Her fierce ultimatum only served to increase his rage. "You're not serious, are you, my darling?" he asked with a disbelieving sneer. "You're my wife, Ava, and don't you forget it."

"Don't dare to threaten me," Ava warned, keeping her sparkling gaze on him. "I want you *out*. If you don't choose to go quietly, I assure you I'll have you thrown out."

"By your lover?" He moved threateningly towards her.

"There will be no need to involve Varo," she said with disgust, not falling back a step as he'd expected, but holding her ground. "Any man on the station would be happy to do it. No one has any time for you, Luke. They never did. I blinded myself to your faults. You kept your true form well hidden until after the wedding ceremony. I've paid for my mistake."

"No, you haven't!" he exploded, feeling a rush of hate and hunger. "You seem to forget I could easily raise objections to your filing for divorce. Why, the separation time isn't even up and you're having it off with another man. Shame on you, Ava."

She laughed at the hypocrisy of it. "The shame is all yours, Luke. You told Varo I had a pregnancy that ended in miscarriage. That was a lie."

He came to a halt, like a statue. "And how exactly are you going to prove that?" he asked, wondering what had possessed her all of a sudden. The change in her seemed profound.

"I would think a medical check-up might do it," she retorted. "I have *never* been pregnant, Luke. I didn't want a child with you."

"But, my darling wife, you confided in Karen," he pointed out, his voice dripping acid. "Don't you remember? Karen surely will. She was as shocked as I was. Angelic old you! You have well and truly blotted your copybook. Karen knows the story."

Ava visibly paled. So he had drawn her cousin into his web. "Even Karen would stop short of telling such a lie for you," she said hardily, praying it would be true.

"Only it *is* no lie." Selwyn kept his eyes on her. "Karen suspected. You simply confirmed it. I was *thrilled* you were carrying our baby. But you aborted it, didn't you?"

Ava was seized by a pain so bad it was agony. "You told Varo I *aborted* my baby?" she cried, blazing with anger. "I don't believe it."

"Didn't he mention it?" Luke asked silkily, shaking his fair floppy head. "I suppose not. I think he was much too shocked to bring up that sad fact. He'd be Catholic, wouldn't he? Practising, no doubt—and his entire family, with their Spanish background. But you did it, didn't you? At some time we all have to take responsibility for our actions, Ava."

"Who would do this kind of thing?" Ava implored. "You disgust me, Luke. You're a truly bad man." Her voice fell away to a whisper.

Heartened, he went to her, grasped her strongly by the shoulders.

She broke away, stepping back sharply. "Keep your hands off me," she warned, very deliberately.

This was too much to tolerate. His meek, vulnerable Ava, blazing like a firebrand. "Ava, I love you," he said, injecting high emotion into his tone. "I understand your shame, your sense of guilt. You did a terrible thing. And the worst part is there was no great pressure on you, Ava—no extenuating circumstances. You weren't single, on your own with little or no money, no support. You had me and my family.

You had a choice and you chose very badly. You *know* you should be punished. What goes around comes around. You need de Montalvo to believe you. Swallow your story. But he won't. He's no fool. Okay, you let him seduce you. You've had your little bit of illicit excitement. Frankly, I didn't think you had it in you. You're such a frigid little thing."

"Not with Varo," she pointed out with pride. "And it hasn't been a case of illicit excitement, Luke. I'm deeply in love with him."

"Rubbish!" Luke exploded, seeing a red mist before his eyes. "Mark my words, you pathetic creature, de Montalvo will very soon be on his way. You're damaged goods, as the saying goes."

Ava was silent a moment longer. "Men *have* caused damage in my life," she admitted in a low voice. "My grandfather…even my father separating from the mother I loved. We weren't able to go to her. Grandfather stopped that. And *you* have done me damage, Luke. You have very dark places in you. You're a narcissist. *Your* needs are the most important thing in the world to you. You don't love me. You don't know anything about love. I entered into a precipitate marriage against all good advice. You enjoyed controlling me. You enjoyed marrying a Langdon—such cachet!"

Ava stepped forward, adrenaline coursing through her. Without another moment of hesitation she hit her husband spontaneously across the mouth. She had known in her bones Luke would provoke her into some sort of action.

Luke was genuinely shocked. He had not been expecting any such action from her. Their life together had been free of physical confrontation. He had played the psychological game. The cat and the mouse. Only the mouse had at long last found its roar.

The blow wasn't heavy, but the antique ring Ava frequently wore had managed to split his lip. He reared back from her, as astonished as if she had morphed into a virago. "Are you *mad*?" he exploded, unable to believe meek and mild Ava had done this.

"Far from it. I've never had this sense of power. It's great. You tried so hard to rob me of all confidence, Luke. That's the ugly side of you." She picked up a handtowel he had left on the bed and threw it at him. "Don't bleed on the carpet. And don't attempt to come down to dinner. I'll have a tray sent up. I mean what I say, Luke. I want you off Kooraki midday tomorrow. I never want to lay eyes on you again."

She went to sweep past him—only in a burst of over-whelming rage he grabbed her.

"I'm the only man you've got," he gritted, close to screaming. There was a wild look in his eyes. "I'm your *husband*—get it?"

That wild look should have made her very nervous indeed, but it didn't. "Let me go," she said, ice-cold.

Luke's good-looking face went white with fury. He shook her hard, much the stronger of the two. "Do you really think I'm going to let you make a fool of me?" he shouted. Then an odd smile spread over his face. "I'm a lot more danger-ous than you think, my darling." He began to rock Ava in his arms. "No way can you leave me, Ava. Till death do us part, remember?" One of his hands closed painfully over her breast. "I won't be going tomorrow. But the Argentine will. You must take your punishment. Then we can get on with life."

Varo had had no intention of allowing Ava to confront her husband with no back-up from him. She had been adamant about his not accompanying her, which was fair enough, and he had made it appear he acquiesced when his true in-tention was to hold himself in readiness some place nearby. He knew the layout of the house well by now. He would take the rear staircase to the gallery. He knew which room Selwyn was in.

Selwyn had deliberately tried to sabotage the relationship between Ava and himself. He had divulged Ava's secret, determining the relationship would quickly burn out. Selwyn wanted his wife back. No one could blame a man for that. But Selwyn wasn't a man. No one who had come close to him would think that. Malyah Man had meted out what could be taken as a genuine warning. Selwyn was *trouble*.

He'd given Ava a good five minutes to mount the main staircase and walk the short distance to Selwyn's guestroom, which was at the far end of the west wing, then made his move. His whole being had felt electric with tension. Even his scalp had prickled. He'd had only one purpose. That was to keep Ava from danger.

At the top of the staircase he'd heard voices. He had seen with gratitude that the door of Selwyn's room was very slightly ajar. Ava had evidently thought it wiser to leave it that way. In his mind he had Selwyn ripping into Ava with his accusations.

Silently he'd moved the short distance to stand just to the side of the heavy mahogany door with its ornate brass knob. Selwyn had been speaking. He'd heard him very clearly.

"Karen suspected. You simply confirmed it," he was saying. "I was *thrilled* you were carrying our baby. But you aborted it, didn't you?"

Selwyn had laughed suddenly with what Varo thought was venom and violence.

My God, was it true then? Was he about to learn the stark facts?

Ava hadn't responded. Perhaps overcome by her feelings, the trauma she had suffered. Then all of a sudden she had exploded. "You told Varo I *aborted* my baby?"

There had been rage in it, but to his ears it had sounded like righteous rage. She'd been utterly incredulous. Was this the most terrible revelation of her whole life brought out into the open, or was it Selwyn's monstrous lie?

Ava had gone on the attack. The attack of the innocent, not the guilty. He had wanted to cry out in triumph. He'd wanted to applaud. An enormous burden had been lifted from his shoulders. Instead he'd stood there, awaiting the right moment when he would thump on the door, then enter without permission.

Selwyn's accusations had continued to stream out. Ava had called him "a bad man". Her voice had been barely audible but the tones were heartfelt. In the next breath she'd switched to a shout.

"Keep your hands off me."

Time to move in on them, Varo had thought grimly. Selwyn was in full flow. He'd called Ava—beautiful, passionate Ava—*frigid*. Anger had welled up in him until he'd heard Ava's impassioned statement like a momentous declaration.

"I'm deeply in love with him."

In love with me! That's brilliant!

Selwyn had put up his worst, and Ava had had her chance to respond. Varo had found himself hanging on her every word. She'd sounded strong, independent. He had felt the fierce pleasure of pride in her. That was what Selwyn would hate—a strong, independent woman. He wanted a woman to control. Ava had broken free of her chains.

Perhaps he should not intervene, but walk quietly away. She was handling the situation on her own.

He was almost at the top of the staircase when he'd heard Selwyn roar, "Are you mad?"

It was followed by Ava's ice-cold retort, "Let me go!"

In a flash he turned back, understanding Ava was in

need of him. He threw open the door so violently it crashed against the wall, rattling a valuable *famille noir* Chinese porcelain vase that miraculously didn't fall over and break. Only who would have cared? Ava was grappling with the brute of a man she had married for all the wrong reasons. He had his hands clamped around her white neck. God, was he trying to *strangle* her?

Varo swooped, his black eyes glittering, his powerful shoulders hunched forward like a heavyweight boxer waiting his moment to unleash his strength. Selwyn was howling now, knowing he was trapped—moreover by a man who looked as if he was about to kill him.

"She had it coming!" he panted. "Everything I told you is the truth."

He got no further. A heavy fist slammed into his ribs, knocking the breath out of him and slamming him back against the French doors.

"Get up." De Montalvo's voice was deadly quiet.

Blood was oozing from Selwyn's lip after Ava's unprecedented attack. Now he faced possible cracked ribs. He threw up his hands as if in defeat.

Concern over what might happen lent Ava strength. She clamped her two hands around Varo's hard-muscled arm. "Leave him, Varo. Please do what I say. He's not worth it. He'll be out of here by tomorrow. I'll lock him in."

She meant it. She wasn't going to have Luke free to wander the house. He wouldn't get out through this door. He wouldn't dream of trying to scale the front façade. He was no mountaineer.

A hard edge was in Varo's voice. "Why don't you let me teach him a lesson?" he rasped.

"I'll have you up on an assault charge," Luke the lawyer suddenly yelled, his expression ugly.

A voice at the back of his mind was telling him Ava

would always come to his rescue. Though no woman would ever measure up to him. Few men either.

"Don't make me laugh!" Varo bit off. "What do you suppose the law would make of a man who attempted to strangle his wife? Can you see the red marks on Ava's neck, you brute? I am witness. I will call the staff to testify. You don't deserve Ava. You never did. Haven't you learned that by now?" He took several steps closer to Luke, who recoiled.

"Don't come any nearer."

"Varo, we don't want more trouble. Leave him." Ava felt her anxiety growing. She knew in her bones she couldn't find a way to Varo. He was tremendously upset.

"This poor excuse for a man doesn't deserve pity," he said with utter scorn. "What if I hadn't been there, outside the door? It doesn't take long for a man to strangle a woman. Particularly a mad man." The tension in his body was like a tightly coiled steel spring. "Get up, you gutless worm."

Luke Selwyn didn't do guts. He remained where he was, holding a hand to his ribs and making weird whimpering sounds.

Varo apparently couldn't care less. He stepped forward and gave Luke a clip across the head. "Count yourself lucky!" he exclaimed. "I believe Ava is the one who should press charges. It would and should end your career."

Luke looked past the menacing Argentine to Ava. "You wouldn't do that?" he asked, like a man amazed. "I'm your husband. I wouldn't have hurt you. I was only trying to shake sense into you."

To his horror, he received another clip over the head. "Strangle, you mean. You're on your knees, so apologise to Ava," Varo told him harshly.

Apologise? Never!

"Can't hear you," Varo said.

"Oh, God, leave him. It's not worth it." Ava's low, mellow voice had turned hoarse. She touched an involuntary hand to her bruised neck.

At that telling hoarseness Varo's strong hand came out, ready to clip Selwyn again.

"Varo, *please*. Leave him for my sake."

Varo gave her a brilliant sideways look. "I will and I am," Varo insisted. "But first the apology. Go ahead, Selwyn. While you're at it, admit your lies. You do realise you're in a very bad position indeed?"

Selwyn was silent.

Varo turned to Ava. "Looks like he's not going to do it. Ah, well!" Contempt was in his face as he stared down at the other man.

Selwyn didn't do bravery either. He broke into a choked apology without actually admitting he had lied. "I only did it because I love you, Ava. I hope you realise that?"

"Thank you, Luke," Ava said. "Tons of self-pity, no genuine remorse. The sad thing is you believe you're a good person when you're a man who knows nothing about love or even empathy. You have no capacity for it. You'll find painkillers in the bathroom cabinet. Take a good long bath. I want you off Kooraki. The chapter in life we shared is *over*."

They were almost at the door when Luke, now up and swaying on his feet, made a final attempt to inflict more wounds and more doubt. "Ask Karen if you want to know the truth," he said, addressing Varo directly. There was a gleam of triumph in his eyes. "Women—even angel-faced women like Ava—are seldom what you think they are. What I told you should be enough to stop you from making a terrible mistake. Heed my warning. Take the path I suggest and see where it leads." He flashed Varo a smile that had nothing to do with friendship or warmth.

Varo didn't smile back. "It's important you stop now, Selwyn," he warned, looking very tense. "It's possible you may have a cracked rib or two. What about a broken nose?"

Luke's moment of feeling back in control crumbled. He had no reply to that. Ribs were one thing. A broken nose would seriously affect his good-looks. He was a man women noticed.

Luke, the king of lies, Ava thought bleakly. *Luke, the rotten liar.* He had taken lying to new heights. The truly depressing thing was that liars had a long history of being believed.

A familiar sick feeling grew in her stomach. Varo *wanted* to believe Luke was a pathological liar, but had all his suspicion fallen away? Luke had had a lifetime of practising lying. Practice had made him very convincing. She fancied she saw an element of doubt in Varo's dark eyes. If he made the decision to speak to Karen she knew she would never recover. Karen was no benevolent soul. Karen harboured the demon jealousy. She had always been Luke's ally in the past. Even so Ava thought her cousin, connected to her by blood, would not go so far as to condone such an enormous sick lie.

Right now all that mattered to her was that Varo believed in her innocence. Where would they be without trust? Trust between two people who loved each other was crucial.

Luke was locked up for the night. A generous tray had been sent up, so there was no danger of his dying of starvation. Another tray was delivered at breakfast.

When Luke's eyes locked with those of the formidable housekeeper, who clearly hated him, he began to wonder if she might have put something in his food. The orange juice tasted a bit funny. He left it aside.

He was burning up inside with fury. As soon as he got

back to Sydney he would arrange to meet Karen; probably he'd take her to dinner if he was fit enough. Put a spin on what had happened. He fully expected Karen to lie for him. He had always had a way with women. Even the strongest of them were weak. Even now he couldn't believe Ava, his wife, no longer loved him.

Give her time, said the voice in his head.

He could almost tell the future in his guts. The Argentine would go away. fade right out of the picture. His accusations would stick. He just *knew* he would have the last word.

Right or wrong, good or bad, Ava's mind was resolved on a single purpose. She had to ask Varo what he intended to do. She wanted a straight answer. If he intended to consult Karen—and even without telling her Karen would soon let her know—she could rule out her heart's desire. Varo would go. And he would go fast. Varo wouldn't be the first man to be blinded by lies. Up until now their hearts had been ruling their heads. Luke's poisonous intervention had changed all that. Luke had brought them to the *big* question.

Did Varo trust her or not?

Varo escorted Luke to the airstrip. He fully intended shoving Selwyn on the freight plane, standing by to make sure he didn't attempt to get off. From the moment they'd get inside the Jeep Selwyn had started up again.

"Beautiful women have a great deal of power. Remember that. They attract sympathy even when they don't deserve it. Men are always the losers. They lose their wives. They lose their kids."

Varo had turned to glance at him. "You never give up, do you?"

"Of course I don't. And you seem to forget I am a practising lawyer. A very good one."

"And you came close to being a criminal. You'd better remember that. You may have missed the bruises on Ava's neck, but no one else did. They will all come forward to speak out against you. I can understand in a fashion why you tried so hard to convince me of your lies, but I assure you I have no need to check out your story with Ava's cousin. I was standing outside your door earlier than you think. It wasn't difficult to believe Ava might have suffered a miscarriage and didn't want to speak about it. Impossible to believe she had her pregnancy terminated."

"Listen—"

"Be quiet now," Varo warned, his mouth twisted with distaste. "In a very short space of time Ava will apply to the court for a divorce. The separation time is almost up. You will offer no resistance. You may harbour a sick desire to hurt her, but you never will. Ava has a powerful brother. And she has *me*."

An hour passed. It was evident Varo had driven off somewhere to think. Ava walked through to the kitchen to have a word with Nula, who was waiting to prepare a late lunch. "I have to go for a walk, Nula," she said.

The housekeeper looked at Ava with concern. Ava was very pale and the marks around her lovely white neck stood out in the first flush of bruising. "A walk where?"

"Oh, just around the garden," Ava said vaguely. "Don't worry about lunch. Varo seems to have gone for a drive. We can have a sandwich and a cup of coffee later."

Ava tried for a smile. Then she walked away.

What had delayed Varo was his offering assistance to the two station hands who had been allotted the job of offloading the station supplies. At first they seemed a bit embarrassed, he supposed because he was a guest, but he took no notice. Three pairs of hands were better than two. Besides, he liked to talk to them about what they did on the station.

When he returned to the house, Nula told him before he even had time to ask that Miss Ava had gone for a walk in the garden. It wasn't any city man's idea of a garden. It was bigger, in fact, than the gardens of Villaflores, which were extensive. No matter—he would find her. He would find her wherever she was. At the ends of the earth. He had come to this extraordinary country for the wedding of a friend. He had found a woman who had caught instantly at his heart and at his imagination. He had found his future wife.

Ava heard a man's footsteps crunching on the gravelled path. Instinctively she opened her mouth to call, "I'm here, Varo. On the stone bridge." This was it. Decision time.

Varo lost no time changing direction. He had come to know the Full Moon Bridge well. It spanned a man-made pond where the great buds of white lotus flowers slowly opened, their giant leaves almost reaching the base of the semi-circular bridge. The sun blazed out of an Outback sky of intense sapphire, lending emerald-green waters a blazing patina of gold.

Ava was standing in the middle of the bridge, gazing down at the glittering water adorned with the great gorgeous blooms. He went to call out an apology because he was a bit late for lunch, only she turned to him as he approached— such a sad, serious expression on her face.

"Ava, what is it?" His heart rocked.

"I thought you might have gone off to think," she said, lifting her remarkable blue-green eyes to him.

"Think about what?" He snaked an arm around her back, letting it fall to her narrow waist.

Slowly he led her off the bridge to one of the small

summerhouse structures in the garden, where it was a great pleasure to sit down in the shade, surrounded by wonderful scents and a wilderness of blossom. The birds and the butterflies loved this place. It was no wonder the Langdons took such pride in the magnificent gardens they had achieved over generations in the wild, he thought. He had already quizzed Ava about many of the native plants, thinking they could do very well in the gardens of Villaflores.

"Well?" He gave her a soft, tender look, fighting down his inner rage at the damage Selwyn had done.

Ava bit her lip. "I don't really know where to begin."

"'Begin at the beginning and go on till you come to the end: then stop,'" he said humorously, quoting Lewis Carroll.

She had to smile. "You're always surprising me, Varo."

"I've got another one of Carroll's," he said, much more seriously. "'I can't go back to yesterday, because I was a different person then.'"

Tears came to her eyes as though they were saying goodbye. "That's true, isn't it?" she said. "But no matter what you do—what you decide to do—no matter where you go, I will never forget you, Varo."

He frowned, then said, "So what is this? You're telling me to go?" She had that look about her. She was so pale. Was she about to break his heart?

"No, no," Ava cried out in a kind of agony. "I thought you would *want* to go. I thought you might have some lingering doubts. Luke is such an accomplished liar. He's made lying an art form."

"You think I doubt you?" Varo asked in amazement. "I may have briefly considered you had a miscarriage and couldn't bear to talk about it. I would understand that. But the rest—never! You are my dearest, most beloved Ava. I trust you with my life. I trust you with my heart. Here—I give it to you." He cupped his elegant hands, held them out to her. His accent was becoming more and more pronounced as his feelings grew. "You *cannot* turn me away. I won't allow it." There was real worry on his stunning face.

"Let you go? You're crazy!" Ava exclaimed, letting her head fall against his shoulder. "I love you, Varo. You are the most wonderful thing that has happened to me in all my life. I would never have experienced *love*—true, undying love—if I hadn't met you. You *can't* go away." She gripped him around the waist, tried to shake him. "I won't let you. The first pregnancy I will ever have—the first baby I will ever hold—will be part of *you. Our* child. I should tell you I want at least four children. Two boys, Two girls. I think that should do it."

Varo stared into her lovely face, his expression deeply serious. He chose that very moment to slip out of her arms, only to drop onto one knee before her. "Some of us are greatly blessed in life," he said with emotion, because he was not a man who was afraid of emotion. "We find our soul mate. You are mine, Ava. I beg you to do me the honour of becoming my wife. Moreover, I insist on it. We will be married wherever you like. If you can't leave your homeland, I will—"

Ava leaned forward and sealed her mouth to his. It was a deep kiss, with an intensity of which there was no doubt. After a while she lifted her shining blonde head, her whole being aglow. "'For whither thou goest, I will go; and where thou lodgest, I will lodge: thy people shall be my people, and thy God, my God,'" she quoted. "I certainly believe in Him. He brought me *you*."

She held out her hands in a gesture of raising Varo to his feet. Then she too stood, to go into his waiting arms. They closed strongly, protectively, adoringly around her.

The moving finger had written. Time now for it to move on.

This was their destiny. They were ready to accept it and all life's challenges head-on. The power of love was awesome. It would overcome all else.

EPILOGUE

WHEN Karen Devereaux was asked by Luke Selwyn to back his shocking claim she refused point-blank, livid with outrage. None of it could be proved. She just *knew* Luke Selwyn had made it all up. Ava had never breathed a word to her about any pregnancy because she had never fallen pregnant to Luke. Karen was furious, deeply resenting the fact Luke was trying to use her. It would be much better if she broke off their so-called friendship.

Word was Ava and Varo were having two wedding ceremonies: one at Kooraki, the other at the Estancia de Villaflores in Argentina. She dearly wanted to go to both. There was even a chance Ava might ask her to be one of the bridesmaids. She had seen a great deal of Europe, the United States and Canada, but she had never been to South America. This was a wonderful opportunity to go.

Dev and Amelia were back from their honeymoon. There was bound to be a *huge* engagement party. She and Ava had always been close. Now she would make it her business to draw closer to Amelia, the mistress of Kooraki. Hadn't they always been a trio? Really good friends? She had always loved and cared for her cousin Ava. Or so she told herself. Luke Selwyn was someone from the past…

* * * * *

CADENCE CREEK COWBOYS
They're the rough diamonds of the West…

Sam and Ty Diamond—these two cowboys have got trouble as their middle name. With chips on their shoulders the size of hay bales, these rough and rugged men think they need a woman like they need a lame horse. Little do they know…

Don't miss any of the action in Cadence Creek!

Sam's story, *The Last Real Cowboy*
—May 2012

With a tip of his Stetson and a lazy smile, Sam Diamond can charm anyone. Except prickly Angela Beck…

Ty's story, *The Rebel Rancher*
—August 2012

Ty Diamond isn't exactly known for his mild reputation. But if he wants to be with Clara Ferguson, he's going to have to show her his gentle side…

Dear Reader,

"All the heroes have not gone. There are many undiscovered heroes left. They are disguised as everyday men and women who touch our lives and help us to be better."

My sister-in-law Julie wrote those words in her eulogy to her dad—my father-in-law—who passed away while I was writing this book. As we sat in the kitchen and typed it up, I got to that part and totally choked up. Part of it was acknowledging the men in the family I married into—strong men, who believe in working hard and loving big. Another part was simply believing in those words. *All the heroes have not gone.* That is, after all, why I love writing romance.

I think those words were partially responsible for how this story turned out, because Tyson ended up being different than I initially imagined. I would expect him to do one thing and he'd turn around and surprise me with a tender side I didn't know he had. I discovered he knew how to be gentle. That he cared very deeply about his family, had his own insecurities and a gigantic sense of honor. Turns out my rebellious hero ended up having a heart of gold.

Heroism comes in many forms. It is standing up for someone, or simply standing beside them as they face their demons. It is honoring a commitment, doing the right thing even when it hurts, or pitching in and lending a hand in a time of need.

Heroes are all around us—all we have to do is look. And sometimes remember.

Warmest wishes,

Donna

THE REBEL
RANCHER

BY
DONNA ALWARD

First published in Great Britain 2012
by Mills & Boon, an imprint of Harlequin (UK) Limited,
Eton House, 18-24 Paradise Road, Richmond, Surrey TW9 1SR

© Donna Alward 2012

ISBN: 978 0 263 89455 4
ebook ISBN: 978 1 408 97131 4

23-0812

Harlequin (UK) policy is to use papers that are natural, renewable and recyclable products and made from wood grown in sustainable forests. The logging and manufacturing processes conform to the legal environmental regulations of the country of origin.

Printed and bound in Spain
by Blackprint CPI, Barcelona

A busy wife and mother of three (two daughters and the family dog), **Donna Alward** believes hers is the best job in the world: a combination of stay-at-home mum and romance novelist. An avid reader since childhood, Donna always made up her own stories. She completed her arts degree in English literature in 1994, but it wasn't until 2001 that she penned her first full-length novel and found herself hooked on writing romance. In 2006 she sold her first manuscript, and now writes warm, emotional stories for Cherish.

In her new home office in Nova Scotia, Donna loves being back on the east coast of Canada after nearly twelve years in Alberta, where her career began, writing about cowboys and the West. Donna's debut romance, *Hired by the Cowboy,* was awarded the Booksellers Best Award in 2008 for Best Traditional Romance.

With the Atlantic Ocean only minutes from her doorstep, Donna has found a fresh take on life and promises even more great romances in the near future!

Donna loves to hear from readers. You can contact her through her website, www.donnaalward.com, her page at www.myspace.com/dalward, or through her publisher.

To Darrell. You're the glue, and I love you for it
and
To Ralph 1940–2011.

CHAPTER ONE

CLARA HAD HEARD A LOT about Tyson Diamond. Some of it good, a lot of it questionable. But none of the reports had warned her that he was over six feet of sexy cowboy with a break-your-heart smile and a devilish gleam in his eye.

And now he was striding this way as Angela, still resplendent in her wedding dress, waved him over.

Clara wondered if she could say her final congratulations to Sam and Angela and escape before Tyson reached them. She'd managed to avoid him up to this point, after all. She'd been helping his father, Virgil, with his rehab after his stroke, and her off-duty hours were spent helping Angela plan the wedding from the safety of Butterfly House, the transition shelter Angela managed and where Clara currently lived. And Ty had been wrapping up his business up north and spending time with Sam as they worked together running the ranch. Somehow she and Tyson had failed to cross paths in the weeks leading up to the wedding.

Until today.

This afternoon he'd turned up spit-polished in his black suit with his hair just a little messy. Her mouth had gone dry just looking at him. Ty was exactly the sort of man she tried to avoid. Tall, sexy, confident and careless. The kind that ate shy girls like her for breakfast. The kind that girls like her could never resist.

Her heart had taken a little jump and she'd caught her breath before she could even put a thought together. But Ty had sauntered in, all long legs and crooked grins, and there it had been. Whomp. Attraction, pure and simple. Nothing in the world could have surprised her more.

He was still several feet away but closing the gap fast, and Clara felt panic start to bubble, making her chest cramp and her breath shorten. She wasn't ready to handle this. She felt as tongue-tied as a schoolgirl only with the sobering wisdom of a woman who'd been through hell. Putting the two together only created chaos in her mind. A quick exit was in order. She turned to Sam and Angela and forced a smile.

"I'm going to take Virgil in now, but I wanted to say happy wedding day to you both." She gave Angela a brief hug. "I'm going to miss you around the house, but you're going to have a wonderful time on your honeymoon."

Sam hugged Clara as well. She didn't feel the unholy urge to pull away and run the way she usually did when faced with someone intruding on her personal space. She'd learned to trust Sam in the weeks leading up to the wedding, especially after he'd stood beside Angela as she faced her own demons.

"You did great today," he said quietly, giving her arm a gentle squeeze. "And you look beautiful."

Heat infused her cheeks at the compliment and at the knowledge that Tyson was nearly upon their little group. "Thank you. Now I'd better get Virgil inside, he was looking tired…."

Sam's voice cut her off as he looked over her shoulder. "Have you met Ty yet?" he asked. "Ty, this is Clara Ferguson, Dad's nurse. You'll be seeing a lot of each other from now on."

Too late. Clara closed her eyes and took a steady breath. She really wished she wasn't blushing as she turned around, but she could feel the heat centered in her cheeks. Dammit.

Tyson's jaw sported a faint shadow of stubble and the suit coat hung awkwardly on his rangy frame. But the style worked for him and his dark eyes held a gleam of approval as he looked down at her. His appraising gaze made something curl inside her uncomfortably. What she wouldn't give for a pair of comfy jeans and a baggy sweater right about now. The sage-green bridesmaid's dress was far too fitted to her figure and made her feel conspicuous. Compliments were well and good, but she was far more confident when she was in her comfort zone.

"Mr. Diamond," she said, setting her jaw defiantly as she held out her hand. She could set the tone between them right here and now. Businesslike—exactly the way it should be between her and Virgil's adopted son.

But it was an utter flop of an attempt. His warm fingers enveloped hers in a strong, lingering grip. A hint of a smile flirted with the corners of his mouth. "It's just Ty," he replied, with a voice as smooth and chocolaty as the dark depths of his eyes. "Or Tyson if I'm on your bad side."

Bad side? Right now she felt as though she might swallow her tongue as she looked into his face. She *liked* the feel of her hand in his. Where was the old reliable revulsion she'd become accustomed to? The instinctive need to pull away and keep her distance? She knew how to deal with that. This was all new territory, and she was momentarily at a loss for words.

His smile widened and she pulled her hand away, hiding her fingers within the clasp of her left hand. "Right," she said, her voice shaking. "Well, I'd better get your dad inside. Good night, everyone."

She couldn't meet his gaze as she scuttled away, but she heard Sam's voice and it made her burn with humiliation.

"Go easy," Sam warned Ty.

"Did I do anything?" There was a hint of defensiveness in Ty's voice that fit with what she'd heard through the grapevine. That things weren't as smooth sailing between the brothers as they seemed.

She quickened her steps so she wouldn't hear Sam's answer. Everything she'd heard around town was right, then. She hadn't been able to tune out the snatches of conversation that had reached her ears today. The return of the prodigal Tyson was a hot topic. Unfortunately so was his track record with the ladies.

Tyson Diamond was gorgeous and he knew it. He was also a wild card and Sam's illegitimate cousin who'd been adopted by Virgil and Molly as a baby. *Trouble.* He was the last person who should make Clara blush and stammer. She was smarter than that, wasn't she?

Now he'd hung up his rodeo spurs and was coming home to run the ranch with Sam. With Virgil still recovering and needing regular care, they were going to see each other *all the time*.

Great. Just wonderful.

Clara helped Virgil get settled, but once she was alone in the quiet house her unease came back with a vengeance, sending tingles shooting up the backs of her legs and making an all-too-familiar weight settle in her chest. It had been a long, tiring day and her defenses were down. That had to be the reason why Ty's simple handshake had made her react in such an uncharacteristic way. Or maybe it was just weddings. Weddings did tend to make people sentimental and romantic, right? She twisted her fingers. Or stupid.

Either way, it was *one day*. It didn't matter a bit if she found Tyson attractive. She had no interest in romance. Not after all that had been taken away from her in the name of "love." She had her eye set on her goal and nothing was going to divert her from it.

She escaped into the first-floor powder room, sat down on the closed toilet and focused on breathing deeply for a few minutes. Once she'd regrouped she got up, ran some cold water over her hands and carefully touched them to her cheeks, soothing the heat there without marring her makeup. She could do this. She'd come too far to go back to hiding away at the first whiff of discomfort. Goodness, a year ago she would never have made it through a day like today. She shouldn't let something like this rattle her.

She stared into the mirror. "Living in fear is not living. I will not live in fear."

The words soothed, both from sentiment and habit. She let out a breath and straightened her shoulders. She opened the door and nearly ran straight into Tyson's chest.

His hands gripped her arms, steadying her from toppling over in the heels she wasn't used to wearing.

"Whoa," he said, his low voice rippling over her nerve endings.

Her faced flamed anew, his word choice making her feel decidedly klutzy and horsy. And he was touching her again. "I'm sorry," she stammered. "I didn't know anyone was waiting for the bathroom."

"I was waiting for *you*," he replied easily. He squatted down slightly so that he was closer to her height and peered into her face. She didn't like the way he was looking at her. As though he was trying to figure her out. The less he knew about her the better. And she planned to keep it that way, no matter how often their paths crossed in the coming weeks.

"Waiting for me?"

"You ran off quite a while ago. I wanted to be sure you're all right."

"Of course I am." His hands seemed to burn through the soft fabric of her dress to the skin beneath. She conjured up the polite smile she'd practiced all week in the mirror. "It took me a while to get your dad settled, that's all."

Liar, her brain protested, but she ignored it. A warmth ran through her at his concern. Usually she managed to fly under the radar, blending into her surroundings like a chameleon. People usually didn't notice if she came or went. But Ty had.

Despite her assurances, Tyson didn't budge from blocking the hallway. His lips curled up in the most alluring manner. Lordy, with a smile like that she bet he didn't even have to try with the ladies. They'd all fall in his lap, wouldn't they?

She stepped around him and he dropped his fingers from her arms. She breathed a little easier once he wasn't touching her anymore. "If you'll excuse me…"

"What's your hurry?" he asked, his soft voice humming over her already raw nerves, making her pause, making her realize once more that they were very alone here in the house while the party went on outside.

"I should get back to Angela, make sure…"

"Angela and Sam have gone. You missed the throwing of the bouquet."

Clara's heart sank. Had she truly been gone so very long? Not that she'd wanted to catch the bouquet by any means, but she'd disappeared into a corner exactly the way she'd promised herself she wouldn't. Once again she'd missed out on good things because she was too busy hiding herself away from something awkward or uncomfortable.

"I thought all the single women fought over catching it." He raised his eyebrows. "You *are* single, aren't you?"

The question was so ludicrous that Clara almost laughed. Single? Absolutely. For now and forever.

"I'm not interested in catching any bouquets," she remarked, finally looking up in his eyes. They were good eyes, she had to admit. They were dark brown but she noticed now that they had little golden flecks around the pupils and crinkles in the corners. His lips were finely shaped, full where they needed to be full and just now curved in what she was realizing was his trademark smile—tilted to one side as if he was sharing a joke. All in all it was a bit lethal, and he was just the sort of man she might have been interested in before.

Before. She looked away from Ty's handsome face and focused on the closet door behind his shoulder. It seemed her life was split into two distinct parts. Before Jackson and after Jackson. The carefree Clara she had been before no longer existed. Jackson had destroyed her.

For well over a year she'd been rebuilding herself from square one. The new Clara stood here now, in a new life and with a new job. She had to remember that. She had accomplished so much. She was a lot more careful now. A lot more cautious. A lot smarter.

"That's a shame," Ty responded, and she heard a laugh in his voice. "Because I caught this."

She caught a glimpse of a blue-and-white lace garter as he stretched it out over a finger. Was he flirting with her? It seemed preposterous. She was plain as ditch water, and to a man like Ty, probably twice as dull. For heaven's sake, she lived in a women's shelter and spent her days as a private nurse. She was distinctly unworldly and unexciting. And Ty was a rodeo star and drifter. They had absolutely nothing in common.

She was therefore surprised to find that she didn't feel particularly threatened by his presence. Ty Diamond was dangerous, all right. A real bad boy from all accounts. Yet somehow she felt…safe.

"Lucky you," she replied dryly, proud that she'd managed to keep her tongue from tying in knots and trying to summon what used to be, in the *before Jackson* days, a ready sense of humor. "Do you have a girl in mind? Tradition says you'll be the next bachelor to be married." She smiled, but it felt forced, like she was baring her teeth. "Who caught the bouquet? A likely candidate for the next Mrs. Diamond, perhaps?"

"Amy Wilson, and I hardly think so."

His displeasure was so obvious Clara let out a half laugh, half gasp. She was familiar with Amy's vivacious and gossipy ways. Amy had had plenty to say about Tyson today and little of it good. It had sounded a bit like sour grapes. "That's not very nice."

He shrugged. "Amy and I have never seen eye to eye. She wanted Sam, you know. And when she saw me catch the garter she hightailed it to the other side of the garden, well out of my reach."

"Why?" She looked up and saw he was still smiling that sexy half smile and she bit down on her lip. "I mean, why doesn't Amy like you?" She couldn't imagine being repulsed by Ty. He might look slightly out of place in formal wear, but it didn't disguise the fact that he was a stunning display of masculinity. Gorgeous enough even to fluster her—someone who'd been immune to any sort of charms for some time now. The new Clara was far too practical to be distracted.

He stepped back. "Easy. The adopted bastard doesn't have the same shine as the heir apparent."

Clara turned away and began walking back to the kitchen so they would be out of the close confines of the hall. The words had been said flippantly, but he hadn't quite been able to disguise the bitterness behind them.

"Did you say that just to shock me?"

In the kitchen, Ty went to the fridge and took out a beer, popping the top as he leaned his hips against the counter. "If I said no, would you believe me?" He took a drink.

She watched him for a few seconds. He wanted her to think he'd been joking but she saw something behind his eyes. Hurt. She was more sensitive to that sort of thing after what she'd been through. All she knew about Ty was that he was really Sam's cousin, and Virgil and Molly had adopted him. What had it been like, growing up at Diamondback, in Sam's shadow? Being a Diamond but still knowing that he didn't quite belong? She found the Diamond house with all its expensive trappings a bit intimidating. Had Ty? Was that why he'd left?

"I don't think I would believe you," she said. "I think you might just enjoy shocking people."

His eyebrow came up and his grin flashed. "You could be right, Clara."

There was something intimate about the way he said her name. Her pulse began to hammer again. How did he do that?

He gestured with his bottle, a careless flick of the wrist. "So, what *would* it take to shock you?"

She swallowed. She might be practical but she understood a come-on when she heard it. Ty hadn't moved an inch but he suddenly seemed much closer. She replayed the conversation she'd heard today to center her thoughts.

Ty Diamond is a flirt and a player, the woman had said. *It's as natural to him as breathing.*

Clara knew she was nothing special. And if this was Tyson's way of making this a game, she wasn't playing. She met his gaze and raised a single eyebrow. "That won't work with me."

He laughed. "You're tougher than you look. Well, here we are anyway, both avoiding all the wedding hoopla. Get you something to drink?"

She shook her head, a bit surprised he seemed to brush off her comment like it was nothing. And he'd called her tough. He probably had no idea how much of a compliment that was. "If Sam and Angela have gone, I should probably be getting home."

Ty leaned a hip against the counter. "To Butterfly House, right?"

She nodded. It was no secret where she lived, but she didn't quite like Ty knowing, for some reason. His dark eyes assessed her a little too closely until she felt like a bug under a microscope. She momentarily wondered if Angela had sent Tyson in on purpose to make sure she wasn't alone. While she appreciated the sentiment, lately she'd found herself chafing against the constant analysis of her every move and thought. Sometimes she just wanted to get on with her life rather than dissect it to pieces.

"Whatever you're thinking, just ask, Tyson. Don't try to guess. And don't stare at me. It makes me uncomfortable." She was learning to stand up for herself, to set her own boundaries, but even so a quiver of anxiety always followed such a demonstration of self-assurance. It was hard to get past the "don't rock the boat" mentality.

"I didn't mean to stare." His gaze softened. "Angela told me you are a…is *client* the right word?"

"It works." Her heart started drumming all over again,

and not in the glorious anticipatory way it had before. He was going to ask. People always got curious when they found out she lived at the shelter, like they were somehow entitled to her story and the sordid details. "Is that why you followed me inside? To get the details?"

He put the beer bottle down on the countertop. He'd undone his tie and the black silk hanging against the brilliant white of his shirt made him seem approachable. Touchable. Not for her, though. He probably had a string of buckle bunnies clear down to Texas. A man like Tyson Diamond would eat her alive and spit out the bones before moving on to the next conquest.

She felt a tiny stab in her heart, remembering how she'd fallen for Jackson only to discover the true man underneath after it was too late. Too late for so many things. Her throat tightened as she grieved for all that she'd lost. Jackson had been handsome and charming, too. In the beginning.

Angela had talked to her about not judging every man by the abuser's yardstick, and in her head Clara knew she was right. Her heart was still a little too bruised, though, to trust her judgment completely. She was perfectly happy going along the way she was. It would be even better when she was completely independent. She couldn't wait to be one hundred percent in charge of her own life.

"You looked panicked out there. I know the feeling, and I wanted to make sure you were okay, that's all."

He wasn't asking about her past. And he was telling the truth. His words were utterly sincere.

"You don't strike me as the panic type," she responded, getting a glass from the cupboard and filling it with water.

"I'm okay—in my element," he responded smoothly. "Garden weddings? Not so much my element. Neither is this monkey suit."

"I imagine you are more of a jeans and boots kind of guy."

"Definitely," he answered. "Anyway, back to my original question. Are you sure you're okay?"

"Of course I am," she replied.

"Okay," he said, sticking his hands in his trouser pockets, making his suit jacket flare away from his hips in a most attractive way. Clara swallowed. She remembered not two months ago, asking Angela about Sam as he chopped wood in the back yard at Butterfly House. She had told Angela there was a big difference between appreciating the package and taking the leap into something more. She'd looked at Sam through the window that day and found him handsome. But Ty...Ty resembled Sam but with an added something she couldn't put her finger on. For the first time since crawling away from Jackson, battered and bruised, she was definitely appreciating the package, all wrapped up in a suit and patent shoes.

Her tongue snuck out to wet her lips and she saw Ty's gaze follow the movement. All the air seemed to go out of the room.

She fought to be rational. Other than his hands briefly on her arms as she came barreling out of the bathroom, he hadn't touched her or made any sort of suggestion that he was interested.

Except...

Except for the dark gleam in his eyes as he stared at her lips. There was just this *thing* hovering around them. It had been a long time since she'd felt it, but it was like riding a bike. Once you experienced it once, it came back to you in a flash—whether you wanted it to or not. Now she found herself staring at his lips and wondering what it would be like to be kissed.

Reality hit like a splash of cold water. "I really should

go," she said, taking a step backwards. Her voice sounded higher than normal and she swallowed. "Your mother will be expecting me here on time tomorrow. Weddings are all well and good, but real life has a tendency to intrude, and your dad has physio in the morning. It was nice meeting you, Ty."

"You're not going to stay for a dance or two?"

"God, no."

The answer came so quickly and with such force that she didn't have time to think about *not* saying it. There was acknowledging the presence of some sort of...*chemistry,* she supposed was a good word for it. But dancing—touching—in front of people? She swallowed. Her progress hadn't quite extended that far. She'd even said no to Sam—who she trusted more than she'd trusted any man since leaving her ex—when he asked for a dance. He'd been perfectly understanding, but she'd stood by the sidelines watching everyone else dance, feeling silly. Like a coward.

Ty's gaze darkened until it was almost black, and she felt his cool withdrawal. Leaving the half-full bottle, he headed towards the deck doors, stopping for just a moment beside her. She could feel the heat from his body and the crisp scent of whatever aftershave he wore surrounded her in a cloud of masculinity. "Miss Ferguson." He nodded, then continued on his way. The click of the French door let her know that he was gone in a swell of country music that was immediately muted; she couldn't bear to turn around and watch him stride away.

She hadn't meant it how it sounded. She'd only been thinking of the idea of being held close in a man's arms. The very prospect was laughable. Dancing was so intimate. The one thing she still hadn't managed to shake in all the therapy sessions and the time that had passed was her aversion to having her personal space invaded. She hadn't been held by a man since walking away. It triggered too many memories of how Jackson had held her and told her he loved her, only to turn around and use those same loving hands to…

She shuddered. But she knew how it must have sounded to Ty. It had been an indirect invitation on his part and she'd refused before he'd been able to take a breath. Right after he'd called himself the adopted bastard. He'd looked at her lips and she'd acted like she was repulsed.

He would think she considered herself just like Amy—a cut above. But he was wrong, so very wrong.

Tomorrow she'd have to face him. He was living here now, and she would be here every day, helping Molly with the household chores and putting Virgil through his physio exercises. It would be incredibly awkward at best if they left things the way they were now. She should at least explain that it wasn't him, right?

She rolled her shoulders back and resolved that she would not have an anxiety attack in the next fifteen minutes. Instead she would take another step towards having a normal life. She couldn't lean on Angela and Sam any longer. "Living in fear is not living," she repeated to the empty room. Wasn't it about time she started putting that mantra into practice? Wasn't it time she did something about the one thing that still held her back?

Her hand tightened on the handle of the French door. She'd be able to face herself—and Tyson Diamond—in the morning.

It was time to move on.

CHAPTER TWO

TYSON PULLED THE TIE from around his neck and rammed it into his pocket. The fall evening was cool and twilight was setting in. White solar minilights were twisted around the garden poplars creating a fairy glow, and chafing dishes held the last remnants of the wedding feast. This was so not his scene. He'd far rather be enjoying a steak in a comfortable pair of jeans. But he'd promised Sam to see out the day and he'd do it.

He hadn't expected the sudden hit to his pride just now, though. He hadn't even had the chance to actually ask Clara to dance before she'd flat-out refused. For the first time in as long as he could remember, his charm had let him down. It was humbling to a man who'd spent a good amount of his youth perfecting his way around women, and with a consistent rate of success. Riding bulls and charming cowgirls was what he'd done best.

And Clara Ferguson had seen right through his act.

He shouldn't take it personally, he knew that. Not considering her past. But he did just the same. The same way he did whenever someone slapped him on the back but offered Sam their hand. Always second-best. Not that Sam had ever bought into the idea. He'd always insisted by word and deed that they were equal brothers.

Oh, he knew there were people who thought that there

was some weird sibling rivalry thing between them, but they were wrong. It was why Ty was willing to come back now. For Sam. And deep down, for his dad, too. Virgil had always picked apart every single thing Tyson ever did. He'd never understood that Tyson loved this ranch as much as Sam did. Trying to get the old man's approval had been killing him, so he'd ventured out on his own years ago to save his sanity. To avoid saying things he might always regret.

Now he was back and already feeling suffocated. But it was time to stop running away. Time to take his place in the family—whether the old man liked it or not.

He frowned and checked his watch. He'd give it ten minutes, and then he was taking his dented pride and packing it in. Tomorrow the real work began—Sam would be gone on his honeymoon, and the day-to-day running of Diamondback would be left to Ty. He was looking forward to the work.

The butting of heads with his dad would start, too, he imagined. He rolled his shoulders, willing out the tension. Virgil had hardly spoken to him since his return two days ago, other than a few grunts and disparaging comments that Ty had, for the most part, ignored, more out of consideration for his mother, Molly, than anything else. Ty knew very well that their father thought that Sam could do no wrong and it was a big mistake to give Ty equal say in running the ranch. He was a damn sight smarter than his father gave him credit for. He always had been. And he intended to prove it. He had ideas. But first he needed to assess the operation and make a plan. Virgil considered Tyson unreliable, but Tyson knew all about calculating risks. He'd been doing it for years.

The hired band whipped the crowd into a frenzy with a

fast-paced polka, and Ty checked his watch again—only a minute had passed.

It had been a mistake to go after Clara. He'd been way-laid by the bouquet and garter catching, but when he'd gone in the house and realized she was locked in the bath-room he'd been alarmed. He knew what Butterfly House was about. He'd felt her fingers tremble in his when they shook hands and had been automatically transported to a day three years ago when he'd interrupted a "situation."

All he'd wanted to do was reassure her that Diamond-back was a safe place…and then she'd run into him, he'd put his hands on her and everything he'd planned to say evaporated. The shocking thing was for a moment he'd thought she'd felt it, too, when the air hummed between them in the kitchen.

It wasn't the first time he'd been wrong.

The music changed and a movement caught his eye. Clara, in her sage-colored dress, tugging a shawl closer around her shoulders against the fall chill. She'd be leav-ing now, then, he thought, and scowled. He'd been an ass, trying to flirt with her. He hadn't mastered the art of polite chit chat and other social graces. Until tonight, they hadn't been required. How did a guy talk to a woman who was in a situation like hers, anyway? He did the only thing he knew how—and came off looking like an idiot. What had he been thinking, asking her to dance?

Clara didn't go around the house to where the cars were parked. Instead she crossed the grass towards the crowd. She looked up and around the throng until she met his eyes and her gaze stopped roaming. His heart gave a sharp kick in response—a surprise. Frightened girls with innocent eyes were so not his type. He was more into confident women who hung around waiting for the bull riders with the big belt buckles. Girls who were only in it for their own eight seconds and no further commitments.

There were at least a dozen reasons why he should stay clear of Clara Ferguson. He could list three off the top without blinking: she had too much baggage, she worked for the family and he'd only cause her trouble.

But she kept coming, her glossy walnut curls twisting over her shoulders like silk ribbons. The cut of her dress was simple and quite conservative, skimming down her figure and showing her curves without revealing much skin. The effect was sexier than it should have been, he realized. She was nothing like the women he dated. Maybe that was why he was noticing her today, but this was as far as it would go. Noticing. And he didn't even need Sam's earlier warning to tell him so.

She stopped in front of him and her chest rose as she took a deep breath. He realized he was holding his and slowly let it out. "Clara?"

She gave him a smile so sweet, so fragile, that it frightened the hell out of him.

"Would you like to dance, Tyson?"

A good puff of air could probably have knocked him over. He stared at her for a good five seconds until her smile began to waver and uncertainty clouded her dark blue eyes. He wasn't sure why, but something had prompted her to change her mind, and he sensed it had taken a lot of courage for her to come out here and ask.

So what was he supposed to do now? She'd been very clear about not wanting to dance—particularly with him. She'd pulled away from him twice now, and if they danced he'd have to touch her. In several places. Odd, but that thought fired his blood more than anything—or anyone—had in weeks.

But he got the feeling that if he declined it would be

about more than refusing a simple turn on the floor. "I thought you didn't want to dance."

She lifted her chin. "I changed my mind. But if you don't want to, that's fine." She started to turn away.

"I didn't say that." Hell, he might have blown it the first time, but she was here now, right? Something had brought her back out here tonight.

She paused, looked over her shoulder at him. Like she wanted him to believe she was in control. He knew better. She had no idea what she was doing. He should walk away right now—it would be better for them both. This whole day had him out of his comfort zone, and Clara was waiting with her sweet, sad eyes for his answer.

He held out his hand and waited. Just because he wasn't a gentleman ninety percent of the time didn't mean he couldn't fake it.

She put her hand in his and he felt the tremor against his palm. Hell. He was not good at this sort of thing. He was used to a not-so-subtle pressing of bodies on the dance floor. An invitation and a promise of things to come. Clara wasn't like that, was she? She was as flighty as a scared rabbit. Innocent.

Ty led her to the dance "floor"—an expanse of even ground in front of the band. As a waltz began, he put his right hand along the warm curve of her waist and clasped her fingers lightly in his left. He had no idea how close to get or if he should say something or… A cold sweat broke out at the back of his neck. Wasn't it hysterical that a man like him was suddenly so unsure what to do?

She'd gone quite pale, so he let go of her waist and put a finger beneath her chin.

Her last partner had abused her—Sam had said as much when he'd issued the warning to tread carefully. Now, as she tensed beneath his chaste touch, he felt an immediate, blinding hatred for the man who had damaged such a beautiful creature, followed by something unfamiliar and unsettling as he realized he was feeling unusually protective.

He lifted her chin with his finger and said simply, "You make the rules."

Emotions flooded her eyes—what he thought was gratitude and relief and maybe even a touch of fear. He was not a particularly good man, and he was certainly not good enough for her, but he wasn't cruel or oblivious. So he waited for her to clasp his hand in hers again before he made his feet move, taking her with him around the dirt floor, making sure there was lots of space between their bodies.

They made small steps around the dance area, neither speaking, but Ty felt the moment she finally began to relax in his arms. He wanted to pull her closer, to nestle her in the curves of his body, feel her softness against him, but he kept a safe distance, honoring his word to let her take the lead. Clara wasn't like other women. There were different rules to be followed. Hell, usually there were no rules.

The first song finished and led straight into another. There was only a pause in their steps and then, by some sort of unspoken agreement, they moved as one again, swaying gently to the music. Her breasts brushed against his jacket, an innocent whisper of contact that he normally wouldn't notice but right now sent his blood racing. Her temple rested lightly against his chin and the floral scent of her shampoo filled his nostrils. There was something inherently sweet about Clara, and he did not normally have a sweet tooth when it came to women. But he couldn't deny that what he was feeling was attraction. Arousal. As the fiddle scraped in the background, his lips nuzzled against the soft hair at her temple and his eyes closed, drawing in her scent that reminded him of his mother's lily of the valley. Her skin was warm and soft and tasted like summer.

The song ended and Ty stepped back, shaken.

But worse than that was looking down at Clara and seeing her eyes swimming with tears. A quick survey showed him that several people were watching them curiously, and why not? It was no secret that Clara was a resident at the women's shelter, and Ty knew his reputation—quite intentional when all was said and done. The cocky, confident rebel image was a lot easier to maintain than the truth, after all.

But Clara didn't deserve gossip or prying eyes. To his dismay a tear slipped out of the corner of her eye and down her cheek.

"Let's get you away from here," he murmured, squeezing her hand, feeling instantly sorry he'd let things go as far as they had during the dance. In another time, another place, with another woman, that sort of soft kiss would have been nothing. But here he'd forgotten himself. The best he could do now was get her away from the gossip.

Her eyes widened at his suggestion. "Away...as in?" He watched as she swallowed.

"Away from busybodies," he said quietly. "I promise you, Clara, you don't have to be afraid of me. I won't hurt you."

She pulled her hand out of his and her face paled. She seemed oblivious to the inquisitive stares of the wedding guests as she stumbled backwards.

"I've heard that before." The words sounded jerked from her throat, harsh and disjointed. "This was a mistake. A horrible, horrible mistake."

She turned on her heel and ran off, dashing out of the garden as she rushed to the house. Her shawl fluttered out of the crook of her arm and settled on the grass. Ty was left standing in the middle of the dance area feeling like a first-class fool.

He walked over to where her shawl lay on the cool grass and picked it up, running the soft fabric through his fingers.

He'd spooked her big-time. It was probably just as well when all was said and done. But now he had an additional reason he wished he hadn't promised Molly he'd move back into the ranch house. He wasn't sure what would be worse—the awkwardness with Clara or the antagonism between him and his father.

She was afraid of him.

The next few months were going to be hell.

Clara kneaded the biscuit dough with a bit more force than necessary, flattening it on the countertop before rolling it and pushing the heels of her hands against it again. She'd put Virgil through his physio exercises already and he'd fallen asleep over his crossword puzzle, tired from the exertions and from all the excitement of the previous day. She'd changed his bedding after his bath, given him his meds and made sure he was comfortable in his favorite chair. Molly was out at a church women's breakfast. And Ty was…

Ty was out in the barns somewhere. Thank goodness.

Just the thought of Tyson made her cheeks grow hot. The few times they'd crossed paths in the days since the wedding, he'd offered a polite greeting and moved on, barely meeting her eyes. And who could blame him? She'd cried, for Pete's sake, and run off. For someone who wasn't into drama or making a spectacle, she'd indulged in plenty. No wonder he kept his distance from her now. Her intentions to smooth the way had been a big fat failure.

Then again, he never should have kissed her either. Even if it hadn't been technically a kiss.

She flipped the dough and kneaded it again, welcoming the rhythmic motion. It was almost therapeutic the way her arm muscles moved and flexed as she pushed the dough around the board. She tended to cook when she needed to empty her mind. And her mind was plenty full.

But so far it wasn't working. Things around the Diamond place were tense. Ty complicated matters—and not just for her. Virgil had been irritable lately, growling at her during his exercises and wearing a scowl more often than a smile. She had half a mind to sit the both of them down and tell them to talk rather than stomp around beating their chests. There was clearly some sort of power struggle at work and it wasn't good for Virgil. It wasn't her place to say anything, though. And sheer embarrassment kept her from offering Ty more than a quiet hello.

She'd fallen quite under his spell while dancing. Their bodies had been touching. Her hands paused over the dough for a minute, remembering. On one hand, it had been a stunning victory over her personal-space phobia. But it had also been a huge mistake. Come on—Ty Diamond? And it had been in front of half of Cadence Creek. She gave her head a shake.

She employed the rolling pin next, rolling the dough out exactly half an inch thick. The more Ty stayed out of her way the better. Virgil needed to stay focused on his rehabilitation, and Ty made Clara feel…

Well, that was the problem, wasn't it? He made Clara feel, full stop. She'd gotten as caught up as any other woman in the romance of the wedding, wooed by the adoring looks Sam and Angela shared, the soft music, the beautiful flowers and pretty dresses. That was the only explanation that made any sense at all.

Clara applied the cookie cutter to the dough with a vengeance, cutting circles and plopping them on a cookie sheet. In the clear light of day she realized he had felt sorry for her. That stung, but she should have retained a little dignity rather than fleeing. She had no one to blame but herself.

She heard the front door shut. Molly couldn't be back already, Sam and Angela were going to be in Ottawa on their honeymoon for another week, and no one else would walk in without knocking. That left Ty. Speak of the devil.

"Morning," he said, coming through to the kitchen in his socked feet. Buster, the family retriever, trotted in on Ty's heels and rubbed up against Clara's leg to say hello with a wag of his tail.

"Go lie down, Buster," Clara said firmly. "Last thing I need is you in my biscuit dough."

The dog obediently found his bed in the corner and curled up on it.

Ty looked around, saw Virgil sleeping, and an indulgent smile curved his lips. She looked down to cover her surprise. The smile changed his face completely, softening his jaw and cheekbones, erasing years off his face and making it appear almost boyish.

Clara slid the pan into the oven, determined to finally put things on an even keel. "Good morning, Tyson." She deliberately kept her voice pleasant and impersonal.

He tilted his head, studying her as she straightened, brushing off her hands. "Ty, remember? Unless I'm in trouble, it's Ty." The smile changed, his lips curving in a devilish grin. "Does calling me Tyson mean you're still mad?"

In trouble? He *was* trouble. It would have been easier if he hadn't smiled, she realized. His smile was the one thing she couldn't get out of her head. At the wedding it had been warm, intimate and slightly lopsided as though he was sharing a joke. The warmth of it had extended to his eyes, the brown-as-molasses depths of them with sundrenched crinkles in the corners.

She avoided his gaze and set the timer on the oven instead. He thought she was mad? Embarrassed, yes. Awkward—definitely. Angry? Well, maybe a little. He shouldn't have rubbed his lips over her temple like that. It was presumptuous. It was…

Glorious. It had made her feel feminine and alive. Lordy, but he was a distraction! She wished he'd get out of the kitchen and back to the barns so she could focus better.

"Miss Ferguson?"

She was surprised that he persisted in addressing her so formally—to the rest of the family she was just Clara. His sober tone turned her head and she bit down on her lip at the sight of him, his weight on one hip, all well-worn jeans and a long-sleeved shirt, the grin no longer in sight. He wore a baseball cap. The curved peak made him seem—for the second time in as many minutes—ridiculously young. She had to stop noticing and simply do her job. It was the most important thing right now, her ticket to a new life. She was saving as much as she could so she could afford her own place. And Ty Diamond wasn't going to screw that up for her.

"Did you want to ask me something?"

He hesitated so long that Clara fought the urge to squirm. The timer on the oven ticked down painfully slowly. Virgil, asleep in his favorite chair in the living room, let out a random snore. It broke the silence, and alleviated a bit of the tension. Clara let out a soft laugh as Virgil snored again and shifted in his chair.

"Your father always falls asleep during his crossword," she said quietly. She wasn't quite sure what to call Virgil in reference to Ty. He was Ty's adopted dad but also his uncle by blood. And the tension between the two sometimes made her wonder if they even acknowledged each other as relatives at all.

"He gets tired easily, doesn't he?"

She nodded. "The stroke took a lot out of him. He's made wonderful progress, though. He did great in his physio this morning. Even if it did take a lot of prodding and a fair amount of sass."

"From you or from him?" Ty's eyes seemed to twinkle at her.

"From him, of course. He's been irritable lately." She met his gaze with a look that told him she knew the source of Virgil's displeasure.

"That's probably my fault," Ty admitted. "He's changed more than I expected. Sam warned me. About a lot of things."

His gaze was steady on her again and the ridiculous fluttering she'd felt at the wedding came dancing back. What had Sam warned him about? That Virgil was more stubborn than ever? That things weren't exactly calm and peaceful around Diamondback Ranch? Or had he warned Ty of something else—about *someone* else? A sudden thought struck. Had Ty asked her to dance because he'd been put up to it?

Each time she thought of that night she regretted it more.

"I'm just his nurse," Clara replied, turning away and taking the rolling pin and empty biscuit bowl to the sink.

"I didn't realize nurse duties included baking." He stepped forward and snuck a small bit of raw biscuit dough from the countertop, popping it in his mouth.

Clara felt a sharp and sudden pain in her heart, watching him sneak the scrap of dough. How many times had she and her brother done that as kids? Bread dough, cookie dough, it hadn't mattered. Their mother would scold but never yell, saying that she hoped they had children someday who did the same thing and drove them crazy. The memory sent a bitter pang through Clara's heart. Life had been so uncomplicated then.

Clara missed her family terribly. She'd followed Jackson to Alberta when he'd claimed he'd make his money in the oil patch and set them up for life. She'd been blind and stupid to leave all the good things behind to chase empty promises. But it was too late to go back home now. How could she possibly explain the changes over the years that had passed? No, the gulf was too wide. Saskatchewan was only a province away but it might as well have been a continent.

"I like to cook, and it gives Molly more of a chance to get out now and again," Clara explained. Besides, if she wasn't here at Diamondback, she was home at Butterfly House, and lately she'd felt more and more dissatisfied with that arrangement. She wanted her own place. Her own space and her own things. She wanted to buy her own groceries and eat on her own schedule and not worry about a set chore list.

"Did you make the pumpkin bread yesterday?"

She wiped her hands on a dishtowel.

"I did, yes."

"It was very good."

It felt so stilted and practiced, Clara realized. She lifted her chin. At least Ty was making an effort for the first time since the wedding. Maybe they just needed to clear the air and find some common ground. He'd never answered her first question so she repeated it.

"Is there something you wanted, Ty?"

The tiny smile threatened to mar the perfection of his

lips. She'd called him Ty deliberately and according to his wishes. Maybe if they could move past the Tyson and Miss Ferguson bit it would be more comfortable.

"Hang on. I'll be right back."

He disappeared up the stairs. Clara ran water into the sink, preparing to wash up her dishes. In seconds he was back, holding her shawl in his hands.

"You dropped this the other night," he said quietly. "I thought you might want it back."

She'd wondered where she'd misplaced it, but was so embarrassed about her quick exit that she hadn't had the courage to ask Molly if it had been found. She dried her hands on a dishtowel and took it from him, careful not to touch his hands. "Thank you. I wondered where it went."

Silence filled the kitchen once more, a quiet of the awkward variety. When she couldn't stand it any longer, she put her dishcloth back in the water and turned to face him. "Was there something else?"

"I don't quite know how to say it," he admitted, then reached up and took off his ball cap. His sable hair was slightly flattened and the band of the cap created a ring around his head.

"Just spit it out," she suggested, her tummy doing weird and wonderful things. Tyson Diamond exuded a carelessness that practically shouted *bad boy*. But most bad boys she'd known growing up had been overconfident and pushy. Not Ty. He was just…there. With his intense eyes and slow swagger. It wasn't much wonder the women flocked to him. Ty didn't have to do anything more than breathe. And here she was, hanging on his every word.

And she knew what it was like to be pressed up against his lean body.

And why on earth was she thinking such a thing?

He frowned, jamming his hands into his pockets. "I'm sorry for the other night. I upset you and I didn't mean to."

Her lips dropped open. Ty was apologizing? He thought she was mad at him—and she was, she supposed, but only a little bit. She'd been the one to ask him to dance. She'd been the one who'd quite unexpectedly melted in his arms. Yes, he'd gotten quite close and then he'd suggested they get out of there, but he hadn't truly done anything so very wrong.

She couldn't have asked for someone to be gentler with her as they'd danced. He'd tipped up her chin and put himself into her hands, letting her take the lead. It wasn't his suggestion that had upset her. It was the fact that she'd wanted to take him up on that offer so badly she'd frightened herself. For a brief, heady moment she'd considered taking his hand and letting him lead her away.

And then she'd come to her senses. She wasn't anywhere near ready to let something like that happen. And then there was the fact that for a few precious minutes she'd forgotten all about her plans and goals and let herself weaken. Oh, she hadn't been mad at Ty. She'd been furious with *herself.*

"You don't need to apologize. Let's just forget the whole thing." She made a show of picking up a set of oven mitts, wishing the oven timer would ding so she could be doing something, anything, rather than feel pinned beneath Ty's dark gaze. She chanced a look up and saw that his eyes had warmed.

"Did you think I was angry?" she asked bravely, suddenly wanting to know. She thought perhaps she'd prefer that to him thinking she was silly and weak.

He opened his lips to answer when the oven timer dinged—just when she wanted to hear his answer.

With a frown of consternation she opened the oven door

and slid out the pan of golden-brown biscuits. She put the pan on top of the stove.

"I wondered," he replied, "because you ran. I wondered if it was because of…you know, your past. I didn't think about that when I…well…it wasn't really a kiss, was it?"

She kept her back to him, closing her eyes. It was a small town and the Butterfly House project was a big deal around here. It was no secret that she came from an abusive background. Of course she was damaged goods.

"I'm not angry. It was just wedding fever or something. I blew what happened out of proportion. You have been perfectly polite and kind to me since you came home."

"Then why won't you look at me right now?"

Her gaze darted up to look into his face. He was too serious. When he looked at her that way it was twice as bad as when he flirted with his saucy grin. "Why did you do it?" she whispered. She didn't need to elaborate for them both to know what "it" was.

"Why did you ask, after you made it clear you didn't want to dance?"

She grabbed a dishcloth and began wiping off the counter. "I thought maybe I'd hurt your feelings."

He laughed, a sharp sound of disbelief as he leaned against the island. "Hurt my feelings? Clara, I think I'm made of tougher stuff than that."

She was getting annoyed now at being put on the spot. "Well then I'm sorry I did it. You can take your unhurt feelings and quit cluttering up my kitchen!"

But it wasn't her kitchen, and they were both aware of it. Silence settled over them, bringing that same, damnable feeling of intimacy she could never escape when he was around.

"You felt good in my arms," he said quietly. "And that's not a line. It's the only reason I have for losing my head.

It's not the sort of situation I normally find myself in. It was innocent, I swear. But I forgot what it's like here in Cadence Creek. It probably opened you up to speculation and for that I'm sorry. It won't happen again."

His explanation—his apology—touched her, though she would rather not let it show. It was better for everyone if they really did forget that stupid dance had ever happened.

"Yes, I think that's best." Thank goodness he was being sensible about it all. "I'm pretty focused on what I want, Tyson. I'm not interested in distractions. And right now my job is to help your father get well."

"I'll stay out of your way," he replied.

He'd been absent during the long weeks when his father was sick. He hadn't come home even when they'd asked him to. But he was here now, and she didn't like the idea that she might be standing in the way of him settling in. Of mending fences. Virgil had a habit of talking to himself and Clara had heard snatches of mutterings and grumblings. Virgil was not happy with his younger son. It wasn't good for him to be stressed. He and Ty needed to sort things out.

"You need to be with your father. I know you stayed away a long time, Tyson. He needs you. As long as we're clear, there's no need to avoid each other, right?"

She bent to get a cooling rack out of the cupboard and started piling the biscuits on the top.

Tyson's gaze caught on the golden-brown biscuits as the warm scent filled the air. She brushed her hands on her apron and stood back. Good God, she was pretty. The dark ringlets from the wedding were gone but now her hair fell in gentle waves to her shoulders. And her eyes... They were the same blue as a September sky over the golden prairie. Her plain apron covered the soft curves of her hips. He was shocked to realize he wanted to put his hands on them and pull her close to see if her lips tasted as sweet as they looked.

But she was sweet, and off-limits. Never mind that he had no idea how to really talk to her. The past ten minutes had been torturous, second-guessing his words and meaning. All his normal self-assurance evaporated when faced with a woman like Clara Ferguson.

He pushed the thoughts aside and nodded at the rack of biscuits. "Mind if I try one?"

"Sure. Here." She gave him a paper napkin and one of the round golden discs. He went to the cupboard and found the carton of molasses. Moments later he'd split the biscuit open and slathered it with butter and the sticky spread.

It was like biting into a buttery cloud. Better than his mother's, if that were possible. In four bites it was gone. Wordlessly she held out another.

"These are delicious, Clara."

"My mother's recipe."

He chewed and swallowed. He had a fair amount of experience dealing with whispers and gossip, and most of the time it ran off him like water off a duck's back. He didn't give a good damn about what Cadence Creek thought. But he found he cared what *she* thought. In some ways she was right. He did need more time with Virgil. He just had no idea how to go about it without starting an argument.

"The reason I stayed away, well, it's complicated."

She nodded. "It usually is. Molly said you didn't even come for his seventieth birthday a few years back. They had a big party I guess. But you wouldn't come."

"I couldn't come," he said.

"Couldn't or wouldn't?"

He wanted her to know why, but telling her could be a huge mistake. He'd had a good reason, but spending a few nights in lockup sounded bad no matter how he spun it. With her history he just couldn't bring himself to say it.

"Do you think it was the right thing for me to come home now?" he asked. He shifted his gaze to look at Virgil, still sleeping in his chair. Virgil had aged so much. He was smaller now than Ty ever remembered, and looked so vulnerable. Ty hated that. Hated that he might have been part of the cause of his father aging, too, by leaving Virgil more of the ranch to handle than he should have.

"Yes," Clara said firmly. "Yes, I do. For your brother, who needed you, and for your mom. Molly missed you and talked about you often. She felt terrible about the rift between you and your dad. And for Virgil, too, of course."

"He criticizes everything I do. He'd be happier if I'd stayed on the circuit and never came home." Even as he said it, he heard how childish it sounded, and he wasn't sure it was true. Virgil had always insisted that it was Ty's place to be at Diamondback pulling his weight. But it was always Virgil's way or no way at all. Ty had chafed against all that authority.

Clara put down the mug she was holding and peered up into Tyson's face. He didn't like that she seemed to see what he took great care to keep hidden. He'd excelled at his chosen path and had the trophies and accolades to prove it. But inside was a boy who always felt second-best.

"You need to patch things up," she reiterated. "What are you waiting for?"

Virgil shifted in his chair and let out a moan as he woke from his nap. What was Ty waiting for? He was excited about his new idea but he knew Virgil would think it was stupid. He wanted to say he was sorry but knew he'd just be told he was being weak.

If he was waiting for unconditional love, he'd be waiting a long time, and it was too hard to take the first step.

Ty reached for his hat, putting it back on his head. "I'd better get back to work."

Clara sighed as the door closed behind him and he passed by the kitchen window, his long legs eating up the ground. "I think the person who needed you to come home the most was you, Ty," she murmured at his retreating back. And she had no idea how to help either one of them meet in the middle.

CHAPTER THREE

As MUCH AS CLARA LOVED her job at Diamondback, Virgil's
care was not enough for the full-time hours she was paid.
Sometimes she felt like a glorified housekeeper. Not that
it was a problem, but one of these days Molly was going
to let her go and she'd have to find a new job. She would
probably have to leave Cadence Creek; her stay at Butterfly House was only temporary until she could get on her
feet. She'd been squirreling away money, but it cost a lot
for an apartment and all the furniture she'd need.

She needed this job for as long as it held out and she
was going to wring every drop out of the opportunity.

But for now she was sitting in one of the spare rooms,
needle and thimble in hand, making tiny, even stitches in
Molly's latest quilt.

She enjoyed doing things with her hands. As a girl she'd
learned to cross-stitch and knit; she and her mother had
spent evenings in front of the television working on little
projects. It had been her mom's way of unwinding after
working all day in an office, and it had been Clara's way
of spending time with her mom.

She'd spent a lot of time thinking about her mom lately.
She'd learned so much from her mother, but the lesson
that Clara carried now was how she had always insisted
that a woman needed a way to support herself. No matter

what, Wendy Ferguson had put in a good day's work and still had time for her kids. As Clara fed the needle through the fabric, she missed her mother something terrible. She talked to Ty about mending fences, so maybe once she was settled she'd reach out to Wendy, too. Maybe they could be a part of each other's lives again.

But for now Molly sat across from Clara, her own needle flashing in and out as she made stitches on the patterned lines of fabric.

"It's almost ready to roll," Molly remarked, tying off her thread and moving to cut a new piece.

The quilt was tied onto old-fashioned wood frames with metal brackets holding the corners. Once they'd quilted as far as they could reach comfortably, the frame would be rolled in and clamped tight. When it was all done Molly would bind the perimeter. But that was weeks away yet, especially since they only sneaked the occasional hour to work on it.

"It's beautiful," Clara replied. "The burgundy-and-green pattern is stunning against the cream."

They stitched for a few more moments, but Clara got the sense that Molly wanted to say something. She shifted in her chair and there was a tension around them that usually didn't exist. Clara's fingers tightened on the needle. Did Molly have a concern about Virgil's care? Or was it something else? Molly, along with the rest of Cadence Creek, had surely seen Clara run from Ty at the wedding. She'd probably seen how close they'd danced, too. And she would be foolish to think the older woman hadn't noticed the strain around the house since his arrival. There was no question that despite breaking the ice, Clara and Ty still tiptoed around each other.

"Is something wrong, Molly?"

Molly put down her needle and sighed. "I suppose so, Clara. I find myself feeling a little bit selfish these days."

Molly? Selfish? Impossible. Clara tied off her thread and snipped it with the scissors. "I don't think you know how to be selfish, Molly." She smiled, but inside she was feeling a bit uneasy.

"No, I am," she admitted. "I have gotten used to having you here. I *like* having you here. And I have taken terrible advantage of you."

Clara's head swam with confusion. Advantage? She had so much to thank Molly for. If anything, Clara felt like she was taking advantage of the Diamonds' generosity. "You gave me a job when I needed one, Molly. You made me feel welcome from the moment I arrived."

"Virgil's care is not a full-time job, Clara, and I feel I've kept you here when you might have found another better position somewhere else. And I've kept you for my own selfish reasons that have nothing to do with medical care."

A cold line of dread snuck down Clara's spine. Was this Molly's gentle way of letting her go? She could look for something else, but it would mean she'd be even longer getting into her own place. She swallowed against the growing lump in her throat. It wasn't just the money either. She'd come to care for Molly and Virgil very much. She already knew it was going to be difficult to say goodbye when the time came.

Molly sighed and began stitching again. "I never had a daughter around, you see. Never had someone to cook with or talk to or sit and quilt with. It was all boys all the time, and I've enjoyed having you here so much. But you're a nurse, Clara, not a hired companion. I just want you to know that if you were to find another position it's okay. I'd miss you, but I'd understand."

Clara swallowed again as relief made her wilt on the inside. "You're not letting me go, then?"

Molly lifted startled eyes to Clara's. "Heavens, no! Was that what you thought?"

Clara's cheeks heated. "I thought you were letting me down easy."

"Oh, goodness." Molly's eyes softened with compassion. "We all adore you. But this is about you, not us."

All adore her? She doubted it. Obviously Molly hadn't included Ty in that equation. Since their talk things had been a bit easier, but it was a long way from being totally comfortable, and adoration was a joke.

"I'll stay as long as you feel Virgil needs my help," she replied carefully. "Honestly, Molly, sometimes I feel guilty taking a paycheck." She offered a smile.

"How much longer are you staying at Butterfly House, then?" Molly didn't look up but her stitches seemed to slow.

"I've been saving up for my own place," Clara explained. "The program is great, but if I can find an apartment, that frees up my spot for someone else who needs it more."

Molly's voice remained conversational as she stitched along a dark green leaf. "This job could easily include room and board."

Clara's heart leapt. Oh, that was generous and so very *Molly.* And a few weeks ago she might have accepted—especially with Angela and Sam getting married and moving into their new house soon. But now there was Ty. It shouldn't matter that he lived here now, too, but somehow it did.

"Oh, Molly, that's so kind of you to offer, but I can't do that. You've been far too good to me already."

Molly's soft eyes met hers. "You're already like one of

the family. It doesn't make sense for you to have to scrimp and save when there is plenty of room here."

But there was every reason, and not just because of Ty. "I wouldn't hurt your feelings for the world, so I hope when I say that this is something I need to do on my own— on my own two feet—you understand. I know you're offering from your heart, and that means so much." Her throat tightened with emotion. "But I can't stay here. I need my own place, my own space. And even though I know you don't mean it that way, I would feel a bit like a charity case."

"Of course I understand." Molly smiled. "I told you I was being selfish. And I'll confess, I'm a bit relieved that you're not going anywhere for a while. You've made all our lives easier."

Except Ty's, Clara thought dryly. She put her needle to work again. Every time he came into a room where she was, he got this weird look on his face before masking it away.

And despite her assertions that she needed independence, she knew darn well she'd be tempted to take up the offer if it didn't mean being faced with Ty twenty-four-seven. Morning, noon and night. Running into each other in the hallways. Sleeping down the hall from each other…

That thought made something delicious hum inside her and *that* was how she knew it was trouble. Trouble she wouldn't touch with a ten-foot pole.

They worked together until they'd each finished the side they were stitching. Molly took a few moments to check on Virgil, who was watching television, and came back with Ty in tow.

"Look who I found hovering around the doughnut jar. Just the help we need to roll the quilt."

Ty's eyes met hers and their gazes caught for one

breathless moment. Goodness, she didn't know why he had the power to make her feel all fizzy and flustered. He looked so *ordinary,* after all, dressed in plain jeans and a plaid work shirt, with his hair still slightly messy. One of Ty's eyebrows rose as he spoke to Molly but kept his gaze locked on Clara. "I haven't rolled a quilt since…"

"Since you were a teenager and still at home, and you and Sam did the rolling while I put on the clamps," Molly finished.

Ty looked down on the top of Molly's head. Clara hid a smile. Ty was what, close to thirty? It had to be constricting for a grown man to be back in his childhood bed again after years of living on his own.

"I haven't forgotten how," he replied, going to one end of the quilt. "Mom, you and I can roll and Clara can do the clamps."

Molly braced her hip against one of the frame pieces and held everything taut while Clara removed the clamps. Then together Molly and Tyson pulled the fabric tight and rolled it under—once, twice, three times.

"Okay, Clara. Put the clamps back on."

She did Molly's corner first because it was harder for the older woman to hold the frame tight and steady. Once that was done she went to Ty's side. But the room was small and she had to brush by him to get the right angle. Their bodies touched—absolutely innocently—but she noticed all the same. She could see the bulge of Ty's arm muscles through his shirt as he held the frame taut. She put the clamp over the intersection of frame pieces but it slipped out of her hands and clattered to the floor.

Rattled, she bent and retrieved the clamp and hurried to tighten it to the frame.

But when they finished they still had to do the other side. And no one was talking. She had to stop clamming up every time he entered a room. Maybe she *should* be looking for a job somewhere else. But then she thought of Molly's kind face and Virgil's rusty laugh and she knew she had to stay. She also knew that refusing the offer of room and board was for the best. She couldn't even roll a quilt with Ty without getting flustered. Living under the same roof would be torture. She wasn't stupid. She had all the signs of being hopelessly attracted to him and yet she shied away from the simplest of touches. Touches that she really didn't want, seeing as touches usually led to other things called complications.

This time she shoved the clamp over the boards and tightened it with sure hands.

"Thanks, you two," Molly said, brushing her hands and looking oblivious to the undercurrents running between Ty and Clara. Perhaps Clara was imagining them. Ty adjusted the stand beneath their corner of the frame and straightened, squaring his shoulders.

"You're welcome. I should get back now." He shuffled past the quilt towards the door. "Lots to do before quitting time."

Ty couldn't get out of the room fast enough, Clara thought. She had to stop letting him affect her like this.

When Ty left, she let out a breath. Why couldn't things stay the way they'd been two, even three weeks ago? Before Ty came back? She had been comfortable coming to work, enjoyed feeling as if she belonged here. Now she was restless, on edge. Feeling that everything was going to change. She'd had enough change to last a lifetime— she didn't need any more.

She knew the answer, she thought, as she stuck her needle into the spool of thread and left it on top of the quilt. Nothing was the same since Ty came because she'd asked him to dance. Because she'd been in his arms and had felt his strong jaw against her temple, his wide hand along the small of her back.

And those few minutes had unlocked something inside her—an old longing, a need for something more. Something she hadn't imagined she'd ever want again. A something more that terrified her to the soles of her shoes. For a physical relationship would only be temporary, and an emotional one would make her far too vulnerable.

Gray clouds had rolled in over the prairie sky hours earlier and the north wind hadn't let up. October was early in the fall for snow, but Ty knew stranger things had happened. A few errant flakes wouldn't surprise him in the least. He shrugged into his jacket, turning up the collar before leaving the barn. He looked up at the house. The lights in the kitchen glowed warmly, but all Ty felt was dread.

His mother was overly cheerful to the point of annoyance right now. He knew she was trying to keep the peace—like today, when she'd pressed him into helping with the quilt. She wanted things to go back to the way they were when he'd been a boy, but that was impossible. Things had been said that couldn't be taken back. He was a grown man. And then there was Clara, all big eyes and as jumpy as a spring frog. She couldn't even get within a foot of him without getting flustered. He'd thought that apologizing to her might ease her discomfort, but today she'd dropped the clamp and hadn't looked at him again before he'd gotten the hell out of there.

And then there was Virgil. All his dad did was scowl. It bugged Ty that Virgil had apparently butted heads with Sam all summer but now it seemed Sam could do no wrong. Of course now Ty was home and he supposed Sam looked like angel in comparison. No matter how he tried to smooth things over, it felt as though all he was doing was stirring up a hornet's nest. One of these days someone was going to get stung.

He slid the barn door shut and latched it. The hell of it all was he loved his dad. Seeking approval that never came had driven him crazy; it had been easier to leave and do his own thing than stay and argue indefinitely, or feel that he could never live up to expectations.

But he was getting older. And so was Virgil. When Sam had called, Ty knew it was time to go home. He thought maybe they'd all mellowed over the past few years. That it would be different.

Mellowed, hah. Ty had walked in the door, Virgil had taken one look and muttered "Humph" before turning away.

It had been a deliberate slap. Ty wished he were a stronger man. That it didn't matter. But it did. Virgil was the only father he'd ever known. He hadn't wanted to adopt Ty, but he had anyway. Ty had spent years trying to prove to Virgil that it hadn't been a mistake. That he was worthy of the Diamond name.

How sad did that make him? He imagined what Virgil would say if he came out and admitted such a thing. He'd tell Ty he was weak. That a man only had to prove something to himself.

An odd whirring sound caught his ear and he paused. There it was again—like a car trying to turn over. He looked towards the garage and saw the bumper of Clara's car, mostly hidden by the farm 4x4.

He sighed, knowing dinner waited inside, knowing she probably didn't want his help but also knowing he couldn't just leave her there. She was going to flood the thing if she kept it up. He made his way over, shoving his hands in his pockets against the raw air. She was behind the wheel, turning the key and looking more than a little frazzled. The late-model car looked as if it was being held together with baler twine and bubble gum. The click-and-whir sounded again as Ty knocked on the window.

She rolled it down—the car was so old it still had manual windows. "My car won't start. I think my battery is dead."

"I'll give you a boost. How old is your battery?"

"Um, I don't know. I bought the car secondhand."

Clearly. It was a "Point A to Point B" car, and even that was being generous. "Don't worry, I'll have you home in no time."

He grabbed the keys from his pocket and went into the garage, starting his car rather than using the farm truck. The engine roared to life, the 454 block engine growling like a leashed lion. The seat was molded perfectly to the shape of his backside. The fact that the classic car felt more like home than the house he grew up in wasn't lost on him.

He backed out and parked it in position ahead of her car. He popped the hood and raised it up, anchoring it in place before doing likewise to her car and then connecting the battery cables. "Try it now," he said, and she turned the key.

The engine sputtered and started and he watched as a big smile filled her face. She looked great when she smiled, which wasn't that often, he noticed. She went through the motions, and she gave pleasant little polite smiles, but not a real, genuine grin like this. She looked like a whole other person when she relaxed. Her whole face lit up—just the way it had on the night of the wedding. It made her eyes shine and her skin glow. At first glance Ty had thought her rather unremarkable. But when she let down her guard, he realized she was quite pretty but in a softer, plainer way than he was used to. Her smile slid away as if she'd just realized she was doing it and was autocorrecting.

He unhooked the cables and backed the car away. When he hopped out, Clara was waiting beside her door, the engine still running. "Thanks, Ty. I guess I'll have to see about a new battery."

"If it doesn't start in the morning, call and I'll come get you."

She drew back a little and he wondered if her assertion the other day that she wasn't afraid was the truth or a convenient lie.

"I should be able to get a battery here in town, right?"

"At Pritchett's Auto."

"I'd better get going. You haven't even had your supper yet. Thanks again."

"You bet."

He had his hand on his car-door handle when her voice called out again. "Ty?"

He turned back. At least she was calling him Ty. She must not be mad anymore.

"Um, shouldn't the voltage thingy go up?"

Yes, he thought, it should. He went back to her car, stuck his head in and checked her dashboard. The car had been running a few minutes now and should be holding a better charge. He frowned and slid behind the wheel, turning off the key. After a few seconds he tried to start it again—dead.

"I don't think it's your battery."

A quick look at the contacts showed little corrosion. "It might be your alternator. Hang on a minute." He went into the garage and came out with a test meter. "I think it's dead, Clara."

"How much will it cost to fix?" She worried her lower lip with her teeth. Ty watched as the supple pink flesh was released, regaining its full, delicious shape. Right. The last thing he needed to focus on was Clara's lips. She was his dad's nurse, for Pete's sake. And she was carrying around a lot of baggage. He had to nip those sorts of thoughts in the bud right now. She couldn't even stand being in the same room with him.

"A couple hundred for the parts, maybe a bit less if you buy a rebuilt one instead of new. And I can put it in for you and save you the labor."

"Oh."

He could almost see the calculator running in her brain. "If it's too much, I can pay for it and you can pay me back a little at a time."

"No!" She stood up straighter. "It's not that. I'm just trying to save up for my own place and stuff. I can dip into my savings."

So she had her own bit of pride, he thought, pleased even though his offer had been genuine. "I thought you were staying at Butterfly House."

"It's temporary," she replied, putting her hands in her coat pockets. "The program is just to get women on their feet as they start over, you know?"

"And you're ready for that?"

She nodded. "I'm ready to be in charge of my own life. But for right now that means putting aside what I can each week so I can come up with first and last month's rent. That sort of thing."

She was stronger than she appeared, Ty thought. At times she seemed unbearably shy and quite jumpy. Her whole body had tensed when their bodies had brushed today. She rarely met his gaze, too. But when she did, it was usually with a determination he admired. Clara Ferguson was no pushover. He liked that.

"Well, you're not going anywhere in that car tonight," he said. "Grab your purse and I'll drive you home."

She hesitated and he knew that despite her words to the contrary, being alone with him made her uneasy.

"You could always call a cab. Or walk." He said the words with a smile. They both knew there was no cab in Cadence Creek and that Diamondback was a good five miles from Butterfly House.

"Funny," she answered dryly, putting her hand on the car-door handle.

The interior of the car was small and felt confined with her in it beside him. Country music played on the radio, filling the space with welcome sound. Clara said nothing, just stared out the window at the brown fields as he put the car in gear and it rumbled down the driveway.

"Your car is...old." She finally broke the awkward silence.

He tried a smile. "I prefer classic."

"What is it?"

"A 1970 Chevelle SS. I bought it for cheap in Edmonton a few years back and restored it."

"You did?"

"Yeah. I worked on it over the winters."

"You're a pretty handy guy to have around. Any other talents up your sleeve?"

He shrugged. "A few, maybe. I like working with my hands. And I got used to doing things for myself."

Silence fell in the car as he turned onto the main road. Several seconds ticked by, feeling interminably long as she stared out the window at the barren fields.

"How's Dad tonight?" he asked, anything to break the awkward quiet. He was starting to wonder if anything would ever be natural between them. If he'd ever stop second-guessing what he said around her, afraid of saying the wrong thing.

"Good. Tired. I think he's getting this cold that's been going around, and I want to make sure it doesn't go to his chest. He's got an appointment on Friday so we'll see how it goes. He ate his supper in his room, though. I've been trying to get him to eat in the kitchen with Molly more often."

"He doesn't do anything he doesn't want to," Ty replied, knowing exactly how tough the man could be when he made up his mind. An immovable brick wall.

"Oh, he's not as tough as you might think. You just have to know how to get around him." She smiled but Ty didn't share in it. After thirty years, he should know how to get around Virgil. But he didn't.

"Maybe you can tell me your secrets sometime," he answered, perhaps a little sharply. He looked over at Clara and let out a breath. "Sorry. I'm a little touchy where my dad is concerned."

She laughed. "Touchy? I hadn't noticed."

Oh, so she had a sense of sarcasm in there after all. He focused on the road but relaxed. "So what'd I miss at dinner tonight?"

"Chicken pot pie."

It sounded like heaven. Creamy chicken and vegetables, sopping up the gravy with fresh bread. His stomach nearly growled just thinking about it. "I'm sorry I missed it."

"You wouldn't if you stopped avoiding the house."

"It's that obvious?"

She nodded. "Yes. I just haven't figured out if you're avoiding your father or avoiding me."

His fingers tightened on the wheel. "Does it matter? It's easier for everyone if I just keep my distance, isn't it?"

They pulled into the Butterfly House yard. He put the car into park but left it running.

She turned in her seat and looked at him. "I don't want to keep you from spending time with your father. He needs that, Ty."

"I don't want to stress him out."

"You could try talking to him."

"Which always ends in an argument."

She huffed. "Good Lord, the both of you are stubborn. If you want to keep things the way they are, then fine. But your father is not going to be here forever, Ty. He might be recovering from his stroke but he is seventy-three years old. You might want to try a little harder."

His fingers tightened on the wheel as the words to explain sat on his tongue. "I'll get the part for your car tomorrow and give you the receipt. Good night, Clara."

Her face flattened. "Good night, Ty. Thank you for the drive."

She got out and slammed the door.

He put his head on the steering wheel for a few seconds as she made her way up the drive to the Butterfly House door.

"Dammit," he muttered, shut off the ignition and got out. "Clara, wait."

She paused by the door.

"I don't know how to talk to him," he said. It felt good to say it at last. And a bit scary.

Clara was standing with the key to the house in her hand. She tucked it back into her purse, turned her back on the house and met his gaze.

"Buy me a piece of pie," she said, straightening her shoulders.

CHAPTER FOUR

THE WAGON WHEEL DINER was the only place to eat in Cadence Creek except the sandwich counter at the gas station.

Clara walked in with Ty and felt a dozen sets of eyes on them. She tried to ignore them. This was not a date. People would always speculate, wouldn't they? And while being in a restaurant with Ty felt weird, it was nothing compared to being alone with him. This was much safer. Another step in her progress, right? Besides, this was about Virgil. The tension between Virgil and Ty was taking its toll. It wasn't good for him to be so stressed. If she could help the two of them meet in the middle it would be so much better for everyone at Diamondback.

Ty led her to a table in a back corner and, to her surprise, held out her chair as she sat down.

Not the first time he'd behaved gallantly. She suspected there might be a gem inside Ty Diamond after all—if he could get rid of the huge chip on his shoulder. Not that it mattered to her. She was only here to help Virgil. The older man had his share of grumpiness but she'd grown fond of him. He had a way of looking up at her with his eyes snapping that made her smile.

Ty had the same look, whether he knew it or not.

"Some things never change," Ty said, pushing aside a menu and relaxing against the wooden chair back. "Martha Bullock's been cooking here for over twenty years and, thank God, has no desire to retire."

"You used to come here," Clara said.

"Since I was a kid. Some kids saved nickels and dimes for candy at the store. I saved it for a piece of Martha's lemon meringue pie."

A waitress approached and took out a small notepad. "Well. Tyson Diamond. Ain't you a sight."

She had to be fifty if she was a day, but her lashes fluttered all the same. Clara rolled her eyes. She'd been absolutely right. All Tyson had to do was breathe and the women fell over themselves. This one was old enough to be his mother!

"Judy. How's George?"

"Gonna take me on a second honeymoon for our twenty-fifth, he says. Told me to pack a bathing suit for Mexico. Can you believe that?"

"You deserve it," Ty said with a wink. "Twenty-five years. Somethin' to celebrate for sure. Have you met Dad's nurse, Clara?"

Judy gave a wide smile. "Virgil still as ornery as ever?"

Clara grinned back. "He's a pussycat."

Judy laughed and Ty angled an appraising look at Clara. "You can see why Mom calls her a miracle worker, eh, Judy?"

Clara felt a glow start deep inside. He'd deliberately made it clear she was here as his father's nurse. Not that it would stop small-town gossip. She'd known that when she suggested it. But he was trying. He understood. And that meant something.

"I missed dinner," she heard him say. "I'd kill for one of Martha's hot turkey sandwiches and a slice of lemon pie."

"You got it. Clara?"

"Coconut cream if you've got it. And a cup of tea, please."

"Coming right up."

With a pat on Ty's shoulder she was gone, leaving them alone with the sound of the jukebox filling up the silence left in her wake.

"All the weeks I've been here, I haven't come into the diner," she said to Ty. An old George Jones tune twanged in the background. "That's a real jukebox, isn't it?"

He grinned. "Some things never change." His smile slipped a bit. "Sometimes that's good. Sometimes not so much."

She folded her hands in her lap. "You're talking about your father." It was so much easier talking to Ty when it was about Virgil, not herself. It almost felt ordinary. It had been years since her life had felt ordinary. It was spectacularly odd and comforting at the same time.

"We never see eye to eye. And the harder I try, the more we argue. That's why I left in the first place. We were going to say something that we couldn't fix, you know? I couldn't do it anymore."

"So you became a rodeo star."

There was that sexy grin again. "It didn't start out that way. I left in rebellion and I went to work at a place in Caroline. I was seventeen and feeling indestructible. A few broken bones, the odd scar, but I was good at it. It was a rush and there were…" He paused, as if measuring his words. "Benefits," he finished, but his dark eyes were sparkling devilishly at her.

"So why come home now?"

He shrugged. "Because I can't ride bulls forever. Because Sam asked me to."

"To make amends?" she asked carefully.

"I don't know if that's possible."

Judy came back with Ty's meal and Clara's pie and tea. Clara dipped the tea bag in the cup, bobbing it up and down a few times before squeezing it along the side with her spoon.

"Of course it's possible," she said quietly. "You just have to be willing to try."

She added a touch of milk to her tea and took a sip. Ty dipped a French fry in gravy, swirling it around his plate thoughtfully. "I don't know what he wants from me. Growing up I never felt like anything I did was good enough. There was so much pressure."

"From him or from yourself?"

His hand stopped moving and he stared at her. "What do you mean?"

She shrugged, picked up her fork and made an effort to cut into her pie. "I just wondered if you were always aware of the difference between you and Sam and if you felt like you were second-best."

He picked up his fork and stabbed the sandwich. "That's blunt." He sawed off a corner of the gravy-soaked bread. "You know, most of the time you have this whole sweet vibe going on, but then you really know how to put a guy in his place."

"Thank you." She couldn't help the smile that curved her lips.

"Thank you?" He popped the forkful of food in his mouth and raised his eyebrows at her.

"A few months ago I wouldn't even have been sitting here across from you, let alone speaking honestly. I know all about low self-esteem, Ty. I struggle with it daily. So telling me I have an assertive streak is a huge compliment."

"I guess you're really not afraid of me, then."

"I wouldn't go that far. It would depend on how you defined *afraid*."

The funny swirling silence enveloped them once more and Clara's stomach turned to butterflies. The first time

they'd truly spoken there'd been attraction. Since then it
had been awkward and stilted. But this—this was a whole
other set of nerves. And it was as delicious as the custardy
pie filling sitting on her tongue.

They knew each other a little better now, and the fa-
miliarity was starting to breed comfort.

"I'm sorry for what happened to you," he replied, putting down his fork. "I might not see eye to eye with my
dad, but I think we can agree that a man should never hit
a woman. I hope you know you're safe with me."

Clara studied his face, debating whether or not she
should reveal any bits of her story. It was so intensely
private. So painful. And yet by keeping it inside like a
dirty secret, she was giving it power, wasn't she?

"Before I met Jackson, I never thought I'd be one of
those women. I'd be smarter. I'd be stronger. And then
there I was, believing all the things he said. Thinking it
was my fault. Too afraid to leave, trying to do the right
things so it wouldn't happen again. Making excuses—for
him and for myself. That person is not who I am. And I've
been working a long time at finding the old me again."

"You will," he said encouragingly.

But her heart felt heavy. "Some days I don't know if I
will. Something changed that can't be fixed. So now I'm
trying to create a new me—with the old parts that I miss
but with the wisdom I've gained."

"That can only be a good thing, right?"

He should be right. Finding herself but being older and
wiser sounded wonderful. But there was the small issue
of forgiving herself, too. She hadn't quite nailed that yet.
Living with the consequences seemed an appropriate pen-
ance most of the time. It ensured she'd never let the same
thing happen again.

"The problem is with the wisdom comes the fear. And

trying to put it all together is really, really confusing. I hope one day I find the right balance. All I know is that from now on, I make my own decisions. The only person I'll depend on for happiness is me."

He reached across the table and laid his hand across hers. "You are one of the bravest women I've ever met. It'll happen for you. After all, there's no timetable, is there?"

She squeezed his fingers and then withdrew her hand before anyone saw them joined on the table top. Besides, she'd liked the feeling of them a little too much. "I'm getting impatient these days," she murmured. "Which I think is a good thing. The idea of moving forward is sounding really great."

"But Dad…"

"I told Molly I'll stay on as long as she needs me."

"And then?"

She shrugged. "I'll have to find another nursing job."

She toyed with her pie. Finding another job didn't hold a lot of appeal at the moment.

"So why did you become an LPN?"

Why had she? She supposed it had to do with growing up poor. She'd wanted to be a chef for a while. But cooking was something you did at home for your family, not a job. Working for minimum wage in a grocery store bakery wasn't a career plan, and whenever she'd mentioned cooking school her mother had flipped. It cost too much. The shorter Licensed Practical Nurse course was what they could afford, but Clara had felt suffocated. She figured that skipping town with Jackson was her way of rebelling. She'd only traded one prison for a much worse one.

"It was practical," she replied stiffly.

"But do you like it?"

She nodded. "Oh, I do. It wasn't my first choice, but

I like helping people. Seeing a patient's progress sometimes…"

She stopped, realizing she was about to say too much. She picked up her tea and took a sip instead.

Ty tackled his sandwich, scooping up a forkful of bread, gravy and peas. "What about a patient's progress?" he asked, popping the food into his mouth.

She avoided his gaze, instead working on scraping some toasted coconut off the top of her pie. "Sometimes seeing a patient improve was the brightest spot in my day."

Ty's leg brushed hers under the table. She looked up, startled, but his eyes were steady on hers. It was a very deliberate touch, but one that was away from anyone's curious eyes. Every nerve ending in her body stood to attention. It did not make her feel small or heavy with dread of what was coming next. It was, she realized, comforting and reassuring. How did he, with no effort at all, accomplish what no one else had accomplished in all these months?

"You realize those days are gone now, right?" His voice was quiet and his knee rubbed hers. "No one is going to hurt you here, Clara. I promise."

She couldn't look at him. If she did she'd blush and lose any coherent thoughts she was scrambling to put together in her head. It wasn't just that she liked how Ty's leg had felt. The simple thing would be to say that she was afraid of it, but that wasn't true either.

"Thank you," she said, her voice coming out sounding a bit strangled.

"I know the rumor mill says I'm a little wild…"

"A little?" she answered quickly, then put her fingers over her mouth. "I'm sorry. That wasn't fair."

His jaw tightened. "You're here to help Dad, and I don't want anything weird between us to get in the way of that.

That's all. I do want it to be better and right now you're one of the closest people to him. And you don't have the kind of bias that Mom does, because you don't have the history with the family. I'm not trying to come on to you, okay? It's not like that."

Of course it wasn't. The tingly feelings she felt were hers alone. Ty wasn't the least bit interested in her. He resumed eating his dinner while her hunger for pie seemed to disappear.

"Does the *wild* label bother you?" she asked, chancing another look up at his face.

He grinned. "I earned it fair and square."

Oh, that smile was lethal. For a second Clara stayed silent until curiosity got the better of her. "So why did you earn it? It sounds like you did it on purpose."

One eyebrow raised and he cupped his long fingers around his water glass. "You probably never did anything to rebel," he replied. "You seem perfectly nice and like…I don't know, like you always do what you should. I wasn't like that. I acted out. Molly should be a candidate for sainthood."

"If you're as stubborn as your father, then I agree." She smiled, but the grin was wiped from Ty's face.

"I never knew my real father," he replied flatly. "I've always said I got my wild streak from my mother and the Diamond stubbornness from Virgil. I really never stood a chance. Funny, I'm probably more Diamond than Sam is—son of one and raised by another—but it's me who's the black sheep."

"I can't imagine Molly and Virgil treating you as less than their own," she contradicted. "They seem very generous and fair and loving."

He shrugged. "I don't expect you to understand. You weren't dropped on a doorstep, Clara, because you weren't wanted by either of your parents. I'll never understand how she could do that. I don't plan on having kids of my own, but you can bet that if I did I'd do a lot better by them than mine did for me. My only link to them is biology. I don't even know if either of them is still alive."

He pushed away his plate. "Molly and Virgil are the only parents I've known. Without them I would have ended up in foster care. Once I graduated I left rather than disappoint them further. Rather than argue all the time."

"We all have choices," Clara responded, intrigued now at Ty's choice of words. Sometimes he called Molly and Virgil by their given names, and other times as Mom and Dad. But she noticed he never called him Uncle Virgil, even though his mother was Virgil's sister. "We just don't always choose the right thing," she added.

"Well, I'd like to do the right thing now. I've been studying the operation and I have ideas on expanding a certain area—and ideas on how to staff it. But I know he's going to tell me I'm crazy and we're going to argue again."

"So why not just put it on hold for a while? Go see him and say hello. Just talk, Ty. Surely there are good memories you can share and laugh over. Start there and see what comes of it. But don't stop trying."

She looked down at her plate, realizing that not trying was exactly what she'd done with her own family. "Maybe I'll even write *my* mom a letter. I haven't exactly been the model daughter."

"You? I can't imagine you doing anything wrong."

Clara pushed away her pie plate. "Oh, Ty." She sighed. "I followed the wrong man even after she told me I was making a huge mistake. And how does a daughter call up her mother and tell her that she's in the hospital because that man has beaten her? How does she say that she went back to that same man over and over?" Her throat tightened. "By the time it got to the point where I could say I found the courage to leave, it was too late, you know?"

This time Ty wasn't circumspect; he reached over and cupped her jaw in his hand. "If it's not too late for me, it's not too late for you." His thumb rubbed against her cheekbone. "I'll make you a deal. I'll try if you will, okay?"

She nodded, the rough texture of his hand oddly soothing against the soft skin of her cheek. "I think that's a good idea."

He withdrew his hand and she was surprised to find she missed the warmth of it.

"Let me look after this and I'll take you home," he said. He leaned forward to get his wallet out of his back pocket and Clara watched how the shape of his muscles beneath his shirt changed with the movement. He took some bills from his wallet, put them on the table, and reached for his jacket hanging on the back of his chair. Even in a cotton shirt, Clara could see there was not a spare ounce of flesh on him anywhere. Her mouth went dry as he shrugged into the coat and pulled up the zipper.

"You coming?" he asked.

"Oh, sorry," she replied, embarrassed at being caught staring. She reached for her coat and was again surprised when Ty took it from her hands and helped her put it on. She hadn't expected him to have such manners. "Thanks," she murmured, putting her purse over her shoulder.

Outside he opened her car door first before jogging around the hood and getting inside.

His chivalry made it feel like a date. Only most of the guys she'd dated hadn't bothered with the niceties either. "You don't have to do that stuff, you know," she said, folding her hands in her lap.

"What stuff?" He put the car in gear and headed out of

the parking lot. It was fully dark now and the headlights lit a swath ahead of them.

"You know. The coat and the car door."

He shrugged. "You've met my mother, right? She'd brain me if I didn't use my manners."

"You're nearly thirty." Clara chuckled as the image of the gentle Molly braining anyone was comical.

"I learned at a young age." He laughed, then sobered. "You asked me a while ago about being wild. I guess I was, but I always try to be upfront and honest. I never make promises I don't intend to keep. I always try to treat people with respect."

"Even the buckle bunnies?" She felt quite daring bringing up such a thing, but Ty was turning all of her preconceptions upside down.

He frowned. "Even them. Don't worry, Clara. They got exactly what they were after. They weren't looking to fall in love and neither was I. Everything upfront and mutual." He angled her a dry look. "And nowhere near as often as people would like to think."

What was it her mother had called her? A danger magnet? Sitting in Ty's muscle car in the dark made her feel just that. He had this edginess about him that was exciting, and yet this penchant for honesty and chivalry that added to the pull.

He pulled up in front of Butterfly House and put the car in park, where it idled with a throaty purr.

"And so what about me?" she asked. There'd been a push-pull thing going on ever since the wedding. "Are you honest with me?"

He turned in the seat slightly so he could look at her. His face was partially lit by the dashboard lights, creating light and shadow along the angles of his cheekbones and jaw. Her heart began beating erratically. How had she gotten here? Only a few short months ago she'd been a scared little mouse. Now she was sitting with Ty in his car in the dark asking him about his intentions.

Scary, but oh, it felt gloriously normal!

"I'm especially honest with you," he said, his voice low and intimate. "You scare the hell out of me, Clara."

It should have driven them apart and broken the spell, but it did exactly the opposite. The air felt warmer and the interior of the car smaller as she watched his tongue wet his lips.

"Me? Scare you?" Her words came out on a squeak.

"I don't know how to act around you. You're different. You've been through stuff I can't understand. I never know if I'm going to make things better or create a disaster. If I mess up or do something wrong, remember I'm trying to do the right thing."

"The right thing," she echoed.

He nodded slowly. "Yes. The right thing." He sighed. "I'm trying to do the right thing for everybody, so I'm bound to screw it up somehow."

Clara fought the urge to reach over and touch his thigh. He was being terribly open, wasn't he? She was starting to realize that beneath the sexy rebel was someone who cared very deeply. Who was kind.

Which made him an even worse sort of trouble.

He cleared his throat. "And now the right thing is for you to get out of the car and go inside and get a good night's sleep."

Clara clutched her purse. With a start she realized how easily he could have leaned over and kissed her. And more shock as she realized she would have let him.

She would have let Ty Diamond kiss her without a second thought.

"You're right," she said, sounding slightly breathless

as she put her hand on the door handle. "Thanks for the pie, Tyson."

"I'll come by in the morning to pick you up."

Nerves bubbled through her. She couldn't let herself get too familiar with him, or start relying on him either. "Don't worry about it. I'll have one of the girls run me over before they go to work."

"You sure?"

Oh, she was sure. She didn't want the added complication. She already cared for Molly and Virgil far more than she expected. She didn't want to come to care for him, too. Despite Molly's assurances, she knew this job wasn't permanent. She knew there was a new life out there for her, and one that didn't include Ty.

He said he tried to do the right thing. She had to, too.

"Good night," she said firmly, and climbed out of the car. It took all she had not to run to the front door, but she put one foot carefully in front of the other, methodically took her keys out of her purse and unlocked the door.

She didn't hear him drive away until she was inside with the door safely locked again.

CHAPTER FIVE

TY STOOD OUTSIDE HIS father's room. He'd been there for a few minutes already, wondering if he was crazy to even try to talk to Virgil about his plans. But the past few days had been rather peaceful, making him think that perhaps Virgil would be open to new ideas. Besides that, Sam was due back from his honeymoon tomorrow. And Sam had already given his approval to at least assess Diamondback's operation and capacity for a different sort of expansion. Ty was ready to talk to him about moving forward.

But he had to talk to Virgil first. Without the old man feeling as if the boys were ganging up on him.

"You gonna stand out there all day?"

Virgil's strong voice made Ty jump, and he pushed the door open as if answering a command. "Dad."

"Something's on your mind if you stand outside my door that long." Virgil pushed himself up in bed so he was sitting, and gave Ty an assessing eye. "Bad news, eh?"

Great. This was not how Ty had planned to introduce things—on the back foot.

"Not at all." He went forward and pulled up a chair close to the bed. "I came in for a cup of coffee and thought I'd check in."

Virgil laughed, and Ty appreciated the rusty sound. It didn't happen enough around here. "Don't kid a kidder,

Ty. You haven't just 'checked in' on me since you got back. What's on your mind?"

"Sam's back tomorrow." There was no use mincing words now. Virgil was mostly bedridden but just as perceptive as ever. "I wanted to talk to you about something before he got back. To get your opinion."

His stomach twisted in knots. Undoubtedly Virgil's opinion would be that Ty was crazy. But Ty had promised Clara to try. He knew this was the right way even if he dreaded the outcome.

"Well, this is a change. You wanting my opinion on anything."

Ty refused to be provoked. "You might be surprised," he replied mildly. "We don't often see eye to eye, but I always valued your opinion. Even when I wished it came in the form of support. Which it rarely did."

How was that for honesty then?

Virgil fixed him with a beady eye, but Ty refused to squirm. They were grown men. Ty wasn't a boy any longer.

"So what hair-brained scheme are you cooking up this time?"

Ty considered the words he'd practiced. If he told Virgil the truth—that he wanted to work with an organization to provide employment to disadvantaged people—he knew what Virgil would say. That Diamondback hadn't become prosperous by being a charity. No, he had to come at it from a business perspective. Solid dollars and cents.

"Nothing hair-brained. I'd like to make a few adjustments, that's all. With Sam and I both back home, we can share the workload."

"Sam and I shared the workload and we didn't have a lot of spare time on our hands," Virgil argued.

But Ty was thirty and healthy and Virgil was in his seventies and slowing down. Ty wanted to point it out but didn't. "I've got nothing but time. Sam has Angela, but I'm commitment-free and ready to put my energy into Diamondback."

"Why now?"

Ty met his gaze evenly. "Why not?"

A reluctant chuckle wheezed from Virgil's throat. "You're just as stubborn as ever."

"I learned from the best," Ty returned. And smiled. They might knock heads over issues but there wasn't a man on earth he had more respect for than his father. Why else would he have tried so hard? Living up to Virgil's expectations had been impossible, but it didn't stop the gratitude. Or the love. If it had, maybe he wouldn't have felt the need to leave rather than face the hurt of being a constant disappointment.

"So you want to expand. How?"

"I want to add some quarter horses for one thing. Sam's biogas plant is making Diamondback greener. We've got the room to keep some good stock in the north barn and put them to good use around here. A lot of ranchers are blending old methods with new technology to make their operations more sustainable." He smiled. "Besides, I like working with horses. I'm good at it. We can add some to our own stock and I can train others into solid working stock—there's a market for it. And I can manage that part alone."

Virgil frowned. "We're a beef ranch. Sam's got this biogas thing going on and now you want to branch into horses. Do you even have any experience in training? What do you think is going to happen to beef production if you boys don't focus?"

Ty sighed. Perhaps Virgil didn't understand that Ty had spent a good many years working at operations big and small. He'd seen what worked and what didn't. "Nothing will be taken away from the beef, Dad. This is all going to make the operation better and more efficient. Diamondback beef is the best in the province, and our reputation is growing. We're working towards reaching sustainability standards so we can have official designation. For Pete's sake, everything Sam and I want to do is to make the ranch bigger and better by looking after the right things. Our priorities are bang on."

Virgil looked away. "You think you have all the answers. You always did."

"Maybe I wasn't always wrong," Ty said quietly.

Virgil said nothing.

"I came here to ask your opinion, whether you think so or not." Ty knew he couldn't possibly bring up the next idea today. Virgil was already riled up with this small little shift. "Is the focus your only concern?"

"How do you plan to pay for the new stock and what goes with it?"

Ty fought the urge to remind his father that Diamondback was a multi-million dollar operation. It had become that way because Virgil had always been diligent about dollars and cents, and Ty knew that in the beginning there had been lean times. He knew what the Diamond family had been. He'd heard the story of his mother often enough. Each time it had stung like a slice of a blade. He was the bastard Diamond. Left on a doorstep for all intents and purposes. He'd felt like a charity case a good portion of the time.

So it was with a fair amount of pride that he straightened his shoulders and said, "Out of my own pocket."

Virgil's lips fell open briefly before he raised an eyebrow. "Your money?"

"That's right."

"What money?"

Ty's temper started to simmer. "Money I earned. You know very well I haven't had a red cent from Diamond-back since I left."

"I never cut you off."

Ty bit his tongue. No, Virgil never had. But Ty had refused any help when he walked away, determined to succeed on his own. To prove he could.

"I can finance whatever needs financing," Ty repeated. "If that's what you're getting at."

"How much?"

"I made some good investments." He didn't want to bring this down to a dollar value. Truth was, he'd lived simply and was fairly comfortable when all was said and done. His answer seemed to have momentarily silenced his dad. He wasn't sure if he was supposed to feel gratified at surprising Virgil, or if he was let down because he knew his dad expected so little of him.

"If you want to stop me, you're going to have to get out of that bed," he said, far more confidently than he felt on the inside. "Stop giving Clara the sharp side of your tongue and put your effort into your rehab."

"Clara hasn't complained." There was a note of petulance in Virgil's voice that made Ty want to smile. Virgil knew very well he'd been a grumpy old bear lately.

"Because she's too nice," Ty replied. He put his hands on the arms of the chair and boosted himself up. "She cares about you. Just because she's on the payroll doesn't mean she deserves your sass." He grinned suddenly. "Save it for me. I can take it. I have years of experience."

Virgil lifted his chin. "Hmm. There may be some Diamond in you after all."

"More than you'd like to think," Ty said, heading for the door.

"Tyson."

He turned around. Virgil had spun about on the bed. There was a wheelchair to one side and a walker on the other. The old man needed to get up and around again. Ty would take all the sharp remarks in the world if it meant Virgil was back to his old self once more.

Virgil nodded. "You and Clara. Are you, ah…"

The question made something funny turn in Ty's chest, something he was afraid to examine too closely. "No," he said. "We're not. She deserves a lot better man than me."

"For once we agree," Virgil replied, but for the first time there was no animosity in the words. Instead there was a camaraderie, the warmth of a shared joke. He was smiling at Ty, and Ty couldn't help but smile back.

"I have a ranch to run," Ty said gruffly. "Until you get off your ass and put me out of a job."

The best sound in the world was the sound of Virgil's laughter following him down the hall.

Things had gone better than he'd dared to hope. But what would Virgil say when he outlined his whole plan?

Clara saw the light on in the north barn and stared at it out the living room window for a few minutes. For the past few days the tension in the house had eased a bit. Virgil had apologized for his dark moods, Ty and Virgil actually sat at the dinner table without arguing, and now Sam and Angela were home and busy finishing the interior of their house, claiming that their do-it-yourself approach to decorating had sentimental value. Their arrival home at Diamondback had prompted a spur-of-the-moment celebration and Clara had been included in the family event. It had been bittersweet, feeling like she belonged and yet somehow knowing she didn't. The warmth, the laughter were all things she was starting to remember about being a part of a family and she missed it horribly.

The fact that her letter to her mother had come back undeliverable only made her feel more down.

Now Sam and Angela had gone home, Molly was in with Virgil, reading while he did a puzzle, and all that waited for her was the sunny yellow room at Butterfly House. Only a few months ago she'd been thrilled to move in there. Now it felt restrictive and, well, not like a home. She often found herself looking for ways to avoid it. What she really wanted was her own place.

But that would have to wait another month. In her pocket was the money to pay Ty back for her car parts. She should have done it before now, but she'd held off, trying not to touch her savings while waiting for payday.

She stared at the light a few moments more before grabbing a sweater and heading out the back door. She paid her debts. And she didn't want to owe Ty anything. He'd been absolutely perfect since the night at the diner. Their conversations had been pleasant and platonic. He'd stopped avoiding the house and came in for a coffee fill-up or simply to check in with Virgil.

But there were times—oh, catch-your-breath times—when their eyes met and she felt that butterfly sensation low in her stomach.

No, she didn't want to owe Ty Diamond anything.

The air was crisp but without the frosty bite that had been present earlier in the week. Her shoes crunched on the gravel of the drive as she made her way to the barn. She pushed the door aside and was greeted by warmth and the pungent but pleasant smell of horses. One whickered softly as she passed by the stalls, heading towards the beam of light slicing across the floor.

She found Ty in a small room. He'd fashioned a desk out of an old table and retrieved a rolling chair from somewhere, using an old wood box as a makeshift file drawer.

His head was bent over a notebook and papers were scattered over the top of the table. A calculator sat by his elbow.

She watched him for a few seconds. Something warm and tender wound its way through her insides. She'd never seen a man work harder than he did. Even with Sam home now, Ty worked from dawn until dusk. He reached for the calculator, punched in a few numbers and frowned. He rubbed a hand over his head—devoid of both ball cap and cowboy hat. The sable strands stood up on end in a careless mess.

In a million years she would not have expected this. She was beginning to care for Tyson Diamond. It was easy to dismiss the good looks and charm, but there was more to him than that. She'd seen it at the diner and she saw it every day. He tried. With the ranch, with his dad. And she'd bet he never thought he was up to scratch either.

"Hey," she said softly.

His head snapped up in surprise, and her heart did a little thump as he smiled at her. He leaned back in his chair and stretched. Her mouth went dry seeing his long arms extend to the side and the hollow of his throat extended. He let out a breath and rolled his shoulders. "Hey yourself. What are you doing out here?"

She found her wits and reached into her pocket. "I came to pay you back for the parts," she said, handing over the folded bills. "I'm sorry it took so long."

She really hoped he accepted it. She didn't want to start a whole "don't worry about it" thing where she felt indebted to anyone. He rubbed his thumb over the end of the bills and considered. Then he tucked it into his shirt pocket. "No problem. Car working all right?"

"Like a top."

He rested his elbows on the table. "Why do people say

that? Tops spin around and around unpredictably, then fall down."

He was in a lazy humor tonight and Clara found she liked it. "Like a dream, then?"

"Dreams are good," he replied, and tingles ran down her arms at the sound of his smooth, deep voice. There was not a soul out here with them in the barn. It was incredibly intimate. What was surprising was that she hadn't even had a second thought about being out here with him. She hadn't required a public situation for support. She hadn't needed a buffer between them. Goodness, she trusted him, didn't she? And other than Angela, she hadn't truly trusted anyone in years.

She blinked past the sting at the backs of her eyes. Ty would never understand the significance of this moment. But she did. It was another huge step in healing. It had begun the night he held her in his arms at the wedding dance.

"Are you all right?" Ty's voice broke through her thoughts and she smiled a wobbly smile.

"I'm great." She desperately wanted to move to another subject, so she waved a hand at the walls. "Sharing your office with a storeroom?"

Ty pushed his chair back. "The cupboards hold a lot of the medical supplies and various treatments we use around here. All it took was shifting a few boxes and I had my own office." He pointed at the floor to a small space heater. "Heat in the winter." He moved his thumb so it pointed at a window. "Air conditioning in summer."

She leaned against the doorjamb. "You could probably set up an office in the house, you know. Molly wouldn't mind and even Virgil seems to be getting used to you these days."

"Here," he said, getting up and retrieving a wooden

crate from the corner and setting it on its end. "Have a seat."

She perched on the crate and folded her hands. Ty sat back down in his chair. The seat was slightly higher than her box so she still had to tilt her head a bit to look into his face. He looked tired, she realized.

"I like it out here," he explained. "If what I want to do actually happens, I'll be making this into an actual office. My own piece of Diamondback, you know?"

"Is this about the horses, then?"

He shrugged. "Partly. There's more to it, but one step at a time. We've got all the facilities right here. We're just not using them. Besides, Sam's the cattle man. I know he plans on helping Angela with the foundation, but beef will always be his baby and that's as it should be." He crossed an ankle over his knee. "Why shouldn't I have something of my own?"

Clara understood that. After all, she had taken this job as a stepping stone to a new life. "I know what you mean," she replied. "Don't get me wrong, I've loved working here. Molly and Virgil have been so good to me. And Angela's foundation—I don't know where I'd be without it. But I want something of my own, too. I've spent years following. I followed Jackson. And when my life blew up I followed what everyone told me I had to do. Now it's time for me to have something for me. I think I'm ready for that."

"Good for you," he said warmly. "You deserve it, Clara."

Silence spun out for a few moments and Clara realized she should get going. Ty showed no signs of stopping work and it probably wasn't the wisest thing to stay out here alone for too long. "Anyway," she said, standing up, "I should get back. Tomorrow's another day, right?"

Ty pushed back his chair. "I'll walk you out. I could stand to give my legs a stretch."

They ambled their way down the barn corridor, their steps slowing more and more as the door drew closer. The horses were quiet now in the dark with only the soft sounds of the odd hoof or snuffle breaking the silence. With only the slightest shift Clara knew her shoulder could be touching his arm. If she reached out the tiniest bit, her fingers would brush with his. They were silly thoughts. Why would Ty want to hold her hand? They weren't shy teens anymore. They weren't even really interested in each other, were they?

They were nearly to the door now and it seemed every nerve ending Clara possessed was on high alert. She *was* interested in Ty. She thought about him far too often and she was way too aware of him. But that wasn't the same thing as being interested in a relationship. They were two very different things. Attraction was momentary. Relationships represented a commitment too scary to even really comprehend.

But it didn't stop the tingling sensations she felt as his arm brushed hers, sliding the barn door a few feet to the side, letting in a chilly puff of air.

"The moon's bright tonight," Ty murmured. His body blocked the door part way; there was no way she could slip through the gap without brushing against him. She swiped her tongue over her lips that seemed suddenly dry.

"It was full two nights ago," she replied, closing her eyes briefly as she realized how breathy she sounded.

"But cloudy." Ty still didn't move. He pointed upwards. "Look. It's so clear the stars go on forever. The unending sky is my favorite thing about the prairies."

She moved forward a bit but her view was blocked by the breadth of Ty's chest. He slid back against the heavy wood frame of the doorway, making room for her to peer through.

The sky was enormous and stunning, full of twinkling stars and the steady, watchful gaze of planets. A cloud of breath frosted the view for a moment as she tilted her head up to watch a satellite cross the sky in a steady, perfect arc.

"What do you suppose it's watching?" she whispered, pointing at the moving dot.

When Ty didn't answer, she turned her head. He wasn't watching the stars at all. Instead he was looking at her. He wasn't smiling. But there was something about him that made her forget the fall air and made her warm all over.

"Look at the stars," she chided softly. "They're beautiful."

"No more beautiful than you."

Her breath caught in her chest, making it difficult to breathe.

"Why did you really come out here tonight?"

She couldn't answer. Instead she bit down on her lip as she stayed suspended in the delicious sensation of being the sole focus of Ty's attention.

He lifted his hand and rested it on the side of her neck while his thumb brushed the curve of her jaw. Breathing was torturous now as Ty's face seemed to come closer. His eyes were open—those gloriously velvet eyes with gold flecks dancing around his pupils. The cotton of his shirt touched the knit of her sweater as their bodies drifted closer.

But Clara was totally lost when he raised his other hand and cradled her face in his palms, as if he was holding something precious and fragile. There was no fear here. No hesitation. There was no darkness, only light.

"Clara," he murmured, and he shifted his head the tiniest bit, closing the remaining gap and touching his lips to hers.

Her lips drifted closed as the sensation rippled through her. His lips were soft and gently persuasive. Instinctively hers parted beneath his, willingly yet carefully tasting what he was offering. What she discovered was sweetness. She hadn't expected sweetness from a man like Ty.

His hands moved from her face to cup her neck, his fingers tangling with her hair, moving through her curls but demanding nothing. All her preconceptions drifted away on the night air. He was the Cadence Creek bad boy. She'd expected him to take. But he wasn't. He was giving, and she rested a trembling hand on his chest for balance as she tilted her head and leaned into the kiss.

He was a solid wall of muscle and man, steady and strong. As she slid her hand up to his shoulder the kiss deepened, losing a touch of its sweetness and replacing it with a wildness that was a promise of what lay ahead. It was an urgency that was somehow unrushed—an acknowledgement of the flare of passion without the need to let it burn out.

It was the most incredible kiss she'd ever experienced.

Ty broke away first, resting his forehead against hers for a few seconds. His breath fanned her cheek in small gasps and she felt the accelerated rise and fall of his chest and shoulders beneath her fingers.

The last thing she expected to see when she pulled back and looked into his face was concern.

"Are you okay?" he asked quietly. "I didn't mean to push. To rush you. I…"

Emotion rushed through her veins—relief and gratitude and affection and awe. She stood on her tiptoes and put her arms around his neck, drawing him into a hug.

"Hey," he soothed, but he didn't push her away. He

looped his arms around her back and rubbed the base of her spine. "It's okay. Right?" His breath was warm on her hair. "Should I have asked first?"

He sounded so unsure. It was a revelation, and a smile blossomed on her lips. She nodded against his neck. "It's okay," she said, the words muffled but discernible. He tightened his arms around her and she wanted to weep with the wonder of it. It was more than a kiss between them. He knew. He understood.

She let him go and tried to get herself together. The last thing she wanted was to cry all over his shirt. He would think she was upset but really it was just a lot of bottled-up emotion that needed to come out. She ran her finger under her lashes and took a big breath. When she could look at him without tears, she met his gaze.

"Thank you, Ty. I..." Her voice caught and she swallowed. "I was so afraid I'd never be able to...to..." She didn't know how to explain the hesitation and fear that had been a part of her life for so long.

"Shh," he said, and to her surprise he turned her by the shoulders and circled her with his arms, so her back was nestled against his chest. "Just look up there for a minute, and breathe."

The stars glittered, perhaps a little brighter than before, as she rested her head against the indent where his shoulder met his chest. His hands rested against the thick waistband of her sweater and she covered them with her own. For several minutes they stood that way, watching the inky sky and the shifting constellations.

"Do you know," he whispered in her ear, "that in the winter, when the conditions are just right, you can see the Northern Lights from here?"

"I've never seen them," she whispered back.

"Maybe you'll be able to this winter," he suggested.

Clara felt a sudden chill. This winter? But she wouldn't be here, would she? At some point Virgil would be able to make do with the extramural nurse a day or two a week, or a drive into town for a physio session. She would be leaving Diamondback behind. She'd be leaving them *all* behind.

She stepped out of his embrace. This had been amazing, wonderful, but it wasn't real, was it? It wasn't practical or advisable. If she kept going on the way she was going she would end up hurt.

"I really should be getting back, Ty. It's getting late."

"I'll walk you to your car."

"You don't have to."

"Yes, I do."

He waited while she grabbed her purse from the kitchen and then walked beside her to her car. When she got there he put his hand on the door handle to open it, but hesitated. When she met his gaze, he stepped forward and kissed her again. Without the breathless hesitation of the last time. It was soft but deliberate. And sexy as hell.

He stood back, opened the door and held it.

Her cheeks flared with heat. Her body hummed with the sense of him—his scent, the feel of him, his taste. "This isn't a good idea, Tyson."

He smiled in the dark. "I knew you were going to say that."

"Not that it wasn't…you know," she continued awkwardly. "Surprising."

"And good?"

Damn him. "And good," she admitted.

"But?"

She sighed. "Yes, but. Tonight was a big step for a girl like me. I haven't allowed myself to be close to anyone, Ty. I felt safe with you. Don't ruin that, please."

His smile turned to a scowl. "You think I'll ruin it?"

She shook her head. "You won't mean to. But we both know this can't go anywhere. You have too much on your plate right now, and I'm going to be moving on. We both know this is temporary. I don't belong here. It's just my job. I care about your family but one day soon I'll have a new job, very likely in a new place. I'm going to build my own life. Getting involved any further would only complicate things."

She put her hand on the car door. "Ty, I'm trusting you to understand when I say that I can't handle complications on top of everything else in my life right now."

"You're not ready."

"I'm not ready," she confirmed. "And that's not the kind of girl for you. You need someone confident and sure of herself, not someone who needs to be fixed. That's not fair to you. Or to me."

"I'm not sorry it happened."

She wanted to reach out and touch him so badly. But she had to be strong. She couldn't send mixed messages anymore. "I'm not sorry either," she murmured. "But it has to end here."

Ty nodded. "Let's just take a step back, okay? Get the ground beneath us again."

Clara nodded, but the bubble of elation from earlier had popped, leaving a thread of unease trickling down her spine. Why did she get the feeling that Ty wasn't going to back off as easily as he said?

Her feelings for Ty had snuck up on her and she couldn't deny they were real. But as she shut the car door and started the engine, she pressed a hand to her abdomen, against an invisible pain. It couldn't go further than tonight. She didn't want to count on someone again. She didn't want to go through losing someone again. And she definitely didn't want the despair of her dreams being destroyed one more time.

Never again.

CHAPTER SIX

OCTOBER'S BRISK, GOLDEN days turned to the gray days of November. The snow still held off, the clouds spitting out random flakes now and then. The days got shorter, and Ty woke most mornings in the dark and then ate his dinner in the dark at night.

It was not his favorite time of year.

Clara still came and went from the house, and Ty tried to keep things on an even keel with her—at least on the outside. He hadn't meant to kiss her that night. Hadn't meant to hold her in his arms. Hell, after their dance he knew she was skittish as a new colt. And she had a good reason.

But he'd been thinking about her too much. And she'd appeared in his cubby hole of an office, all wide blue eyes and wearing that thick, completely unsexy sweater like body armor, holding out money that he wanted to tell her to put back in her pocket.

He turned up his collar against the wind and nudged Strawberry forward, holding the reins loosely in his gloved hand. The mare hadn't had much exercise lately and he'd decided to give her a treat with a ride out to the west butte. It had given him time to think, too. He'd been putting off really talking to Virgil for days. Ty had known all along that he could finance his project on his own. Sam had loved the idea. No, it was one tiny detail that kept sticking to Ty like a burr under a saddle. He was afraid of disappointing Virgil once more.

He took Strawberry into the barn, removed her saddle and bridle and gave her a good rubdown before turning her out in the paddock. The fresh air had worked up his appetite, so he thought a cup of coffee and a slab of the marble cake Molly had whipped up yesterday might hit the spot.

The house was quiet inside, but the coffee was hot in the pot. He poured a cup and cut a slice of cake, standing over the kitchen sink to eat it. Crumbs dropped into the stainless steel sink as he looked out over the barnyard. It was good to be back. He'd been gone a long time, but he was glad now that Sam had made the call and asked him to come home. This was where he belonged. Things would work out. They had to.

He turned from the sink and saw Clara's tote bag on the hook by the front door. He had no idea what to do about her. One part of his brain knew she was right—they both knew this was a temporary position and that she would be moving on. Another part of his brain reminded him that she'd been through hell and it was a lot for her—and a potential partner—to overcome. So he'd backed off like she'd asked.

The thing getting in the way was his heart. When he'd set foot back on Diamondback soil the last thing on his mind had been getting involved with a woman. Especially not a shy, buttoned-to-the-neck nurse with a wagonload of baggage as big as his own.

But there she'd been, right from the first night. And kissing her under the stars had unlocked something inside him. Something he suspected he'd been searching for for a long time. He didn't have to pretend to be someone else with Clara. He didn't have to put on a show or hide away.

His heart didn't want him to back away. His heart wanted him to hold on and he was having a heck of a time deciding exactly what he should do.

So as he finished up his coffee and wandered down the hall to his dad's room, he decided that he'd simply keep on as he had been—waiting. There was no rush, was there?

Virgil was making his way from the bathroom to his bed with the help of his walker. Was it just Ty or did the shuffling steps seem shorter than before? Clara was there beside him, quietly encouraging. As Ty appeared in the doorway she looked up and smiled. But before the smile he caught the shadow of concern in her eyes.

"Look who's come to see you," Clara said brightly as Virgil sat on the edge of the bed. "Just the person to drag you out of your doldrums."

"Dad," Ty said, stepping inside. He smiled at Clara and nodded. They were in this together. Clearly Virgil wasn't having a very good day and they were going to do their best to bring him around.

Maybe it wasn't the best time to talk about what was weighing on his mind after all.

"It looks like it's cold out," Virgil remarked as Clara helped him swing his legs over the mattress.

"It is. I took Strawberry out for a ride. Air's brisk. Maybe we'll have snow tonight."

The weather was a good place to start, right?

"Been thinking about what you said." Virgil let out a labored breath. "About the horses. If Sam's in agreement, I won't stand in your way."

Ty frowned. Just like that? Why was Virgil giving in so easily? Not that he wasn't pleased. But it wasn't like his father to back down. He'd expected more of a fight.

"I appreciate that. I've crunched some numbers and talked to Sam. I also thought I'd convert the storeroom in the barn into an office." He pulled the chair next to the bed closer and sat in it. "It's not fair to Sam, or to you, for me to tie this to Diamondback. Other than the space, this will stay completely separate from the cattle operation."

"You don't have to do that. I trust you."

Ty sat back in his chair, flummoxed. "You do?"

Virgil nodded.

Clara was quietly tidying up around the room. Ty wondered if this was the opening he'd been waiting for. With his heart in his throat, he reached for his father's hand and clasped it between his own.

"Then I should tell you about the rest, Dad."

One of Virgil's eyebrows went up. "There's more?"

Ty nodded. "I'm going to need to hire some help, some new hands. I've talked to Angela, who has agreed to make some connections for me. There are a lot of people out there who are stuck for one reason or another—a bad choice, a disability…people who haven't had the advantages I had. Some people who need a fresh start and someone to give them a chance." He swallowed and when he continued his voice was thick with emotion. "Where would I be now if you and Mom hadn't taken me in? I was lucky."

Virgil's eyes were wide. "If you were so lucky, then why did you leave?"

Clara was beside the door, ready to sneak out but Ty shook his head. "Stay," he said quietly. "I've got nothing to hide."

She hesitated, met his gaze. For a long moment he was remembering the feel of her in his arms as she'd hugged him. Why didn't he care if she knew the truth? He'd been so careful to keep it hidden for years.

Was he falling in love with her?

She took a chair across the room and picked up a ball of yarn and knitting needles. He watched the points flash back and forth as she worked on something that was dark gray with red stripes. Looking at her made him feel better. Calm rather than scattered. Settled.

He shook his head and turned back to his father. Falling in love was impossible. And right now he needed to patch things up with his dad. Enough time had passed. They had to make amends.

"I left because I always felt like I somehow disappointed you. Like you wished I was more like Sam. Sam was yours and I was the charity case."

"You were my son."

The plainly spoken words went straight to his heart. "It didn't always feel that way. Sam always seemed to do everything right. I idolized him. Heck—" he grinned suddenly "—I still do." The smile slid from his face. "And I always felt like I fell just a little bit short of your expectations. I felt like a burden."

"Tyson."

"No, I need to say this. I heard you once," he continued. "When I was eight. I'd gotten in trouble at school for fighting. You were talking to Mom and you said that you hadn't even wanted to adopt me."

Virgil said nothing.

"I knew you didn't want me. I tried to earn my way but the harder I tried the more I screwed up, and the more I screwed up the more we argued, until I knew we were going to go crazy. That's why I left. I couldn't stand disappointing you anymore."

Virgil had closed his eyes, but when Ty finished he opened them. The dark depths were swimming in tears. "Stupid boy," he murmured. "My sister did beg me to adopt you. When she showed up and begged me to take you, I resisted. I thought you'd be better off with her— your real mother. But Molly saw what I didn't. That Junie was an addict who'd gotten pregnant and was in no way ready to be a mother. I didn't want to believe it, but after you'd been here a week I knew we couldn't give you up. I never regretted it. Not even when you drove me crazy. What you heard was only part of the truth. I hadn't wanted to adopt you, but I was never sorry. I loved you even when you made it difficult."

Ty's heart expanded and he blinked back tears. In all his life he'd never heard Virgil say he loved him. "Then why did you push so hard? Why did you make me feel like such a failure?" The words came out as a hoarse whisper.

Virgil shook his head. "I never meant to, son. I only wanted you to grow up to be a good man. You already had baggage, knowing where you came from and the circumstances. I wanted you to be better than that. To be bigger than that. I wanted more for you than you thought you deserved. I could see the potential in you and you only seemed to throw it away. I had faith you could do better, even if you didn't think you were capable of it yourself. It was frustrating as hell to watch." Virgil finished talking and coughed.

"I didn't know that," Ty whispered, trying desperately to hold on to his emotions. Why hadn't they talked about this sooner? Why had it taken a call from Sam for Ty to finally come home? He swallowed around a lump in his throat. Stupid pride.

"I pushed too hard and I drove you away."

Virgil dropped his head and his chest shook. Ty hadn't truly thought his heart could break until that moment. He had never seen his father cry. Not ever. Virgil was a shadow of the strong man he'd used to be, reduced to being bedridden most of the time, frail and weak. And now Ty had made him cry.

He got up on the bed beside his father and put his arms

around him. "It's okay," he whispered. "I'm here now. We can fix it."

As he held his father he became incredibly aware how much smaller the big man had become during his illness. He lifted his eyes and looked over at Clara. She'd dropped her knitting into her lap, her hands resting on the forgotten needles and her eyes shimmered with tears. Ty fought the urge to wipe his away. He hated that she was seeing him this way, but he had to put his discomfort aside. For once, something was more important than the barrier he usually built around himself.

He squeezed Virgil's arm and cleared his throat. "Okay now, Dad?"

Virgil nodded. A tissue appeared by Ty's arm—Clara holding it out—and he took it and tenderly wiped the tears from Virgil's cheeks.

"We should have talked a long time ago," Ty decreed, still uncomfortable with all the emotion but somehow feeling lighter than he had in ages.

"Stubborn. You get that from the Diamonds," Virgil replied. When he smiled Ty noticed his mouth was still a little lopsided from the lingering effects of the paralysis.

"Who, me?" Ty looked back at the chair, expecting to see Clara, but she'd disappeared. It was just as well. She'd gotten an eyeful today and it definitely wasn't Ty at his best.

Virgil tried a laugh, but he began coughing again. "Here," Ty said. "Let's fix your pillows and get you a drink."

Once his father was settled Ty sat back in the chair. "About the staffing, Dad. I want to give people a chance. People aren't so different from animals, you know." He smiled. "They just need some dignity and encouragement.

I spent so long riding bulls and wandering around. It's time I did something really important. Something meaningful."

Virgil's gaze—still sharp despite everything—met Ty's. "Proud of you," he said with a sigh. He patted Ty's hand. "Proud of you."

"You should get some rest now." Ty got up and shoved his hands in his pockets. Now that they'd opened up, he felt awkward and oddly vulnerable. They'd patched things up, but somehow the heavy feeling of expectation remained. Ty knew he had to make his plan work. He couldn't fail. His father had put his faith in Ty, and Ty couldn't bear the thought of disappointing him again.

Clara finished washing out the mugs and placed them in the drying rack. Since Ty had talked to Virgil two days before, a change had come over the house. A peacefulness of sorts and a positive energy that had been missing. Molly was thrilled that Ty and Virgil had mended fences, Virgil had lost his ornery attitude, and Ty smiled more, which always put a glad feeling in Clara's heart.

So it made no sense whatsoever that she was on edge, with the uneasy feeling that something was horribly off. No matter how she tried, she couldn't shake the sense that something was wrong.

"Penny for your thoughts."

The mug she was holding slipped from her fingers and shattered on the ceramic tile of the kitchen floor.

"What the…" Ty stepped around the pieces of pottery and peered into her face. "I didn't mean to startle you. Are you okay?"

Heat rushed into her face. "I was just preoccupied. And feeling silly now. I'm fine. I'll just get the dustpan and clean this up."

"I'll get it." Ty went to the broom closet and pulled out

the broom and dustpan. "Sit down. You look as though you're ready to tip over."

She hadn't been sleeping, that was why. She worked all day and then went home and made sure she carried her weight at Butterfly House, taking her turn at laundry and meals and dishes according to the house schedule. She had started knitting some wool socks for Virgil to wear as the days got colder—anything to keep her hands busy and tire her out so she could sleep at night. But each night she lay awake. She couldn't stop thinking about Ty. About how it had felt to kiss him. About how afraid she was to care for him. And how the unfamiliar longings pulling at her lately were completely at odds with the plans she'd made.

She wished she'd never witnessed that conversation Ty had had with Virgil. She'd cared about him before. But she'd seen something more that afternoon that only made her more scared and confused.

"I can do it," she replied, hearing a snap in her voice she instantly regretted. She tempered her tone. "Don't mind me. I've just had a lot on my mind lately."

He waved her away and stooped to sweep the pieces into the dustpan. "So you said. Maybe you need some fresh air."

Deep down she knew what she needed. She needed to move on, find her own place, be independent. Here in Cadence Creek—at Diamondback—she was pulled away from what she knew was the best course for her. She was too personally involved. Yet how could she up and quit? Molly relied on her. So did Virgil. She'd feel as though she was abandoning them all.

It had nothing to do with missing Ty, she told herself. She told herself that a lot lately. And perhaps if she said it enough times it would be true.

"Maybe," she murmured, watching Ty dump the dust-pan in the garbage.

He put everything back in the broom cupboard and turned around. "I came in for my gloves. Why don't you bundle up and come with me? I've been trying to spend some time evaluating each of the horses. There's a gelding you could ride. He's an old fellow who is as calm as can be."

Clara hadn't been on a horse since she was a girl. And yet an hour outside in the fresh air sounded heavenly. "I'm pretty inexperienced," she said, "and I'd just slow you down."

He laughed. "It isn't a race. Besides, Herb needs some activity, too. You're perfect for each other."

"Herb?" She tried not to snicker, but failed.

Ty smiled, that secret, lopsided smile that made her go a little lightheaded each time she saw it. "Yes, Herb. He came to us years ago with the lofty handle of Conqueror. You'll understand when you see him."

"Well…"

"Don't 'well' about it. Put on your coat. Did you wear a hat?" She shook her head, but he was undeterred. "We'll grab one of Mom's, then. And you'll need gloves. It's brisk out there today."

She let herself be convinced because it really did sound like fun. She'd spent a long time doing what "needed" to be done, she'd taken barely any time for herself. She'd al-most forgotten what fun was. The closest she'd come was pie at the diner with Ty. "Let me put on my boots," she replied. "I'll meet you in the barn."

CHAPTER SEVEN

SHE FOUND TY in the corridor with a gorgeous chestnut cross-tied. Ty hefted a saddle over the horse's back, swinging it as if it weighed nothing, centering it on the blanket and adjusting the position just a little. He wore his black cowboy hat and a brown jacket with a heavy collar. He was the very picture of a rugged cowboy, and for a moment Clara caught her breath. He was so strong and capable—far more than he gave himself credit for.

She finally found her tongue and stepped forward. "Is this Herb?"

Ty looked up, his face pressed against the horse's smooth hide as he tightened the cinch. "Of course not. This here is Rattler. Seven years old and too smart for his own good. A little too much horse for a greenhorn." He flashed her a quick smile. "No, that's Herb." He pointed his thumb towards another stall where a horse waited, tacked and ready to ride.

"Of course he is," Clara said, immediately understanding, and she let out a laugh on a delighted breath. His bones were too sound to be called a nag. But the dappled gray had a low-maintenance look. His wide eyes had a knowing look to them, his forelock hung shaggily down the center of his nose, and she smiled widely at the sight of one back hoof resting jauntily on its edge on the floor as if to say, "Whenever you're ready. Take your time." All in all he *looked* like a Herb—not a Conqueror at all!

"Can you lead him out?"

Clara reached over the stall door and rubbed Herb's nose. Sure she could do this. She stepped inside and grabbed the reins. "Come on, Herb."

His hooves made slow clopping sounds on the concrete—Herb wasn't one to hurry—and then they were outside, standing on the hard gravel while Ty followed with the high-stepping Rattler. Clara looked up into Herb's brown eyes. He looked trustworthy. Surely riding a horse was like riding a bike, right? Determined to take the initiative, she put her foot in the stirrup, grabbed hold of the saddle horn and none too gracefully hauled herself up, swinging her leg over the saddle before plopping down heavily in the seat. Herb looked around as if to say, "Hey, take it easy back there!"

She could hear Ty's light laughter behind her. "That's the spirit," he said, and moved closer to adjust her stirrups. She looked at Rattler, who had stopped his prancing and was standing quietly even without Ty's hands on the leather. Ty held his gloves in his teeth as his sure fingers adjusted the buckles until her boot was cushioned in the stirrup. When he was done, he slipped the gloves back on his hands, took Rattler's reins and then slipped into the saddle with the balletic grace of a dancer.

"Warm enough?"

She nodded, and then as an afterthought pulled the knitted hat down over her ears. It was a thick, mismatched hat and the green color clashed with the red of her coat, and she knew that she must look comical next to Ty's cowboy perfection. But today she was leaving her insecurities behind. In the sharp bite of the cold air and the wide-open prairie, what did it matter if she didn't match? If she were less than perfect? She'd needed this—to get out for a while. Shake off the cobwebs and swing her arms a bit.

"Let's go then," he said, and led the way at a leisurely walk.

For several minutes Clara was happy to ride beside Ty in silence. The ranch land spread out before them: brown, undulating fields that stretched on forever, broken only by the odd stand of trees or winding creek. The clouds were steel-gray and forbidding, but the rhythm of the horse's slow stride was comforting and the basics of riding came back to Clara without much trouble. She breathed deeply and let out the air, relaxing in the idea that for the foreseeable future the only thing she had to do was ride until Ty said to turn around and head back. Nothing could touch her out here. Not her painful past, not her worries about the future. Not the niggling feeling of dread she'd felt in the house lately. None of it mattered. The center of her universe was a man and his horse. She wondered if, in a different time and place, he might have been *her* man. Or if he could be now, if she were only brave enough to speak up?

Brave. Huh. She definitely wasn't that, and she wondered if she ever would be. No matter how much she found herself drawn to Ty, there was always something—that little bit of fear and uncertainty preventing her from taking a step forward. It was the pain, she realized. When she'd left Jackson there hadn't just been fear. There'd been pain over what she'd lost. There'd been blame, too, and feeling as though she'd let so many people down. And she simply couldn't find a way to get past how much it hurt. Maybe she never would.

When they reached the creek, Ty stopped and dismounted. "Might as well let them have a drink," he said, taking Herb's reins and holding him while she climbed out of the saddle. She already felt the impact of an hour

astride in her thighs, and she gave her legs a little shake
as she laughed.

"I'm very out of practice."

"You're doing fine. You looked like you needed some
fresh air."

"I did." She chafed her hands together as Ty looped
the reins around the saddle horn and let Herb wander to
the creek alone. "You don't worry about him wandering
away?"

Ty chuckled. "Not this guy. Or Rattler either. Especially if I take out the apples I have stuck in my pockets."

She smiled, but the silence that followed was awkward,
as if they were waiting for the other to say something. Finally Ty spoke up.

"Clara, about the other day…"

She looked up and met his gaze. She was right. He was
feeling uncomfortable.

"Why did you leave?"

She shrugged. "It seemed like it was a private moment
between you and your father. I felt like I was intruding.
And the two of you obviously needed it, Ty." She didn't
mention that seeing the two of them had done something
to her emotionally, something so strong that she'd had to
retreat to a corner to shed her own tears. The men she'd
known all her life had never shown their feelings like that.
She hadn't known men could. Seeing Ty with his arms
around Virgil, opening himself up to that vulnerability…

She swallowed.

"You heard what I plan to do then. My hiring plans?"

"I think it's wonderful." She tilted her head. "It just
made me wonder…"

"Wonder what?"

Herb came back from the creek and, true to form, nuzzled his nose at Ty's pocket. Ty reached inside and took

out an apple. He squeezed it in such a way that it broke in half, and he held out the first piece on his palm. Herb gathered it up in his lips and munched.

"Wonder why you hide the generous and compassionate man behind the facade of a…" She faltered. What was he exactly? Charming. A player? Perhaps at one time, but not now. She'd known him over a month and she had yet to even hear of him going on a date let alone playing the field. An egomaniac? Playboy? None of the names seemed to fit.

"A what?"

Herb nuzzled for the second half and Ty held it out mindlessly as he kept his gaze locked with hers.

"I don't know. You came back to Cadence Creek with this reputation. Of being a ladies' man. Of being cocky. The smooth rodeo star who says all the right things to make the women blush. But that's not you, is it?"

"No, it's not. It was just easier than being myself. Except when I'm with you…"

Her heart started pounding. "When you're with me?"

"I don't want to be that person. I feel like if I even tried it, you'd see right through me. It's a pain in the ass, to be honest. You've totally blown my cover."

She laughed and held out her hand for an apple. He took out another, split it, and gave her a piece. Rattler came over and she took off her glove, letting the apple sit on her open palm. The flesh and juice were cold and Rattler's lips were velvety soft against her skin. On impulse she lifted her hand and rubbed the horse's neck. The hair there was coarse but smooth.

Ty joined her, resting his palm against the firm hide. "Clara, I want to tell you the real reason why I wasn't at dad's seventieth birthday a few years back. He's never asked, and things are still pretty raw between us. I'll explain to him someday. But I want you to know, because of what you've been through. Because of what's happened between us."

The smile slipped from her lips. Ty was being terribly serious. "Okay."

"Let's walk," he suggested, snagging Herb's reins and handing them to her. They walked side by side as they led the horses away from the creek bank. Clara's boots crunched against the frosty blades of grass and she tucked her free hand into her pocket for extra warmth. The air had a bitter bite to it now, and she wondered if they weren't finally due for that snowfall.

"I spent a few nights in jail," he explained. "I was all set to come home. I'd told myself I'd hold my tongue and put on a pleasant face and show up for the old man. Mom had asked and even Sam called. I was planning on leaving and driving down, but I'd loaned something to one of the hands I was working with at the time. I drove by to pick it up—and interrupted something."

Something heavy seemed to settle in Clara's stomach. "What did you interrupt?"

"Him, trying to keep his wife in line."

The heavy weight did a sickening twist.

"What did you do?"

"Put him in line instead."

"Oh, Tyson."

He sighed. "I know what you're going to say. Violence doesn't solve other violence, right?"

"That's probably what I should be saying."

"But you're not?"

She shook her head. "No, I'm not." She hesitated for a second and then said, "There were so many times I wished someone would come in and give Jackson a taste of his own medicine. That they'd swoop in and rescue me. But I finally realized that it wasn't up to anyone else to rescue me. I had to do it for myself. For my…"

She halted, and Herb's hoof beats quieted.

"For your?"

She'd almost come right out and said it, hadn't she? The thing that only the doctors and the social workers knew. That she'd been pregnant during that final beating.

Ty somehow made her forget that she had any secrets left at all. This one was too close, too painful to share. She shook her head and resumed walking, Herb following obediently beside her. "Never mind. Tell me what happened after that."

Thankfully he let his question drop. "She called the police."

Clara's brow furrowed. "How did *you* end up in lockup then?"

He gave her a pointed look and she suddenly understood. "She called the police on you, not him."

"Right the first time."

Clara sighed. "I know it doesn't make sense, but it happens more often than you'd think. For so many complicated reasons, Ty. At least you tried to help."

"I'll admit I didn't make it easy for the officers. I didn't exactly go quietly. They put me in a cell to cool down. By the time I got out, it was too late to drive home for the party. Then I'd have to explain why I was late and also the condition of my face."

"The charges were dropped?"

"The next day there was a 9-1-1 call from the house. He'd taken my interference out on her. There wasn't much reason to keep me in jail. But I figured it was time I got out of Dodge. I quit and moved on to a new place outside Fort McMurray."

"So it looked like you were guilty anyway."

He shrugged. "I suppose it did."

"But Ty—" She stopped again, clutching the reins in her hand. "Surely you must have known your parents would understand. You were just standing up for someone."

He stopped, too. Stepped a foot closer and his face softened. He was looking at her almost tenderly, she realized, as the all-too-familiar thumping of her heart started again. He put his gloved palm against her face. It was cold and smelled like worn leather and horse. It was a scent she knew she'd always associate with him.

"Sweet Clara," he murmured, looking down at her. "Even after all you've been through, you look for the best in people. You accept them. I wish I had been more like you. Maybe I wouldn't have stayed away. Maybe I never would have left at all."

She stepped back, stunned. She considered herself distrusting at best, jaded at her worst. Cautious and careful. But Ty didn't see her that way. He saw her the way she'd always wanted to be but thought she fell short.

"But I'm so withdrawn," she replied, frowning. "Cold. I see it in myself and I wish I wasn't. You're wrong, Ty."

He shook his head. "I don't know how to explain it." He adjusted his hat on his head as if trying to shake up the right words. "You don't hold other people away from you. You hold yourself away from them. There's a difference."

It shouldn't have made sense but it did. She loved Molly, and Virgil, Angela and even Sam, she supposed. She felt affection towards them all. But he was right. She stopped just short of offering herself. She allowed them to welcome her in—she accepted them—but she didn't let them accept her in return.

"I'm sorry," she murmured.

"Don't be. I get it. Maybe better than you think. It's not other people you don't trust, Clara. It's yourself."

His dark eyes were warm with understanding and once more she felt something pulling them together, just like it had the night in the barn under the glittering stars.

"Maybe," he whispered, "one day you won't feel the need to hold back so much. Maybe one day you'll trust yourself enough to let someone in."

When had he gotten so close? All she'd have to do was lean forward the slightest bit and she could feel the warmth of him. Another step and she could tilt up her face and touch her lips to his. Just one more...

Rattler got sick of standing still and tossed his head, shaking Ty's arm and making his bridle hardware jingle in the clear, cold air.

"We should mount up," he said, but his voice sounded all husky and soft.

"We should," she murmured, and then threw caution to the north wind, stood on tiptoe and pressed her mouth to his.

She clutched the reins tightly to keep her hands from reaching out to him. The contact of her lips on his was enough. More than enough. The hard wall of his body was against hers and even through the heavy jacket it felt intimate. Just this much. She wanted just this much to hold close to her heart. When he kissed her this way she could temporarily forget all the ways she'd failed. All the mistakes she'd made.

"Drop the reins," he murmured against her mouth. "Please, Clara."

She obeyed, letting the leather dangle to the ground as he also let go of Rattler's.

The next moment she was in his arms. One hand cupped her head, warm against the knitted cap, while the other pressed against the small of her back, pulling her flush against his body as he spread his feet, anchoring the both of them to the hard ground. The kiss lost its sweetness and blossomed into something wild and primitive and beautiful, and she clutched at the shoulder of his coat, a lifeline to keep herself from coming completely unglued.

"Clara," he murmured, sliding his lips along her jaw and touching the hollow just below her earlobe. A delicious shiver ran down her body and she heard herself gasp as he tasted the spot with his tongue. The hand that had been cupping her head moved, grazing her shoulder as it traveled down the front of her coat. Shock rippled through Clara's body. If it weren't for the coat he would know exactly what his touch was doing to her. She swallowed, tried desperately to clear her head. She wasn't ready. Her body was crying out for her to be but she wasn't. She captured his hand in her fingers.

"I can't," she whispered. Even in the brisk breeze, her hushed words were clear as a bell.

He squeezed her hand, but his lips were still busy doing marvellous things to her earlobe and the delicate skin of her neck. "I'll slow down," he suggested, his breath warm and slightly damp and altogether far too arousing.

For the space of a few seconds she gave in, letting out a shaky breath as her head tipped back, allowing him easier access to her throat. But when his arm tightened around her again, pinning their bodies together, she knew they had to stop. Now.

"Please, Ty, please don't do this." She nearly sounded like she was sobbing and she wasn't sure if it was from fear of taking this to the ultimate conclusion or if it was just all too much for her senses to handle.

He loosened his grip, hesitated, then pressed one last heartbreakingly sweet kiss on the sensitive side of her chin. "You're killing me, Clara."

"I didn't mean to. I just wanted to kiss you."

Oh, good Lord. She sounded about thirteen and just as green.

"Mission accomplished." She felt his lips curve against her cheek. "God, woman. What am I going to do with you?"

She relaxed, knowing he'd finally heeded her plea and he wasn't angry. "I don't know. I like you, Ty. I care for you. But I'm not sure I'll ever be able to give anyone anything more. I'm sorry I misled you. You're probably used to women who are more confident."

She couldn't make herself look him in the eye.

"I'm not mad. Frustrated? Maybe." His voice was rich and seductive. "But you didn't mislead me, Clara. Not ever. And I wouldn't want you to change one hair on your head. You're worth far more than any of those other girls."

Her cheeks felt hot, even in the wintery air. "You don't have to say that."

He tilted her chin up so she was forced to look at him. There was no teasing on his face. And he wasn't just being polite. He was absolutely sincere. "I said it and I meant it. I shouldn't have pushed. I got caught up." The corner of his mouth turned up in a boyish smile. "That's what you do to me. You make me forget all my good intentions."

She sighed, but then caught him staring at her lips again. "You'd better mount up," he warned softly, "before I change my mind."

She scurried off to grab Herb's reins and with weak knees put her foot in the stirrup.

Ty was the honorable one here. Ty was the solid, stable one who despite popular opinion really did seem to always do the right thing.

This couldn't happen again. No more time alone. No more sneaking away just the two of them. It was too tempting. Because it wasn't Ty who'd run scared when it was all over. It was her.

She had fallen under his spell, but this wasn't what she wanted. There was no future for them. There was only her future. She'd never let anyone have the power to hurt her again. She'd never again let anyone break her heart again. And Ty was just the sort of man who could do it. He was already doing it.

She didn't wait for Ty's command. She pointed Herb in the direction of the ranch and started for home. It was time she stuck to doing her job and locked her personal feelings away. Because Ty, without even trying, made her forget all the important lessons she'd learned.

The snow held off overnight, but by the time Clara arrived at Diamondback the next morning, the first hard, flinty flakes were starting to fall, promising a miserable day ahead. The kitchen, however, was bright and warm and welcoming; Molly had a pot of coffee perking and the air still smelled of bacon and pancakes and maple syrup. The scent of it was homey and sweet.

This was exactly the sort of thing she couldn't get used to. She had to remember that this wasn't her home, and this wasn't her family. Ty was right. She did hold people at arm's length, refusing to let them too close. There were reasons for that. You let people in and soon they discovered your vulnerabilities. And then they found ways to exploit them. Jackson had been a champ at it. He'd used his innate charm—the man he showed the world—to win her over time and time again. To give her hope. She'd hoped that telling him about the baby would change things. She'd seen him with his nephews. "Uncle" Jackson had been warm and caring and gentle. Getting pregnant had been unintentional, but she'd deluded herself into thinking Jackson would change once he knew.

She hadn't expected the jealous rage. The accusations.

She'd stayed awake long into the night last night, thinking about it. There had been two sides to Jackson and she'd seen them both. She knew Ty was different. But was she willing to take a chance on being wrong? She'd been wrong before, after all.

Molly had her hands in a sink full of dishwater as a troubled Clara hung up her coat and tucked her scarf into her sleeve, determined to let her dark thoughts go. She had a job to do.

"Oh, Clara," Molly said. "I nearly called you and told you to stay home today. I fear the weather's going to turn nasty."

"It's okay. I can always put Virgil through his paces and then head back at lunchtime." The prospect of a short workday suddenly held a certain appeal. The one bright spot in her evening last night had been arriving home to find a letter on the table. She'd written to her aunt, who had gotten in touch with Clara's mom, and now her mom had replied with a letter and an open invitation to visit her new condo anytime.

Clara wasn't sure what would happen next or when, but they'd made contact. It was an exciting first step. Maybe if she went home after lunch she could write a response, or even call the number her mom had written on the bottom of the letter.

"There's lots of room here if the roads get bad." Molly smiled and wiped her hands on a dishcloth. "You know how he perks up when you're around. You're good for him."

Clara assumed Molly was talking about Virgil and not Tyson, but a warmth spread through her just the same at the compliment. What was it about Diamondback that felt like coming home? Yet it did. This house—that she only visited—felt more like home than her own room with her belongings did at Butterfly House. Yet another feeling Clara knew she shouldn't get used to.

Molly's face fell, though, as she reached for a tray that still contained a plate of uneaten breakfast. "Virgil barely touched his breakfast, even though I made bacon and buckwheat pancakes, his favorite."

Clara frowned, shifting her brain into work mode. Virgil always ate a hearty morning meal. To not eat—especially his favorites—was definitely out of character. "Did he take his meds okay?"

Molly nodded. "Yes, with his juice. He said he was tired so I left him to nap, oh, maybe an hour ago?"

Clara forced a smile. The heavy, persistent feeling she'd had lately came back, sending tingles down her spine. Ever since the day Ty had spoken to his father, Virgil had been quiet. He'd done his exercises but without the ornery, determined edge Clara was used to. He hadn't been eating as well, either, picking at the meals Molly made him. Clara had chalked it up to not being as hungry. Now that the weather was turning cold, Virgil spent less time outside, and she'd thought maybe his appetite was adjusting according to his activity level.

But for him to barely touch a favorite? Clara thought back over the last weeks. She compared that man to the one who had been so insistent that he'd walk Angela down the aisle.

Virgil had been failing. She hadn't done her job, had she? She'd seen the signs but hadn't wanted to believe it. She'd taken his vitals and put him through his paces but she'd ignored the other obvious tells because she'd wanted to believe he was getting better. She'd put it down to simple aging. What if it was something more?

"I'll tiptoe in and check on him," Clara suggested. And if he was awake, she was going to give him a stern talking-to and let him know that from now on she was going to be dogging his heels big time. No more meals in his room. She was going to have him up and about and at the dining table three times a day.

She made her way to the bedroom, her footsteps slowing as she walked on the soft hallway carpet. Virgil had a doctor's appointment in a few weeks, but perhaps it was time to call and move it up. To make sure there wasn't something going on that they didn't know about.

The door was open a crack and she pushed it gently so she could peer in. Virgil's eyes were closed, his face peaceful. Clara's eyes burned. She'd seen that look before. Too peaceful.

She went inside, felt for a pulse, bit down on her lip. Swallowed around the lump in her throat. All the resolutions she'd made during the walk down the hall evaporated. It was too late.

For a long moment she stood there, unsure of what to do next. It didn't seem possible that he could be gone—just like that. Molly was going to be so devastated, and Ty and Sam…

The air seemed to burn a path into her lungs as she gasped for breath. Poor Molly. Finally Clara moved into action. She straightened the blankets, tucking them neatly around his chest. Tenderly brushed his hair with her fingertips until it lay flat and smooth. When Molly came in, Clara wanted her to see a loving husband who had simply gone to sleep. It was a moment Molly would always remember. Clara couldn't take away the pain but she could do this one thing to perhaps make the memory easier.

A barrage of emotions threatened to break free, but Clara held them in, knowing she had too much to do right now to fall apart. This family had given her a second chance. Maybe Ty had been right. Maybe she did hold herself away from them all. And she'd just resolved to distance herself even more.

Those thoughts evaporated in the face of Virgil's death. She would be there for them. Help them through this as best she could. As Virgil's nurse. But more than that—as a friend. They deserved more, but she could give them that much.

She laid her hand on the blanket one last time. "I am going to miss you," she whispered, and sniffled. The tears she hadn't wanted to shed slid free and burned their way down her cheeks. It didn't matter what she said or how she rationalized anything. She *loved* this family.

She should have done more. She shouldn't have let herself get so personally involved that she wore rose-colored glasses where Virgil was concerned. She'd failed him, hadn't she? And so she'd failed them all by letting her feelings blind her to what was happening before her eyes.

She swiped the tears away with the back of her hand, determined to pull herself together. She would miss him. His garrulous teasing, the way he winked at her, even the way he grumbled during physio. She'd miss the way his eyes lit up when Molly came in the room. What would it be like to have that sort of love? It made her heart hurt just thinking about it.

Then she took a breath, squared her shoulders and set about the terrible job of telling Molly the news.

CHAPTER EIGHT

THE CHURCH WAS PACKED with mourners, the overflow parking a line of cars and heavy-duty half-ton trucks along the shoulder of the road. Angela had kindly offered Clara a seat with her and Sam, but Clara had refused. Today was for family. She sat, instead, about halfway back and by herself.

The snow that had held off for so long had arrived in earnest the night after Virgil's death. Outside, the prairie was pristine and white. Every time the church door opened, a gust of frigid air blustered its way in; it was cold on her legs and she tucked them farther beneath the pew. Her black skirt and sweater provided little warmth against the subzero temperatures, so she hugged her arms around herself, waiting for the family to be seated and the service to start.

When the minister escorted the family in, Clara's hand flew to her mouth in alarm. Tyson looked terrible, as though he hadn't slept for days. He was clean-shaven and once more in the dark suit he'd worn to Sam's wedding just a few months earlier. But the careless disorder of his hair was now severely tamed, and he had bags beneath his eyes.

Her heart broke for all of them, but particularly for Ty. He'd just gotten his father back only to lose him once more—and forever. She watched as he sat between Molly and Sam, and she stared at the breadth of his shoulders. They looked somehow narrower now that he was hunched over slightly. Molly leaned over and whispered something in his ear and he nodded and attempted a smile.

But Clara knew what Ty's smile looked like, and that wasn't it. Everything she knew—and loved—about him was buried beneath his grief, and her heart broke for him.

The service itself was lovely, a true testament to the pillar of the community that Virgil had been over the years. Sam delivered a heartfelt, emotional eulogy that had Clara, and several others, wiping their eyes. But it was when he mentioned Ty's return that Ty's head snapped up and he met his brother's gaze. "Only one thing meant more to my dad than Diamondback," Sam said. "And that was his family. He was so happy that Ty had come home. That his boys were going to be working Diamondback together, the way it was meant to be. Dad, your life wasn't quite finished, but I know your heart is at rest, because the family is back together again."

Sam paused, collected himself and carried on. But Clara saw Angela slide over on the pew next to Ty and put her arm around his shoulders. Clara reached inside her purse for a tissue and wiped her eyes and nose. This had to be killing him. And she suddenly regretted not accepting the invitation to sit with the family. This went beyond her own fears and resolutions. Ty was a friend. She should have put her own issues aside for today and been there for him.

When it was over, the family exited first. Ty's eyes were red, and for a fraction of a second his gaze caught hers before he looked away. The pain in his eyes cut into her with the sharpness of a knife blade. Virgil was gone. None of them would ever hear his rusty laugh or see his smile and twinkling eyes again. He had been more than a client. It had been more than a job. She might as well stop pretending otherwise. For all her trying to keep the Diamonds at arm's length, they'd managed—all of them—to sneak past her defenses. Especially Ty.

He would always hold a piece of her heart, even as she prepared to leave Cadence Creek forever. There was no real reason to stay now, was there? She no longer had a job. And she had her own family waiting.

Angela touched her arm in the vestibule. "There's a reception back at the house. The church ladies have put together sandwiches and sweets and coffee. You should come, Clara."

"I will," she answered.

Angela's face blanked with surprise. "That easily? You were so hesitant earlier."

"I was wrong." She squeezed Angela's fingers. "Ty's a wreck, isn't he?"

"He was fine for a while. You remember. He rolled up his sleeves and did what needed to be done."

Clara did remember. After she'd broken the news to Molly, Molly had called Sam and Ty. Sam had cried but Ty had remained dry-eyed, holding everyone together. While Sam and Angela and Molly talked about arrangements, Ty had done the practical thing and looked after the stock and chores. Clara had asked what she could do but there was nothing. In an effort to do something helpful, she'd spent a few hours putting together some food while the family followed the ambulance to the hospital and from there to the funeral home.

But she had gone home to Butterfly House before they returned rather than feel like an intruder, arriving home ahead of the snowstorm.

She'd told Ty to call if he needed anything.

He hadn't called.

"But?" she asked Angela. She knew there was a *but* coming.

"But yesterday it became clear he wasn't sleeping. He's running on autopilot and I'm not sure how much longer he can keep it up. I know you're not involved, you know, romantically, but he needs a friend."

Not involved? Clara blinked. She was in it up to her eyeballs. Ty hadn't slept but she hadn't either for worrying and wondering how he was coping. And then the invitation from her mom had come and more decisions were up for grabs. The tossing and turning was getting to her, too.

This was the last thing she could do for Ty before she had to say goodbye, she supposed. Someone needed to be there for him rather than the other way around.

"I'll get my coat and meet you there," she assured Angela.

The house was already crammed with people when she arrived. She had to park along the side of the driveway, a long way away from the house, and she made her way carefully along the ploughed surface in her heels. When she got to the porch, she saw Buster tied outside. He was lying in a back corner of the verandah, his nose between his paws, and his eyes were the sorriest eyes she'd ever seen on a dog. He'd lost his master and he'd been evicted from his warm bed. She took a moment and went to him, squatting down and resting her weight on her high heels as she stroked his fur.

"Hey, boy," she crooned, rubbing the silky crown of his head. "Lost your place today, huh? If it weren't so cold, I think I'd rather stay out here with you in the quiet. All those people...hmmm."

He lifted his head, and when she stopped patting he nudged her palm. She laughed lightly.

"Feels good, doesn't it?" She patted his neck. "Don't worry, Buster. It's only temporary."

"It's nicer out here, isn't it?"

The deep timbre of his voice surprised her, and a shiver of pleasure rippled up her body before she could even think about it. "Ty."

She looked over her shoulder. Goodness, he looked even more terrible up close. Haunted, she realized. She pushed up from the squat and brushed her hands down her skirt, unsure of what to say next. I'm sorry? She'd already said that days ago.

"I'm glad you came," he said quietly, taking a step forward.

"Of course I did." And then she did what she'd wanted to do since first seeing him at the church: she went to him and wrapped her arms around him.

He didn't hug back right away, but after a few seconds his arms tightened around her middle and held her close. "I needed this," he murmured in her ear. "Thank you."

"Anytime," she said back, but knew she was a liar. She wouldn't be here long enough to make that true.

He let her go and stepped back. "You must be freezing. Let's go inside. I could do with a cup of coffee."

Inside the house was loud—how could it be otherwise with so many people crowding up the living room and kitchen? The dining table had been extended with every leaf and was laden with platters of sandwiches and squares. A catering-size coffee urn was on the butcher block next to a stack of foam cups and wooden stir sticks. Everywhere around her, voices expressed sympathy and shared stories of Virgil's life. Molly was in the middle, smiling and holding a paper plate with a few sandwiches and sweets. But Clara noticed she wasn't eating them. Not a single bite was taken from the triangles of bread with some unnamed filling inside.

Ty held a cup of coffee in his hands but nothing else. "When did you eat last?" she asked him, pouring herself a cup of tea. She took a sip and blinked. It was strong enough to dance the Hornpipe on, so she added extra milk and hoped for the best.

"I'm fine," he replied, nodding at a passing neighbor who was on his way to the door.

"You're not fine." She stood in front of him so his body afforded her a bit of privacy from the eyes of the room. "You're tired and gaunt and not eating properly. Let me fix you a plate."

"You're not going to let it go, are you?"

"No."

"Fine. I'll eat something."

She went to the table and selected what looked like roast beef and minced ham sandwiches, leaving the pretty but insubstantial offerings like cream cheese and cherry to more delicate tastes. Beside that she added sliced pickles and several pieces of cheese, a brownie and what looked like something lemony with a coconut topping. When she presented it to him he raised an eyebrow. "I went for the most manly items I could," she said.

"How long do these things usually last?"

She shrugged. "Hopefully not long. You all look exhausted."

"I'm fine."

She picked up a sandwich from his plate and bit into it, hoping a little competition would get his appetite going. "So you said." Her tone definitely let him know that she didn't believe a word of it.

Molly approached and put her hand on Ty's arm. "Oh, good, you're eating."

Clara gave him a telling look and he scowled back at her.

"Thank you for coming, Clara. I'm afraid we seemed a bit lost without you here the last few days. It's good to see Ty actually eat something rather than promise to and then hardly nibble."

Molly's words made her feel even worse for staying away. "Oh, Molly, I wish you'd called. I would have come. I didn't want to intrude on family time. If there's anything you need…"

But again there was a bittersweet edge to her words. She meant them and yet she knew that her time was limited. It was simply a platitude and she hated that she'd done that. She'd been on the receiving end of too many over the years.

"We're fine," Molly said. "It'll get easier. I have my boys here and Angela and I hope you'll come to see us even though…"

Molly's eyes suddenly misted with tears. "Oh, dear."

Even though Clara no longer had a job. No one really had to say it, did they?

And so Clara spoke from the heart when she said the next words. "You were always more than an employer to me, Molly, you know that."

"The wedding ring quilt still needs finishing. One last roll before I bind it off. You're welcome to pick up a needle and thread anytime."

Clara's heart seized, thinking of the lovely times she and Molly had shared stitching the beautiful wedding ring pattern. She wished she could be here and for a moment almost reconsidered. But it wasn't practical. She had a home waiting in Moose Jaw and a job to look for and she couldn't remain at Butterfly House forever.

Instead of replying she did something she hadn't done

before—she hugged Molly. A genuine, squeezy, heartfelt hug.

Molly hugged back.

They pulled apart and sniffed a little. "I'd better keep moving," Molly said. "So many people."

Clara turned back to Ty but he was gone. She saw him across the room talking to one of the ranch hands who had put on his best jeans and starched shirt for the somber occasion. Was it just her or had the lines around Ty's eyes eased just a little bit? Why hadn't someone made sure he was taking care of himself?

Then again, it wasn't her job, was it?

After another hour, the church ladies packed up their tins and Tupperware and coffee pots. Clara helped move leftover sandwiches to a platter for the fridge—an easy meal for the family later. The stragglers made their way until it was just Sam, Angela, Molly, Ty and Clara left standing in the silence.

"I suppose I should pick up the things from Mr. Burgess," Molly said, referring to the funeral director. She let out a long sigh.

"Let us do that," Sam suggested. "You've had enough, don't you think?"

"I'm fine."

Clara stepped forward. "I've heard that from someone else today, too. A good gust of wind would topple you right over. You're exhausted. Let us look after you."

The lack of a reply told Clara all she needed to know.

She looked at Sam. "I'll stay. You and Angela look after what you need to. I'll putter around here and make sure Molly takes it easy."

"You're a gem," Sam replied, dropping a kiss on her cheek. She found she didn't even mind. When he straightened he took Angela's hand in his. Clara had noticed them holding hands a lot today. They had each other, loved each other, were there for each other. What did it feel like to love someone and feel so utterly secure that you could trust them with everything?

Ty nodded at his brother. "I'll help Clara and look after the stock."

"Sounds good." Sam gave his mother a kiss and pointed a finger at her. "Do what Clara says, and let us handle the rest for today."

Clara shooed Molly to bed after Sam and Angela were gone, and returned shortly after with a small tea tray holding a cup of hot cocoa and two warm scones topped with Molly's favorite jam. "Your favorites," she announced softly, stepping inside the bedroom. She'd only been in this room once before—Molly had always stayed in the downstairs room with Virgil after his stroke. But this had been the master bedroom, and Molly looked tiny and fragile in the middle of the king-size bed.

"What would I do without you, Clara?"

She sat down on the edge of the bed. "I'm sorry I wasn't here the past few days. I didn't want to get in the way."

"I thought Ty would have called you. Or perhaps this was too hard for you for some reason."

"Ty doesn't like to ask for help," Clara pointed out. "Anyway, I'm here now. And I'm going to make you promise to drink every sip and eat every bite and then have a nap."

"Yes, ma'am." Molly held up the cup and took a drink of the rich cocoa.

"Right. I'll come back for the tray in a bit."

She was at the door when Molly's voice called her back. "Clara?"

She paused, her hand on the door. "Hmm?"

Molly's voice thickened. "Virgil loved you, you know.

We used to talk about it alone. We understood you'd had a terrible time, but I think he had a secret hope that you and Ty might…well, you're good for our son. He's a different man since he came home."

Nothing Molly might have said could have cut any deeper. Ty had kissed her and there was definitely something between them, but he'd never even breathed a word about anything more permanent. And what if he did? Clara was smart enough to know that she'd probably go running for the hills. A woman could only take so many disappointments, after all. Maybe Ty was a different man but she still doubted she was the woman for him. He was the rodeo star with the belt buckles and a wagonload of experience. She'd only ever been with one man, and it had been enough for a lifetime.

"If Ty is different, it's all down to him," Clara replied. "Maybe he grew up. It takes some people longer than others."

She shut the door with a quiet click and leaned against it. And sometimes people just stayed stuck, didn't they? Like her. Would she ever have a normal life where none of this mattered anymore?

Ty couldn't bear the thought of going back to the house.

The chores were done and the watery afternoon light had dimmed to a thin twilight, casting gray shadows over the snow. He stood in the barn doorway and saw the lights glowing warmly from the kitchen windows; looked farther up the length of the driveway and saw Clara's car still sitting halfway to the road, a bump on the otherwise lonely stretch of gravel. She was still here. And he was too raw to face her right now. To face anyone.

Today had been about saying goodbye, but he hadn't been able to. Not at the funeral, surrounded by all those

people. Not sitting next to Molly, who was counting on him
to hold it together, or next to Sam, who'd been the apple of
Virgil's eye for over thirty years. He'd had nowhere to put
his grief and instead it had built and built until he stood
here in the barn and thought he might explode with it all.

Even the physical exertion of mucking out stalls hadn't
been enough of a displacement activity.

He fisted his hands, pressing them against the massive
door frame. He should have come home sooner. He should
have made amends sooner. Should, should, should. All
the things he'd put off, all the mistakes he'd made. Regret
tasted bitter in his mouth. If he'd been here all along, he
could have spared Virgil some of the heavy load of running Diamondback.

Now it was too late. And the man he'd loved and respected and even at times despised for pushing him so
hard was gone.

The breath left Ty's chest as the grief finally struck,
hard and sharp and with the jarring thud of hitting the dirt
after being bucked off. For a moment he stood, paralyzed
with it until he heard the first harsh sob escape his mouth.
The sound was so foreign, so unfamiliar that it frightened
him. It was followed by another, and another.

He had to get out of the doorway. He stumbled down
the corridor, past the stalls to the storeroom and his office. Once inside he sat on the edge of the fold-out army
cot Sam had kept there for long nights during animal
births or illnesses. He put his head in his hands and let it
come, finally—all the pain and hurt and self-loathing and
other myriad emotions he couldn't even name but that had
threatened to overwhelm him for days.

He'd loved his father—and Virgil had been his father
in all the ways that truly mattered.

His biggest regret was that he'd never been man enough to say the words. And Virgil had died not knowing.

When Ty didn't come back from the barn, Clara started to get worried. Molly was sound asleep and there wasn't a speck of dirt to be found in the kitchen. She looked out the deck doors towards the barn. The lights were off—all except for one tiny glow from the room she now knew Ty used as an office.

She put on her coat and borrowed a pair of Molly's boots, slipping out the door and heading towards the long, low structure.

Inside was quiet and dark, until she heard a low, muffled sound. Her stomach knotted as she followed the noise, down the corridor with her boots making soft steps on the concrete. The door to the office was open a few inches, and peering inside, she saw him—sitting on the army cot and weeping.

For the space of a breath she considered tiptoeing back out and leaving him to his grief privately, but in the end she couldn't make herself walk away. She pushed the door open, went to his side and put her hand on his shoulder.

"Tyson," she whispered.

His head snapped up, his face a terrible mixture of pain, surprise and embarrassment. "It's okay," she murmured, squeezing the wide shoulder beneath her fingers. "Let it out."

His arms looped around her hips, drawing her close, and she felt his breath through her jacket and hot against her belly as he pressed his face against her. Touched, drowned in sympathy and love for him, she rested her hands on his head, gently stroking his soft hair as he cried.

"He didn't know," Ty said, his breath hitching. "Dammit. I didn't want to fall apart like this."

"What didn't he know?"

Ty shuddered. Clara slid out of his embrace, taking a seat beside him on the cot. She reached over and took his hand. "What didn't he know, Ty?"

"How I felt about him. I couldn't ever say the words. He…he took me in even though doing it meant admitting his own sister was a failure. He stopped being my uncle at that moment and became my father. But I always resented him. I felt sorry for myself. I told myself he loved Sam more than me."

"But he didn't. You know that."

Ty shook his head. "I was such a screwup. I had something to prove and I didn't care who I hurt to do it. Mom, Dad, Sam… I was good at what I did and it was an added bonus to rub their noses in it."

"Ty," she said softly, knowing he had to get out the feelings but also knowing they weren't accurate. "This is the grief talking. You're being too hard on yourself."

"No," he insisted, resting his elbows on his knees. "I was wrong. I knew it long ago but was too proud to admit it and come home where I belonged. It took an invitation from Sam and a request for help. I was so proud that I had to be *needed*, don't you understand? And now he's gone. I gave up the chance to show him what I could do. To show him I've grown up. That I loved and admired him."

"He knew."

Ty shook his head. "How could he possibly know?"

"You're human," she soothed. "You're strong. You're independent. And most of all, you're a good man, Ty. He knew that. Look how he felt about your new plans. Believe me, he gave them his stamp of approval far easier than he gave it to Sam this year. He loved you for exactly who you are. He was proud of you—for your accomplishments, for your successes. Love, Ty…" She swallowed as she folded his hand inside her own. "Love isn't conditional on never making mistakes, or being flawed, or afraid. It just is. So go ahead and grieve for him and miss him. But please, please, don't regret what can't be changed now. You came home and made amends. It was the greatest gift you could have given him."

His face was tear-streaked, his rich brown eyes rimmed with red and his cheeks were chapped from rubbing them. But as Ty lifted his face and gazed into her eyes, she knew she was done for. She loved him. Not for his charm or sexy swagger, but for the heart he kept so closely guarded inside. She loved him for his flaws and insecurities and all the things that made him want to be a better man when he was already pretty darn amazing to begin with.

And because she loved him, it killed her to see him hurting so much. She cupped his face in her hands and leaned in, kissing each of his bruised eyelids as her lip wobbled uncontrollably. Never, never in her life had she felt this raw and exposed with anyone. And while that was terrifying in itself, the truly amazing thing was that it felt *right*.

Her lips lingered on the crest of his cheek as she hesitated. Their breaths mingled as something extraordinary shifted, curling deliciously through her body as they both froze, paused in the prolonged moment, on the edge of something monumental.

She forgot how to breathe.

Then his hand was on the nape of her neck, holding her in place while his mouth clashed with hers, full of passion and pain and acceptance.

There was no fear. No hesitation, no questions, nothing but Ty and the feel of his mouth on hers and the energy flowing between them. Desperately she clung to his shoulders, well aware that they were perfectly alone in the dark with only the pale circle of the desk lamp's glow giving any light in the room and leaving the corners black and hidden. The kiss was edgy and full-on and held nothing back, and it was glorious and devastating and out of control.

With trembling fingers she reached for the buttons of his flannel shirt, needing to make a connection in the midst of her own confusing grief, needing to touch his warm skin. She shoved it off his shoulders and he broke off the kiss, sitting back and searing her with his gaze while he hastily pulled it off his arms and dropped it to the floor. Her heart leapt as his voice came soft and husky in the dimness. "Touch me."

He was warm and smooth beneath her fingertips as she ran her hand down the center of his chest, over the taut skin of his ribs and back up to his shoulder. Her fingertips touched a puckered scar by his rotator cuff and she wondered how he'd got it. His eyes closed and his lips fell open and she marvelled that she could possibly have such an effect on a man like him. Momentarily she paused, daunted by the idea of the experienced women who had come before her. But then Ty opened his eyes and reached for her coat. "I want to see you, too," he said.

She didn't answer as he unzipped her coat and let it fall behind her. She was still in her sweater and skirt and he reached for the hem of the sweater, pulling it up and off with tantalizing slowness.

She sat before him in her bra and felt her face flame. What was she doing? She should get up and leave right now before they got to a point where they couldn't turn back. But her feet felt as though they were made of concrete blocks and she didn't move. Goosebumps erupted over her skin, tiny points of sensation as he pulled her close, and for the first time in two years she was pressed, flesh to flesh, against a man.

It was so different. So warm and alluring and…luxurious. His skin was warm pressed against hers and he kissed her again, longer, slower, with promises of things to come.

Wonderful things, she realized, giving herself over to the sensation. Ty would not hurt her. She trusted him completely. And even though a tiny voice inside her head echoed with a smidgen of common sense—that Ty was acting out of grief, that they both were—she ignored it.

She was lying on the cot now, looking up at him as his tough, lean body pressed her into the mattress. "I need you," he murmured, touching the soft skin at her temple with a finger.

"You have me," she replied, reaching for him.

CHAPTER NINE

SUNLIGHT FILTERED weakly through the office window as Clara turned her head and the full impact of what she'd done slammed into her.

Ty slept, his lashes peaceful against his still-tanned-from-the-summer cheeks. A rough blanket covered them both, but he'd pushed it down on his slice of the army cot so that it bunched around his hips. Even relaxed she could see the curves and dips of the muscles in his chest and arms. He was beautiful. And he'd been…

She stopped the thought before she could finish it. Her cheeks flared with heat. She didn't want to think about how gentle he'd been. How intense. How consuming. She'd been shameless, caught up in the emotion of the day, needing that connection with another human being, needing to be there for him when he was hurting so much.

Making love to Ty had been nothing short of perfect—beautiful, without fear, without agenda or power. It had been giving, not taking. She hadn't known it could be like that. Hadn't known it could make her feel so…full.

And now that it was over, and the sun was coming up, it was scary as hell.

She needed to get out of here before he woke up. He couldn't see her this way. She shivered as the cold air touched her bare skin, raising goosebumps. How could she have forgotten all her rules so easily? Had she really thought she loved him last night?

She looked down at him one last time, tenderness washing over her. She *did* love him. In a way she hadn't known she could love. It threatened to swallow her up with its hugeness. What about her plans? She'd let her feelings for someone derail her before, hadn't she? And that had ended in the worst sort of disaster. It had taken everything from her. The one thing she'd been sure of since the day she walked away was that she was going to be completely self-sufficient. How could she do that if she kept getting swept up in Tyson?

And then there was her family. She wanted to get them back again. To reconnect. How could she turn her back on her mom's invitation to stay with her? To set back the clock and start again?

Clara slipped out from beneath the blanket and off the army cot as Ty took a deep breath and exhaled. She froze, hoping his eyes would remain closed. When he stilled once more, she reached for her panties and bra and slipped them on, followed quickly by her skirt and sweater. She kept her gaze on his face as she stuffed her pantyhose into a ball and shoved her feet into Molly's boots. Last night was supposed to be nothing more than a hug and a healthy dose of empathy. A kind ear to listen as he talked it out.

But there'd been little talking. From the moment she'd found him, the simple hug of sympathy had blazed into a passionate fire that quickly burned out of control the moment he'd touched his lips to hers.

On tiptoe she crept out of the tack room. Right now she had to get back to the house and from there, home. He wouldn't follow her to Butterfly House, she knew that. She'd be safe there. With a pain in her heart she realized she wouldn't be back. There was no need for her now. Her job was over. It was all over.

She was nearly to the door when his voice stopped her. "Clara."

It wasn't a question. It wasn't quite a command. But it stopped her in her tracks and made her bite down on her lip. She didn't turn around, but folded her arms over her chest as a blast of cold air came through the open barn door.

"You're running away?"

He had come up behind her, close enough she could feel the heat radiating off his body and smell the warm, male scent of him. She trembled, so incredibly tempted to turn and find shelter in his arms again. But she had to be stronger than that. Ty wasn't for her. They both knew it. And yet there was an edge of hurt in his question that snuck past all her resolve and hit its mark.

"I didn't want to wake you."

It sounded weak even to her ears, and he hadn't bought it either as he huffed out a bitter laugh. "Right. Well, I deserve that. I mean usually I'm the one sneaking out, right? Ty Diamond the player, isn't that what you said before? What am I now? Your dirty little secret? After all, I doubt too many residents of Butterfly House do the walk of shame that often."

If he was trying to sound flippant he was failing miserably. He flayed her with his words, each one a little stinging whip of insult. There was such bitterness in them, such pain. She remembered the words she'd nearly said to him last night and felt relieved she hadn't said them out loud. At least she wouldn't regret *that*.

She didn't know what to say and seconds ticked by. Why couldn't he just turn around and go back in the barn? Let her go? She should be the one to walk away. This was his home. And yet the pain in her chest persisted. Last night had been the first time she'd been intimate with a man since walking away from Jackson. It was the first time she'd *enjoyed* it in longer than she could remember. Ty had made that possible. He would always be special because of it. No matter what he said now, she wouldn't let him take that away. She hadn't frozen, like Jackson had so often accused her of doing. She'd let herself feel every sensation and emotion and it had been heavenly.

"I'm sorry," she whispered, turning around.

It wasn't the right thing to say. His face that had been so relaxed and beautiful in sleep had a hard edge now, a mask to hide any sort of emotion. She'd seen that look more than once over the past weeks when he'd crossed swords with his father. It was his brittle protective layer. Lately it had been gone, and she hated that she was the one to put it back. She should have known better last night. She should have walked away and let him grieve in peace.

He shrugged as if her apology meant nothing. "I just thought you might want this so no one else found it and asked questions."

He dangled an earring from his fingers. The smile on his lips wasn't tender, but hard-edged and mocking. But there was something in his eyes—a flicker—that sent a spiral of guilt curling through her. She'd hurt him. She'd only wanted to help and instead she'd made it worse.

They'd made it worse.

She took the earring from his fingers. "It's not like that, Ty. I'm not ashamed."

He shrugged again, making the muscles in his shoulders flex, as though it didn't matter if she was or wasn't. He'd slipped his shirt on but left it unbuttoned, revealing an alluring slice of chest. Was it any wonder she'd fallen under his spell? He was the most beautiful specimen of manhood she'd ever seen, hard and honed from years of hard work and rodeo. He had his share of scars but he'd healed and come back for more.

As if he was punishing himself.

"It's exactly like that, Clara. There's no sense in pretending it's not."

Panic started to grip her. Realizing she'd abandoned her rules was one thing. Doing an analysis after the fact was terrifying. She was torn between needing to escape and needing him to understand. He had taken something that had made her so afraid and made it beautiful, relaxed and liberating. But to explain meant she'd have to admit that she had feelings. She couldn't have made love to him otherwise.

"Secret, yes," she admitted, forcing herself to stare directly into his eyes. "But not dirty. I would prefer to keep this private, Ty. It's no one else's business and it's not going to happen again."

"You're sure about that?"

She swallowed. "Aren't you? I'm not a girl. I know what last night was. It was grief and emotion and needing someone. I'm…I'm glad I was there for you. We were there for each other—I've got my share of grief, too, you know. And a few of my own regrets. You don't hold the corner on that."

"Two ships in the night, is that it? Solace in a time of grief?"

"Wasn't it?" she challenged.

He didn't answer, but she saw doubt cloud his face and wished things could magically be less complicated between them. Wished that they might have met under different circumstances. What if he'd never left home and had run the ranch with Sam, and what if she'd never made such a horrible mess of her life?

You have to play the cards you're dealt, she told herself, lifting her chin.

"I don't for one second think that you love me, Ty. I think you needed me last night, but this is this morning. It's different now. Besides, I'm no longer needed here now that…" Her throat tightened. "Now that Virgil is gone."

"Who says you're not needed?"

Oh, he was going to make this difficult. Why couldn't he have slept on so she could have made her escape? "I was his nurse. What job is there here for me now? Please believe me, Ty. Keeping this between us has nothing to do with being ashamed of what happened. You have a far lower opinion of yourself than anyone else does. And I can't fix that, Ty. Only you can do that."

Oh, wasn't that rich. She was the last person who should be offering advice about self-confidence and worth.

"And yet you're still running away." He shoved his hands in his pockets and she stared at the space where his shirt wrinkled over his wrists. An image flashed through her mind, a picture so vivid and erotic her whole body heated.

An image so intoxicating she knew she wanted it again. Her gaze traveled up to his face once more and now the smile was knowing. He knew exactly where her mind had gone, didn't he?

She couldn't want him again. This couldn't happen again. Because again would lead into what? An affair? A relationship?

Ty Diamond didn't do relationships. Neither did Clara. And an affair with Ty would end in someone getting hurt—specifically, her.

"I've been in contact with my mom," she said quietly. "She's offered me a place to stay and help finding another job. I'm going back to Saskatchewan in a few days. It's time I made up with my own family, don't you think?"

She began to back away. "Just let me go, Ty. Let's leave last night as a nice memory. You're not in the market for anything more than that, and neither am I."

Before either of them could say another word, she ran through the snow to the house.

And she never looked back.

The last place Ty wanted to be was at Butterfly House, surrounded by its residents, Sam, Angela, Molly and of course Clara.

The rambling yellow house was the sort of big, cozy place that welcomed large families, a lot of noise, and generally had a swing set in the back. The kind of place he'd envisioned as damn near perfect growing up, the sort of place you saw on television movies and sitcoms.

The kind of place he'd pictured when he'd thought about what it would have been like to grow up with his real mother and father—if things had been different. Not that Virgil and Molly hadn't been wonderful parents. But as a kid there had always been that knowledge, that bit of sting of the unknown. What it might have been like to know his birth parents. Wondering why it had been so easy for them to hand him off. He couldn't imagine doing that to his own kid. Not that it had ever been an issue. He'd never wanted the wife and kid and white picket fence that everyone seemed to think was necessary.

But there was no swing set in the yard or children laughing here. Instead of growing families, Butterfly House sheltered healing souls. And he'd been unable to resist his sister-in-law when she'd said with shining eyes that her very first resident was preparing to leave, just the way the program was intended. Angela was happy and proud that Clara was beginning a new phase in her life. To mark the occasion, they were having a potluck dinner as a send-off.

He climbed the porch steps carrying a bachelor's offering to such an event: a paper bag of fresh rolls from the bakery. The door opened and the sound of women's laughter bubbled out, making his heart clench.

He was supposed to be celebrating Clara walking out of his life today. He was supposed to be sending her off with a smile and a good-luck wish. Not a single soul knew that they'd spent the night together. Not one person knew how he regretted the sharp words he'd flung at her when she'd tried to sneak out of the barn.

That had hurt. He hadn't known how much a woman walking away *could* hurt until the right woman did it. And instead of being honest about his feelings, he'd lashed out. He sighed. He'd always been the guy with all the right words and moves. Why did those things never work with Clara?

"Ty! You came!"

Angela greeted him at the door, and he pasted on a smile. "Of course I did."

He stepped inside and held on to the paper bag. He heard Clara's sparkling laugh and something twisted inside his gut. He needed to apologize. And he needed to let her go. Over the past forty-eight hours that had become crystal clear. He didn't want her to ever live with the same regrets he had. She needed to be with her family and make things right.

The party was taking place in the large kitchen. The oversized dining table was set for nine, one side squeezing in four spaces so everyone could fit. The island in the middle of the room was already filling with food—salads were laid out and a cake waited in a domed plastic container. A Crock-Pot bubbled with something delicious-smelling, and as Ty put his bag down on the countertop Molly reached inside the oven and took out an enormous chicken-and-broccoli casserole.

Clara came from the pantry and stopped suddenly at the sight of him there. He was gratified when the color rose in her cheeks.

"Clara."

"Tyson," she said quietly.

He forced a smile for the second time in five minutes. "Big day for you. Congratulations."

She swallowed. Conversations flowed all around them, providing a protective bubble as they spoke. "This isn't quite the way I envisioned it happening," she replied. For a moment her eyes deepened with some sort of emotion he didn't want to try to decipher.

"A new start. You're obviously very happy about it. And Angela is thrilled with the first success of her program."

She finally smiled. "There is that. This program was supposed to help me get back on my feet. It's certainly done that."

Silence fell between them, a lull in conversation where he didn't know what more to say, especially with a potential audience.

"But—" Her sad eyes met his again. "I'd trade it for having Virgil back. How are you?"

For a moment anger flared. How dare she ask in that polite tone, as if something bigger hadn't happened between them? Maybe she could pretend that it had meant nothing, but he couldn't. Yes, he'd been overwhelmed. With grief and fatigue and needing, somehow, to feel connected to another human being.

But not just anyone. To Clara. The kind of woman who'd always scared the living hell out of him.

"I'm fine," he replied sharply, and felt like a heel when her face fell. Damn. They'd spent weeks getting to know each other, learning to relax and trust each other. And now he was right back to wondering what to say and do.

Angela and Sam stood by the head of the table and called for everyone's attention, saving Ty—and Clara—from trying to come up with further empty platitudes. He moved to stand beside Molly, taking the time to look at each of the women present. They were all here for the same reason—because they were building a new life for themselves after escaping abusive relationships. A few were relaxed and smiling, listening to Angela speak. One held back from the others, just a bit, trying to stay under the radar. He ran a finger over his lip. She was a wallflower, much in the way Clara had been when they first met. Uncertain and shy. That first night she'd run away from him after the tiniest kiss on her temple. He hadn't known how to deal with her that night.

And now he knew what it was to make love to her. To hold her heart in his hands. He knew the kind of soul she had inside and the hurts that had shaped her life. She had achieved so much whether she realized it or not. She had a bright future ahead of her, with so much more than he had to offer.

She wanted independence and options.

He was locked into Diamondback and he wouldn't have it any other way. It was where he belonged.

The kindest thing was to let her go, wasn't it? To let her have the life she'd worked so hard for?

After the meal Clara was shooed from the kitchen, absolved of kitchen duties on this, her last night in Cadence Creek. He heard Molly talking with a couple of the ladies about starting a weekly craft night, and Sam and

Angela were chatting with the new director about foundation business.

Ty looked at Clara, who was putting her teacup in the dishwasher. "Walk with me?" he asked.

"I guess that would be okay," she answered. "For a minute."

He held the door for her as they stepped onto the front porch. Somehow he had to make things right in the next few minutes. He had to come up with a way to let her go and wish her well. It was the right thing to do. And after years of making mistakes, Ty knew it was time he started doing the right thing instead of the easy thing.

Clara pulled on her mittens as she led the way down the steps and onto the walkway. Dinner had been excruciating, having to smile all the time like she hadn't a care in the world. Truth was, everything was about to change—again. And the ugly truth was she should be more excited about reconnecting with her family and starting over.

But she wasn't. Because there was still a hole in her heart that was distinctly Ty-shaped. And now he'd asked her outside for what she could only assume was a private goodbye.

His boots sounded on the concrete blocks leading to the driveway, and her pulse did the odd patter that it often did simply when he was near. Despite the cold that was a permanent thing now that snow had finally arrived, Clara felt overly warm in her coat. Another consequence of being near Ty. She wished he hadn't asked. Wished he'd just said his goodbye at the door and gone. It would have been easier than *this*.

She stopped next to the farm truck, knowing it hid them from view of the house and also knowing that if she stopped here he'd be able to get in and drive home once they'd said what they needed to say. Briefly she thought of his car, remembering the night he'd taken her to the diner and brought her home afterward. Sitting in the dark that night she'd wondered if he'd kiss her. Standing in the dark now, with just the streetlamp lighting the street, she wondered the same thing. And just like then, she was torn between wanting him to and scared to death he actually might.

He'd put his hat on his head, the dark brim shadowing his face as he shoved his hands into his coat pockets. Clara swallowed, knowing she'd always remember him this way: tall, sexy and with a dangerous edge. The problem was she knew what was behind the edge, and it made it so very difficult to say goodbye.

"Thank you for coming tonight."

He nodded. "You're heading out in the morning?"

"Yes." She clenched her fingers inside the fleece pocket lining. "It'll take me most of the day to get there."

There was silence, then the far-off sound of a train to the northwest. Clara couldn't stand it any longer. One of them had to say something about it. Clear the air so they could leave it behind. "Ty, I'm sorry about the other day. About running off like I did."

She looked up at him but couldn't tell what he was thinking. The angle of the streetlamp's light and his hat made it impossible to see his eyes. He hunched his shoulders and then straightened them again.

"I said some things I shouldn't have, too. I didn't want it to go that way."

"Then why did it?"

Even though she couldn't see his eyes, his gaze seemed to bore into the very center of her. "Because you were running away. I know I'm not the kind of man for you. I know us being together would be a mistake. But you were running like you were ashamed and I was mad on top of everything else."

Ashamed? That was what he thought? It had been fear, pure and simple. She'd worked too hard to find herself again only to lose herself in another relationship. She didn't trust herself. He'd been right about that. And throwing love into the mix made it ten times worse. How could she possibly tell him that, now that he'd said straight up that anything between them was a mistake?

She couldn't, so she looked at her feet and said, "I wanted to get out of there before anyone would notice my car in the driveway."

The harsh, dry laugh was bitter and she saw his boots turn away. He walked a few feet before turning back. "Clara Ferguson," he said clearly. "You are a lot of things, but I never, ever took you for a coward."

Frustration simmered. Why did he have to make this so hard? He should just let her go, right? What was one night to a man like Ty? He'd broken hearts before, she was sure of it. Had each one been entitled to this touching goodbye? The sarcastic words sat on her tongue. The only thing keeping her from blurting them out was that he was, unfortunately, right.

"What happened between us was a by-product of grief, that's all."

He said nothing. Clara's nerves began to fray under his steady gaze. She was no good at this. She had no experience in it. It sounded as if *she* was giving *him* the brushoff, which was ridiculous, wasn't it?

"I didn't ask you out here so we could replay our mistakes," he said softly. "Though for my part, I don't have any regrets. I hope you don't either, Clara. I never wanted to hurt you, or take advantage of you in any way."

"You didn't," she whispered. If anything she felt as

though she'd taken advantage of him. "You were a gentleman from the first, Ty."

"I didn't know how to act around you. I knew what you'd been through and I never knew if I should touch you or turn away, talk about it or ignore it. I just knew things were better when you were around. You made me understand a lot of things, and because of it I was able to make amends with my dad. So thank you, Clara." He reached out and pulled her hand out of her pocket, folding it within his, warm even through his glove and her mitten. "I hope your new life is everything you wanted. I am so glad that you're reconnecting with your family because I know how important that is. And I hope you'll look back on your time at Diamondback as something good and positive and not colored by the last week."

A stinging began behind her nose. This really was goodbye, then. She hated that a part of her heart had wanted him to say something more sentimental. Hated knowing that she might have reconsidered leaving if he'd admitted he'd fallen in love with her the way she'd fallen for him. But he didn't. Because he'd been honest, right? Ty didn't fall in love. He'd told her that at the very beginning.

"Of course I will," she answered, unable to stop the quiver in her voice.

"I'm so happy for you. It's a whole new start, and you'll have your family back. But I'll miss you, Clara. I wanted you to know that before you went. I'll miss you."

She clenched her teeth together, trying to hold her emotions in, but they got the better of her. Her lower lip began to wobble as she looked up…and he took off his hat.

His eyes. Oh, his eyes were dark and tortured and she thought for a minute that he might reach out and pull her close and tell her it was all a mistake. But he didn't. Instead he held out his hand, offering it to her to shake. She stared at it, not wanting to take it. It seemed less than it should be between them somehow. And to not take it would leave such a bitter taste for both of them. She couldn't let things end that way. Not after all he'd given to her. All the things she couldn't say. He'd given her back her confidence, he'd taken away her fear with his gentleness. He'd taught her to laugh again and made her feel as though she had something unique to offer the world. He'd done all of that simply by being Ty.

So she held out her hand, put it in his and felt her insides tremble.

"Good luck with Diamondback, Ty. You and Sam are going to do great things, I just know it."

Her gaze landed on his lips. She'd done so well by coming out with a platonic wish for the future. But then she'd looked at his lips, and then back to his eyes, and everything they'd been holding back seemed to sizzle between them again.

He squeezed her fingers almost painfully. "And good luck to you, Clara, and your shiny new life. If anyone deserves it, you do."

One of them had to let go. One of them had to make the first move and slide their fingers out of the clasp. And yet it went on, and on, hovering on the brink of becoming more, holding back.

Finally Ty pulled his hand from hers and put his hat on his head. The lump in her throat got bigger as silently he tipped a finger to the brim and then reached for the door handle of the truck.

Then he paused, left the truck door open, came back and pressed a kiss to her cheek. His lips were warm and soft, and she desperately wanted to pull him to her and just tell him how she felt and ask if she could stay.

It was only the crushing realization that her feelings

wouldn't be returned that held her back from confessing it all. And if she did, she'd know that once more she wouldn't be making the smart decision for her life but the one based on her feelings for a man who didn't feel the same way about her.

"Goodbye, Clara," he murmured, and she closed her eyes, imprinting the feel of his lips, the warmth of his breath, the masculine scent of him on her brain one last time.

"'Bye, Tyson."

He hopped into the cab of the truck and started the engine as she stepped back onto the shoulder of the road, out of the way.

Then he was gone in a cloud of exhaust. And she was left standing there, on the brink of a whole new shiny life that suddenly didn't feel quite as shiny as it ought.

CHAPTER TEN

A WARM CHINOOK had come over the Rockies, pushing through Alberta into Saskatchewan and providing an uncharacteristic springlike feeling to the air considering it was only February.

Clara parked the car in the garage and shut off the key, resting her head on the steering wheel for a moment. She was so tired lately, and getting up in the night to pee wasn't helping her much either. She often got back in bed and couldn't nod off again as she kept thinking about Ty, and Diamondback, and the consequences she hadn't seen coming from their night together.

She was going to have to tell him. Soon. This was not something she could keep a secret. Ty deserved to know he was going to be a father. She'd only held off this long because she'd wanted to be sure.

She'd wanted to get through the first trimester safely before sharing the news. And she'd wanted to give herself a little time to think—to sort out her feelings and make some sort of plan. There was no question about going through with the pregnancy. She'd already been given one second chance in her life and she wasn't about to squander another. But that in itself created so many questions that the more she tried to sort things out, the more confused she became.

The door connecting the garage to the house opened. "Clara, you coming in?"

She looked up at her mother, holding the door open. Wendy's face was creased with concern. Clara hadn't been able to keep the pregnancy secret for long once morning sickness kicked in, and the whole story had come tumbling out. She'd forgotten how wonderful it was to be held in her mother's arms and told it would all be okay. But she also knew that her mother worried about her plenty. She dropped the keys into her purse and slung it over her shoulder as she opened the car door. "Sorry."

"Dinner's almost ready. Beef stew and spinach salad."

Clara's stomach growled at the good news. "Lots of iron. Maybe that's what I've been craving lately."

Wendy Ferguson shrugged. "Gotta keep you and that little one fed." She smiled. "Oh, and that friend of yours called. Angela? She asked if you'd call her back at her house. I told her I'd pass on the message."

Clara's appetite took a nose dive. What did Angela want? For the first month they'd kept in touch briefly. Part of that was Angela keeping tabs on people who had gone through her program. But now it was different. Clara didn't like keeping secrets, and talking to Angela did nothing more than remind her of Diamondback and Cadence Creek and how much she missed them all.

"I'll call her later. Thanks for making dinner again."

"Your turn's coming. I'm back to work on Monday."

They'd been doing a fair job of splitting the housekeeping duties, with whoever was home taking over cooking meals and throwing in a load of laundry when time allowed. For Clara, it was more like having a roommate than living at home with a parent, and for that she was glad. Reconnecting with her mother had helped fill a space that had been empty for a long time. She'd been welcomed back with open arms and a few tears. She'd even spoken to her brother on the phone, all the way from where he was living in Australia. Bit by bit she was getting back the pieces of her life that had been scattered.

All except one. Her feelings for Ty hadn't dimmed in the least. How were they ever going to manage to parent this child with everything so complicated?

Once dinner was over she grabbed the phone and went to her room to talk to Angela in private. Perhaps it was nothing, just a follow-up from the Butterfly Foundation as usual. Angela answered on the first ring and Clara laughed. "Were you sitting on the phone?"

"Just about," Angela said. "It's good to hear your voice, Clara."

"You, too," she answered, and it really was. Angela had been more than her social worker. They'd been friends. She'd been Angela's bridesmaid, after all, and along with Ty and Molly she missed Angela, too. Looking back, Clara supposed it was odd that she'd never confided to Angela that she'd developed feelings for Ty. But then it had been pretty obvious, hadn't it? And while no one had breathed a word about seeing her car in the drive the morning after the funeral, Clara knew it was foolish to think no one had noticed.

"I'm calling with a specific invitation," Angela chirped. "Molly's birthday. It's coming up a week from Monday, but we're having a party on Saturday night to celebrate. Just a few close friends for dinner at the new house. Tell me you have the weekend off."

She did, so there was that excuse out the window. She hesitated, searching for an excuse not to go. "It's an awfully long drive, Ang, and it's still winter."

"Well, we can't control that. If it's storming, you won't come of course. But otherwise you will, right?"

She needed to see Ty, but this was not how she wanted to do it. She wanted it to be on her own time, in her own way, when she was ready and with a clear plan. "I don't know…"

"Come on, you can stay here. We finally have a real spare room and you can be our first guest. Or you can stay at the ranch. Though Ty's there…"

"What's that supposed to mean?" She asked the question before she could stop herself.

"Just that, well, things seemed kind of tense between you before you left. Did you argue or something?"

Tense didn't begin to cover it. Clara had fallen in love with a man who didn't love her back.

"There was a lot going on, that's all." She tried to pass it off as nothing. "There are no hard feelings or anything."

"Then you'll come?"

Clara thought for a moment. What better excuse would she have for driving all the way to Cadence Creek? And she did have to tell Ty about the baby. Soon. It wouldn't do to show up at his door in maternity clothes or carrying a car seat with a bundle of joy. They should talk now so they had lots of time to make calm, rational decisions.

"Would it be okay if I came on Friday?" That way she could talk to Ty privately, beforehand.

"I'd love that! Let's pray for good weather and I'll see you then."

"See you," Clara echoed, as they finished the conversation and hung up.

A week. She had barely a week to come up with a plan that would allow her to raise her baby, allow Ty to be a father, and keep her heart intact.

Easy peasy, she thought skeptically, sinking back onto

the pillows of her bed and wondering why the nausea, which had been so much better this week, was suddenly back.

The Chinook of the previous week had missed Cadence Creek, and the fields were still blanketed with white as Clara drove past the main house and headed to Sam and Angela's. The two-story Cape Cod was welcoming, with lights glowing through the windows as afternoon waned. It had taken Clara most of the day to get here, and she was looking forward to stretching her legs in a big way.

And she had to find a way to talk to Ty. Maybe in the morning, when they were both fresh and she'd had a chance to sleep on the words she was preparing to say. She'd decided she wanted to stay close to Moose Jaw, with her mother, at least for the time being. She'd have wonderful support and flexible hours working at the local hospital. She hoped Ty would support her in her decision, especially when she told him that she wanted him to be involved as much as possible. It wouldn't always be easy, but surely they could work out visitation. They were adults, after all.

She knocked on the door, carrying her overnight bag on her shoulder. First she needed to pee—pregnancy bladder was killer—and freshen up her makeup. She wanted to be completely prepared and collected when she saw him again.

She was firmly in control when the door opened. And that control went sideways when Ty stood in the breach.

"You!" she said, and her bag slipped off her shoulder and hit the step with a thump.

"Hi to you, too," he said. Oh, how she'd missed that voice. A little soft, a little smooth, completely masculine.

Her mouth opened and closed a few times, and all her

practiced words flew out of her head. He was here. Right now. Looking the way he always did—careless, casual and gorgeous.

And his baby was inside her.

She reached down and picked up her bag, willing her hands not to tremble and taking calming breaths. When she straightened her head got a little fuzzy, as it often did when she made quick changes in position these days. She forced a smile. "May I come in, then? It's cold out here."

He stood aside and opened the door so she could enter the foyer.

The house was new and quite grand by Clara's standards, all wide, white woodwork and polished hardwood and gleaming light fixtures. "I thought Angela would be here," she said, hearing her voice echo in the vaulted hallway.

"She's just popped up out to the diner for pie for dessert."

The diner. Clara felt a familiar twist in her stomach thinking of that night and how Ty had smiled at her and talked about Virgil. She remembered too how she'd put her fingers on his when he'd explained how he came to be at Diamondback as a baby. Their closeness had really begun that night, hadn't it?

"So you're staying for dinner?" She chanced a look up at him.

He nodded. "I was invited. But if it makes you too uncomfortable…"

The front door opened and Angela stepped through, her cheeks rosy and a paper sack balanced in her hands. "You're here! Yay! Let me put this in the kitchen and come back and hug you properly!"

She hurried through to the kitchen and Clara raised an eyebrow. "She's so, wow. Excited? Bubbly." It was more than that. Angela was so open with her affection now. Angela had fought her own demons and won, but she'd still had a bit of reserve that kept her at arm's length some of the time. That seemed to be completely gone. "I've never seen her like this."

"I think it's called happiness," Ty remarked dryly.

"Do you suppose it's catching?"

"I guess we can hope, right? It looks good on her."

She smiled, a genuine smile this time rather than strained politeness. This was the Ty she'd liked from the start. Easygoing, charming, with a ready smile.

Angela bustled back and enveloped Clara in a welcoming hug. "You look great," she said. "Doesn't she look great, Ty?"

Angela was fishing now and Clara felt heat rise in her cheeks. "Great," Ty said quietly, and her eyes found his immediately. The warm brown depths held a gleam of approval that sent her heart thumping in an all-too-familiar way. This was what was going to make it difficult, wasn't it? Her feelings hadn't changed. And it was going to be hell trying to keep them out of the way.

"Come on in the kitchen and tell me what you've really been up to," Angela suggested, taking Clara by the hand. "Ty, why don't you find out what's keeping Sam? Dinner's in half an hour."

"If that's your not-so-subtle invitation to get out of the way so you can have some girl-talk, I accept," Ty replied, flashing a grin. "And I'll make sure Sam's here on time."

Clara was tugged away towards the kitchen and as they entered the large room, she slipped her hand out of Angela's. "Can you point me in the direction of the bathroom? It was a long drive."

"Oh, look at me! Of course. And let me show you to

your room instead. You can freshen up or whatever until dinner. I'm sorry, I'm just so happy to see you again."

"I'm happy to see you, too," Clara admitted. Being here felt like coming home—was it possible for someone to have two homes?

Angela changed direction, taking Clara upstairs instead as she kept chattering. "We'll have plenty of time to catch up later." She stopped in front of a white door. "We can curl up on the sofa with hot cocoa tonight and whisper to our heart's content."

She opened the door. The room was beautiful. Clara stepped inside, putting her bag on the floor at the foot of the bed before spinning around. "Oh, Angela. You must love your house."

"I do. It's exactly what I always dreamed of, even as a kid. I'm so lucky. So happy." She leaned against the door and smiled wistfully. "And you. You're back home with your mom. It's good, right?"

"It's been wonderful. All the things I remembered, though the house is different now because she moved into a townhouse, and some of those good things are just memories. But she kept a lot of the things I remember and she hasn't changed a bit. I feel like I got myself back, Ang, and that's all thanks to you."

"Nonsense. But I'm so happy for you. I won't lie—we miss you around here. Anyway, there's an ensuite through that door that's yours. Take your time."

When she was gone, Clara explored the ensuite and freshened up, then perched on the window seat for a few moments, staring out the window. It overlooked the gate and driveway and she saw Sam and Ty drive in, and Ty's long legs as he hopped out of the truck. She wondered what he would say when she told him. He didn't want kids of his own, did he? He'd said that he'd never want to be in the position his birth parents had found themselves. That he'd always been careful.

But they hadn't been careful, had they? They'd been reckless and emotional. Fine beginning for a child. Her head began to ache and she knew she had to find a way to speak to Ty soon. Dragging it out wasn't going to help at all. Once dinner was over and the dishes tucked away into the dishwasher, Clara touched Angela's arm. "I need a favor."

"Of course. Name it."

Clara met Angela's gaze. "I'll explain later, I promise, okay? Is there a place where I can speak to Ty? Alone?"

"You can use my office. Are you okay?"

Clara lifted her shoulders and dropped them again. "To be honest? I don't know. But I have a feeling I'll need that cocoa later, okay?"

"You got it." Angela squeezed her shoulder. "He's a good man, Clara. And I think he's been a bit lost since you left."

Oh, that was not what she wanted to hear! She swallowed against the unease building in her throat. "Thanks, Ang." She went to the door of the living room and cleared her throat. "Ty?" she asked. "Could I have a word?"

"Sure," he replied, surprise blanking his face but he rose instantly.

"Angela said we could use her office."

There was a hint of alarm flattening his features now and his eyes, usually twinkling with mischief, darkened with concern. "Lead the way," he said, standing beside her shoulder.

She shut the door behind them and closed her eyes, taking a restorative breath.

"What's wrong?" He was in front of her in an instant. "You're pale, and you've had this funny look since you arrived. Are you sick? Is everything okay in Moose Jaw? Are you in trouble?"

Oh, Lord, his genuine concern was almost too much to bear. Then he put his hands on her upper arms, rubbing his thumbs along the surface of her shirt and creating a lovely warm friction beneath his touch. She blinked a few times—she was determined to get through this conversation without turning into a waterworks. "I'm not in trouble. Not the way you're thinking, anyway." She tried to smile but it felt crooked and odd. "I've got a good job, and sharing a condo with my mom has been wonderful. Truly."

"Then what is it?" He squatted down a bit and looked her dead in the eye. "Why do you need to talk to me alone?"

His cheeks turned slightly ruddy. My goodness, was Ty Diamond blushing?

"If it's about the last night you were here…what I said… is it…" He cleared his throat roughly. "Do you still have feelings for me? I swear I didn't mean to hurt you, Clara, I…"

She slid out of his grasp and took a few stumbling steps. "No! I mean, that's not why I wanted to talk to you," she amended, feeling the conversation already getting off track. She faced him and lifted her chin as much as she dared, gathering all her strength and composure. "Ty, about the night we spent together…"

He stilled.

She locked her gaze with his. "We didn't use any protection, Ty," she said gently. "And I'm pregnant."

For the space of a second his eyes widened and his lips dropped open. Then he put a hand over his mouth and scraped it along his chin as he absorbed the hit.

"Pregnant."

"I was as surprised as you are."

"When did you… How long have you known?"

"Since before Christmas."

His gaze narrowed. "And you waited until now, why?"

This was the hard part, wasn't it? The real reason she had kept the news to herself. It wasn't just about her feelings for Ty, but her own insecurity and guilt and the resulting fear. It was finding out the news and feeling happy and terrified and confused and wanting to cherish the knowledge and keep it to herself in case something went horribly wrong.

The last time she'd thought being pregnant would fix things, but she'd been younger and her thinking had been skewed and she'd been so utterly wrong. She was older now. She knew better. And so she'd held the secret inside until her conscience told her she couldn't anymore.

"I…I…" She hated that she sounded so weak. "I didn't know how, Ty. It was such a shock at first. And you'd just lost your father. The last thing you needed was more upheaval. But you deserve to know. Angela's invitation came and I knew I couldn't keep you in the dark any longer."

"Oh, man," he breathed, sinking down on the futon next to the wall. "I'm going to be a father."

"I know it's a shock."

"You've got that right."

She wanted to go sit beside him but didn't. She needed the distance to keep her perspective. To stay strong. That wouldn't happen if she sat beside him. He'd be too close. She was already far too aware of everything about him.

"I've thought about it, Ty, and I definitely want you to be part of this baby's life." She tried to smile. "I've got things pretty good now—my mom's been wonderful and I have a great new job. I won't be without any support this…" She broke off the sentence, a tiny pain clutching at her heart. "Anyway, I'm ready to raise him. Or her. And

I know we can work it out so you can see him—or her—whenever you want. We're grown-ups. We can…"

"Like hell," he interrupted, standing. "I can see the baby whenever I want?" His lip curled. "How long did you rehearse, Clara? Did you really think you could sell me on this farce of a parenting proposal?"

Hope plummeted. "But you don't even want to be a parent!"

"What I wanted and what's to be are two very different things. You know that." He went to her and gripped her wrist. "How could you ever think that I'd let my own child be raised miles away, to see them what, a few times a year? A week in the summer and every other Christmas?" His eyes blazed at her now, sparking with indignation. "No child of mine will ever feel unwanted or pushed aside! After all you know about me. After all I told you. I'd never told anyone before, did you know that?" He let go of her wrist, pushing it aside as if it were distasteful. "I thought you knew me better than that. I thought I knew *you* better than that."

The insult hit its mark and she inhaled sharply. "That's not fair. Neither of us planned this! What am I supposed to do, Ty? I just found my family again. I just started over with a job and a whole new life!"

"So you don't want it?"

Hurt seemed to seep through her, right through her very bones. She went to a meeting chair and perched on the edge, trying to catch her breath. "I want it so much I can hardly stand it," she whispered. She hated that he was angry. Hated that this was the situation her baby would grow up in. There should be harmony, not conflict. Working together, not against each other. "Oh, Ty," she breathed. "I have had so many second chances. I'm so afraid of blowing this one. I always thought I'd be too afraid to be pregnant again, but now I am and it's the most terrifying, humbling, wonderful thing. I know we can find a way to work this out. We have to, don't you see?"

Ty had grown dangerously quiet. "Again?" he asked softly.

Panic blossomed. She'd said that, hadn't she? She'd said the word *again* when Ty didn't know about before. How could he? It was *her* deep, dark secret.

And finally the strain was too much to bear. She put her face in her hands and began to cry.

Ty hadn't expected tears. He hadn't expected any of this. When she'd called him in here tonight, he'd seriously thought she'd found herself in trouble again and needed his help. That perhaps she hadn't quite been ready to go it alone as she thought.

But a baby? His baby. As he'd stared at her, he'd flashed back to that night in the barn when it had been conceived. There had been grief, but there'd been more than that, too. It had been beautiful, and right, and for the first time ever, Ty had let himself give up emotional control when with a woman. He'd bared himself to her in a way he'd never done before. He doubted she knew that.

There'd been no one since either.

He knelt beside her and touched her hair. "Tell me what you mean by 'again,'" he said quietly. There were layers to Clara he still hadn't unwrapped. Things he figured he should know before this went any further.

She didn't answer, and he saw a tear sneak below her palms, dropping off her chin to the rug below her chair. It damn near ripped him apart to see her cry. Clara, the cheerful one. Clara, the woman who looked after everyone else. She was weeping quietly as if her heart would break, and even though the whole thing was a damned mess, he gathered her in his arms and let her cry it out.

"Clara," he finally nudged gently. "You're killing my legs here. Let's sit on the futon."

She nodded against his shirt and stood, shaky at first, as he pushed up out of the crouch and led her to the futon. She sat, avoiding his gaze. Her face was red and puffy from crying and her hair was a tangle around her cheeks, the odd strand stuck to the skin with tears. She was still the most beautiful woman he knew. More beautiful now that she was carrying his child. But she wanted to raise it a province away without him. He couldn't let that happen. What was she afraid of? He was sure that was the key to everything.

"Can you tell me now?" he asked, rubbing her hand between his. "What did you mean by again? Do you have another child, Clara?"

"Do you see another?" She wrinkled her brow. "That question doesn't make sense."

"Sure it does. You might have given one up for adoption. Is that what you meant by a second chance?"

She shook her head. "No. The decision was taken out of my hands." Again she paused. And sighed. "I've never told anyone this. Not even Angela. Oh, Tyson, it's so hard."

"Just say it," he said. "I need to know, Clara."

"Yes, you do." She sounded resigned as she leaned back against the cushion of the futon. "It was when I was with Jackson, you see. I found out I was pregnant. I thought if he knew that maybe he'd let up, you know? He'd been so good to me at first. I thought maybe it could be that way again." She met Ty's gaze with sad eyes. "I know now how stupid that sounds."

"Not stupid," Ty murmured. "Desperate."

"Well, regardless, I was wrong. He flew into a rage.

Said it wasn't his, and accused me of sleeping around."
Bitterness crept into her voice. "When would I have time
to do that? When I wasn't at work, he practically kept me
under lock and key."

"He beat you when you were pregnant?"

"Three fractured ribs and a broken nose and a lot of
bruises. And a miscarriage."

Ty felt as if someone had punched him in the gut. Even
suspecting what was coming, he couldn't comprehend a
man who could do that to a woman. Not when she was
carrying a precious baby inside her. All the air came out
of his lungs and he gripped her fingers tighter.

"So now you understand," she whispered, "why I want
it so much. Why I want to do it right this time. I couldn't
tell you before because I wanted to get past the first trimester and be sure things were okay. I needed to wrap
my head around the idea of being a mom and being me."

Nothing about sorting out her feelings for him, then.
He knew he shouldn't be hurt by that. They'd had a one-
night thing during an emotional storm. They'd cared for
each other but neither of them had used the word *love,*
had they? Clara had always made it clear that she wanted
her own life and her independence, and it appeared she
was still determined to have it. If he admitted he loved
her now, wouldn't she think he was trying to manipulate
her to get his way?

Would he be? His head was spinning so much right
now that he couldn't even be sure. All he knew was that
no child of his would be raised without him there every
step of the way.

There could be no solution tonight. Clara looked exhausted and he wasn't sure where to go next. He looked
at where her shirt lay over the zipper of her jeans and his
heart gave a little kick. His baby was in there. The one

they'd created together. And that baby deserved better than this.

"May I?" He held out his hand, letting it hover over her tummy. He wished he didn't have to ask. Wished that things were different, that they'd gotten the news together, that they'd shared in it and worried about it as one. But they hadn't, because none of this had been supposed to happen. Now they just had to roll with it, right?

She nodded. "Yes, of course."

He put his hand on her still-flat belly. "There's no bump there yet," he murmured, the warmth from her body seeping into his palm.

"Soon," she replied. "My waistbands are already getting a little tight. Thank God scrubs have drawstrings."

He should remove his hand but it felt too good. Instead he looked into her face. It hit him then, with the force of a brick upside the head. He *did* love her. Not just love... He was *in* love with her. All the way, headfirst without a safety net, in love with her. With her sweetness, with her tender heart, with the life she carried inside her. Nothing in his life—not even the first moment when she'd said the words *I'm pregnant*—had frightened and exhilarated him this way. How could a man feel as though he could take on the world and be so terrified of failure at the same time?

"Nothing needs to be decided tonight," he said, finally sliding his hand off her tummy. "We both need time to think. I know we can work this out, Clara. We both want to do what's right, and that means we will. Somehow."

"I wish I had your confidence. Some people might find it cocky, but I admire that."

"We'll make a good team," he replied, the beginnings of something flickering inside, expanding into a glow of certainty. "You care about people, Clara. You always have, even when you were hurt and distrustful. You'll make a wonderful mother."

"I appreciate that more than you know."

"It'll be okay," he said, stronger. "I have a lot to think about, and you need some rest, right? I'll see you tomorrow for the party?"

"Of course."

"And you'll be okay now?"

"Ty." She smiled. It was good to see her smile without the strain that had been around her eyes since…well, since the night they'd spent together, if he were being truthful. "I've had longer to get used to the idea. It's okay to freak a little."

He leaned down and kissed her forehead, wondering what she'd say if she really knew what he was thinking. "I'll see you tomorrow, then."

He left the office and headed straight to the foyer. His head was swimming with so many things right now— pregnancy and fatherhood and being in love and how to make it all come together in the right way without sending Clara running in a panic. He wished his father was there to talk to. Virgil would have known what to do. He wouldn't have minced words either. Ty had hated that bluntness for years, and had hated that Virgil always seemed to be right as well.

But right now he missed what he realized had been guidance and love all along.

"Ty? Is everything okay?"

Angela stopped at the end of the hall and folded her arms, a look of concern wrinkling her features.

"It will be," he answered. He nodded towards the office. "Clara could use a friend, though."

Angela came forward. "I knew something was wrong. She was far too quiet at dinner. Is she okay?"

"Don't worry," Ty said, wishing he felt more of the confidence Clara seemed so sure he possessed. "I'm going to make everything right."

As he stepped out into the frigid air, he turned up his collar. He would come up with the solution. And he'd do it before Clara left on Sunday.

CHAPTER ELEVEN

CLARA SIGHED WITH frustration as she tried to button the trousers she'd brought for the party. Things were starting to not fit. The faint bubble of her belly wasn't really visible, but it would be soon. Especially if she were popping buttons and zippers all over the place.

The button finally went through the hole and she frowned, looking at the reflection in the mirror. Thank goodness she'd brought a flowing kind of blouse to wear over top. It would cover the ill-fitting waistband. She put her hands over her tummy, and the frown slid from her face. Things were so very complicated but she couldn't find it within herself to be sorry. She was going to be a mother. And she was going to do everything possible to be a good one. She'd make the right decisions this time.

Except there was the small matter of Ty to consider. She got the feeling he'd have ideas of his own. And she also got the feeling that he might not go along with her plans as easily as she hoped.

Angela knocked on the door and stuck her head inside. "You ready to go?"

Clara nodded. "As ready as I'm going to be." She picked up her purse and followed Angela down the stairs. "You're not going to say anything to Molly, right?" Angela had been so concerned last night that Clara had confessed about the pregnancy. Angela had been shocked but not totally surprised that something had happened between Clara and Ty. "Ty and I need to talk before anyone else is brought into it. You understand."

"Of course I do. I won't breathe a word."

The drive to the main house was short and Clara swallowed thickly as they approached the house. She'd done a lot of growing here. She'd found her heart again at Diamondback. Moving back to Moose Jaw had been the right decision, and it had given her something back that had been missing.

But Diamondback…it felt like home.

Molly met them at the door, and before Clara could catch a breath, she found herself enveloped in a tight hug. "My goodness, girl," Molly said, stepping back and grinning from ear to ear. "It's good to see you. You look wonderful. Just glowing."

Buster bounced around, barking and offering his own doggy greeting with wags of his tail. Clara nearly swallowed her tongue but recovered quickly. "It's the winter air putting roses in my cheeks. How are you, Molly?"

"I'm doing okay. House seems awful big these days. But Ty's here. I can't be lonely when I have family all around, can I?" She looked at Angela and raised an eyebrow. "Now all I need are a few grandbabies to cuddle."

Clara scurried aside, hiding her face as she unbuttoned her coat and hung it on her customary peg behind the door. Molly couldn't possibly have said anything that would make her more uncomfortable. Even Angela had an odd, tight look on her face, but at least that could be explained away by being put on the spot.

"What's the rush?" Sam interjected smoothly, giving his mother a kiss on the cheek. He winked at Clara. "Where's Ty? I figured he'd be where the cake is."

The timing of the question was perfect as Ty stomped in, clearing the light snow from his boots. "Someone ask for me?" he grinned. "I was on food duty, remember?" He held up a gigantic paper bag. "Mom requested Chinese. The birthday girl gets her wish."

Molly took the bag from him and put it on the butcher block. "We'll have to heat this up a bit, but it won't take long."

Angela and Sam went to help, and Ty turned his attention towards Clara. His gaze was warm and soft as he looked at her, and she felt herself turning to jelly. He'd always been able to do that, right from the first. And now there was something more in that light of approval in his eyes. There was the knowing. Knowing each other intimately. Knowing they'd created another human being. It was a powerful force.

"Clara," he said simply, and her heart turned over.

"Hi," she replied softly, watching as he took off his jacket, hanging it beside hers. He looked so good, maybe even better than she remembered. The tan brushed-cotton of his shirt brought out the glints of gold in his eyes, and it fit across the breadth of his shoulders as if it had been tailored for him. With a stutter of her heart she realized that she hoped she had a boy just like him—big brown eyes and a lightning grin and a mop of stubborn dark hair.

"How'd you sleep last night?" He stepped closer and kept his voice low, letting the chatter behind him provide a little bit of cover.

But now he was very near and her pulse started leaping around. Why couldn't she keep her reactions to him under control? Co-parenting was going to be hellish if this kept getting in the way. Maybe it would get better in time. It had to, right?

"Okay." She tried a smile. "To be honest, I've been worrying so much about telling you that I think I slept better because it was such a relief to have it over with."

She looked over his shoulder; Sam and Molly and Angela were still putting food in dishes and there was a steady hum as Angela started the microwave.

"How about you?" she asked.

"Not so good. I did a lot of thinking."

"I'm sorry."

"Don't be." He frowned, then pinned her with a direct gaze. "Things won't be ready for a while. Can we talk? Somewhere more private than the living room?"

"Sure," she answered. Not that she was in any hurry to be alone with Ty, but she sure as heck didn't want them to be overheard either.

He led her through the living room and up the stairs. "I hope this isn't awkward," he said. "My room is probably the best place to avoid being interrupted."

His room? Clara paused, but what else could she do? He was right. Anywhere downstairs they'd risk being interrupted or overheard. She stepped inside when he opened the door and took a fortifying breath.

The door shut with a quiet click and Clara immediately felt the intimacy of being closed away in his personal space. The bed was made of sturdy pine and covered with one of Molly's handmade quilts in cozy shades of tan and chocolate and cream. A sturdy shelf covered one wall and was full of huge trophies and accolades. Goodness, he had been successful, hadn't he? It seemed a little bit glamorous to Clara and there was a sense of awe in knowing this was the sort of man who'd fathered her child.

His window overlooked the north pasture and the view extended for miles, the odd house and barn of neighboring ranches dotting the rolling landscape here and there. From this view Clara truly began to realize how big Diamondback was. What a responsibility it was for Sam and Ty, and her respect for them both—and for Virgil—grew.

She turned away from the window and faced him. The bed was behind her and she had the persistent thought that it was quite inappropriate, under the circumstances, to be so very aware of it. To be aware of him. She wanted to be in his arms. To feel his lips on hers once more. Oh, how she'd missed that. But it went against everything she wanted to accomplish, so she clasped her hands together, bit down on her lip and waited. Last night she'd said her piece. Clearly Ty wanted to say his.

"You're nervous," he said gently, standing just in front of the door. Not moving any closer, but not getting any farther away either.

"I'm fine," she contradicted, but he shook his head.

"You always bite down on your lip when you're uncomfortable, did you know that? It's quite attractive, actually."

"Ty…"

This time he took a step forward. "I thought about it all night, Clara. Thought about you and the baby and Diamondback, and I know what we have to do."

She wasn't sure she liked the sound of this. He seemed very sure of himself, and considering she'd already explained her proposal this meant he wasn't likely to go along with it. She tangled her fingers tighter together and replied as evenly as she could, "I already told you what I'd like to do. This doesn't have to change anything, not really. I can keep my life and you can keep yours, and we can work it out so that our baby has both a mother and a father. Right?"

Somehow in the twisting of her fingers, she managed to cross hers, hoping he would see reason.

Another step closer, and this time he was shaking his head. "That doesn't work for me, Clara. I can't be a father from hundreds of kilometers away." He reached out and pried one of her hands loose, clasping it in his strong, warm fingers. "What makes the most sense is…"

He paused, then got down on one knee while her mouth fell open. No, no, no! This couldn't be happening. He couldn't possibly be proposing. It would ruin everything! She didn't want to get married. Didn't want to lose herself in another relationship where she wasn't loved in return. Why couldn't he just be reasonable?

She tried to slide her fingers out of his but his grip was too firm. Oh, God, he was looking up at her with those heart-on-his-sleeve eyes and she couldn't look away.

"I want you to marry me," he said softly. "Come home to Diamondback, and we can raise our child together."

Panic threaded its way through her body. "We don't have to get married to be parents," she answered, adding a nervous laugh to the end that fell completely flat. Ty's brow furrowed and a wrinkle appeared just above his nose.

He got to his feet and Clara realized once more how very tall he was. Ty had such presence that he tended to fill a room with it without even trying. It was hard to go toe-to-toe with that. But the truth was Ty had mentioned absolutely nothing about love. He had asked her, but for all the wrong reasons. And it would be a disaster to marry without it. They would end up resenting each other and then what sort of parents would they be?

She had to make him understand that somehow. "Ty," she tried, praying for calm, "getting married would be a mistake. We'd end up regretting it, I'm sure of it. And then there'd be a child stuck in the middle. If we're calm and practical now, it'll be so much better, can't you see? We'll make rational decisions rather than running on emotion."

"Of course there are emotions involved. We're not talking about buying a car or taking a job. We're talking about a baby here. My baby."

"And mine," she reminded him.

A muscle in his jaw ticked. This wasn't going the way she wanted at all! It had never crossed her mind that he'd propose. He didn't love her. She wasn't a naive little girl, after all. She knew that one night of passion and grief did not a love affair make.

"You're asking me to make an impossible choice, do you realize that?" He ran his hand through his hair. "I either have to try to be a father on special occasions and holidays, or…"

He dropped his hand. "Damn," he muttered.

"Or what?" she asked, wondering what choice she'd possibly forced.

"Or leave Diamondback."

Her lips dropped open. "You'd do that?"

The chocolaty eyes she'd drowned in earlier now hardened. "What choice would I have? You should know me better, especially after everything I told you." His voice turned accusing. "You know my history. You know how I feel about what my parents did. Thank God Virgil and Molly were there, but what if they hadn't been? Don't you think I know how it might have ended up for me? Maybe this was unplanned, but I could never turn my back on my own child. I could never put them second in my life and I thought you understood that."

And now she saw his eyes glisten with the barest sheen of moisture before he blinked and turned away from her.

"But you love Diamondback," she said weakly.

"Yes, I do." His voice was hoarse with emotion. And he didn't need to say anything more. If she insisted on staying in Saskatchewan, he would leave the ranch behind. His birthright. His family.

"All last night I asked myself what my dad would do in my place," he said. He faced her once more, the harsh anger gone from his features but replaced by naked anguish. "I wished I had him to talk to. But in the end I knew what he'd do. Because he'd already done it—with me. He put me first. He'd done what was best and that was give me a family and security and love. Our baby deserves at least that much. I blew my chance with my father too many times to count. You're not the only one with a second chance, Clara. I wasn't the best son, but I can damn well be a good father. I know in my heart the best way to do that is for us to make a home here, at Diamondback. To be a real family."

Clara's resolve was weakening and she knew she had to say the word they were both so assiduously avoiding. "How can you be a real family without love?" she asked.

A shadow passed over his face. "We'll have love for our child," he replied. "And maybe for us, too, in time." He offered a weak smile. "Haven't we always gotten along? I mean, we wouldn't be here if we didn't. Maybe we just need to give it time."

Her heart wept a little. This was not the way marriage was supposed to start out.

Was it enough? She knew it wasn't. And yet how could she ask him to give up Diamondback without at least compromising? She knew they weren't idle words on Ty's part. He was determined and stubborn and he'd do it. He'd leave Diamondback and he'd be a good father but miserable.

And there was the niggling reminder that she loved it here. She was happy she had her family back in her life and she liked her job, but this felt like home. She'd be stupid to deny it.

"I don't know, Ty."

He sensed her weakening and hit her with one more

emotional shot: "It would kill Mom to have you both so far away. She's already started bugging Sam and Angela about babies. She's wanted grandchildren for years. With Dad gone now this would be so good for her, Clara."

"What if it doesn't work out? What if…"

Ty stepped forward and cupped her face in his hands. "It will. I promise. It's too important not to."

He touched his lips to hers, a faint whisper of contact but it rocketed through Clara like a lightning bolt.

"Marry me," he murmured against her lips.

She nodded. How could she resist when deep down Ty was what she really wanted? How could she say no when her only reasoning was to prove a point? How could she ask him to give everything up so she could be selfish and have her own way?

And perhaps she'd learn how to swallow her fear and believe that one day he might come to love her, too.

When they entered the kitchen again, three pairs of eyes watched them curiously. Clara felt her cheeks heat as she realized they'd been gone several minutes and that they'd kept the meal waiting. Angela sent Clara a sympathetic look and Sam was grinning at Ty like an idiot. Molly's face, however, had fallen into wrinkles of concern. "Is everything all right?" she asked.

"Fine," Clara answered before Ty could get a chance. "Sorry we held you up. Everything smells delicious." Truthfully she didn't care a bit about eating but she'd put on a good show. Anything to put things back to normal.

Angela gave Molly a plate and everyone dished up the food buffet-style, but even though snatches of conversation picked up, the atmosphere remained strained. They sat at the table and Clara saw Angela give Sam a kick. He winced and then picked up his water glass. "Well, I sup-

pose we should kick off the festivities. How about a toast?"
He beamed at the table in general. "To Mom, on her birthday." Everyone clinked glasses and drank, but Sam wasn't
done yet. "And to family. All of us being together."

Ty grinned at his brother, and Angela aimed a perturbed look at him; poor Molly only looked confused.
"All right," she said, putting down her glass. "Would one
of you care to tell me what's going on here? The atmosphere's so thick you could cut it with a knife and I know
I'm completely in the dark."

Clara froze. Ty reached over and took her hand and
squeezed. He wouldn't. Not so soon. Not now...

"Clara and I are getting married," he said clearly.

Sam let out a whoop and Angela gawped and Molly sat
back in her chair, stunned. Clara smiled weakly, wishing
she could throttle Ty. There was no backing out now, was
there? Just the way he wanted it. She looked at him and
saw a hint of apology in his eyes. Then he squeezed her
hand again and she felt a bit of her anger dissolve. What
was the point in waiting? It didn't change anything. And
time was ticking along.

"You're really getting married?" Molly asked, her eyes
wide.

Clara met her gaze and nodded. "Yes, we are."

"Oh, dear." And then Molly pushed back from the table,
came around the corner, and Clara got up to meet her.
Molly put her arms around her and hugged her for the
second time in an hour. "Thank you," she said, and Clara
heard tears in the older woman's voice. "It's just what I
wanted."

Clara started to laugh. Resistance was futile, wasn't
it? She loved this family. All the quirks, the dysfunction,
the love. She hugged Molly and then leaned back so she
could see her future mother-in-law's face. "We didn't really

plan it to be a birthday present," she said. "That comes later. With cake."

"Oh, presents be darned," Molly declared.

Ty looked at Clara. "Should we tell her, then?"

"Tell me what?" She let go of Clara and gave Ty the evil eye. "What are you up to, Tyson Diamond?"

Ty looked into Clara's eyes and gave her a slow smile, one that reached inside and took hold and made her want her own birthday cake so that she might close her eyes and blow out the candles and wish that this was all real and not just a forced, desperate decision. "I think you should," he urged.

Clara took a deep breath, gazed one more second in Ty's eyes, then took Molly's hands in hers. "Molly, remember that grandbaby you wished for?"

Molly's eyes grew even bigger as the words sank in. And Clara took one of the wrinkled hands and put it on her abdomen. "Happy birthday," she whispered.

"Oh," Molly breathed, and Clara saw tears form in Molly's eyes. "Oh, my. Oh." Her lip trembled. "I wish Virgil could be here for this. He would have been so happy. He always thought there was something special between you."

The words cut into Clara's soul just a bit; something special, yes, but it wasn't all it should be. She met Ty's gaze and she could see he was troubled, too, but then Molly kissed her cheek and Angela was hugging her gently and Ty rose to shake Sam's hand and get a clap on the back. "You've just bought us some time, brother," he said to Ty. Molly gave Sam's arm a swat as she went to hug Ty as well. Sam gave her an easy hug and smiled down at her. "This makes me Uncle Sam," he said, puffing out his chest.

Clara leaned in. "Don't get too cozy," she warned in an undertone. "When women see babies they get clucky.

And it wouldn't take much for your wife to get that glint in her eye."

At Sam's look of alarm she burst out laughing. Everyone took their seats again, and it seemed the cloud of uncertainty had lifted as people dug into their food.

She had a fork full of chow mein halfway to her mouth when she looked over at Ty and found him looking at her. He smiled.

It would be so easy to get used to this. To pretend it was all real. To want it to be real.

What had she done?

Ty put the overnight bag in the back seat and shut the door. Now that the weekend was over, Clara had to go back to Moose Jaw. She'd said yes and they'd told the family. It all seemed like a whirlwind of craziness. But as he held open the driver's side door for her, he couldn't stop the uncertainty that weighed heavily in his chest. He was terrified she'd change her mind the moment she was away from him. From Diamondback.

"I should get on the road," she reminded him.

He swallowed. Her breath made puffy clouds in the air and her eyes seemed unusually blue in the winter morning light. "Drive carefully and call me when you get there," he said. But he still didn't move to get out of the way so she could get behind the wheel.

"I will," she replied.

There had been a time yesterday—when she'd asked about love—that he'd considered confessing his feelings. He thought about it now, too. But he knew how it would look. Would she even believe him if he said it? He doubted it. He knew exactly how it would look—that he was saying it in reaction to the circumstances and not because he really meant it.

With Clara, he had to prove it. He knew the words were not enough. And he had to give her time. Because she'd had all the opportunity in the world to say the words yesterday, too—and she hadn't. In fact, she'd asked, "How can you be a real family without love?"

It wasn't the usual progression of things—baby, marriage, then love—but then nothing about his family followed the usual pattern. It didn't mean it couldn't work. He just had to take it slow. Their family depended on it.

"Clara, I…" He swore lightly. "Honestly, I think about everything I'm going to say about ten times before I say it."

She smiled. "Relax. I'm almost over being mad about yesterday."

He shifted uncomfortably. He hadn't exactly played it cool. And yet time was so short. Less than twenty-four hours later here she was, getting ready to leave. "I'm almost sorry about it," he replied, but he smiled back. "About the wedding, like I told you last night, whatever you want is fine."

"I thought about it. Something small, Ty. Just us and our families. And soon. I'd like for us to have some time to get settled before the baby turns things upside down." There was a sweet upturn to her lips. "I hear they do that."

"And I want to share the rest of the pregnancy with you, too," he added. "I want to be there for you from the start."

How much more plain could he be without actually saying the words?

She gasped and zipped open her purse, searching for something. A moment later she held up an envelope. "Here," she said. "I nearly forgot. I meant to give you this, but in all the commotion…" She handed it over.

"What is it?"

"Ultrasound pictures. I had them done last week. Everything's normal, but I'll have them done again in about six weeks."

Pictures. Of his child. He clutched the envelope in his hand.

"I've really got to go," she said. "I promise I'll call."

He moved aside and she climbed behind the wheel. He shut the door and listened as she started the engine, letting it warm for a few seconds before putting the car in reverse and turning it around on the parking pad. As she drove by him, she raised her fingers in farewell.

He stood in the driveway, watching until she turned on the road and out of sight. Then he opened the envelope and stared at the strange black-and-white film.

It would all work out. It had to.

CHAPTER TWELVE

SPRING CAME EARLY to Cadence Creek, and Ty and Clara's wedding day was unseasonably warm. Ty had heeded her request for a small wedding, but instead of her suggestion of the Diamondback living room, he'd convinced her to let him book the nearby bed-and-breakfast for the afternoon and night. Intimate and classy, Clara realized she was going to have a fairy-tale wedding after all—even if it was a scaled-down version.

She stood in the room they would share later, gazing at her figure in a cheval glass. She put her hand over her belly and the bump that was there now. Not just a bump but also the first little flutters of movement. Ty hadn't felt them yet, but she had. And each time it happened she thought of Ty, and Diamondback, and the future, and prayed that she was doing the right thing.

The fact that she still wasn't sure was troubling.

There was a knock on the door and she opened it to find Angela, Molly and Wendy standing with wide grins and white boxes. "The flowers are here," Wendy said. "And we wanted to see you before we go downstairs."

Molly and Wendy had hit it off immediately, and at the rehearsal dinner Clara had heard them promise to exchange quilting and knitting patterns. They were both thrilled about becoming grandmothers. And Ty had charmed the socks off his future mother-in-law. Now the two of them came into the suite in brand-new dresses and heels and matching smiles.

Angela took the lid off the first box. "This one is yours, Clara."

It was simple but stunning, a nosegay of red roses and baby's breath and white satin ribbon. Clara held it up and sniffed deeply. It all felt so surreal. After Jackson she'd never thought she'd get married. Never thought she'd have a family. And here she was, standing in a simple white dress with a bridal bouquet, and her matron of honor and two mothers looking on.

"Let's see yours," she said to Angela, and Angela took out the second bouquet—a smaller version of Clara's but all in white, contrasting with her deep red dress.

"You both look gorgeous," Wendy said.

Molly gave her a kiss on the cheek. "I'll second that. And I was going to wait until later to tell you, but I'm giving you and Ty the wedding ring quilt as a wedding present. You should have it. So many of the stitches are yours." She dabbed at her eyes. "You were part of the family long before today."

Clara fanned her eyes. "Oh, that's not fair! I just fixed my makeup." But she hugged Molly. "Thank you, Mom," she answered, and then there were sniffles on both sides.

Wendy gave Clara a final hug. "I'll see you downstairs. Love you, honey."

Clara blinked to keep from smudging her mascara. "You, too," she said, giving her a quick hug.

She'd worried about telling Wendy about moving back to Cadence Creek, but Wendy had been surprisingly supportive. "I lost you once before," she'd said. "Having you back in my life is the most important thing. Knowing I can visit you and the baby and knowing you can come visit us is enough."

And now the big day was here. Molly and Wendy left together and now it was just Angela and Clara left in the room. Angela arranged one of Clara's curls just right and stood back, admiring the dress. "You look amazing," she said. "When you said a short dress, I was skeptical, but it's perfect."

Clara ran a hand over the skirt, willing away the nerves that persisted in swirling in her stomach. The sheer cap sleeves were modest and feminine, and the skirt flowed to her knees where it flared slightly in a delicate, feminine ruffle. Tiny white satin heels completed the outfit, and her curls were frosted over by a simple short veil.

She was getting married.

To a man who didn't love her.

"Are you all right?" Angela asked. She took Clara's bouquet and put it on the bed. "You got pale all of a sudden."

Clara smiled weakly. "This has all happened so fast," she confessed. "I just need a minute to get my bearings."

"Oh, honey." Angela led her to the bed and they sat down. "Are you sure this is what you want? You went from telling Ty to being engaged all in a weekend, and here you are barely a month later getting married."

"I love him," she said to Angela, and despite her mascara fears, two tears slipped over her lids and down her cheek.

"Well, I'm relieved to hear that," Angela said, her voice thick as she reached for a tissue from the box beside the bed. "Isn't it a good thing?"

"But it's not why he's marrying me," she answered. "It's all because of the baby. And because he is so determined to do the right thing by our child that he said he'd leave the ranch behind to be with us. How could I ask him to do that? He was willing to give up so much for us. And I love it here. It would be selfish."

Angela rubbed her arm.

"I just don't know how to do this and still keep my heart intact."

Angela wiped her eyes and blew her nose. "Ty is the most honorable man I know—with one obvious exception," Angela said. "He wouldn't have asked you to marry him if he didn't have feelings for you."

Clara didn't know how to explain it any further. Feelings were not the same thing as love. It was hard to build a life on "feelings." It was hard to trust your heart to feelings. And expressing her doubt made her feel ungrateful and selfish.

"I'll be fine," she assured Angela. "It's just last-minute jitters."

There was a discreet knock on the door. It was time.

"Here." Angela dabbed beneath Clara's eyes. "That's better." She picked up her bouquet and handed Clara hers. "All set?"

"As ready as I'm going to be," Clara answered.

Ty waited in the parlor, locking and unlocking his knee nervously. A small fire blazed in the fireplace behind him; he could feel the heat against the back of his legs. The minister stood beside him, and the handful of guests sat in chairs brought in from the dining room for the occasion. There was the smell of roses in the air and Ty heard a small knock and then a door opening and shutting.

It was really happening.

Sam put a reassuring hand on his shoulder. "Breathe," he instructed.

Angela appeared in the door, stepping slowly and smiling at Sam in a way that made Ty's heart clench. She stepped to the side and then there was Clara, standing in the doorway, her fingers clutching her bouquet.

My God, she was beautiful. Catch-your-breath beautiful, in a floaty white dress and filmy veil over her hair. He smiled, but the smile slipped as he saw her face go white and her teeth worried her lip.

She always did that when she was afraid and unsure. Cold panic ran like ice water through his veins as he saw the wild look in her eyes—a split second before she turned on her heel and disappeared.

Angela took a step to go after her, but Ty stalled her with a hand. "No," he said. "I did this. It has to be me."

It was hard to breathe. The breaths were coming short and fast and Clara felt slightly lightheaded from it all. She stumbled through the back door of the B and B into what would, in the summer, be a back garden for afternoon tea or an al fresco breakfast. Right now it was slightly soggy and brown with a few brave spears of new grass poking through. She dropped her flowers in a dry bird bath and rested her hands on the cool concrete edge. She had to breathe.

"Clara!"

The screen door slammed with a bang and she heard his footsteps behind her. Humiliation burned through her. She should have put a stop to this from the beginning. It never should have gone this far.

"Clara," he said, quieter now, gently. "Breathe, honey. It's all right."

She hated that his soothing tone worked. Hated that she'd come to rely on him this much, hated that she loved him so much that the thought of marrying him when that emotion wasn't returned was too much to bear. She couldn't look him in the eye. And she had no idea what to do next. There was just a bunch of nothingness stretched out before her. Clara, who was always able to see one step ahead, even when times were at their worst, had ground to a complete standstill.

"It's okay," he said, still not touching her with anything but his voice. "I shouldn't have pushed so hard. I thought…" He stopped, cleared his throat. "I don't want you to marry me if you don't love me, Clara. I should have listened to you. We can figure the rest out, I promise. I'll be the best father I can. But I won't ask you to go into a marriage with a man you don't love. I was wrong to do that."

Her fingers tightened on the bird bath. It was the only thing holding her upright. Had he just said… But it made no sense! Was he saying he was in love with her? But that wasn't exactly what he'd said, was it? Only that he wouldn't pressure her to go into a marriage if *she* didn't love *him*.

"What about you?" she finally asked, closing her eyes. "You were willing to marry a woman you didn't love. And you didn't back out, did you? You were going to see it through." Her voice caught on a sob. "I don't know what's wrong with me, Ty!"

"Who said I was marrying a woman I didn't love?"

The words echoed through the bare garden for a heart-stopping moment. Slowly she turned to face him. Her heart started beating again, a little too fast. He was so dashing in his suit and serious eyes and unsmiling lips. He was a man filled with purpose, she realized. And that purpose was her. Joy pierced her like a shining beam of sunlight.

"You love me?"

"I do. I have for some time. Maybe from the first moment I took you in my arms and danced with you at Sam

and Angela's wedding, but I was too stupid to realize it.
But I've known for sure since the night you told me you
were pregnant."

Her mind spun back to everything that happened that
weekend. Everything that had been said. "Why didn't you
tell me?" she wailed. "It would have made things so much
easier!"

"Because," he said, coming closer. "You would have
thought I was only saying it because of the baby. You
would have wondered if it was true or if I was trying to
manipulate you into getting my way." Another step. "And
because I knew you didn't feel the same way about me and
I wasn't willing to put myself out there like that."

"Didn't feel the same way?" Clara let her fingers release the bird bath and faced him full-on. "Tyson. I have
loved you since the night you kissed me under the stars.
You made me believe in *me* again. You made me feel
whole again. Do you think I could have made love with
you otherwise?"

He took the final step and gathered her in his arms,
lifting her until her toes barely touched the hard ground.
"Thank God," he said close to her ear. "I didn't know I
could even fall in love. And I certainly didn't know if anyone could fall in love with me."

"Because you never showed anyone who you really
are. But I saw it. And that's the man I fell in love with. I
was just too scared to admit it. To let myself be that vulnerable again. To trust anyone and give them the power
to hurt me."

He put her back down on the ground but kept his arms
around her. "Do you trust me now?"

She nodded. "Everything you've done has been to try
to do the right thing. If I'd been smart, I would have seen

with my eyes what you didn't say. I guess we're both a couple of blind fools."

"Not anymore."

"No, not anymore. I used to have a saying, did you know that? 'Living in fear is not living.' But that's exactly what I was doing. I was so afraid to love you." She cuddled into him, drawing strength from him just as she'd always done. "I was wrong about that."

He stepped back a little and held her fingers in his. "So, are we going to do this thing? Because I'd sure like to marry you today, Clara Ferguson. Marry you and make us a family."

"I'd like that." This time her smile was free and it felt glorious. "I'd like that a lot."

"I love you," he declared. "Just to be perfectly clear."

"And I love you. Let's get married."

He grabbed her roses from the bird bath, put them in her hands, and she gave a delighted little laugh as he swung her up in his arms and carried her over the threshold to a brand-new life.

EPILOGUE

CLARA TUCKED THE tiny feet into frilly bottoms and buttoned the row of tiny buttons up the front of the pink-and-white dress, quite efficiently when all flailing legs and arms were considered. She laughed as she lifted baby Susanna into her arms. Today was a special day and deserved a fancy dress. It wasn't every day that Uncle Sam and Aunt Angela celebrated an anniversary.

Molly tiptoed into the nursery. "Is the coast clear?"

Clara laughed. "Oh, she's bright eyed and bushy tailed. No need to tread softly. I think this is a girl ready for a party. Come on, Susanna Banana."

"Come to Grandma," Molly crooned, and took the infant from Clara's arms. "There's my girl." She looked up at Clara. "My, Virgil would have loved her."

"I wish he could have been here," Clara agreed, smoothing the back of the dress and smiling. "But I think he's probably somewhere feeling very satisfied about the part he played in bringing this all together."

"I think you're right. Okay, little one, there's a party happening around here. Let's get some cake."

Ty was coming through the deck doors with a platter of steaks, and Angela was in the kitchen putting together a salad. Sam had given Buster a bone and put him in the back yard to gnaw to his heart's content.

Her family.

Ty came over and planted a kiss on her lips while Molly perched on a chair and bounced Susanna on her knee, saying a silly rhyme. But when dinner was ready, they all gathered around the table for a celebratory toast. Clara did the honors of popping the champagne she'd bought especially for the occasion, and she filled five glasses, handing them around.

This time Ty did the honors. "Happy anniversary, to my brother and the woman brave enough to put up with him."

"Ty!" Clara exclaimed, but everyone laughed and tilted their glasses. Except Angela…

Molly's eagle eye noticed. "Something wrong with the champagne?"

Angela met Sam's gaze and they shared a tender glance before she turned back to Molly. "Well, Ty and Clara got the birthday announcement. We figured we'd save it for the anniversary." She put down her glass and put her fingers over her belly. "Is it too soon for another grandchild?"

"Never!" Molly jumped up and hugged Angela tightly until Susanna began to fuss and complain. She lifted the baby and her grin was from ear to ear.

"You are going to have a cousin," she announced. Then she looked at Sam and Ty. "Cousins," she remarked, "as close as siblings."

Tucking the baby on her arm, she raised her glass and took a healthy sip. "Ah," she said. "Is there anything better than family?"

There really wasn't.

* * * * *

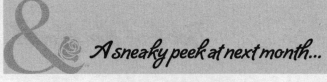

A sneaky peek at next month...

Cherish™

ROMANCE TO MELT THE HEART EVERY TIME

My wish list for next month's titles...

In stores from 17th August 2012:

❑ The Rancher's Housekeeper – Rebecca Winters

& The Cowboy Comes Home – Patricia Thayer

❑ A Doctor in His House

& A Marriage Worth Fighting For – Lilian Darcy

In stores from 7th September 2012:

❑ Her Outback Rescuer – Marion Lennox

& Mr Right, Next Door! – Barbara Wallace

❑ The Princess and the Outlaw – Leanne Banks

& Stand-in Wife – Karina Bliss

Available at WHSmith, Tesco, Asda, Eason, Amazon and Apple

Just can't wait?

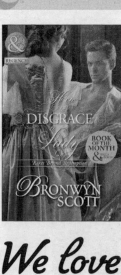

www.millsandboon.co.uk/freebookoffer

Or fill in the form below and post it back to us

THE MILLS & BOON® BOOK CLUB™—HERE'S HOW IT WORKS: Accepting your free books places you under no obligation to buy anything. You may keep the books and return the despatch note marked 'Cancel'. If we do not hear from you, about a month later we'll send you 5 brand-new stories from the Cherish™ series, including two 2-in-1 books priced at £5.49 each, and a single book priced at £3.49*. There is no extra charge for post and packaging. You may cancel at any time, otherwise we will send you 5 stories a month which you may purchase or return to us—the choice is yours. *Terms and prices subject to change without notice. Offer valid in UK only. Applicants must be 18 or over. Offer expires 31st January 2013. **For full terms and conditions, please go to www.millsandboon.co.uk/freebookoffer**

Mrs/Miss/Ms/Mr (please circle)

First Name

Surname

Address

                                                    Postcode

E-mail

Send this completed page to: Mills & Boon Book Club, Free Book Offer, FREEPOST NAT 10298, Richmond, Surrey, TW9 1BR

Find out more at
www.millsandboon.co.uk/freebookoffer

Visit us Online

0712/S2YEA

Have Your Say

You've just finished your book.
So what did you think?

We'd love to hear your thoughts on our
'Have your say' online panel
www.millsandboon.co.uk/haveyoursay

- 🌹 Easy to use
- 🌹 Short questionnaire
- 🌹 Chance to win Mills & Boon®
  goodies

Visit us Online | Tell us what you thought of this book now at
www.millsandboon.co.uk/haveyoursay

YOUR_SAY